"In his plotting, dialogue, and empathy for the bad guys, Goldberg aspires to the heights of Elmore Leonard. For those who miss the master, *Gangsterland* is a high-grade substitute." —*The New York Times*

"For many of us, *The Godfather*, book or movie, ushered us into a second boyhood, teaching that the incorrigible vitality of a first-rate gangster story could temporarily inoculate us against adult sanity. For readers of a like mind, Tod Goldberg's *Gangsterland* will arrive as a gloriously original Mafia novel: 100 percent unhinged about the professionally unhinged . . . Torridly funny . . . The novel swells with a spiritual but jazzy tone." —*The New York Times Book Review*

"*Gangsterland* explores the question: What would happen if a hitman were forced to fake being religious? . . . That led to the nuances of *Gangsterland*—to not only become a page turner, but also to expand beyond that . . . into an environment of faith and spirituality." —*San Francisco Chronicle*

"The setup is blackly comic, the plotting a tad rococo, the payoff grim but sly . . . Goldberg's new book is clever bordering on wise, like *Get Shorty* on antacid." —David Kipen, *Los Angeles Magazine*

"As sharp as a straight razor. But a lot more fun. Count me a huge fan." —Lee Child, *New York Times* bestselling author of *Personal: A Jack Reacher Novel*

"*Gangsterland* is rich with complex and meaty characters, but its greatest strength is that it never pulls a punch, never holds back, and never apologizes for life's absurdities. If this novel were a person, you could ask it for a bookie." —Brad Meltzer, bestselling author of *The Fifth Assassin*

"Complex characters with understandable motivations distinguish this highly unusual crime novel . . . Goldberg injects Talmudic wisdom and a hint of Springsteen into the workings of organized crime and FBI investigative techniques and makes it all work splendidly." —*Publishers Weekly* (starred review)

"Sal's transformation—and intermittent edification—into Rabbi Cohen is brilliantly rendered, and Goldberg's careening plot, cast of memorably dubious characters, and mordant portrait of Las Vegas make this one of the year's best hard-boiled crime novels." —*Booklist* (starred review)

"Clever plotting, a colorful cast of characters, and priceless situations make this comedic crime novel an instant classic." —*Kirkus Reviews* (starred review)

"Unlike many of his literary forebears and contemporaries, Goldberg, it seems, has not been seized by self-evisceration or self-doubt. There's no scolding messaging about universalism here, just respect for a group that looks after its own . . . As Rabbi Cohen observes, who wants to hear the same old stories? For those who don't, there is *Gangsterland*." —Los Angeles Review of Books

"Not into gangster capers? The skillfully spun *Gangsterland* could convert you . . . A cleverly spun novel that forced me to abandon my wiseguy moratorium. Goldberg has an amusing flair for contemporary hard-boil, and he knows his crime and crime-fighting procedures." —*Las Vegas Weekly*

"Tod Goldberg's wickedly dark and hilarious new book will remind you of everything you love about Walter White (or any Coen brothers antihero, for that matter)." —*Purewow*

"The Mafia plus the Torah makes for a darkly funny and suspenseful morality tale . . . The man can spin a good yarn." —Edan Lepucki, *The Millions*

"This tale of witness relocation-by-mob—part Elmore Leonard, part Theatre of the Absurd—is a compelling examination of salvation, which comes in various guises and moves in elusive ways. A wholly unique tale from a wholly unique voice." —Gregg Hurwitz, *New York Times* bestselling author of *Don't Look Back*

"Tod Goldberg is a one-of-a-kind writer, and this is his best novel to date. Harrowing, funny, wise, and heretical, *Gangsterland* is everything a thriller should be." —T. Jefferson Parker, author of *Full Measure*

GANGSTER NATION

GANGSTER NATION

TOD GOLDBERG

COUNTERPOINT
BERKELEY, CALIFORNIA

GANGSTER NATION

Library of Congress Cataloging-in-Publication Data
Names: Goldberg, Tod, author.
Title: Gangster nation : a novel / Tod Goldberg.
Description: Berkeley, CA : Counterpoint Press, [2017]
Identifiers: LCCN 2017024769 | ISBN 9781619027237 (hardcover)
Subjects: LCSH: Criminals—Fiction. | Mafia—Fiction. | GSAFD: Suspense
    fiction. | Mystery fiction.
Classification: LCC PS3557.O35836 G35 2017 | DDC 813/.54—dc23
LC record available at https://lccn.loc.gov/2017024769

Paperback ISBN: 978-1-64009-106-1

Jacket designed by Jarrod Taylor
Book designed by Domini Dragoone

COUNTERPOINT
2560 Ninth Street, Suite 318
Berkeley, CA 94710
www.counterpointpress.com

Printed in the United States of America

10 9 8 7 6 5 4 3 2

For Wendy, who makes me a better man

Whoever destroys a soul, it is considered as if he destroyed an entire world. And whoever saves a life, it is considered as if he saved an entire world.

—THE TALMUD

PROLOGUE

P eaches Pocotillo never got to kill anyone anymore. All those years he'd spent perfecting his craft had led to bigger and better things, which in this case meant a mid-level leadership position in the Native Mob, overseeing tribal gang consolidation and farming operations in Minnesota, Wisconsin, Illinois, even into Nebraska. He had Native Gangster Disciples reporting to him, Native Vice Lords, Native Crips, Native Bloods, Peaches the one guy everyone listened to, the one guy who could get everyone to the table, the one guy who you didn't want to cross, because, man, he used to kill people for *nothing*, son.

That reputation got him in the room. Still had to make the sale. But he was good at that, too.

So he was the guy they'd send to sit down with some Native Crip shot caller to explain, patiently, why co-opting the iconography of a Los Angeles gang that would kill him on sight was bad business. It put everyone in jeopardy. So, sure, call yourself a Crip while you're out tending the dirt fields in Nebraska. But you come to Minneapolis, Green Bay, or Chicago? You either called yourself Native Mob or you called yourself dead. Then he'd paint a more optimistic picture: *See all this reservation farmland? See all those beets? See all that kale? Shit no one likes to eat. Imagine it green with marijuana. Don't worry, we got*

1

the recipe. Don't worry, we'll front you the cost of machinery. Don't worry, we got the protection. Don't worry, we got distribution.

That advice? That's fifty thousand dollars. Big bills are fine. By tomorrow. Next day? It's seventy-five. End of the week? Don't worry, we'll give your mom something to help her with the bills.

Now, three in the morning, crossing over the Blackburn Point Bridge from Osprey, Florida, onto Casey Key, sitting in the passenger seat of a rented Ford Taurus—big trunk but it handled like a rhino, American cars absolute crap these days—Peaches could see his middle management career coming to an end. His own thing on the horizon. He was forty-five years old. The time for waiting was over.

His nephew Mike, who he liked but didn't think was exceptionally bright, pulled up in front of the Pirate's Cove Apartments and cut the engine. The Pirate's Cove consisted of six low-slung white bungalows surrounded by stumpy palm trees and beds of hibiscus that had begun to grow wild, climbing up toward the blue Bermuda shutters that were pushed out, letting in the gulf breeze. It had been hot and humid all day. Mike's Midwest blood was not suited to this Florida bullshit, even this late in the year, but Peaches liked it, particularly now that it was in the sixties and the air finally thin enough to breathe.

"Uncle," Mike said, "this place is nice."

It was. Or, well, the land was. The Pirate's Cove was a dump but it was surrounded on either side by mansions—only a few hundred yards east of the Gulf of Mexico, a few hundred yards west of the Intracoastal Waterway. Prime real estate. Worth maybe a million, a million and a half. Even more if the bungalows were torn down. Peaches knew about real estate, had made it his specialty, had his broker's license, was happy to sift through public records, knock on doors, talk about gentrification, talk about curb appeal, talk about market value, talk about how, for his tribe the Chuyalla, real estate was the ticket to prosperity. That if they wanted to move real weight, they had to take their casino profits and roll that into durable investments, which sometimes meant buying up land that had once been theirs in the first place.

Lately, though, he'd been all about buying up commercial space, medical buildings, but especially any empty plots next to phone company switching stations, particularly in shitty little towns, Peaches thinking ahead, seeing how the Internet was changing business. Phone companies were going to need that space. Build server farms. Data was a more durable crop than weed, but that wasn't something Peaches was confident his soldiers could cultivate. So he knew something about how to improve investments and he knew no one had bothered to update these bungalows since 1953, which is when Ronnie Cupertine's father, Tom "Dandy Tommy" Cupertine, bought the land in the first place.

Almost fifty years later, the Pirate's Cove was in the name of an LLC and was operated by a property management company in Chicago. In all that time, though, the property had never been sold. Peaches stumbled on it while searching the records for every bit of residential property in the Cupertine family name, going all the way back to the early 1900s, looking for plausible safe houses for the Family, as far away from Chicago as possible. The Pirate's Cove had been quit-claimed thirteen times up through the 1980s, but since then, nothing. It took Peaches about three months to plow through microfiche and old deeds and records, since he had to do it all by hand, couldn't get some file clerk on the Family payroll interested in what he was looking for, not that anyone in Osprey looked particularly mobbed up.

Next, Peaches rented a house up the block from the Pirate's Cove and spent a month walking up and down the beach, making friends. Started wearing linen, started to take to it, actually. Bought tortoiseshell glasses. Played the part. Sat out on the beach in front of the Pirate's Cove a couple nights a week, chatted up the tenants coming in and out, found out Terrance worked the line at Casey Key Fish House, also dealt a little coke, neighbors showing up on Friday nights in their Audis and BMWs, Peaches picking up a few lines, too, for Halloween. It was crap. Baking soda and Adderall. The kind of shit that would get you killed in the real world. Out here, they were just happy for the bump. Sandi and Lisa, they were Jet Ski instructors at the Gulf Resort and Spa. Rob was the bartender at the Beachcomber, nice place if you liked tiki bars. Pasqual was teaching at a private school in Sarasota, just lucked into a spot on the water. Becca and Tony were servers at the Charthouse. Frank and Doreen, they were the on-site managers. Married couple. Super nice, everyone said so.

Frank and Doreen, they didn't get any mail.

Frank and Doreen, they didn't have any friends. No kids. Not even a cat.

Frank and Doreen, they didn't talk too much, had Chicago accents so thick it was like sitting in the bleachers at Wrigley.

"Two minutes," Peaches said. "Three at the most."

Mike rolled down his window. Sniffed. "It's so wet out here, Uncle, I'm gonna have to double up."

Back in the day, Peaches worked alone. But this was a two-man job, and Mike had shown himself to be pretty good with accelerants. He didn't know why Mike needed to sniff to figure out the wetness in the air, but whatever. Everyone had their moves.

"Do what you need to do." Peaches reached into the backseat, unzipped his travel bag, took out a steel-headed drilling hammer. He didn't have any guns with him, because he'd be tempted to use them, and this wasn't the type of neighborhood where people would sleep through a gunshot.

Frank Fishmann had been driving a truck for Kochel Farms for twenty-five years, so his back was fucked up, his knees were shit, his night vision was half gone. He was fifty-five, about thirty pounds overweight, and he hadn't been bright enough to decline the job of hustling the Rain Man out of town in the back of his refrigerated meat truck. Well, Peaches considered, maybe that wasn't exactly true. He probably didn't have a choice. Frank *was* bright enough not to come forward to the FBI with information on where he'd dumped Sal Cupertine, even though that information was worth a $500,000 reward. Instead, he'd spent the last two years hiding out on Ronnie Cupertine's dime. The one guy still alive, other than Ronnie, who knew where Sal Cupertine might be living was spending his days on the edge of the continent, ocean view. Probably the best years of his life.

Mike popped the trunk, came out with three gas cans, headed into the darkness. He'd set the fires on their way out, if Peaches thought they needed the cover, or in case things got messy. Peaches walked over to Frank and Doreen's bungalow, the one closest to the street, the stench of gasoline already starting to waft toward him, pounded on the door, waited, pounded again. A light came on.

If Doreen answered, that would be too bad.

A shadow crossed the peephole. Peaches raised his left hand and waved, gave a faint smile. "It's me," Peaches said. "So sorry to bother you in the middle of the night." Whoever was on the other side of the peephole took another few seconds, probably contemplating the risk. If this were Chicago, a bullet would already be through the peephole and out the back of their head. "So sorry," Peaches said again. "Frank? Is that you? It's me. Mr. Taylor." That's what Frank knew him as. The neighbor up the way. A real nice guy.

The porch light came on and Frank opened the door, stepped onto his small front porch, closed the door behind him. Had on a pair of pajama bottoms, no shirt. A tattoo of an eagle on his chest. That was unexpected. "What's going on, Mr. Taylor?" he began to say, honest concern in his voice, but before he could get it all out, Peaches hit him flush on the right temple with the hammer, caving in the side of his head with a single blow. Maybe breaking his neck, too, judging by the way Frank went to the ground, his body kinked into an S.

Peaches hit him three more times, regardless, stopping only when he saw brain matter.

Frank Fishmann's whole life ended in three seconds. Maybe fewer. That's all it took, if you knew what you were doing.

Mike appeared out of the shadows and they picked up Frank, carried him to the Taurus, dropped him in the trunk, closed it. Looked around.

Nothing.

Peaches checked his watch. Three minutes, start to finish. Almost exactly.

"All right," he said, more to himself, really. "All right." He could still do it. He wasn't just about the business. That was good to know.

"We good?" Mike asked.

They'd left a fair amount of blood and hair and viscera on the porch, but once Doreen realized Frank was gone, what was she gonna do? She was a felon, at this point, even if she wasn't before. She could call Ronnie, but Peaches didn't imagine she knew his number. Or his name. Probably had no idea of anything, if Frank was any kind of decent. She couldn't go back to Chicago, that was for sure. Best thing for her, really, was to pretend nothing happened. Live her life. Hose off the porch.

"What's the word, Uncle?"

Peaches loved Mike. He did. Twenty-two. His little sister's kid. But still.

This is why Peaches usually preferred to work alone. If he didn't want to worry about Mike flipping on him one day, Mike had to have his own crime tonight, something bigger than an accessory beef, which the government didn't mind turning their heads on. So Mike had to have it worse. Burn half a dozen people to death while they slept? You didn't plead down on that charge, no matter what you gave up.

"Light it up," Peaches said.

•

TWO DAYS LATER, back in Chicago, Peaches went through an OG in the Gangster 2-6—the Mexican gang the Family used to move drugs—to make the meeting happen. Lonzo Guijarro middled heroin and meth out to the hinterlands, so he and Peaches had done a few deals over the last couple years. Fair prices, no drama, Peaches able to get some good shit for the tribes, Lonzo getting credit for opening up a new market, everyone square.

Even with that shared past, Peaches still had to deliver ten Gs in a Trader Joe's shopping bag to Lonzo that morning, the two of them meeting at the Diner Grill in Lakeview, where Lonzo liked to eat breakfast. Peaches set the bag between them on the counter like it was filled with organic bananas and locally sourced honey.

"This is nonrefundable," Lonzo told him. He didn't even bother to look inside or count the money. "If the boss doesn't like the way you walk or thinks you got bad breath or some shit, that's not my problem. You cool with that?"

"I'm not a complainer, Lonzo," Peaches said. "Mr. Cupertine doesn't take to me, that's fine. We don't need to be friends. You and me, we don't need to be friends either."

Lonzo shifted on his stool. The Diner Grill was an old railroad dining car, so it was just twelve stools up against a Formica counter, one guy working the grill, another guy taking orders, both dressed in white shirts, white soda jerk hats, everyone overhearing everyone, if anyone bothered to listen. "All's I'm saying," Lonzo said, "is that the boss is keeping it low. You feel me?"

Peaches couldn't say he blamed him. Ronnie had spent the better part of the last year trying to unfuck himself after the *Chicago Tribune* detailed widespread corruption within the Chicago FBI's Organized Crime Task Force, eventually tying Sal Cupertine's murder of three undercover FBI agents and a CI at the Parker House to a series of gangland and jailhouse killings of Family and Gangster 2-6 soldiers and associates, and then what appeared to be some modicum of complicity with the FBI, suggesting that a network of high-level snitches were working both sides of the aisle, culminating in the faked death of Sal Cupertine. The Family had Sal shipped out of town in a refrigerated meat truck—the one driven by Frank Fishmann—and then dumped a couple of their soldiers' bodies in the Poyter Landfill, along with Sal's ID, and everyone played nice, acted like Sal Cupertine was dead, case closed. It all fell apart courtesy of a tip from a former FBI agent named Jeff Hopper, who conveniently disappeared, too, until his severed head showed up in a Dumpster in Chicago a few weeks after the first stories hit.

Peaches read about it just like the rest of the city did, except he saw a crack opening. So when the DOJ ended up cleaning house locally, putting on some show trials down in Springfield, then rousting half of the Family on a variety of charges, hollowing out the organization of the real earners, low-level guys copping to every crime they could, Peaches made note. The middle management was loyal, willing to save their boss from prison, probably for a little something when they got out. Do a couple years in Stateville or Joliet, come out, get a bar or a restaurant in Elmhurst? Easy. But it also meant Ronnie Cupertine was going to have a vacuum in the middle of his organization.

Because in the end, the feds never did find Sal Cupertine, and they never did find the last person to see him alive, either, so they had dick on Ronnie Cupertine himself.

Lonzo pointed out the window. "That your guy in the Lincoln?"

Mike was idling in a blue zone out front. "My nephew."

"That's a five-hundred-dollar ticket, parking there," Lonzo said.

"He has a handicapped placard," Peaches said. It was impossible to park in Chicago, and Peaches wasn't going to be one of those assholes who got shot walking to his car in some dark parking structure. Handicapped parking was always well lit, always close to the door.

Lonzo raised his eyebrows. "No shit? I'll have to look into that." He reached into the Trader Joe's bag, came out with two twenties, dropped them on his plate, then pointed out the diner's window. "Get what you need from your car and then tell your guy you're riding with me. He can go park somewhere, read a book or something. Leave the space for someone with a real problem."

"That's not how I work," Peaches said.

"Wasn't a request," Lonzo said.

Lonzo wasn't a guy who got off making threats. Peaches looked down the counter. There were two uniformed cops sitting at the far end, staring straight ahead, drinking coffee, eating toast. An old lady, oxygen tank at her feet. A black guy sitting with a white girl, eating off each other's plate. Two older men in suits, sipping coffee, reading the paper, not a fistfight between them.

When he looked back at the cops, they were both staring at him with notably blank expressions.

Okay.

"Expensive help," Peaches said.

Lonzo downed the rest of his coffee, slid off his stool. "You in it now for real."

TWO PATROL CARS followed behind Lonzo's red Escalade all the way until he parked in front of a house on West Junior Terrace, a street lined with old growth Buckthorn and two- and three-story homes, a few blocks from Montrose Beach. Peaches was familiar with the properties here, at least on paper. They'd been in the Cupertine family for decades. Three houses on one side of the street, two on the other, another down the block. Sometimes there were families living in them. Sometimes there were girlfriends. Sometimes they were just empty. They weren't safe houses, not in this neighborhood, where the average home price was getting close to a million five. They weren't places where people were getting done dirty, either, since every house on the block had security cameras and their own private security patrols, Peaches not really sure who the neighbors thought was gonna walk up on them here . . . though, fact was, there were two bad guys parked on the street right now.

Peaches started to get out, but Lonzo said, "Hold up."

One of the cruisers double-parked down the block, on the corner of North Clarendon. Peaches looked over his shoulder, saw the other cruiser parked on the corner of Hazel, boxing the block in.

"You always roll with cops?" Peaches asked.

"Only on Family business," he said. "Hard to get used to it at first, but fuck it. It is what it is." Lonzo pointed at the house in front of them. "Go on in. Ronnie's guys are a little much, but he's cool. Like talking to a congressman. Friendly but about that business."

"You talk to a lot of congressmen?"

"You'd be surprised," Lonzo said. Peaches retrieved his briefcase from the backseat. It was filled with cash. The cost of doing business with Ronnie Cupertine was you had to pay for his time. Lonzo had already looked inside it, felt around, made sure Peaches wasn't trying to smuggle in a hand grenade. Though he did have a little something extra for Ronnie Cupertine under all the cash. "Last thing," Lonzo said. "You come out and I'm gone for some reason? That's bad news. Those cops? They're here to protect the boss. Not you."

"I get it," Peaches said, knowing it wouldn't always be like that.

AFTER HE FRISKED him, a beefy guy calling himself Donte, wearing a Kevlar vest under his suit, guided Peaches downstairs into a finished basement, which connected to another finished basement through a long, narrow hallway. *Okay*, Peaches thought. *I'm next door.* But then they went through two more corridors, these ones crooked, Peaches's sense of direction getting fucked up after about two minutes of winding around. Peaches thought he was across the street now, or maybe right back where he started. They ended up in another corridor that fed into yet another basement, and this one looked like a fairly decent rumpus room from the 1970s: shag carpet, wood paneling, a leather recliner, L-shaped sofa, dartboard, wet bar. Ronnie Cupertine shooting pool by himself.

"You can leave us alone," Ronnie said to Donte, though Peaches didn't think they were alone, since he saw that there were cameras mounted on all four walls. This guy was more paranoid than Nixon. "You play?" Ronnie asked once his guy left.

"No," Peaches said.

"No one does anymore," he said. He lined up his shot—the six in the corner—and hit it, missed wide to the left, though he did manage to sink his cue ball. "Shit." Ronnie stood up straight, cracked his neck. "Problem with no one wanting to play with me is it's easier for me to cheat." He walked to the other side of the table, dug out his cue ball, and rolled the six into a pocket, too. He set his stick across the table. "So, who the fuck are you?"

"I'm here representing the Native Mob," Peaches said, which Ronnie knew. Peaches figured he had to peacock a bit, put on his show, be about that business after he figured out a few things. Ronnie wasn't the boss of bosses, but he ran Chicago, and for that alone, Peaches had admiration for him. He'd been at the tip of the spear since 1972, though one Cupertine or another ran the game since forever. Peaches had been hearing about Ronnie Cupertine his entire life. Plus the commercials for this car lots ran on every TV and radio.

"I always wanted to ask," Ronnie said, "do you call yourselves the Native Mob? Or someone else call you that?"

"We chose it," Peaches said, though he didn't actually know if that was true.

"The Family," Ronnie said. "The Outfit. Not a lot of nuance there, but enough to hide behind on a tape. Anyone can be a family or working for an outfit. It's just funny to me, how you guys start calling yourself the Mob, spray-painting it on billboards, screaming it before you shoot somebody. Seems a tad obvious, no?"

"No more obvious than a man in a suit wearing Kevlar," Peaches said.

"Maybe so," Ronnie said. He walked over to the bar, poured himself a scotch. "You drink?"

"Not when I'm working," Peaches said. He didn't ever drink. He liked to take some pills. An Oxy every now and then. Made shit smoothed out. A little weed. Coke to fit in, if need be.

"Who's that guy keeps getting arrested?" Ronnie said. "In Michigan? Indian with an Irish name? Collins?"

The Native Mob wasn't run like the Family, with one guy at the top. Instead, it had a council, decisions made democratically, things like drug profits getting split up evenly. When casinos and bingo rooms were involved, however, it got more complex; no one wanted to share anything. Richard Collins was part of the tribe opening casinos in Michigan, from Acme to Williamsburg. Doing it right. Spas and condos. High end. Problem was that he was also moving weight out of Canada. Landed a private plane filled with cocaine on reservation land. Now Michigan was dead, Native Mob telling everyone to stick to their places, don't come up there, let shit cool down. Peaches had other plans.

"He's not involved in this," Peaches said.

"You guys need better lawyers," Ronnie said. "Been getting fucked by the government for a long time now."

"I'll mention that to my boss."

"Your boss know you're here?"

"*Your* boss know I'm here?" Peaches said. He pointed at the cameras. "Or is that the feds on the other side?"

"That's funny," Ronnie said. Not that he laughed. "You come here to make jokes?"

"I wasn't making a joke," Peaches said. "I just know you've been lucky with the government and so I wondered why. Then I saw those cameras and thought maybe I was in an interrogation room."

"You think I answer to *anybody?*" Ronnie swirled the ice around in his drink, took a drink. Sniffed. "You wearing perfume?"

"I think you're worried that you'll have to," Peaches said, ignoring the second question, "or else you wouldn't put cameras in your own home."

"I don't live here," Ronnie said. "But your auntie? In Green Bay? I say the word, she's living underneath floorboards here by the end of the day. Your cousin right next to her. But personally? I'm not worried about anything." He took another sip. "You done measuring your dick in front of me, son?"

All right.

Everybody knows everybody.

That was fast.

"I'm not trying to insult you, Mr. Cupertine," Peaches said. "You're getting the wrong impression." He walked over to the wet bar, looked up at the camera mounted above it. State of the art for about 1985. These fucking people. All their operations were anti-quated. "If you've got someone on the other side of this camera? You answer to them. That's just a fact, Mr. Cupertine. I'm just pointing out a logistical concern you should have. Problem happens? You're down here, they're up there. You're dead already, yeah? What's the big deal if they witness the crime but can't stop it?"

"Who's to say you'd make it out alive?"

"Nobody," Peaches said. "I wouldn't expect to. But also? I don't give a fuck what you do to my auntie. I don't give a fuck what you do to my cousin, either. Kill them both right now. You and me, we still have business." He went over to the sofa, lifted up one of the cushions. There was a pull-out bed inside. Man. If it was up to Peaches, he'd fill this basement with cement, all the way to the roof. Science left these people behind. "I see things differently, Mr. Cupertine, and that can work to your advantage."

"Why don't you open that briefcase," Ronnie said.

Peaches came back to the pool table, popped open the case, set it on the green felt. He had fifty thousand in used twenties, so it was going to take a minute to unpack. "Case in point, Mr. Cupertine? I know you're not gonna go kill my auntie, because that's not how the Family operates. You don't kill families. So before you stand here and threaten me with it, you gotta do it sometimes to make it plausible. Not farm that shit out, either. Actually send a couple fucking Italians out there to kill an old lady." He started to put the cash down, one stack at a time, fifty in total. "This place you got here? Don't get me wrong. It's peaceful. But this carpet contains the DNA of every person who has stepped foot in here. Same with that sofa and that recliner. The grout in your wood paneling is rubber, which means any bit of hair or skin floating around in the dust is stuck in it. Blood, spit, snot, same deal. You could set fire to this place, cops could probably still dig hair and fiber out of the walls." He ran a hand across the top of the pool table. "This felt is a problem, too. You may as well cover it with mugshots." He put the last of the cash down and then took out two padded mailers that were on the bottom of the case.

Ronnie took a sip from his drink. "Aren't you a smart mother-fucker," he said after a while.

"I'm trying to be," Peaches said.

"What is it you're interested in?"

"You need partners," Peaches said. "Your best guys are in prison, or they're missing, or they're dead. Gangster 2-6, they're going to run out the door soon as the Cartels make them a decent offer, particularly now that they know you dumped one of theirs in a garbage pit trying to deke out the feds. I respect the game, but those Mexicans? They don't give a fuck about you. They just want your product. The Cartels can get them all the weed and coke they want and they don't need to go through you."

"They don't have access to heroin," Ronnie said. "Not like I do."

"Not yet," Peaches said. "You get that good stuff, I agree. Afghanistan and shit. It's nice. But people, they don't need the good stuff. They just want the stuff. So they'll take the dirt the Mexicans are making and the Cartels will sell double the amount while you're cranking out that artisanal brand. You're gonna price yourself out in two, three years, by my estimation."

"I don't worry about the Cartels," Ronnie said.

"You should," Peaches said, "because they don't worry about you." Ronnie put down his drink. "No?"

"You got submarines and missile launchers? Because they do." Ronnie thought for a moment. "Go on," he said. There was the congressman.

"Mexican gangs keep coming in and burning our crops, snitching us out, it's getting tiresome, but I don't have the capital to fight them. Or the relationships. So, before they turn on you, I was hoping you might assist us in getting ourselves a foothold."

"What's in it for me?"

"I help you modernize a bit, keep you out of the newspapers, clean up some dirty dishes you still got sitting on the counter," Peaches said. "And we're opening a casino up north. We could use your expertise on a few things."

"The Family is out of the casino business."

"Not by choice, right? Everything being equal, you'd rather still own Las Vegas, right?"

"No," he said, after a while. He picked his drink back up, tossed it back. "I wouldn't be happy paying workmen's comp insurance for a thousand employees. I don't need that."

"You wouldn't be doing that with us," Peaches said. "And Howard Hughes won't be showing up to buy you out. We're looking at a capital infusion and then you can name your involvement. Because Mr. Cupertine, I'm looking around? And I don't see your next foray."

"I don't need a next one," he said.

"And yet," Peaches said, "you can't stop your soldiers from knocking over liquor stores."

Ronnie smiled then. "I'm almost entirely legal now."

"Which only means you're still a crook," Peaches said. "War is coming. Isn't gonna be guys in suits shooting each other on the streets. It's gonna be some sixteen-year-old in a lowered Honda Civic shooting an AK out his window at you and your kids while you're walking into Wrigley. You want to survive? You gotta move rural. That's the next wave. That's where the money's going. And you want to beat the Cartels, you get out of that junk bullshit and get into pills. Oxy. Klonopin. Ambien. No one gets shot picking up a prescription from CVS. And tribes, we've got our clinics, our own doctors, our old folks' homes, our own health insurance. There's a lot of us, yeah? And we've got our own land and our own cops. What we don't have is someone like you. The boss of bosses."

Ronnie said, "Why haven't I met you before?"

"I don't get invited to social functions."

"I bet," Ronnie said. "Where you from?"

"You don't know?"

"I want it on tape," Ronnie said. Wasn't he a smart motherfucker.

"Wisconsin," Peaches said. "Been down here a few years. Did a couple years in West Texas, living with some cousins. Did a spot in Joliet."

"How long?"

"A year."

"On what?"

"Assault with a deadly weapon." He'd put a guy's head through a television.

"A year is fast."

"I know how to behave," Peaches said. "Plus, it happened on reservation land."

Ronnie flipped through a stack of twenties. "How you know all this about fibers and DNA? You watch *CSI* or something?"

"No," Peaches said, "I read books. Take criminology classes at a couple community colleges. This stuff, it's all out in the open. You just gotta know where to look."

"I pay people for that," Ronnie said.

"Not enough," Peaches said. "FBI could be on those cameras in five minutes. Take a sixteen-year-old probably half that time."

"No one knows I'm down here," Ronnie said. Peaches handed Ronnie one of the mailers. He opened it up, looked inside. It was filled with papers. "What's this?"

"Every piece of property you own and every piece of property you've hidden in the last three decades. Including that one that burned down the other day."

"The fuck you talking about?"

"In Florida."

"Donte," Ronnie said, though he kept his eyes on Peaches.

The door opened up and there was that big motherfucker with the Kevlar, gun in his hand, and then behind him two other guys now. So here it was.

"Tell the boys upstairs to give me three minutes off camera," Ronnie said.

"Okay," Donte said. He looked at Peaches, then back at Ronnie. "You all right alone?"

Ronnie stared at Peaches for a few seconds. "Yeah," he said. "I think I'm fine." When Donte left, Ronnie put a finger up. "Don't speak," he said. He looked up at the cameras. When the red light went off on all of them, he said, "All right. You've got three minutes. I don't like what I hear, you're leaving in a bag."

"I had a problem solved for you," Peaches said. "An impediment to us having any kind of fruitful association."

"For me? An entire fucking block of residential properties burned down," Ronnie said. Peaches hadn't seen that. Mike really had a sheet now.

"That wasn't the intention."

"I got cops picking bones out of the ashes down there. It's gonna cost me all the insurance money just to keep people quiet. So tell me, what fucking problem did you solve?"

"A transportation problem," Peaches said. He tore open the second mailer, dumped out Frank Fishmann's eyes, ears, tongue, and the skin that once covered his face. "Let's have a conversation about Sal Cupertine."

I

AUGUST 2001

That Rabbi David Cohen wasn't Jewish had ceased, over time, to be a problem. He hardly thought of it anymore. Not when he was at the Bagel Café grabbing a nosh with Phyllis Rosencrantz to go over the Teen Fashion Show for the Homeless, not when he was shaking Abe Seigel down for a donation to the Tikvah scholarship over a bucket of balls at the TPC driving range, nor even when he was doing Shabbat services on a Saturday morning at Temple Beth Israel.

It didn't cross his mind when he was burying some motherfucker shipped in from Los Angeles or San Francisco or Seattle, like the low-level Chinese Triad gangsters they'd been getting lately. The last one—David thought he was maybe nineteen—went into eternity under the gravestone of Howard Katz, loving husband of Jill. Or at least *some* of him went into eternity. Katz didn't have much of a face left and David had his long bones extracted for transplant, then disposed of his organs, so basically he performed a service over metacarpals and phalanges in a bag of skin. Same day, David also put Morris Brinkman down, and that was fine, too. Eighty-seven years old, always crinkling butterscotch wrappers during minyan, the kind of man who still called black guys *schvartzes?* His time was up. Long up.

Hell, not even brises really got to David. That was all the mohel's show, anyway, and a RICO-level scam in its own right. Schlomo

Meir did the cuttings at every synagogue in town, a fucking monopoly on the foreskin business, but David didn't see any way to move in on that. There were training courses and accreditations involved, most Reform mohels these days were nurses or EMTs, no one really wanting some shaky-hand from the Old Country wielding the knife on their son. Since David was about the only person in the room who wasn't queasy around a blade and a little blood, it was actually a fairly pleasant affair. He could zone out for a few minutes, not worry about a tactical team kicking down the door.

No, the only time the Jewish thing crept up on David was on a day like today, the last Sunday of August, presiding over the quickie wedding of Michael Solomon to Naomi Rosen. They were too young, in David's opinion, Naomi only twenty-two, Michael a few months younger, both just out of UNLV with degrees in golf resort management, which was a thing, apparently. The rub was that Naomi was three months pregnant and that wasn't going to fly, at least not with her father. Jordan Rosen came to David a few weeks earlier to get a spiritual opinion on the matter, wanting to know where abortion fell among the irredeemable sins.

They were sitting in David's office at Temple Beth Israel. He'd rearranged it since taking over from Rabbi Cy Kales, moving out the two sofas that faced each other in favor of four uncomfortable chairs surrounding a narrow coffee table. He didn't want people staying longer than they had to.

"Talmud says it is acceptable," David told him, "if the baby isn't viable, or if it's making your daughter want to harm herself." This was, admittedly, a pretty modern interpretation. "In either case, it's not a choice you get to make for her."

"What if she's not in her right mind?"

"Is that the situation?"

"Seems like it," Jordan said. "When I was her age, you know what I was doing?" he asked. "Nothing. I was doing nothing. That's how it should be. Make no important life decisions until you're at least twenty-five. That's what my father told me. Makes sense to me now. At the time, it was just a free pass to screw up without any real ramifications. It was liberating." Jordan squeezed his thumb and index finger over his slim mustache, thinking. Then: "What about killing the kid who knocked her up? What's the ruling on that?"

"Is he threatening your life?"

"In a way."

Jordan Rosen was in his late fifties and had amassed a decent fortune developing gas station mini-marts around the city, all of them called Manic Al's. His latest venture was a carwash over on Fort Apache and Sahara that catered to the Summerlin country club set. Leather sofas. Recessed lighting. A wine bar. A cigar lounge. Seven pretty girls in knock-off Chanel suits running the front of the house like they were FBI, everything handled via earpieces, cuff mics, and disinterested stares.

Friday afternoons, Rosen brought out minor Las Vegas celebrities for meet and greets, so guys coming to pick up their Bentleys might run into Danny Gans or Charo or even Ralph Lamb, the cowboy sheriff who supposedly roughed up Johnny Roselli back in the day. It was one of those famous stories David heard growing up in Chicago, but which, when he thought about it now, seemed like it was probably made up. Good for tourism, shitty for reality. Because it turned out, what the fuck did it matter? Mob was still in Las Vegas and Ralph Lamb was still swinging his dick, fifty years later, eating free lunches for *maybe* smacking a guy who spent his days producing movies and counting cards. Real tough guys, both of them.

Jordan calling the car wash Manic Al's wouldn't fly in Summerlin, so he opted for the Millionaire Detail Club, started running commercials on KNPR, pulling in those sensitive types who listened to classical music and shopped organic but still wanted to feel like a boss, then priced everything at a markup: The most basic wash was $35.99. The Platinum Care Package ran five bills and included a blacked-out, supposedly bulletproof Suburban that would shuttle you back and forth to your home or office while your ride was getting cleaned. The Diamond Experience? Rosen didn't bother to advertise a price on that, nor explain what it entailed. You felt the need to ask, it wasn't for you.

David didn't get it. It was all just water and soap. And yet there was always a line of cars waiting to get washed.

"What does your wife think?" David asked.

"Sarah's losing her mind with glee. She's been preparing to be called Nana her entire life. Throw in planning a wedding and she might combust." Jordan stopped rubbing his mustache, but left his thumb in his rather pronounced Cupid's bow, then pointed at David. "Can I ask you a personal question, Rabbi Cohen?"

"If you feel you have to."

"Growing up, what did your parents want you to be?"

"My own man," David said. That was what his mother wanted, at any rate, back when David was still her son Sal, back before he started doing hits in Chicago for the Family, back before he became the Rain Man, when she'd still acknowledge him. What his dad wanted? Sal didn't know. He'd been dead since Sal was ten, so what he remembered about him now, almost thirty years later, were small things: How he'd pay Sal a quarter for a hug. How he read the comics in the *Sun-Times* first thing every morning. How he always had scabs on his knuckles.

Sometimes, Sal thought about the sound his father's body made hitting the ground in front of the IBM Building, about how when someone gets thrown out of a fifty-two-story building, they've got a long time to make noise, and his father did. Screamed for a good five seconds. And then it was a liquid crunch, a spray of blood, and nothing. Sal Cupertine never did anyone like that. It wasn't fucking human.

Rabbi David Cohen tried not to think about those things too often. He was about keeping his rage in check these days. Every morning, he wrapped tefillin on his strong arm, to remind himself of this. As a Reform Jew, it wasn't needed, but David had adopted it anyway, thought the imagery was good, and it served a higher purpose. David couldn't always be dialed to ten, or else he'd have nowhere to go when he really needed to be angry. Six or seven, that was his sweet spot.

"I imagined Naomi would be a vet. She always had hamsters and silkworms and whatnot," Jordan said. "Made me sponsor a puma adoption at that gypsy zoo over on Rancho. Have you been there?"

"I don't believe in zoos," David said.

"She didn't either. That's why I had to sponsor the puma. She wanted to bust it out. Place is a dump. Anyway. I don't know. I guess that's just me imagining a life for her." He stood up, cracked his neck—an annoying habit that David had noticed over the course of the last few years—then walked over to one of the three bookshelves in the office. They were six feet tall and crammed full of books on Jewish philosophy, Jewish thought, even a bit of poetry and self-help, titles like *Understanding the Mishna, Understanding You.* "You read all of these?"

"Most of them," David said.

He pulled out a book of poetry, flipped it open. David didn't like people touching his books, much less reading what he wrote in the margins. "Truth is," he said, "I don't really know Naomi anymore." He closed the book, slipped it back into its slot, upside down, pulled out another. "Maybe a kid will put us into each other's orbit again, you know? I guess that would be a side benefit."

"Do you know the boy?"

"Yeah," he said. "It's the Solomon kid. The oldest."

"Robert and Janice's son?"

"No, the other Solomons. The yenta and the ear, nose, and throat guy."

"Oh. Scott and Claudia?"

"Good family, I guess. It could be worse. Few years ago, Naomi was dating a Vietnamese kid. Father dealt cards at the Orleans. One of those pinkie-ring guys who smoked funny? You know, like he held his cigarette with the wrong fingers? Anyway. Kid's name was Binh but he called himself DJ Bomb Squad. Had it painted on his car, left stickers on light poles, even had T-shirts. I'm of the opinion it put

Naomi's grandfather into the grave prematurely." He snapped closed the book in his hand and put it away, right side up, then flipped over the poetry book, too. "It was fine with me," he added eventually. "I sort of liked DJ Bomb Squad. He was enterprising. I knew what I was getting with that kid."

"What happened?"

"Who knows. One day, he's everything, next day, Sarah tells me never to mention DJ Bomb Squad again. I almost felt sorry for him. He probably never saw it coming." He paused for a second, stared directly at Rabbi Cohen, which made him slightly uncomfortable. It wasn't that he didn't like eye contact—though that was true—it was more that he didn't like people studying his face too closely, especially now when it felt like his face was collapsing; his jaw a fucking mess, the skin around his left eye starting to droop, and a fair amount of nasal problems were plaguing him of late, too, leaving him stuffed up half the time. There wasn't a decent doctor he could see. Hard to get a new specialist and explain why you have titanium rods to elongate your jaw, plus a new chin and nose, and no medical records.

There was only so much his beard and a pair of glasses could hide, particularly since half the congregation were doctors of some kind. Maybe he could fake Bell's palsy at a temple in Oklahoma, but it wasn't going to go unnoticed in Summerlin.

"I'm not trying to be rude," Jordan said, "but you ever think about getting Botox?" He made a circle in the air with his index finger, pointing, generally, to David's whole head. "Just a cosmetic type thing?"

"No," David said. If another question about his appearance were proposed, there was a chance the next time anyone saw Jordan Rosen, it would be his photo on the news when he was reported missing.

"I ask," he said, still pointing, "because my wife, she had that problem with her eyelid. Started to hang over her left eye?" David remembered. She looked like a retired boxer. "She got it lasered and then botox froze the nerve, I guess. Something like that might help your eye. You know, if you care about such things."

"Talmud says all paths are crooked."

Jordan put up his hands. "Fair enough," he said. "But don't you ever think about getting married, Rabbi Cohen?"

That was now three personal questions Jordan Rosen had asked him. It was three more than David felt comfortable answering, though the marriage one was getting to be so common as to be impersonal.

"I may well have to at some point," David said. It was, in fact, among his worst fears. Because Sal Cupertine was married. His wife, Jennifer, and son, William, were still in Chicago, Sal keeping watch on Jennifer's movements in whatever way he could, even looking at her credit report online a few months back. She was racking up debt on her cards. Five grand on the Chase card. Another seven on the Citibank. A month behind on her Amex. Even the fucking Discover card was maxed out. Three and a half years since he'd seen his wife and kid and the closest he could come to them was this: peeping on their lives like some kind of pervert. He'd been able to get her money once, but since then it had become too difficult. The problem with embarrassing the FBI, turning on the Family, and pissing off the Gangster 2-6 was that it didn't exactly make life easier.

"It changes your perspective," Jordan said. "Sometimes, I hardly recognize myself, truth be told. Maybe it's what Naomi needs."

This was how it often went with the Jews: They'd come in with a problem and ask questions they'd answer themselves, as if all they needed was for David to witness the process in order to make it divine. Jordan took a deep breath, then peered around the office, as if he were seeing it for the first time even though he had spent a fair amount of time in it over the years, first meeting with Rabbi Kales and now with David. "You should get some pictures in here," Jordan said after a while. "Something personal."

"You want to know a man, read his books."

"That in the Talmud?"

"No," David said. "I made that one up myself." Though, in fact, he hadn't. He read it somewhere. Emerson or Whitman or maybe it was George Washington? Used to be people thought Sal Cupertine had a photographic memory, hence all that Rain Man shit, but the truth was more complex than that, David understood now. It wasn't that he remembered every single detail of every single experience with 100 percent accuracy. He retained a lot, but that didn't mean everything got filed with the correct headings. The last couple years—at least since all the plastic surgery—he'd felt like things weren't quite as accurate as they'd once been. Maybe getting discount anesthesia wasn't great on the cerebral cortex.

"Rabbi Kales always had a lot of tchotchkes, is all." He stepped over to the shelf where David kept his doctored diploma from Hebrew Union in a frame on a stand.

"He still has them," David said. Rabbi Kales lived in an apartment in an "Active Senior Living" complex off Charleston now, on the second floor with a view of the courtyard between the two sides of the facility—the "active living" portion, which was three stories and held about seventy-five people who needed only to have someone cook their meals or remind them to take their pills—and the "assisted living" side, which held another hundred people on a rotating basis, seeing as it was reserved for those sliding into death, mostly in full dementia or straight-up hospice care. David thinking that if he needed to be assisted in order to live, he'd fix that quick.

"Sarah bumped into him at Smith's a while back." Jordan pulled out another book, read the back for a few seconds. "Said he was confused as hell."

"Some days he's good," David said, "some days, not." That was the problem with Rabbi Kales—he wasn't getting *actual* dementia fast enough. He could pretend pretty well when he needed to, but then pride would take over. David reminded him periodically that if he wanted to stay aboveground, he needed to spend a bit more time out in the world acting inconsistent, particularly once his son-in-law, Bennie, was free. Rabbi Kales couldn't drive anymore—that was part of the plan, couldn't very well have him diagnosed as having early onset dementia and also let him keep his license—so his daughter, Rachel, either drove him places or paid for a Town Car.

"He still makes it to services fairly regularly." David hadn't seen Jordan at services since his youngest, Tricia, went off to college at Berkeley last fall. She used to come, help out with the little ones, tutor, that sort of thing. She also worked down at the Bagel Café, too, telling David she liked making her own money. David missed seeing her around. He also missed the fact that she was a shitty waitress and occasionally got his order wrong, which meant he was periodically able to wolf down a piece of bacon or sausage on the down low.

"Well, tell him I said hello," Jordan said. He turned the book in his hand back over, looked at the cover, then held it up. "You mind if I borrow this one?"

It was a collection of notable transcripts from the Nuremberg trials. Not exactly light reading.

"Be my guest," David said.

Jordan tucked the book under one arm, then took his wallet out and thumbed through his cash, pulled out two hundreds and two fifties and set them on the coffee table. "Appreciate the counsel, Rabbi. Come by the car wash this week," he said. "Donny Osmond is signing autographs."

NOW NAOMI AND Michael were exchanging a series of vows that David was pretty sure were cribbed from a pop song. The three of them stood under a chuppah in the Rosens' backyard . . . if you could call anything with an acre of grass with an outdoor wine bar surrounding a private lake a yard. The Rosens lived in the Vineyards at Summerlin, a few doors down from Bennie Savone and his family, in an exclusive development that was supposed to evoke the Italian countryside except with German cars and Mexican domestic staff. David had never been to Italy, never even made it to the Venetian on the Strip to ride in a gondola, on account of the facial recognition cameras all the casinos had—they weren't looking for average bad guys, by and large, but Bennie told him it was a no-go zone—but he couldn't help wondering if there were housing developments being built on the Amalfi Coast modeled after Las Vegas, Italians living in peach-colored tract homes with brown lawns.

David viewed weddings as sacred affairs and took his role seriously—of all the vows he'd taken in his own life, it was the only one that had actually stuck—and if Naomi and Michael wanted to seal their love by quoting Kid Rock in front of a few hundred of their closest friends and family members, who was he to judge? Those were just words. A vow was something you believed in, and that didn't require spoken words. Besides, it was David's job to give them the true blessing, the sense that what they were doing had some continuity with history, so even though they weren't particularly faithful Jews, and they exchanged bullshit vows, at least David was doing his part.

Which was the problem.

There was going to come a time, pretty soon if David had his way, when Rabbi David Cohen would be replaced again by Sal Cupertine, and by no fault of their own, Naomi and Michael's marriage would be a sham: David's blessings upon them little more than a minor fraud perpetuated by a professional Mob killer, this otherwise mild summer day a footnote in a series of criminal acts, and no matter how much David wanted Naomi and Michael to have a good life, free of the shit and violence and deception he'd been party to since he was ten years old . . . man, one day? There they would be, right in it, forever.

David could see the *Dateline* episode already: Keith Morrison sitting across from Naomi and Michael, asking them if they'd ever noticed anything . . . *odd* . . . about Rabbi David Cohen, a man they'd trusted to bless their union, bless their unborn child. Hadn't he seemed . . . *different?* Though, of course, it wasn't as if Naomi's father would want anyone poking too far into his life, what with his business relationship with Bennie. A couple years earlier, Jordan had become infatuated with a dancer at Bennie's club, the Wild Horse, and ended up owing a hundred thousand dollars, plus an increasing vig, for lap dances and VIP-room hand jobs, which wasn't exactly a check he could write without his wife noticing. So now Bennie was a silent partner in some of Jordan's real estate holdings out on what used to be the butthole end of North Las Vegas, down on Craig Road, but which was suddenly a hot property. Trilogy and a dozen other developers were talking about building their own master-planned communities out there, 2002 promising to be the year that everyone moved into supermax prison complexes in the desert, replete with open-concept floor plans, travertine floors, and armed rent-a-cops patrolling 24/7.

So . . . maybe it wouldn't be Naomi and Michael on camera.

Maybe it would be Rochelle and Lee.

Andrea and Brent.

Tara and Neil.

How many couples had he married in the last three years? Twenty? Thirty? Which didn't make David feel any better. His entire life as Sal Cupertine had been lived as a ghost, and now here he was, rolled up in the lives of common civilians.

"That was beautiful," Rabbi Cohen said when Michael finished his vows, something about Naomi's smile making him think of brighter days ahead. David was pretty sure Michael was high. His eyes were almost entirely black, nothing but pupils staring back. Probably did a couple bumps before the ceremony, or chopped up his little brother's Ritalin, maybe stole a prescription pad from his father's office and got himself and his best men Adderall for the big day, since all six of them were fidgeting messes.

Or maybe it was just that Michael was shit-scared. David had seen that look once or twice before in people, back in his old line of work. *This kid is fucked,* David thought, but wasn't absolutely certain who he was thinking of: Michael, Naomi, or the unborn child in Naomi's belly, who was already named Dakota, even though they didn't yet know the sex.

David poured two glasses of wine and set them between the bride and groom, along with a third empty glass.

"In our tradition," he said, "wine is a symbol of the transformations we go through as people. From the dirt grows the vine, which grows the grape, which is picked and goes through the sour period of fermentation, and then becomes the wine itself, which becomes the warmth of your body when you drink, which creates a sense of euphoria in your mind." David paused then, as he always did during this portion of the ceremony, and made a point to look directly at both the bride and groom, as Rabbi Kales had taught him: *Tilt your head, smile, but not with too much joy. Think of something sad at the same time, so that there is also something slightly mournful in your face. Sigh before you begin again. Lower your voice an octave. It will sound like you're quoting something even if you are not.*

"Such is the beautiful journey we make as people, and, together, Michael and Naomi, you'll make as husband and wife." David poured both glasses of wine into the third glass, then held it up. "From many, we have one."

He handed the glass to Naomi and she took a tiny sip, barely enough to wet her lips. Naomi gave the wine to Michael, who downed it like he was doing a shot, wiped his mouth with the back of his hand, and pumped his fist. In that moment, David saw Michael's entire life unfold in front of him. It was a future of SUV payments he couldn't afford, tight black short-sleeved V-necks under sport coats, and vague notions that maybe having someone knock off his physician father would alleviate some of his financial burdens. Thing was, a few years ago, Sal Cupertine would have taken that job.

David began the chant of the Sheva Brachot, the Seven Blessings, first in Hebrew—*Barukh atah Adonai Eloheinu melekh ha-olam, bo'rei p'ri ha-gafen*—and then in English. David thought the blessings were fine, if a little generic—thanking God for creating everything, essentially—but it was the sixth one where he really had a beef: *Blessed art Thou, O Lord, King of the universe, who has created joy and gladness, bridegroom and bride, mirth and exultation, pleasure and delight, love, brotherhood, peace, and fellowship. Soon may there be heard in the cities of Judah and in the streets of Jerusalem the voice of joy and gladness, the voice of the bridegroom and the voice of the bride, the jubilant voice of bridegrooms from their canopies, and of youths from their feasts of song. Blessed art Thou, O Lord, who makest the bridegroom to rejoice with the bride.*

David didn't believe God created joy and gladness any more than he thought God was responsible for pain and suffering. He'd dealt enough in those last two to know that God was very rarely involved. It wasn't God who'd put Sal Cupertine on the streets of Chicago disposing of people for the Family. It wasn't God who packed Sal Cupertine into a frozen meat truck and hustled him off to Las Vegas, sold him into this long con after he killed three feds and a CI. No, that was his cousin Ronnie.

However, if God was responsible for anything these days, David thought it was for moments like today—when there was a real spirit in the air, when love felt like a tangible thing, yet somehow otherworldly—and the fact was he felt pretty Jewish in those situations, since he was the one who was supposed to be keeping the candle lit, so to speak, and if there was one thing he did, it was his fucking job.

David finished the blessings. Took in the guests. What Rabbi Kales called "accounting": See who is being moved. Add them to your list. Then, at a later date, make them account.

Jordan Rosen openly sobbed with joy, clutched his wife's hand, kissed it.

Tricia Rosen, back from Berkeley with short hair now, dabbed at her eyes and nodded at Rabbi Cohen in that way young people do when they believe in something beyond their present emotional experience.

The flower girl was asleep across Mrs. Solomon's lap, Mr. Solomon stroking her hair.

The grandparents, the aunts, the uncles, the cousins, the second cousins, the friends, the alter kockers who flew in from Portland and Seattle and New York and Toronto and Israel, everyone paying a debt for having shown up for some other distant cousin's wedding or bris or funeral. Jews were pretty good about showing up, no matter the occasion. They all looked too much alike for David's comfort. All brown hair, thick eyebrows, pale-to-light-olive complexion, too much hair on their forearms, too many gold necklaces, too many Coach handbags, too many of those pimp watches with gold bracelets young men seemed to be favoring of late, constantly spinning them around their wrists, the links catching hits off the sun. Not enough men in ties. Too many women in sandals. It just wasn't right. You come to a wedding, you should dress with the dignity of a funeral, because who the fuck knows when you'll ever see the couple again, and who the fuck knows when they'll see you again. So you get your look right, you don't glam it up, you don't whore it up, even though it's Las Vegas. No one ever got kicked out of a place in Las Vegas for dressing elegantly. If David was going to wear the tallith, the least everyone else could do was put on a fucking tie and some closed-toe shoes.

In the back were the professionals: the lawyers, the accountants, the doctors, the investment guys, the real estate team, the city councilmen, the casino executives, Andy from Summerlin Rolls-Royce, Carter from JetVegas, Kendra from Caesars Palace Forum Shops Private Shopping Concierge Services, the local ABC meteorologist—Ginger or Bianca or something in between those names—in a plunging red dress, all of them clustered near the bar, talking the whole fucking time, but pausing now, David's eyes on them, sensing that the big moment was about to happen, when God left and the party started. Behind the professionals, the tuxedoed catering staff set up the elaborate dinner under pitched white tents. The three-piece wind ensemble unpacked their instruments.

And, watching from his lawn, stood Bennie Savone.

David wrapped the wineglass in a clean white towel and held it aloft for all the guests to see. "Talmud says the breaking of the glass is a symbol of the fall of the Temple of Jerusalem," David said. "But I believe it is to remind us that there are sharp edges in life." Pause. Chin tilted up half an inch. "Thus." Pause. Octave down. "We must temper joy with the remembrance of and preparation for sorrow." David found the oldest person in the audience—one of the Solomon clan, David had met him earlier, cousin Louis from New York, wearing a yarmulke made of fine silk, Louis telling David its entire provenance, which involved a tragic summer in Poland, a month stuck at Ellis Island, his mother dying at thirty-seven, and then, eventually, a very successful furniture business in upstate New York, where he was considered the Sleeper-Sofa King of Troy—and extended a hand in his general direction, everyone turning to look at the old codger, as if he were the living embodiment of the Exodus. "For we are the witnesses of history." Pause. Raise the voice. Smile. Tilt the head back down half an inch. "Love needs no permission. For we are taught that *ahev* is a natural convergence of giving and being open to emotion. And so, Michael and Naomi, I tell you to make your own traditions, but keep, too, our shared history close, remembering, always, that your people are our people."

Rabbi David Cohen set the wineglass down in front of Michael and Naomi and was just about to tell them they could kiss, but he didn't get the chance. The couple both began to curb-stomp the living shit out of the wineglass. Then Michael swooped Naomi up into his arms and kissed her flush on the mouth, both of them wide-eyed and laughing through the kiss, everyone shouting *Mazel tov! Mazel tov!* even though Naomi had sliced her foot open on the glass and had stained the hem of her wedding dress with blood.

2

"Lovely ceremony, Rabbi," Bennie Savone said. He was standing at the bottom of his lawn, eating from a bag of sunflower seeds and watching Sophie, the youngest of his two daughters, pedal boat around the lake. He wore a polo shirt and shorts, no shoes, a court-mandated ankle bracelet. Technically, David could visit Bennie whenever he wanted, since house arrest allowed for visits from clergy, but Bennie didn't want to take that chance. He'd done six months inside on a Conspiracy to Obstruct Justice beef related to the vicious beating of a patron at the Wild Horse by two of his bouncers, still had another five months of home detention, and didn't want to give the feds any reason to start looking at his associates. But he'd sent a message through Rabbi Kales.

"I expected to see your wife at the ceremony," David said.

Bennie said, "Rachel and Sarah aren't currently speaking."

"Since when?"

"I don't know," Bennie said. "Rachel doesn't tell me shit these days." He offered Rabbi Cohen the bag of sunflower seeds, but David demurred. "My guess is that Sarah told Rachel something she didn't want to hear, like maybe she didn't want some criminal's wife at her daughter's blessed day."

"There were plenty of criminals there," David said.

"Maybe she just doesn't like me," Bennie said, which was probably true, too. She had good reason.

Bennie had been picked up in 1999 and charged with conspiracy, which meant the feds had free rein to find whatever shit they could uncover, though the only thing that stuck was the obstruction charge on the beating, which wasn't even a federal charge. Bennie kept his books clean, paid his taxes, made sure his boys at the club paid theirs, made sure the girls did, too. Not that they were running an entirely legal enterprise, only that Bennie wasn't dumb enough to make it obvious. Bennie's lawyer, Vincent Zangari, got him a quickie plea deal just in case the dentist died before they could get to trial, which would have been bad, since then Bennie would be looking at an accessory charge on a murder, which was a mandatory twelve-year RICO sentence. As it was, the fucker was paralyzed and breathing through a hole in his neck, which made him a pretty convincing witness, even if he couldn't talk.

Bennie called in some favors from the judicial bench, made sure he wasn't going to be doing time in some ass factory, ended up getting six months in the minimum-security wing up at Warm Springs in Carson City—which was like doing time at a Radisson: shitty, but not torture—followed by six months home detention.

And that calmed shit down.

For a while, anyway.

Then the owner of Panthers Gentleman's Club—a local named Vic Acosta, doing front work for some low-level Miami boys—skipped town after getting indicted on tax evasion a few months ago and the feds seized his club. The IRS was owed fifteen million, which they weren't gonna get selling the building, so they figured they'd recoup it on the pole. They brought in the U.S. Marshals to run the joint, which wasn't great for business, even after they dropped the price of lap dances from twenty dollars to ten. When that didn't work, they got a food license, started to move steak and lobster in addition to tits and ass, tried to cater to gentlemen, as if gentlemen still came to Las Vegas. Still nothing. So they tried an Italian buffet, started giving the girls health benefits, since they were now federal employees, figuring they'd get some high-class girls that way, not realizing conventioneers didn't want a high-class girl. Their last big move was a billboard on the Strip advertising ACTUALLY LEGAL GIRLS.

That got the national media interested, everyone from *20/20* to the *Today* show to the *National Enquirer* coming to town to do stories on how tax dollars were paying the hourly wages of lap dancers, which eventually dovetailed into tales of how antiquated the Italian American Mafia had become. While the Chinese Triads were training teenagers to hack half the world, the Mafia was still running protection schemes for a couple grand a month. While the Russian Mob was counterfeiting credit cards and stealing a million dollars a week from gas and oil companies overseas, the Mafia was running sex rings and blackmail scams. The Mexican Cartels owned an entire fucking country . . . and the Mafia was breaking city councilmen's legs for unpaid debts on the Super Bowl. And who was scared of the Mafia anymore, anyway, when kids on the block had automatic weapons? People got shot in the head just for waking up and going to school.

Then they made it personal: Talking about how Al Capone had morphed into that Teflon pussy John Gotti. How Joseph "The Animal" Barboza, who ate the faces of his enemies, gave way to the likes of Sammy the Bull, who only stopped snitching long enough to write a tell-all book and flirt with Diane Sawyer on TV, all while still under witness protection. Or how Whitey Bulger had skipped Boston with the FBI's assistance—not that he was real Mafia, just a dumb Irish thug, not that it mattered to Al Roker, that giggling fuck—long before Sal Cupertine, the Chicago Family enforcer known as the Rain Man—Matt Lauer acting up, too, the fuck: "I see that, I think of Dustin Hoffman, don't you, Al? Not threatening in the least"—got away with killing three FBI agents and a CI, and then got shipped out of the city in a truck full of frozen meat. And now this fuckwit Vic Acosta, who lost his club to the government and didn't even have the good sense to burn it down first.

David caught it all one morning while he sat at his kitchen table, eating his oatmeal, the one food that didn't hurt his jaw. His old face flashed on the screen for ten seconds, the first time David had seen it in a couple years, along with some grainy video of him ordering a tuna sandwich inside a Subway in Chicago. David thinking how nice it would be to eat a sandwich without it sending white hot pain into his nasal cavity and out his ears, thinking, *Shit, I hope Jennifer doesn't see this.* Thinking, *Shit, I hope my mother doesn't see this.* Even if he hadn't seen his mother in fifteen years.

First couple years after he dropped out of high school, he was deep in the life, and she was still in Chicago, going by her maiden name, Arlene Rigliano, because she'd given up the Family. He'd bump into her on the street, she'd act like he didn't exist, and he was so hard, he didn't want to believe he'd ever been someone's kid, so what did it matter?

Except one time. He and Jennifer were in Target, buying mouthwash and cereal and greeting cards, that real-life stuff, and suddenly his mother came around the bend in the paper towel aisle. It was just the two of them there under those bright white lights—Jennifer still lingering in the vitamin row, adding up how much they'd spent; Target an indulgence for them in those days, they were so broke, they had to keep track of every dime, bouncing checks not the kind of thing Sal Cupertine wanted to get nicked for—Sal done up in a leather duster like he was in a western, Arlene white haired, wearing high-waisted pants, pushing a cart filled with laundry detergent, ice cream, cottage cheese, Diet Pepsi, the opposite of how Sal remembered her. When his dad was alive, his mother was always in designer jeans and ribbed turtlenecks, coral lipstick, perfect hair, a glass of wine or a Marlboro red in her hand. Then his dad got thrown off a building. Maybe it would have been different if they both hadn't seen it happen from Billy Cupertine's convertible, waiting for him to come back down from an errand he had to run, *be gone two seconds*, that's what he said, and then fifteen minutes later he came back down all right. After that Sal's mother couldn't even put a comb through her hair for a few years, barely made it out of bed, started to take up with men who drove TR7s. By then, Sal was under Ronnie's sway.

"Look at you," she said, stopped there at the end of the aisle, right next to a display of Bounty, the contempt in her voice metallic. "A real professional."

"That's right," Sal said. He was twenty-six. He didn't know shit. Wouldn't for years. His mother was just the lady who didn't want him to be in the Family. If he had a time machine, man, he'd use it to punch himself in the gut.

"They murdered your father," she said.

"Someone was going to," he said.

"If only they'd waited a few years," she said, "you could have done it."

A boy and girl came running into the aisle, chasing a blue ball that came bouncing past, stopped, looked at Sal, and ran in the other direction. He had that effect.

She tilted her head to the right, tried to look around Sal, saw Jennifer back there. "She looks well."

"She is."

"You have any kids?"

"Not yet."

"Don't," she said, then she just turned around, left her cart where it was, and walked out. Sal played that scene in his head a hundred times, a thousand times, all the different things he should have said, though never once did he tell Jennifer about it. His mother lived in Arizona now, remarried, that was the story, which meant she was close by, could be in Las Vegas, even, dumping quarters into the slots at Treasure Island.

Then his face on the TV melted away into a shot of a U.S. Marshal in a shirt and a tie, sitting in his office at Panthers, talking about the perils of running a strip club. The Mafia in Las Vegas a big fucking joke.

David didn't think it was funny. As it was, every time some hump in New York or Chicago or Miami got busted doing some gangster shit, they'd drag Sal Cupertine back into the news for a few days, sure to mention that the FBI was offering a $500,000 reward for his capture now that they admitted he wasn't dead. David conveniently got a head cold whenever that happened, kept his face away from the public, since Las Vegas was filled with bounty hunters, professional and amateur, the town the last stop for fugitives. Every other week *America's Most Wanted* would feature some pedophile asshole who was last spotted on camera inside the ice cream parlor at the Frontier, or would note that some white supremacist militia wacko was apprehended in the parking lot of the Fashion Show Mall, the trunk of his car filled with ropes and handcuffs and diapers and brass knuckles and *The Anarchist's Cookbook*. It was only a matter of time before John Walsh spent thirty minutes talking about Sal Cupertine and then what? Jennifer would see that, for sure. His mom, too. And everyone else, everywhere. David would have to fake shingles for a month.

Everyone thought Las Vegas was the kind of place you could hide in, that you could fuck up all you wanted. But the truth, David had learned, was that Las Vegas was a small, mostly conservative town and more isolated than a Hawaiian island. Five miles out of the city limits, going in any direction, sat the wild desert, hundreds of miles and several hours from the next big city, which meant you saw the same people everywhere . . . provided you didn't go to the Strip, which David never did, and neither did any other local, unless they were going to their jobs, but even then, you saw your neighbor, one blackjack table over, everyone in everyone's business, and all of it now getting captured on camera, the video processed and stored on a hard drive somewhere, waiting for a subpoena. Casinos *used* to be a place you could fuck off in, not worry about being an asshole, and maybe that was still true, but now, all the while, you were also being mined for your data, David reading about how all these big gaming companies were tracking your every move: how much you spent, how long you stayed in one place, your betting patterns, your body language, did you smile when the cocktail girl walked by, even how long you sat in the toilet, since they had a camera on you walking in and a camera on you walking out.

Being home wasn't much different.

If someone strange showed up in your Summerlin or Henderson or Green Valley neighborhood, didn't go to your church or your temple, didn't wave hello in the morning, never got Nevada plates on their car, let their pit bull shit on your lawn, watered their own lawn with a hose instead of sprinklers, never finished their backyard, then you could bet the Mormons on the street would make a fuss, put in a call to the HOA. If you kept fucking up, the HOA would eventually call the cops, the cops would bring in the sheriff, sheriff would bring in the marshals, next thing, there would be a standoff, shots fired, and a body being wheeled out of your community draped with a white sheet, and it turns out you've got a grow house on the block, not Cartel level, but enough to fill Centennial High School and Bishop Gorman High School with narcotic-quality weed.

Thus, David recognized the need to be prepared. He wasn't going to be caught slipping again, like when that agent showed up. The national news had already rolled into Las Vegas just to talk shit in light of the Panthers debacle, and eventually some enterprising reporter would realize Panthers was only two blocks from the Wild Horse, whose owner, they'd learn, was Bennie Savone, also a reputed wiseguy, who was arrested on some RICO shit that didn't stick . . . was currently doing time on the beating of a Nebraska-based dentist . . . and then that reporter and a cameraman would be knocking on the door of the temple to get some background color for their story . . . and, well, that would not do.

Even on a night like tonight, behind the walls of the Vineyards, whose security was tight—Bennie couldn't live in a place where anyone could walk up to him on the golf course and kill him—David had his butterfly knife in his pocket. If the FBI showed up with an assault team tonight, he recognized he couldn't kill them all. But if it was just one or two guys, well, he could knife one guy, take his gun, and kill the other guy. He'd done that before. Average room filled with average people, there weren't many who'd stick around after seeing someone bleed out through the neck or get a knife in the ear—which was a bad way to kill a person, since it was hard to get a knife out of someone's head—or hear someone screaming when they got their eyes slit in two, which wasn't fatal, but it was some horror movie shit, the kind of thing David was prepared to do if he needed to get out of a crowded room, fast.

He kept a Glock cut into the passenger seat of his Range Rover, easy enough to get to when he was driving, since he never rode with anyone, and not easily found in a cursory flashlight search if he got pulled over, not that Rabbi David Cohen ever got pulled over in Summerlin, but he didn't keep it on his person out in public. Couldn't very well be golfing with a city councilman and have his Glock fall out of his bag. Even if everyone in Nevada pretended to have a gun, that whole Wild West ethos a *thing* in Nevada, David was of the opinion that rabbis couldn't be Wyatt Earping motherfuckers on the street. Anyway, David knew that most people had no real idea how to use a gun—even cops were scared of killing somebody—unless they were on a shooting range, fitted with noise-suppressing head-gear, protective goggles, and ceramic vests. It wasn't like TV, where everyone was a trained assassin waiting for the right moment to show their disregard for human life.

But David was. That was a difference that mattered.

"I saw that the weathergirl from Channel Thirteen made the show," Bennie said now. "Jordan still sleeping with her?"

"I don't know," David said. "He doesn't confess to me."

"Any other notables I gotta worry about?"

"The guy from Channel Eight who believes in aliens was in the back, drinking White Russians."

"That Kenny Rogers–looking guy?"

"Yeah," David said.

"Like there's not enough bad shit in the real world? You gotta go searching for worse things in space? Makes no sense to me."

"It's entertainment," David said.

"That's what worries me."

David never worried about the local media surprising him, since they came out to the temple somewhat regularly for events—the

Kugel Bake Off for Social Justice, the Jewish Book Festival, the annual Hanukkah Carnival and Menorah Lighting event—and besides, they never seemed to be sure whose side they were on when it came to organized crime, only that Mob business was good for everyone's bottom line.

One day, Harvey B. Curran, the *Review-Journal's* Mob gossip columnist, would be insinuating that more trouble was about to come down on local wiseguys, that the feds were massed outside the gates of the Vineyards, had put recording devices into the neighborhood cats, were buying houses in the Scotch 80s, had moles in the gaming board, were running anthropologists around Lake Mead as the water receded, pulling out dead bodies, running DNA, capturing plates out front of Piero's, strong-arming UPS drivers, bribing maids, everyone about a week away from a major indictment, the whole city about to be tossed up. Nothing anyone could confirm or deny.

The next day, Curran would be going on about what assholes the corporate casino billionaires were, how life was better when the Mob ran the Strip, since at least you knew where you stood with those guys.

The day after that, there'd be a half-page ad for happy hour at the Wild Horse, some nineteen-year-old blond jerking off a bottle of champagne. By Sunday, there'd be a color photo of Mayor Oscar Goodman in the same space, pimping at a fund-raiser for the Mob museum he wanted the city to build smack on the spot where Estes Kefauver held hearings on Cosa Nostra back in the day, David wondering if they'd be building museums for the Crips and Bloods and Mexican Mafia, too. Maybe toss one up for the Skinheads. Come with a prison tattoo, get a free tour. He thought maybe he'd write a letter to the editor, get on the record about how stupid this idea was, that the Jews didn't support celebrating the Mob, any mob.

But before he could put pen to paper, the *Mercury*, one of those shit-rag weekly papers, would do an investigative piece, send a girl into a strip club and have her report back on the dark shit she'd witnessed, the local Mob so fucking stupid that they didn't even run background checks on their dancers. The *Mercury* would get photos of known felons counting stacks of cash in the break room, guns out, like they were waiting for someone to tell them to go to the fucking mattresses, and David would think: *Build a museum and bury these dumb fucks in the foundation. Start fresh.*

It wasn't, David understood, the right frame of mind to have in this situation.

"You get a copy of the guest list?" Bennie asked.

"I will," David said.

"Get the photos, too," Bennie said, like this was David's first gig.

"I will," David said. The temple had provided the wedding planner and the photographer, which made procuring these things no problem. David was the middleman on everything these days, which meant paperwork and spreadsheets and calls on Saturday nights with questions about chevron vs. amphitheater seating arrangements for the ceremony and did he have a preference in terms of a wireless mic or a handheld? David was most comfortable not speaking at all, though you couldn't be a rabbi and stay silent. He couldn't avoid people taking his picture, but he could mitigate, when possible, how clear he looked. Lately he'd become one of those guys who could wear a hat. Initially he'd adopted the look so he wouldn't have to worry about cameras catching his face, but now he sort of liked it, though you couldn't exactly rock a fedora while officiating a wedding.

"Let Rachel pick out the nice ones to give to Naomi," Bennie said. "She's got an eye for that sort of thing." David didn't particularly like spending time with Rachel Savone. Not that he disliked her, merely that she knew he wasn't what he seemed, had figured out he'd had plastic surgery, had even confided in him that she was thinking of leaving her husband. But that hadn't worked out. Not yet, anyway. "I don't want Rosen getting any of this shit before we go over it, got it? He'll have you on a fucking poster in his car wash if we're not careful."

"I don't think you need to worry about Rosen," David said. "Not for a little while, anyway. He's not looking for trouble. Not if he's inviting his mistress to his daughter's wedding."

"Rosen is always about thirty minutes from going balls up." He pointed at the wedding reception going on across the way. "I paid for more of that than he did. Two months I've been waiting for some word on this project we've got cooking up on Craig Road. Supposed to be getting funding from the Japs or something." He shook his head. "Fucking money pit, is what it is. Best thing that could happen is if the city decided the ground was polluted and could only be zoned for a nuclear dump. Get a government contract, write our own ticket." He paused, thinking. "You ever drive out that way?"

"No."

"See what I'm saying? I should have just made the motherfucker pay me."

"He would have called the cops," David said.

"You'd think so," Bennie said. "But they don't. This town? People would rather be in business with me than risk embarrassment. Isn't that something?"

A helicopter swept up in the air from the Vineyards' helipad a block away, behind the clubhouse, climbed a few hundred feet, then flew up and over the wedding party and spun back toward downtown. That was one thing the Mob didn't have: air support.

"Who's that asshole?"

"Probably the mayor," David said. "He showed up to the reception."

"How's he looking?"

"Had on a nice tie," David said.

"How much you think Spilotro and Scarfo paid him over the years?"

Tony Spilotro, a Chicago Outfit guy—the Family's rivals—and Nicky Scarfo, the boss of Philadelphia, were two of Goodman's clients, back when he was a lawyer, but then so were all the Vegas hoods. "Not enough," David said. Spilotro was dead and Scarfo was doing fed time in Atlanta, scheduled to get out when he was 133 years old, no chance of parole. That RICO shit was no joke. "If he was any good, they wouldn't have needed his services so often."

When the helicopter disappeared, Bennie turned his attention back to his daughter Sophie. There were four houses surrounding the lake, each with its own private dock where they kept electric boats, dinghies, and more bright yellow pedal boats like the one Sophie was tooling around in. Sophie was seven and a little chubby now, unfortunately growing into a body that more closely resembled her father's than her mother's. "Goodman still going to Beth Shalom?"

"That's the word."

"You talk to him?"

"No. He just shook some hands. Couple minutes, in and out. Guess Manic Al gave him some cash on his election campaign."

"That's my fucking money," Bennie said.

"Maybe you'll get your own exhibit in the museum."

"Worst secret organization on the planet," Bennie said. "I find myself wondering why anyone is surprised when someone snitches. But you know, I figure running a city is worse than being in the game. Mayor can't kill anyone and he has to work with those Waste Management fucks. I've got it easy."

David considered that. In Chicago, the Family had run the garbage business since the turn of the twentieth century. Back then people didn't want to pay, they had to dig a pit and burn their garbage. Now it was just taken out of their property taxes. Government got their bite, the Family got theirs, everyone happy. Fact was, when the mayor was in a room, David left it. If there was one person in the city who could smell a gangster, it was probably that guy.

"I'll have Rabbi Kales give him a call around Hanukkah, maybe he'll be in a generous mood," David said, "give us a donation for the birthright trips."

Bennie shook his head. "Rabbi Kales should be in a nursing home." He paused. "Or whatever comes next."

"He's fine for now."

"He pissed on my sofa the other night. The leather one? You know, in the den? Just sat there and pissed himself. Good thing Sophie was asleep and Jean was off doing whatever the fuck fifteen-year-old girls do." Across the way, Naomi and Michael and their wedding party gathered along the Rosens' dock for a photo, everyone looking sharp in their rented clothes. "*Omerta* has shit on the secret lives of teenage girls."

"Maybe ask more questions," David said, "before it's too late."

"You assume I want the answers." He pointed at Sophie. "That one still tells me everything, snitches on her sister every ten minutes. Benedict Arnold thinks she's hard to trust."

David tried to imagine what his own son, William, looked like these days. He and Sophie were about the same age. William's seventh birthday was only a few weeks away.

David could remember being seven.

Walking to school with Fat Monte, that poor dead fucker, sneaking into Cubs games, Monte lifting pocketbooks from ladies' purses, the two of them getting loaded on Carnation Frozen Malt cups in the bleachers, snapping those wooden spoons into shanks, playing at being tough guys. Which got David wondering: Who was William playing with? Did he *have* any friends? If Jennifer was smart, she was keeping him far away from his cousins, away from any of the kids of the old crew. David hoped William wasn't playing video games with one of Sugar Lopiparno's dumb-fuck sons, like the one who had to get his stomach pumped after he ate a handful of pennies.

Did William remember his father at all? Because it was getting harder and harder for David to accurately recall his son. He could remember *experiences*—his first birthday, chocolate frosting and yellow cake all over everything; Christmas, ripping up wrapping paper and throwing it everywhere, not giving a shit about the presents; Jennifer giving him haircuts by putting a bowl on his head—but they'd known each other for only a few years. Hard to make any kind of permanent *memories*. In a year, maybe less, William could walk by him on the street unnoticed.

Sophie pedaled out into the middle of the lake, right in the line of the photo shoot, so Bennie cupped a hand around his mouth, shouted, "That's too far, Soph," then waved her in with two fingers. He dug some shells from between his bottom lip and teeth, crouched down on one knee, wiped his fingers on the grass, motioned David down, too. "Everything going okay with the Chinamen?"

"No problems," David said.

"Ruben said they've been coming in pretty steady."

Ruben Topaz was Bennie's guy at the Kales Mortuary and Home of Peace, the temple's funeral home, and the only other person on the planet Bennie trusted to handle his business while he was away. Ruben didn't know the truth about David, though he probably had some suspicions.

"Yeah," David said. "Some kind of hostile takeover going on. Can't last much longer." They'd put ten guys down in the last few months. Unless they were importing new guys from China, David couldn't conceive of a way for them to keep pace and keep ahead of the law, too. You disappear one guy, maybe their families and friends keep quiet, because that's the life, but you start getting toward a dozen missing gangsters, someone is going to say something, and either the cops pick up a lead on a wire or someone walks into a station and starts telling stories.

"It can always last longer." Bennie shrugged. They weren't his men. "How's the back end?"

"Slow," David said. He'd been moving body parts to Jerry Ford, who ran a tissue and organ donation shop called LifeCore for a few years now. It was a good partnership. The funeral home provided him with product, Jerry provided the funeral home with money, and in between there weren't a lot of questions. Still, even Jerry Ford had some simple standards. "Their lungs are shit and there's too many livers Jerry says he can't use, so, mostly, he's taking some bones, skin, a few corneas. But these Triad fuckers have a real thing about hot pokers into the eyes."

"Language, Rabbi," Bennie said.

He was pretty good about controlling his vernacular until he got around Bennie, then all the old ways would come right back to the surface. Bennie Savone was the kind of guy Sal Cupertine had known his whole life. It was easy to drift. "My point is," David said, "our return hasn't been what it could be. Least not on these. Unavoidable, I suppose."

"Now would be one of those opportunities to say you're sorry."

"I'm not sorry," David said.

It *was* his fault, however. David had fucked up their supply line with many of the traditional families when he wouldn't let his cousin Ronnie muscle in on their operations after Bennie got pinched, not that Bennie knew the whole story. David hadn't told him how he'd killed that FBI agent, Jeff Hopper, who'd shown up at the temple. Didn't tell him he'd pretended to be Hopper when he dimed out the whole Family to the *Chicago Tribune*. Didn't even tell him how he'd worked the game perfectly, getting Hopper's head to a Dumpster in Chicago a few weeks later, right after the story hit the streets. All he'd said was that Ronnie had tried to buy in after Bennie was arrested and that David—well, Sal—had threatened to kill him if he didn't keep to his own business, that his Vegas card was pulled.

Not that it mattered. They were triple fucked. Once Sal's faked death was talked about on *Good Morning America*, no families east of the Mississippi would touch work that went through any part of Chicago, and likewise, Bennie wasn't keen on having any direct or indirect communication with the Family, not while he was in county jail working on his own beef. And since the Family had vouched for Bennie's burial service to Detroit and Cleveland after Bennie bought Sal from Ronnie, everyone now considered Bennie to be Chicago-affiliated. A fucking mess all around.

"Every now and then," Bennie said, "saying you're sorry even when you're not is a thing you should do. Makes you seem human. People like the sentiment."

"Guys the Chinese are sending," David said, like Bennie hadn't even spoken, "are young. Street kids."

"And?" Bennie said. "You get birth certificates before you did a job?"

"I'm just saying," David said, "teenagers got parents who give a shit."

On top of that, David just wasn't comfortable with a bunch of Chinese guys who were obviously not Jews sitting on the tables. Bennie knew the Triads from the Wild Horse, where they moved girls in and out over the years, Bennie and the Triads' guy in San Francisco having done business since the late '80s, escort shit, laundering chips, even pills back in the day, though Bennie was out of that now. Drugs, you depended on addicts and criminals not smart enough to get off their own block to do business.

Bennie Savone wasn't putting his livelihood in the hands of people who were still wrapped up in what public housing development they represented, and upper management in the Triads didn't get down like that, either. They were a cash-and-influence business stateside. That was Bennie's game, too . . . though David was beginning to wonder how much of either was enough. David was in the game to earn a living, initially, and then he was in the game because he couldn't get out of it even if he wanted to, but he didn't want to, not until he fucked everything up, and now? Well, now he was in the game for good. Bennie, on the other hand, had enough money that he could live comfortably out of it all . . . if it wasn't for the fact that he knew where all the bodies were buried, literally, and that meant someone would come for him if he tried to walk away. Which is probably part of why he bought David in the first place, in addition to his desire to run this long con.

"Our options are limited right now. I get out, we can be pickier." Bennie paused, working through something. "You trust them? The Chinese?"

"I don't trust anybody," David said. "But I'm not working with the living ones."

Bennie nodded. "Ford asking any questions?"

"Never," David said.

"That's good," Bennie said, still working in his mind. The thing about Bennie Savone: He liked people to think he was stupid, liked people to underestimate him. Because he wasn't stupid and he shouldn't be underestimated, and that gave him an advantage in everything, self-awareness not exactly a trait of most crooks. David hadn't taken him seriously to start with, seeing as he was used to working for Ronnie, who was a good businessman, but didn't see the bigger picture like Bennie did. Bennie liked the slow bleed. "Any collection problems?"

"Everything is smooth," David said. "First-quarter tuition comes in next week." Temple Beth Israel had a preschool, the Tikvah, and a K–12 operation rolling now, the Barer Academy, six hundred students, the temple minting money every day, never mind that they were also loaning tuition money out to families who couldn't afford the full out of pocket, charging 12 percent interest, which was a shitty vig in David's opinion, but it would be bad PR to be charging more than Citibank did. Though if you were late, that number jumped to 23 percent, which was better, but still six points less than Visa.

If someone missed two payments, the temple would start getting liens right away, none of that Fair Debt Reporting crap, the temple got every family to sign contracts allowing property liens, never mind the public shame aspect. Worst-case scenario, David figured if someone had to accidentally get electrocuted at home to get their life insurance to pay the debt, well, then he'd go and fuck with their pool light. It hadn't come to that, thankfully, because the nice thing was that everyone was rich as fuck these days.

"How the donations looking?"

"We'll get our bump a little early," David said. "Rosh Hashanah and Yom Kippur hit in mid-September." David knew that Bennie had no concept of how the Jewish calendar worked, and the fact was David didn't get it either. Rabbi Kales had tried to explain the lunar calendar, the concept that there were no hours in a day, only light and the absence of light. David just couldn't get the reasoning behind it, when science had it all pretty much settled. Rabbi Kales told him, eventually, that if he had a problem with it, he should take it up with Maimonides.

"Shit, that's another six, eight weeks."

"There a problem?"

"Some liquidity issues, that's all," Bennie said, a touch too dismissively. He yanked a handful of grass out by the root, smelled it, tossed it into the water. "That dentist fucker? His family has me in civil court. They already got two million from the insurance company and now they're trying to get another five out of me. Pay for his long-term care, lost wages, everything. Fucker could live fifty years or he could die in his sleep tonight."

"I'd write the check," David said.

"You got an extra five million sitting around?"

In fact, David had about two hundred grand in cash squirreled away in safe deposit boxes around the city, and that was just what he'd been able to skim. He didn't dare keep the money in his house, since Bennie had closed-circuit cameras hidden all over the fucking property, plus if trouble came down and his house was surrounded, last thing he wanted was for the cash to go to the feds. That money belonged to his wife and kid. Anyway, nice thing about Las Vegas, *everyone* kept cash in safe deposit boxes. Monday morning, 9:00, there was a line of strippers, bouncers, bartenders, dealers, and pit bosses making their deposits from the weekend and none of them were putting it into their checking accounts, and no one thought any different about it.

David figured he needed closer to a million, cash, before he could make his move. Get his wife and kid, fly to South America, wherever Butch and Sundance ended up; that seemed nice, until the army showed up. But he wouldn't get there if Bennie kept getting nicked. Or if Bennie kept running the business himself, since he controlled the flow of cash. It was a double-edged sword David hadn't quite figured how to grasp. Bennie had assured him from the start that he'd be getting paid handsomely, had shown him the ledgers, but didn't let him hold his own money.

"I pay," Bennie continued, "every pervert who got punched in the mouth at my club is gonna come after me. I'll be in court the rest of my life." He picked a seed from his teeth, then flicked it out from under his fingernail.

"They don't want to be embarrassed, you said so yourself," David said. "First guy who sues you, get a picture of him in the newspaper, have a girl from the club tell Curran that she remembered the guy shooting his load on her, and believe me, they'll be happy to settle for next to nothing. Maybe you have to cut a couple checks. Two, three grand and they get to tell their buddies they beat the Mob, big deal."

"Look at you," Bennie said, "spending all my money." He rubbed at the scar on his neck, from where he'd had his thyroid removed. It made him look hard core, like his throat had been slit and he'd lived, which, David supposed, was true, but it was actually a nervous habit Bennie had, the only one David had noticed, other than his propensity to pace. He was quiet for about a minute, thinking. David sensed his idea was taking root.

Bennie Savone wasn't a boss like Ronnie Cupertine was a boss, didn't run a crew of a hundred-plus guys, wasn't moving all the opiates in five states, plus back and forth into Canada, didn't have a Mexican street gang on his payroll, wasn't running multilevel rackets and gambling businesses, basically didn't get down like Chicago at all. He ran his strip club, he ran Temple Beth Israel (kind of), had his construction outfit, took a little juice on some books, but was largely an independent contractor providing an indispensable service with the funeral and burial business, which made him unique. Didn't answer to Chicago, New York, or Florida, never mind any of those Dixie Mafia or LA pussies. Bennie Savone had his own thing and, yeah, when an outfit came to do business in Las Vegas, even though it was an open city, they tended to come through Bennie first, not the other way around. But there wasn't the structure of the Family in Chicago. No underboss. No capos. None of that *Godfather* shit. It was all a series of firewalls. There was Bennie. There was

David. There used to be Rabbi Kales, but he'd been put on the farm. There was Ruben, handling the funeral business, and then there was Bennie's crew, not that David ever saw them. Oh, he saw the construction workers hitting nails on the temple's campus, but those were mostly Mexican laborers and actual employees of Savone Construction Partners, not guys running jobs.

"If I were you," David said, "I'd take the dentist out. You already did your time on him. If he dies now, you're done. He's off the books. And then I'd give his family money anyway."

"You would?"

"Some appropriate amount."

Bennie cocked his head. "He's in a care facility in Omaha."

"I could make a road trip," David said.

"No," Bennie said, "you couldn't."

"You afraid I'll run?"

"No," Bennie said. "You got nowhere to go." He fished through his bag of seeds, but it was just husks and salt, so he dumped the remnants into the grass, tossed the empty bag into the water, watched it float there. "You know someone in Chicago calls themselves Peaches?"

"No. I don't know anybody named Peaches."

"What's with you guys and the names and shit?"

"I don't know," David said. "Tradition, I guess."

"I'm hearing some words about him being the new number two out there," Bennie said. This was what Bennie really wanted to talk about, though it was all connected. Every problem they had stemmed from the same tree. "And that he's putting people in the ground."

"Like who?"

"Mothers and fathers and wives and kids and sisters and shit," Bennie said. "Going into nursing homes and hotshotting old-timers. Taking motherfuckers out on the street in Boca. Staging car accidents. All kinds of shit. I don't know what's real and what isn't."

David tried to think of anyone who might be calling themselves Peaches, but it didn't ring any bells. But then it occurred to him that the order of succession was probably pretty jacked up in Chicago these days. The only close blood relative Ronnie had in the game was . . . well, Sal Cupertine. And Sal's son. Ronnie's own son, James, was slow. "He from out of town?"

"Personally? Sounds to me like Russians," Bennie said.

David used to not give a shit about the Russians. He didn't like the way they operated in Chicago, in an ethical sense, killing families and pets, or all the purported ex-KGB fucks in Suburbans running counterfeit schemes and protection rackets out in Skokie, or that high-stakes poker shit they started to get in on for a while around the colleges, juicing twenty-year-olds for their student loan money, or even those old-school Chi-West Ukrainians with their goofy sweaters and allegiance to a bleak series of gray streets, stabbing Puerto Ricans for looking at them wrong. No, these days, because of the stories of his congregation, he thought about shit that had gone down in 1917. All that Pale of Settlement mishegoss. Pogroms and show trials and Cossacks chasing down toddlers with dogs. That shit pissed him off like it happened yesterday, because, in effect, it had. Three years ago, he was blissfully unenlightened. Now, could be he went to work and Gordon Simon would be waiting for him, wanting to talk about his nightmares, how he'd seen his little sister Lizi being killed on the streets of Odessa in his dreams again, set on fire, her ashes left to blow in the wind.

"Ronnie wouldn't be in business with Russians," David said.

"You think I'm working with the Triads because I enjoy their company?" David supposed not. "Global economy, Rabbi. Get used to it. That provincial shit is twentieth-century thinking. We're twenty-first-century gangsters now."

"You know the story of the Jews of the Roman ghetto?"

"Let me guess," Bennie said, "they suffered and then died?"

"No," David said, "they were the one people who never knelt before Caligula. Fifteen hundred years of Holy Roman emperors and what the Jews did was never change, never paid homage to the

ruling assholes. They set themselves on fire before they'd let someone baptize them."

"So, yeah, they suffered and then they died, like I said."

"They died pure of belief, souls intact."

"You saying you want us to go back to selling whiskey in olive oil
bottles and stealing cigarettes?"

"No," David said. "What I'm saying is, root pulls are some shit
from the old times. Burn the graves and salt the earth. All that." He
thought about it for a second. Thought about what it might mean for
Jennifer and William. Thought about getting on a fucking bus, getting to Chicago in a few days, breaking into his house in the night,
taking his family, running to . . . where? Wasn't that always the question? "I don't see it with the Russians. They wouldn't kill for the
Family. And they'd be no one's number two. They got too much
invested in Europe to have word get out that they're doing dog work
for Cosa Nostra, you know? Because Ronnie's just gonna flip them
to the FBI eventually and the story will be that the Russians tried to
muscle the Mafia out of Chicago and lost. And then it's a war. No
one wants that."

"What about the Indians? Native Americans," Bennie said.
"Whatever the fuck they're called now. Fuck if I know. If you people
made it easy and went by normal names, I wouldn't need to DNA-
test my information with you. Give me a motherfucker named Scott
every now and then."

Across the way, the string band was playing "Unforgettable" and
David could see some of the old folks were already taking to the
dance floor, the bride and groom not even back from taking pictures
yet. Put on Nat King Cole and old Jews slow-danced. He saw it at
every wedding and bar or bat mitzvah he went to.

Doing business with the Russians and Chinese didn't make
sense to David. If some shit went down, they could just run back to
their own countries. Working with the Gangster 2-6 back in
Chicago made sense—the only place they had to flee to was their
block or back to prison, two places they could be taken out if the

need arose. David didn't see himself flying to Beijing to kill a motherfucker. But Ronnie was never going to have someone from the 2-6 at his shoulder.

Chicago had controlled the street gangs for decades. It was never equal footing. Hard to see the boys falling in line with that. They'd just call Detroit, muscle up. Align with Memphis if they had to.

The Native gangs, that was different. They owned property. Casinos. Farmland. Had their own cops. Made better sense.

"Could be," David said.

"You been in contact with anyone out there?" Bennie asked.

"No," David said, which was true, save for getting his wife some money after all this shit with Hopper went down, but nothing since. But now he was thinking about it. Because this news? It was out of the ordinary. And out of the ordinary meant Ronnie was making some kind of move. He'd survived David tipping off the press about his operations, but he was weak now. He really only had two moves left, if shit got untenable: Kill Sal, or give him up to the authorities, hope he got a plea deal out of it.

"Haven't tried to get in touch with your wife?"

"I don't have a wife."

"Say you did. Would you be talking to her on the down low?"

"Never," David said, which was a lie. If he thought he could, he would. But he wasn't about to put Jennifer and William in jeopardy. One consensual phone call with Jennifer and she could be looking at time; feds might even try to put fifteen accessory-to-murder charges on her if they were feeling particularly litigious.

"Comes to it," Bennie said, "you may need to go underground for a bit. We gotta stay nimble, understand?"

"You put me in another meat truck," David said, "you better be next to me."

Bennie then cupped his hand around his mouth, shouted at his kid, "Come on in, Soph, let's get you some dinner." The wedding party on the dock turned and looked, the bride and groom giving a big enthusiastic wave to Bennie, Bennie waving right back. Best day of their lives, all right. "You better get back to your duties, Rabbi," Bennie said eventually. "Looks like the bride and groom are about to make their big entrance."

"'The vineyards of Israel have ceased to exist,'" Rabbi David Cohen said, "'but eternal law enjoins the children of Israel to celebrate the vintage.'"

"An empire of clean cars for the both of them," Bennie said.

David tried to laugh, just to make Bennie feel good, but he couldn't get his mouth to quite work in that direction, so what came out sounded like someone getting stabbed in the throat.

"Christ, Rabbi, maybe don't try that again, at least not in public."

"Listen," David said. "I need to see someone about my face."

"I'm working on that," Bennie said.

"Work faster," David said. Bennie couldn't respond, since Sophie was climbing from the pedal boat. She had on a bright yellow one-piece swimsuit and David could see she was burned on her shoulders and neck, too. She practically glowed. There'd be blisters by the morning.

David watched Bennie and Sophie walk off, until they faded into the shadows the Red Rocks had cut across the expanse of the Savones' lawn. David's night vision was turning to shit. All this and he needed glasses, too? A few minutes later, Bennie and Sophie reappeared, as if by magic, walking up the red brick steps into the house. In the Talmud, they hung witches who practiced magic. Time came, Bennie Savone probably wouldn't get off much easier than that.

I just need to make it through September, David thought. He'd have enough money then to start working his plan, because when Bennie got off house arrest and could look closer at the books, David wasn't sure how much he could pinch. David had maybe four months to get his face fixed, make his nut, get word to Jennifer, secure passports good enough to get him, his wife, and his kid into and out of some small airports, good enough to get them into Mexico, at least, where he could throw around some cash and it wouldn't matter what their passports looked like, and then . . . Argentina? Maybe. There were Jews in Argentina.

If he wanted to live with his wife and son, it would have to be somewhere foreign. The FBI wasn't just going to forget about the Mafia. They hadn't for the last seventy years, anyway. Didn't stop during WWI, didn't stop during WWII, Korea, Vietnam, or Iraq. They never stopped coming . . . but also never fully completed the job, because the feds needed job security, too. Good to leave a few loose ends, so you could round them up into a ball every few years and then start again. But they didn't give up on people who killed their men. Sal Cupertine would be on their to-do list until they had his head in a noose.

Pain shot up into David's right eye and he realized he was gritting his teeth, which had become a bad habit. He let his mouth open half an inch, exhaled, waited for the pain to subside.

It didn't.

It just lingered there, his face throbbing.

The sun would be completely down in an hour or so. There would be toasts. Rabbi David Cohen would dance the hora, would pose for photos, would engage the congregants of Temple Beth Israel with talk of next month's High Holy Days, would touch women on their elbow, men on their shoulder, would chastise the old and the young for eschewing yarmulkes on a wedding day. Rabbi David Cohen would leave the wedding at an appropriate hour, would drive the five miles back to his guard-gated house inside the Lakes at Summerlin Greens, would strip off his suit, stuff his yarmulke into a drawer, go to his in-home gym and work the heavy bag for an hour, until he felt like Sal Cupertine again, made sure he knew who the fuck he still was.

3

Matthew Drew should have shot Ronnie Cupertine in the back of the head. That would have solved a lot of problems. Stopped everything. But nothing was going according to plan, and Matthew Drew was a guy who needed a plan.

For one thing, it was barely six in the morning—Matthew always pictured killing Ronnie around midnight—and for another, he was twenty miles northwest of Milwaukee, inside the shitter at the Chuyalla Indian Casino, not in a warehouse in Chicago with a bat in his hand, contemplating where he was going to bury the body of one of the biggest crime bosses in the country.

Matthew always imagined beating Ronnie Cupertine to death inside an abandoned warehouse. Black Visqueen over the windows. Graffiti on the walls. Ronnie tied to a chair. An old stuffed bear on the ground, though Matthew wasn't sure how the bear got there.

Funny thing was Matthew didn't think he'd ever *been* in an abandoned warehouse, didn't know if warehouses got abandoned. Yet in movies and TV shows, that's always where the bad shit went down, as if criminals had access to all the prime unoccupied industrial real estate. Most people, if they got murdered, it either happened inside their own home or the home of their killer. Usually in bed. Or the car.

That wasn't going to work for Matthew. He wasn't some criminal.

So Matthew had gone out and done the physical recon, just like he'd been taught at Quantico. Developers were turning old timber plants along Wolcott—the half-abandoned industrial corridor of

Chicago—into loft spaces, and now artists were moving in, setting up coffeehouses and artisan bread stores, places to get henna tattoos, galleries where on Sundays they'd hold open mics and poetry slams. At night, however, the area was still a little rough, so all the artists locked their doors, turned up their music, and pretended not to hear the sirens. Kaufman and Broad had gutted three warehouses down to the studs for a development they were calling the Timber Factory Lofts, but for two years, nothing had come to pass; the sign offering EXECUTIVE LOFT SPACES STARTING IN THE LOW 800s! didn't even have a phone number on it. So Matthew broke in one night—which was hardly breaking and entering, since there wasn't even a lock on the door—scoped out a suitable space, set up the chair, rolled out some Visqueen, even found an old Teddy Ruxpin at Goodwill and tossed it on the floor, came in one night with a boombox, blared a mixture of punk rock and Sarah McLachlan for forty-five minutes, checked the acoustics and the taste of the neighbors.

Warped Tour or Lilith Fair, no one said a thing.

He could take a hacksaw to Ronnie Cupertine, and as long as he played music at the same time, no one would give a shit.

Then Matthew proceeded to phase two, which entailed watching Ronnie for months.

He didn't have anything else to do.

Two years ago, he'd spent six months hiding out in Jeff Hopper's house in Walla Walla after Hopper turned up dead, trying to piece together what the fuck happened. Hopper had gone to Las Vegas, Matthew to Palm Springs, to follow a lead on Sal Cupertine's disappearance, after Hopper figured out that Cupertine was smuggled from Illinois in a frozen meat truck, most likely to Nevada or California. The two of them were to reconnect in a few days, make their next move, except Matthew never heard another word from Hopper. He just disappeared. Then he turned up dead. But not before telling the *Tribune* everything Jeff and Matthew had learned in their investigation . . . save for any mention of Matthew's name, which was probably why he still walked the earth.

It didn't make any sense. It was the opposite of everything he and Matthew had been working toward, their entire focus being the capture of Sal Cupertine for the murder of those three FBI agents and the CI. Delivering actual justice, not this media bullshit. Going to the press before he had Sal Cupertine in cuffs, and without telling Matthew ahead of time? No. That wasn't his style. And neither was the giant picture of Hopper that graced the front page of the paper, right next to a grainy photo of Sal Cupertine. Jeff would never consent to that.

After leaving Walla Walla, when Hopper's estate was settled and the bank sent a sheriff over to give Matthew the boot, Matthew spent another month at a Ramada in Springfield waiting to get called in on the corruption trial of Kirk Biglione, his former boss at the FBI. That never came to pass, either. Biglione took a deal before anything went to the jury, the FBI admitting that they'd disregarded evidence to keep a long-running—and ill-fated—surveillance program of the Family going, even admitting that they delivered a box of ashes to Sal Cupertine's wife, Jennifer, that were actually the remains of Chema Espinoza, a soldier in the Gangster 2-6 who was doing scut work for the Family and ended up in that landfill for his troubles. That would have been a decent civil lawsuit if Sal Cupertine hadn't been a Mafia hit man and if Jennifer Cupertine was interested in being deposed, which Matthew figured she probably wasn't. Biglione didn't even get any time, just a suspended sentence, and was now doing big-money corporate security in Detroit, making a hundred times the salary he pulled from the government.

Matthew kept tabs on him, waiting for his next fuckup. Biglione had fired Matthew for doing the right thing. That wasn't something he was going to forget. Ever.

But Matthew kept tabs on everyone these days . . . which made tracking Ronnie Cupertine easy. Ronnie had come out of the whole FBI corruption scandal without a single charge against him, his crimes dumped on Fat Monte Moretti, who was dead, and Sal Cupertine, who was in the wind and on his way to becoming something of an urban legend, and then half a dozen soldiers and capos willing to take a five-year bid for shit they didn't do. If the courts, the FBI, or the media couldn't hold Ronnie Cupertine accountable, Matthew Drew figured he could.

Catching him? That was another matter.

Ronnie Cupertine's Gold Coast manor had a six-foot wrought-iron gate out front, topped with cameras, and there was a private security guard out front, some rent-a-cop with a badge, flashlight, Glock, and walkie-talkie, usually sitting in the front seat of an ARMED RESPONSE squad car—not unusual in a neighborhood where Cupertine's neighbors included most of the Cubs roster and a quarter century of Chicago's robber-baron industrialists. What was unusual was that Ronnie also owned the house across the street and the one next door, on the corner, giving himself a de facto compound, all on public streets, which was smart. You couldn't bug a public street. Likewise, Matthew couldn't just park his car in front of Ronnie Cupertine's house, not unless he wanted his plates run, the Family good about having tendrils in mundane government operations like the DMV. He also didn't like the idea of getting shot at from three different angles, since those two houses were filled with a rotating band of Ronnie's guys.

But half a block away was a brand-new Starbucks where Matthew could sit all day if he pretended to peck away at his laptop. So he'd grab the big chair by the window, nurse latte after latte, and watch Cupertine pace his sidewalk, taking calls.

He always had one of his kids with him, usually the little girl, Cupertine knowing no one would take a shot at him with his kid right there. Still, one of his Family guys would always be a few steps behind, thick with Kevlar; even the Mafia had body armor these days. With a sniper's rifle, Matthew could take Cupertine out from that distance, no problem, and not even get blood spatter on the kid. Could put one in Ronnie's body guy with no problem, too, since he wasn't wearing Kevlar on his face. Might even put a bullet into the ARMED RESPONSE vehicle down the block, just for kicks.

But he wasn't an assassin.

Not yet, anyway.

So Matthew waited for Ronnie to slip—run outside in his underwear to get the newspaper, step out for a smoke by himself on the day his body guy had the stomach flu—thinking then that maybe he could poison the security guy . . . or involve himself in a minor hit-and-run, if need be.

Matthew just needed a tiny opening.

It never happened.

Ronnie Cupertine was never alone. He never fucked up. There wasn't a single moment when Matthew could have exacted his plan without needing to kill two or three other people in the process. Ronnie flew out of town, he flew with three guys. He drove to Trader Joe's for some artichoke dip, he drove with two guys and a second car running interference. He went to his daughter's ballet recital, there was a guy at the front door, a guy at the back, a guy on his body.

Not that any of them ever noticed Matthew. They were meat, plain and simple. But they were human beings. Just because they had shitty jobs didn't mean they deserved to die.

But then, one day, Matthew woke up in the Chicago apartment he was back to sharing with his sister, Nina, two miles from the FBI office he was legally barred from, and didn't pretend to go out on a job interview—instead he actually *went* on the interview, not because he wanted to, but because the night before, Nina walked into his bedroom and handed him a Post-it with a phone number. "You got a call while you were out," she said, "doing whatever it is you do."

"Great," he said. He stuck the Post-it to his desk calendar, which he hadn't changed since 1999.

"It was about a job."

"Wonderful," he said.

"They called yesterday, too," she said.

She stood there in his doorway, arms crossed over her chest, not moving. "Look at you. What are you doing to yourself?"

"I'm trying to figure a few things out," he said.

"By doing what?" He couldn't exactly tell her he was stalking Ronnie Cupertine, not that she didn't already know enough to be worried. When the world flipped after Fat Monte's suicide, he'd taken her with him to hide out in Walla Walla, Hopper worried that the Family might come after them, which hadn't transpired. "Look," she said, "I don't pretend to know what it's like to be up in your head, but Matt, I'm right here, and I need you." She sat down on the edge of his bed. "Also, wash your sheets. It smells like a frat house in here."

"How do you know that?"

She waved him off. "Mom says she can't send me any more rent money," she said, "and that she'd appreciate it if you'd return her calls every now and then, too." Their mom lived alone, back in the family home in Maryland, which she was trying to sell. Matthew had shared this apartment with Nina for two years, splitting costs while they both got on their feet, Nina in college, Matthew at the FBI. He'd kept paying half the rent even after he lost his job, with the money Hopper gave him, because Matthew didn't want her with a bunch of roommates. He told her he didn't think it was safe, which, he recognized now, was silly. Nothing is safe. Nowhere is safe. But that money was gone. And his unemployment was up, too.

The last few months, they'd both subsisted on a little bit of inheritance they'd received from their father's life insurance.

"I'll call her," Matthew said.

"I'm worried," Nina said. She leaned back on Matthew's bed, closed her eyes, and shook out her hands and feet, an old habit she'd carried from childhood.

"I'm fine," he said.

"Clearly you're a liar," she said. She sat back up. "Mom doesn't think she can help out on tuition, either. I'm going to get a loan."

"No," Matthew said. "You don't have to." He tried to sound bright. "I'm going to take care of everything. Okay?" He picked up the Post-it. "I'm going to call this, first thing."

And then he actually did. It was a headhunter for a new Indian casino opening outside Milwaukee, who told Matthew that he'd been referred to them. Matthew figured it was someone at the FBI doing him a favor. They needed a head of security to run the whole shop, six figures, moving expenses, everything. The headhunter told him he could write his own ticket, maybe end up in Las Vegas in a few years, get a house with a pool, no more winter, basically be retired for the next thirty-five years . . . if he spent two, three years making it work in Milwaukee. It was close enough to Chicago that he could still keep an eye on Nina, but far enough away that he wouldn't be running into Gangster 2-6 shot callers and Family enforcers at Target. It also meant he couldn't drive over to Cupertine's house whenever he wanted, couldn't roll by his car dealerships (not that Ronnie Cupertine ever showed up at any of them), couldn't wait out by one of the Family's bars in Bridgeport or Andersonville, couldn't run by his murder warehouse to check on the Teddy Ruxpin.

And, all things considered, that was probably a good thing.

Because what Matthew Drew had come to realize was that he was obsessed with Ronnie Cupertine, but Ronnie Cupertine didn't give a shit about him. Probably never had. Hadn't even noticed he was being stalked. Matthew had lone wolfed him for so long, he wasn't even sure he knew why he wanted to kill him anymore. Oh, sure, he blamed him for Jeff Hopper's death, but the fact was he didn't even know if Ronnie had been directly responsible. Matthew could dig up the bodies of Al Capone and J. Edgar Hoover, piss on them, rebury them, and the net result would be the same as putting one between Ronnie Cupertine's eyes: Jeff Hopper would still be dead, his men would still be dead, and both of their killers would still be out there. Matthew's career would still be over, and the Mafia would beat on, the FBI would beat on, history forgetting about it all, the minor wars of thugs and government agencies usually not enough to merit any civilian review whatsoever.

You wanted to be remembered, you had to kill innocent people.

Sal Cupertine, wherever the fuck he was, would never know any different. Ronnie Cupertine was a Mob boss, a killer, sold shitty cars, but he wasn't the only one. Every crime these days was organized. The Cartels moved heroin and coke into the cities, the Mafia middled it to the gangs, the gangs sold it to the people, the people got hooked, lost their jobs, had to rob a liquor store for the fifty bucks they needed to score . . . and the cycle started all over again. That wasn't Ronnie Cupertine's fault. That was just his job.

The obsession, Matthew then understood, had become the result of the thing, not the thing itself.

The thing was Sal. He'd killed the FBI agents. He didn't *need* to do that. He *wanted* to do that.

It was disorganized.

No planning.

The thing was Sal Cupertine. If he had to, Matthew would get that tattooed on the back of his hand so he wouldn't forget going forward. Every time he raised his fist, he'd know why.

•

NOW HERE IT was, Saturday morning at the ass end of a twelve-hour shift running the casino's security, Matthew ducking into the high-roller restroom, the one with all the marble fixtures. Bottles of Drakkar, Polo, Grey Flannel, and something called Joop lined the countertop—high rollers in a Wisconsin Indian casino being a relative thing, at least as it related to their smell—along with an array of toothpicks, mouthwash, mints, and Hershey's chocolates.

The Chuyalla were the biggest employer for miles, the hotel and casino the best thing to happen to the region since a women's prison was built up in Fond du Lac a few years earlier. In fact, the tribe had its own cops, its own courts. The Chuyalla was one of the few Wisconsin tribes that operated its own justice system, everything except prisons.

There was an old guy in a velvet vest named Curtis who sat on a stool next to the sink and expected money for handing you a towel.

When Matthew felt low—which was often lately—he thought about Curtis, who had to be pushing eighty, and how he spent his whole day listening to, and smelling, people's bodily functions. Not even doctors got paid enough for that indignity, not even the ones who were curing cancer or doing brain surgery. Because people never did really heal, always waiting for the next thing to break.

But he didn't really empathize with Curtis. At some point, he'd made a choice—this was his life. So when he spied Curtis there, with the jaundiced caste to the skin around his eyes and the picked-open scabs on his forearms, Matthew didn't want to help the man out with a dollar. He wanted to tell him to move to Oregon, where they had assisted suicide. Stop waiting for the end. It was already here.

"How you doing, boss?" Curtis asked.

"Fine," Matthew said. He was heading to his preferred stall, the handicapped one at the very end. In Matthew's experience, anytime someone called you "boss" what they were really saying was: *I think you're a fucking asshole.*

Matthew closed the door to the stall and locked it, sat down, closed his eyes, counted backward from two hundred. Then he started over from three hundred and did it again and again and again. He didn't even need to go to the bathroom. He just wanted to not worry about anything for a few minutes. It's bad when your one sanctuary is literally the shittiest place on earth, but that's where Matthew Drew found himself these days. He was working in a fucking Indian casino because he needed the money, looking the other way when Native Mob OGs bought chips in the morning and cashed them in at midnight, never once playing a single hand in between and beating up on any rival gangs who showed their face on the game floor.

Lucky to even have this job.

Twenty-seven years old going on infinity.

TEN MINUTES LATER, Matthew stepped out of the toilet and found Ronnie Cupertine at the pink marble urinal, one arm propped up against the tile wall. Curtis was gone from his spot, probably at the buffet, getting his free breakfast of pancakes and yesterday's link sausage. Matthew was pretty sure he was hallucinating. He'd only ever seen Ronnie through his binoculars or on TV, acting like a tough guy in his car dealership commercials, always in a trench coat and hat, blowing holes into credit-rating reports with his fake tommy gun.

In Matthew's head, Ronnie Cupertine was maybe six foot two, six foot three, but wasn't it funny how distance and anger made someone bigger in your mind? Because Ronnie couldn't be more than five nine, Matthew saw, even with the little heel on his dress shoe. Back in the day, Ronnie was supposed to have been a hands-on bad guy, hammers and blowtorches and dismemberments with rusty screwdrivers and such. It seemed inconceivable, looking at him now in his tailored slacks, his perfect white shirt, his platinum President Rolex, his manicured nails, his understated black cufflinks. But Matthew had listened to the old FBI wire recordings, had read all the files, had seen the pictures of the decomposed bodies: Tino Loria, under the floorboards of his mother's house in Wheaton; his brother Frank, missing his hands, feet, and ears, under a swing set in a backyard in Buffalo Grove; Mike Zornes, built into the community pool in Mundelein; of course, Chema Espinoza, cut up, burned, and dumped in the Poyter Landfill.

Ronnie was always smart about having his boys bury their bodies away from the crime, out in the suburbs where no one bothered to look, at least not until someone snitched or new construction came along. The exception was when he wanted obvious messages to be sent, which was usually when he had his cousin Sal shoot someone in the back of the head, in public, because who was going to say anything? Or the time Ronnie and his boys pushed Sal's father, who they called Dark Billy, right off the IBM Building while it was still under construction. Newspapers called it a construction accident, except Dark Billy Cupertine never did a day of construction work in his life, other than building a network for heroin distribution. Ronnie Cupertine probably hadn't personally killed someone since then, maybe longer, but only because he'd been effective enough to get other people to do that work for him.

"Good morning, boss," Matthew said, and Ronnie jerked back from the urinal, splashing piss onto his thousand-dollar shoes.

"Jesus fuck," Ronnie said.

It was him all right.

Ronnie glared at Matthew for two, three, four seconds like he was trying to figure out if Matthew was some asshole up from Memphis, hiding out in the bathroom waiting to kill him. So Matthew gave him that smile he used with people he was meeting for the first time, the one that showed off his perfect teeth and the one dimple on his left cheek. Matthew was always bigger than most, always more imposing, and it helped disarm them. He felt normal about his size only when he was playing lacrosse or, later, when he worked for the FBI, and everyone seemed like they'd been cut from the same fabric, physically, at least. Nina always had to tell her friends he was as friendly as a St. Bernard, which wasn't true in the least. But he could look like one when he needed to.

"Didn't mean to startle you," Matthew said, then turned his body slightly to the right so Ronnie could see his gold arrowhead-shaped name tag, the one that said CAPTAIN MATTHEW DREW, like he was commanding a whaling ship. The Indians were funny about giving everyone a rank. "You're safe here."

"My one bit of luck all night," Ronnie said. He looked over his shoulder at the door, shook his head once, muttered, "Fucking idiots," then went back to his business, the poor bastard squirting dashes of piss every few seconds like a sprinkler. Matthew's dad had been like that a few years ago. One day it was an enlarged prostate, the next day it was cancer, the next day he was dead. That's what it seemed like, anyway.

Matthew stepped over to the bank of sinks, started to wash his hands. He was in the gray suit he liked to wear on the Friday night/Saturday morning shift. It was big through the shoulders, so he was able to wear the harness holster he preferred, his .357 SIG under his left arm, a sap under his right. It wasn't legal in Wisconsin for private citizens or security guards to conceal a sap, strictly speaking, but the rules on Indian land were fungible, and who was going to stop him?

Nine months he'd been working security for the Chuyalla tribe, splitting his time between the casino and the hotel, his bosses happy to tell potential convention clients how Matthew was ex-FBI, as if the accountants, notaries, travel agents, and paralegals renting space might need someone qualified for tactical assault to assist them with their awards banquet. Matthew wasn't sure why the Indians wanted some former fed on their security payroll. Everyone else was local talent—ex–tribal cops and Desert Storm vets, guys who looked the part, anyway, even if they were shit at their jobs. Maybe they liked that he wasn't Chuyalla, so he wasn't constantly kicking his cousins out of the casino. Or maybe they just liked that Matthew didn't mind putting blood on the floor.

Earlier that night, he'd sapped a Latin King who'd walked into the casino to play some craps. Matthew made him and his girl on the parking lot cam, had his picture run through their facial-recognition database before he even hit the tables. Ten minutes later he had a positive ID on one Desmond Christopher, called his info into the tribal police, who gave him his sheet: thirty-nine years old, five foot nine, 227 pounds—not fat, just swollen with prison muscles like a linebacker, though he looked skinnier now, probably the meth—known Latin Kings shot caller and meth wholesaler with two years down in Stateville on trafficking, another nine months for pimping, five years at Waupun for attempted murder on a Gangster Disciples soldier, which wasn't surprising since the dumb shit had *Killer* tattooed across his forehead in Old English script.

The Chuyalla were sensitive about providing a family environment, and they hated the Mexican gangs working their way north into Native land, so Matthew went down to the floor to encourage the gentleman to take his drug money elsewhere. They were more tolerant toward the Native gangs, since the Chuyalla rented them a ballroom once a month to hold their council meetings; plus most of them were Chuyalla, and those that weren't were careful not to show too much disrespect. The Native Mob controlled all the interests on reservation land, but the Mexican gangs were creeping closer and closer, the Cartels down south emboldening them with better guns and extra cash, which helped when they ended up getting arrested. Bloods and Crips kept to the big cities, but even still, on a weekend night, they'd roll in to wash their money at the tables, at least until Matthew pulled them out by their faces.

"Time to go," Matthew told Killer, then reached down onto the craps table, picked up Killer's bet—fifty on the hard eight; all these street gangsters bet the hard eight—and dropped it back on his chip stack. He had maybe another four grand piled in front of him. If he wasn't washing money, he was doing a pretty good job faking it.

"Me and my girl come here all the time," Killer said. He wasn't angry. Not yet, anyway. Probably because he knew he was caught. Last thing he wanted was the cops coming to see him. A felon with his sheet, he was always a parole violation waiting to happen. His girl was maybe twenty-two, and though she didn't have any tattoos on her face, she did have an ace of spades playing card the size of a fist on her neck, prison ink for thieves and con artists. Consorting with her was probably a violation in itself.

"Don't make a scene," Matthew said, "and you won't go back to prison."

Killer looked around the table. There were two Red Hat Society ladies, a couple white boys with the backwards baseball caps and bottles of Michelob, an old-timer with his lip filled with dip. A bachelorette party, one woman in a veil with a balloon penis taped to her forehead, all her drunk friends in matching black tank tops that said MANDY'S HITCHED! across their chests. "One of you got a problem?" Killer asked. They all kept their eyes down. "See? I'm just out on Friday night, keeping my own. No one said shit when I lost five bills here last week."

"Yeah," his girl said, and she got up into Matthew's face, pointing a finger at his chin like she was shooting a gun. Getting loud. "Everyone was real nice to us." She pointed at the craps dealer now, a Chuyalla who everyone called Puny because he was a good 400 pounds. "Right, Puny?" Puny didn't respond, which was good, because he would have been out of a job. "D, this pussy can't tell you what to do."

"Chill," Killer said.

"I don't need to chill," she said. "This marshmallow mother-fucker needs to chill."

The casino floor was filled with an Elderhostel group, fifty retirees in town for some kind of educational tour of Milwaukee, and they were all craning their necks around the slots now, standing up at their five-dollar blackjack tables; a couple ladies even had their cameras out, getting a real education. This wasn't a show Matthew really wanted to put on.

"I'm not going to ask again," Matthew said.

"You didn't ask in the first place," Killer said. "I know my rights. Fourteenth Amendment and shit. You can't just be discriminating against me."

"I don't know," Matthew said. "Felon in possession of a hooker? That seems like a crime. But you can check with the ACLU."

Killer stared at him. "I say the word your whole family is in the ground."

There it was. He'd been waiting for it.

First two smacks of his sap went on either side of Killer's head, right across the ears. Matthew had to hold Killer up by his shirt so he could get his second shot in, since the first probably would have knocked him to the ground, and Matthew had a point to make, something Killer could take back to the rest of the Latin Kings: Listening is important.

The shot across the lips? Well, that was for talking shit. Matthew busted Killer's mouth open to the bone and out came most of his teeth, including two gold ones, his girl shrieking like Matthew had hit her, too, which he wasn't planning on doing.

He then dragged Killer through the casino by the throat, out through the loading dock, bounced his open wound of a face off a few Dumpsters, giving him a better-than-average chance of picking up a staph infection, and dropped him on the pavement, away from the cameras, not that it mattered, since Matthew was the guy who handled the video. Killer screamed the whole time, or made a noise that used to be screaming, back when his face worked right.

"I don't want you walking back in here," Matthew said. Then he did the only thing he thought would emphasize the point, which was to stomp on Killer's ankles until they snapped. He then went back inside, found Killer's girl crouched under the craps table trying to find all of her boyfriend's teeth, told his floor guys to get her a bag and get her the fuck out of the casino, since looking at her there on the floor, she didn't seem all that threatening anymore, just a woman who had terrible taste in men but loved one enough to pick up his teeth. That was worth something.

Was it all an extreme response? Maybe. Washing a few Gs through the casino wasn't a hanging offense—hell, it was practically why casinos in the Midwest existed—but it was about the point: Matthew Drew hadn't qualified for assault team work at Quantico, hadn't made it all the way to the FBI's top shop in Chicago, so people with their crimes cataloged on their faces could dictate his behavior. That's just not how life worked.

And yet.

He'd somehow missed Ronnie Cupertine walking through the door, as did everyone else working the Eye in the Sky, not that anyone would have complained, least of all any of the Chuyalla management. Ronnie Cupertine was a celebrity, so famous for running the Family that people didn't really believe he ran the Family.

It was . . . impossible.

And yet.

Ronnie Cupertine gave everyone credit at his half a dozen car dealerships around Chicago. Warrantied every purchase for two years. Paid for the entire Little League from Chicago to Springfield.

Donated a million dollars to establish Hope from Fear, a battered women's home on the South Side. Pumped a couple hundred grand into AIDS and cancer research at Northwestern every year. The Chicago Historical Society needed money to preserve a building? Ronnie Cupertine wrote a check. The Field Museum was short fifty Gs for an art exhibit? No problem. Ronnie Cupertine even gave money for an independent film festival and attended the gala, shook hands with the actors and actresses, his wife on his arm draped in diamonds and furs, because Ronnie Cupertine? He was the philanthropic king of Chicago.

So he occasionally had a motherfucker killed.

At least Ronnie Cupertine didn't have a tattoo on his forehead.

Ronnie zipped up and flushed, made his way over to the sink next to Matthew. Up close, Matthew could smell the liquor seeping out of Ronnie's pores. How long had he been at the casino? How many times had Matthew missed seeing him? Ronnie ran the hot water for a few seconds, then took a towel, soaked it, and scrubbed at his face, letting out an exasperated grunt when he was done.

"Tough night?" Matthew asked.

"Too much smoke in this place," Ronnie said. "Feel like it's in my skin, you know? Lungs are all congested. It's unhealthy. Even Atlantic City has better ventilation." He leaned toward the mirror, inspected his face, licked his pinkies, used them to push down his eyebrows. "Fuck it. Can't tell an Indian not to smoke, right? It was their tobacco in the first place, right?"

"Everyone's got their culture," Matthew said.

"You believe that," Ronnie said, "then you should work for me." He took another towel, dried his face, then reached into his pocket, slipped a fifty from his billfold into Curtis's tip jar. "You new here?"

"Been here a few months."

"I haven't seen you before."

"I bought my car from you, actually."

"Yeah?" Ronnie looked at Matthew in the mirror. "You from Chicago?"

"Not originally," Matthew said. "Relocated for a job. Didn't pan out. So here I am."

"You recognize me from TV?" he asked.

"That's it," Matthew said. How much time did he have before one of Ronnie's boys came in, looking for their *actual* boss? Two, three minutes? Maybe five, at the most. It would be disrespectful to walk in on a boss while he was taking a shit, so maybe it would be more like ten. But that seemed like an excessive amount of time to be guarding the door, which Matthew presumed they were doing. They must have swept through and somehow missed seeing Matthew's feet in the back of the handicapped stall. Or they hadn't looked very hard. Matthew reached into his pocket, took out his car keys, jingled them. "You sold me a Mustang."

"You get a good deal?"

"Not bad," Matthew said. "Carburetor gave out after twenty-five thousand miles."

"I replace it?"

"You did."

"I don't welch," Ronnie said. It was a catchphrase from one of his commercials, so popular it was even on the flyers that came in the junk mail and inside the *Tribune* on Sundays. "My opinion, that's the problem with Detroit these days," he continued. Ronnie checked his face in the mirror again, picked a piece of lint from his chin. "It's like they forgot how to build muscle cars. Give me something with a big trunk, big tires, and nothing with the name of some country we bombed the shit out of on any of the materials, right? Every time I see a Japanese or Korean car I ask myself what the fuck we fought for, right?" He paused. "Not that I'm not happy to sell them. But I don't want to drive one."

"You fought in Korea?"

"Nah," Ronnie said. "Before my time."

"So you were in Vietnam?"

Ronnie pointed at his feet. "Bad arches."

"My dad fought."

"Yeah? He come back all messed up?"

"Got cancer eventually," Matthew said. "I don't know if it was the Agent Orange or the two packs a day."

"You know quitting cigarettes is harder than quitting heroin?"

"No," Matthew said. "I didn't know that."

"There's no secondhand heroin," Ronnie said. "You want heroin, you gotta go find it. Cigarettes are everywhere. Fucks with your head." He paused. "Your old man ever try to quit?"

"Not once."

"Sounds like he had a death wish."

"He was complicated," Matthew said. "But he signed up to fight. Didn't wait for the draft. I feel like I would have done the same. And if they said I had some physical impairment, I would have asked for a waiver, snuck back in, whatever it took."

"You say that now," Ronnie said. "Wait until some shit goes down." He selected a toothpick, dug out a spot of food jammed above his incisor. "The weapons back then were shit and, pardon my language, who the fuck wanted to sit in a jungle waiting to get captured? End up like John McCain? All bent in thirty different directions? Nah." He rubbed his top front teeth with his index finger, then leaned back from the sink, adjusted his shirt, made sure his collar was straight, adjusted his belt. "If it was up to me, I would have told the generals to bomb Berkeley, that would have ended the war fast." He took out his billfold again, came out with a business card. "You got a pen?"

Matthew did. It was a black Smith & Wesson tactical pen, the kind you could use to bust out your car window if you found yourself rammed off the road into a frozen lake, or as a weapon if you were fighting up close. He handed it to the head of the biggest organized crime outfit west of New York, who started to scrawl a message on the back of the card.

"Next time you're in the market, bring this card into any of my dealerships, my boys will take good . . ." Ronnie began to say, but Matthew didn't let him finish.

He grabbed Ronnie by the hair and slammed his face into the sink, crushing his nose and snapping his jaw in a single move. Slammed him a second time, across his eyebrows, shattered his orbital bones. Split his forehead open like it had a zipper. Third time, he turned Ronnie's head slightly to the right, aimed down an inch, then severed the top of Ronnie's ear on the sharp marble edge of the counter, and dropped him face-first onto the tile floor. What teeth Ronnie had left clattered around him.

Improvisational skills were a hallmark of good FBI agents. The Bureau even had its agents-in-training work with acting coaches and comics to refine the skill. Matthew liked that aspect of the job. Pretending to be someone else. Day like today, Matthew wasn't sure if he was someone different or who he'd always been.

Matthew got down on one knee, tipped Ronnie on his side, examined the damage.

It wasn't easy to tell the difference between Ronnie's mouth and his nose, his eyes and his scalp.

He'd live. Not happily. But he'd live.

Matthew could put him out of his misery. Drag him into a stall, flip him onto his back, let him choke to death on his own blood. Maybe Matthew could pinch Ronnie's nose to help death along. He'd last a minute, probably less. Even if his boys came in and found him, there was a good chance Ronnie would asphyxiate enough to get some decent brain damage, spend the rest of his life watching cartoons and eating Jell-O.

Tough to run the Family with mush brains.

But that was the easy way out.

Painless, in the end, really.

It had been three years since Sal Cupertine was disappeared. Matthew and Jeff couldn't find him. The rest of the FBI couldn't find him, not that they'd given it much effort. The public hadn't spotted him, not even after all the news programs ran his photo. If Sal Cupertine was still alive, he was doing a good job of pretending he wasn't, which was curious to Matthew. Unless he was living in a cave somewhere, he'd need a new face by this point, and it wasn't like the movies: You could get all the plastic surgery you wanted, but your face was still your face. Maybe all this new facial-recognition software wouldn't make an exact match, but a 50 percent match would be enough to get a warrant if everything else lined up. The FBI did a dry run at the Super Bowl a few months earlier, running 100,000 people in one day, arresting a couple dozen wanted felons. Small database searches made it easier—if Sal Cupertine showed up somewhere the government was looking for the most wanted criminals on the planet, he'd pop right up. And the technology was only getting better: The system they had at the casino updated every few months with new patches, predictive biometrics that could spot extensive makeup, nose jobs, Botox, even artificial aging, what the techs called Tanning Salon Soul Man Face.

If it had a nickname, you were already beaten.

So, yeah, maybe Matthew should have dragged Ronnie into a stall and tortured him for answers, but then what? Ronnie wasn't the boss of Chicago because he was stupid. Maybe Ronnie Cupertine knew where Sal was at one time, but surely that time had passed. Sal Cupertine had spent fifteen years on the streets of Chicago killing with impunity. He knew people were looking for him. If he'd left his wife and kid alone for three long years it wasn't because he was enjoying his life. He'd poke his head up eventually. And Matthew would be there waiting.

Matthew picked up his Smith & Wesson pen and Ronnie's business card, took some time to wash his hands, strands of Ronnie's hair filling up the sink, buttoned up his jacket so the flecks of Ronnie's blood wouldn't be visible on his white shirt, slipped his arrowhead name tag into this pocket. Wet one of Curtis's towels, wiped Ronnie's blood, hair, spit, and skin from the edge of the counter, tossed it in the trash. Checked his reflection in the mirror, then had a thought, got back down on the floor, shoved his hand in Ronnie's pants pocket, came out with his billfold. Counted the cash.

Five grand. He'd give it to Nina, save for fifty bucks to get his suit and shoes cleaned, then headed out, just as Ronnie Cupertine let out a low moan and shit himself.

THERE WERE TWO guys lingering outside, heads down, pacing, backs to the door, talking on their phones. They wore identical Adidas sweat suits, though one guy had on white Nikes, the other old-school black Pumas. It was odd, since the Family guys tended to dress like they were in business, at least the ones who went around with Ronnie. These two weren't even wearing Kevlar. He scanned them for weapons, saw both were going for fashion over utility, guns stuffed in the back of their waistbands, like in the movies. Matthew could shoot both of these guys between the eyes, or simply walk up and disarm them, before either realized how stupid it was to keep their guns behind them. At Quantico, during live-action fire drills, they'd practice on guys like this, since most of the time, if you're FBI, you're rousing assholes from their houses, not shooting it out with bank robbers armed with AK-47s on the streets of LA. These guys hadn't received the memo, Matthew thought, that rolling with nines shoved up your ass was no way to conduct modern warfare.

Everything was slower in Wisconsin.

"Excuse me, boss," Matthew said to the one in the white Nikes, and the guy turned around, surprised to find someone standing there. He had a cross tattooed on his neck—one with the full body of Christ splayed out, though it wasn't especially well done, shitty prison ink making Jesus look more like a melted Kris Kristofferson—and one of those pencil-thin goatees.

"What?" he said. He wasn't Italian, which was odd. The Family didn't usually use their affiliates for personal security. They didn't mind having them sell their drugs or do their scut work, like Chema and Neto Espinoza had done; but it wasn't exactly a ringing endorsement for a positive work environment, Chema chopped up and dumped in a landfill, Neto murdered in Stateville. But every-one had bills.

"You with the guy in the bathroom?"

"Why do you care?"

"I think he fell down," Matthew said.

"Shit," the man said, flipped his phone closed, pushed past Matthew, grabbed the other guy, and both disappeared into the bathroom, still not pulling their guns. Matthew could follow them into the bathroom and plug them both in the back of the head if he so wished.

Instead, Matthew headed to his office upstairs.

He still had another fifteen minutes on the clock, so he took a little time to run through the security footage, found the feed of himself walking in and out of the bathroom, wiped it from the sys-tem, wiped it from the backup system, too. The perk of being in charge. Tomorrow, he'd come in early, track Ronnie Cupertine's movements through the casino, see who he played with, see if he met with anyone. Ronnie Cupertine could fly to Las Vegas if he wanted to gamble for real money, so there had to be something else to get him up to this shithole in the middle of the night.

Matthew Drew, who'd spent six months as an FBI agent and another six months pretending to be one while searching for Sal Cupertine, locked his office and headed out through the service exit, saw that housekeeping hadn't managed to get all of Killer's blood out of the carpet, took a mental note to have that taken care of on Sunday, too, then made his way to the employee parking lot, where he was the only non-Chuyalla with a reserved spot. Found his Mustang, the piece of shit, got in, and called 911 from his cell, the operator telling him an ambulance was already on its way, again.

4

Jennifer Cupertine had come to arrange her life into three tidy segments: *William. Work. Waiting.* The William part came first now that he was back in school. Every weekday morning, like today, the last Monday of August, she'd drive him from their house in Lincolnwood out to Mount Carmel Academy on West Belmont, idle on the street until he walked through the front doors, not leaving until the security guard on duty gave her a nod in recognition. The guards probably thought she was nuts, waiting out there every day like that in Sal's old Lincoln with the broken odometer, but that was fine. *Everyone* at Mount Carmel thought she was nuts, the result of never taking part in any of the car pools, never letting William take the bus on field trips, if she let him go on the field trips at all, insisting that she always drive him everywhere.

If someone on the streets came for her son, Jennifer Cupertine was going to make them take her, too. She wasn't going to let Becky the Soccer Mom die in her pink Juicy track pants just because it was her day on the calendar to drive the brats.

So let them think she was crazy. She was saving their lives.

Jennifer checked the clock on the dashboard: 7:39 a.m. The guard would be out in two minutes, three tops, then she'd head over to her office at the Museum of Contemporary Photography. *Work* had a predictable monotony: a few hours of filing down in the archives, followed by some time at her computer on digital restorations, for which she'd found a surprising facility. The museum even picked up the tab for her night classes at UIC once she showed some promise, had eventually bumped her up to full-time, which was nice, though she got paid less than everyone else, since she'd only ever done a bit of junior college. Even the nameplate on her office door was slightly smaller than her office mate Stacy's. The restoration work was meticulous and time consuming—she worked pixel by pixel on old photos, trying to correct color or fill in holes and tears, fix resolution, get them ready for shows—but it focused her mind, kept that free-floating fear from descending on her before she was adequately prepared.

It wasn't until Stacy went to lunch that she'd get online to look for Sal. She didn't have the Internet at her house, not because she couldn't afford it—though she couldn't—but because she was pretty sure the FBI was watching all communications that came into and out of her home. She didn't know if they could get into her computer, but she asked herself what Sal would do in this situation, and she remembered him telling her, years ago, when she finally understood what he did for a living, "Don't open the door to strangers and don't open the door to cops." And then he paused and said, "No one we know would show up unannounced. But if they did, it wouldn't be good news. Just . . . don't open the door for anyone."

And what was the Internet but a big open door? So she used only Stacy's computer to search newspapers for stories that might show evidence of Sal's presence in a city—people getting killed "execution-style" was her prime indicator—or used only Stacy's phone to make calls to hospitals and morgues when there were reports of people with Sal's basic description found in ravines, or in trunks of cars, or washed up somewhere. She'd see if the person had a crappy eight-ball tattoo on his arm, raised and mottled. Sal's wounds never did heal right, which made that tattoo a dumb idea in the first place, but that was before Jennifer exerted any control over his life. Sal was always getting infections—he'd break a toe and set it himself, it would grow back crooked, then the nail would fall off and he'd just suffer through it, maybe grab a couple of Jennifer's amoxicillin from the medicine cabinet, until it became some festering thing and he'd finally haul himself to a free clinic, a place where he could use a fake ID and no one would care, people only really caring about who you were if they wanted your money.

How Jennifer's life had changed in the three years since Sal disappeared. How wary she'd become. Predictability was the one intangible thing in her life that Jennifer Cupertine appreciated. It all worked into a simple ebb and flow. Still, she woke up every morning a little farther from the person she'd been. If Sal ever came back, would he even recognize her? That was the *Waiting*. Waiting for her husband to return. Waiting for their next move. Waiting for someone to show up, knock on the door, and tell her the waiting was over, that Sal was dead—*really dead* this time—or that her time was up, too. A bullet to the brain for both mother and son.

The bell rang and the last few straggling kids ran up the front steps of the school and then, one minute later, the guard came out, just like always. Except Jennifer didn't recognize him. That gave her a moment of pause, but it wasn't terribly unusual, the school did cycle through security personnel somewhat regularly, and someone would eventually tell the new person about the Crazy Lady in the Old Lincoln. But then the new guy walked all the way down onto the sidewalk, to the drop-off lane where Jennifer was parked, and motioned for her to roll down the passenger window.

"How you doing, Mrs. Cupertine?"

The guard's name tag said he was called Horace. He was in his forties, but already had a belly that slid over his belt like an avalanche. He held the top of the walkie-talkie on his belt like it was a gun, probably an old habit; the school was real big about letting parents know that all of their security guards were either current or ex–Chicagoland PD. There wasn't going to be some Columbine situation on their school grounds.

Not that it mattered to Jennifer. She didn't trust cops. Half of them worked for Cousin Ronnie, the other half were looking to kill her husband. If she came home and found burglars in her house, she'd let them walk out with her TV before she called 911. Last thing she was going to do was invite a cop into her house, since either way she'd probably end up dead.

"What is it?" Jennifer said.

"That's real good," Horace said, not actually answering the question Jennifer had asked. He was looking into Jennifer's backseat. It was littered with stray toys, this morning's empty juice box, two binders full of photos she took from her office three days earlier, with the idea that she'd get some work done from home, but which instead had languished back there all weekend. "Reason I come by today, I just wanted to tell you, Billy's a real nice kid . . ."

Before he could get the "but" out, Jennifer interrupted him: "William."

"Pardon me?" Horace looking at her now.

"His name is William."

"People here call him Billy, so that's what I know him as."

"That's not his name," Jennifer said. "If I wanted people to call him Billy, I would have named him Billy."

"I get it, Mrs. Cupertine," Horace said. "I mean no offense." He smiled at her, though he didn't seem particularly happy about anything. "Thing is, these first two weeks of school, he's already been getting into it with his classmates. You know, scuffles on the kickball field, pushing and shoving, nothing big, probably not even enough to warrant this conversation just yet. But what's horseplay today, tomorrow could be three, four, five kids getting him on the ground. It's just, I know you worry about him."

"How do you know that?"

He shrugged. "I see you're real conscientious about his safety."

"If William is having a problem," Jennifer said, "I'm sure one of the Sisters of Mercy will call me."

"Maybe." Horace nodded, as if he was considering this possibility. "But anyone here ever call you?"

They hadn't. Not even when she was late making tuition payments, which she had been for a few months, though she'd been smart about holding on to the money Sal had sent her, using it only for William's school stuff, his clothes, whatever he needed to get along like the rest of the kids. But then the pipes burst last winter, and her cushion had a few less feathers in it. Some people in Chicago, ones with a little bit of history in town, knew you didn't hound someone with the last name Cupertine about money. Not that the phone company or the electric company gave a shit. It was all automated now. The red overdue notices weren't scared of her married name and no one was putting a gun in the face of the asshole who kept calling about her Discover card. Then last week she heard Cousin Ronnie had suffered some kind of neurological episode out on the golf course. Sunstroke or something.

"I'll talk to him," Jennifer said.

Horace nodded again, straightened up, kept one hand on the nub of the passenger window, looked both ways, like he wanted to make sure no one was watching him. "Thing is," he said eventually, "Mrs. Cupertine, everyone here knows who you are. Difference is, I don't hold you personally responsible for the actions of your husband."

"I'm *not* personally responsible for his actions," Jennifer said.

"See, it's good to know you feel that way," he said. "Because this is my part-time job here. Nights, I'm working in Evanston, at the college? Doing community policing. And only authority I have here, at Mount Carmel," he pointed his thumb over his shoulder, "is to get that door locked, make sure no strangers come onto the campus and start killing kids. Same basic job as at the college, but there they give me a gun. Here I'm just a human shield. You understand?"

She was beginning to. Jennifer glanced into her rearview mirror, half expecting some blacked-out Suburban to be behind her, sort of hoping the FBI was tailing her, since at least they now made a pretense of not being crooked, unlike these cops. Instead, she recognized Tom Gehrlein, one of the single dads who seemed nice, pulling up in his gold Lexus. He was mid-argument with his daughter, Jennifer able to make out tears on the girl's face.

Good.

If need be, Jennifer could throw her car into reverse, slam into Tom's car, cause a scene. Maybe Tom's daughter would get whiplash. Small price to pay. Girl that young shouldn't be sitting in the front seat, anyway.

"I'm running late for work," Jennifer said.

"That's fine," Horace said. "I'll only keep you a minute longer." He reached through the window with surprising quickness for a big guy and pulled her keys from the ignition, tossed them into the backseat.

"If you're trying to scare me," Jennifer said, "get in line."

"Scare you? I'm trying to protect you."

Jennifer wished she kept a gun under her seat or in the glove box instead of just in the crawl space of her house. But she'd made a choice to not have guns around William. To not talk about guns. To not watch TV shows with guns in them. To not even have guns be part of William's vernacular.

A car door slammed, hard, startling both her and Horace, both of them turning to watch Tom Gehrlein's daughter storm away from her father's car and up Mount Carmel's front steps. What was her name? Bethany or Britney or Whitney. One of those names that didn't exist ten or fifteen years ago, except in movies, and then as a joke. She reached the locked doors, yanked on them one, two, three times, making a racket, then turned and glared in Horace's direction.

"One minute, sugar," Horace called, then turned his attention back to Jennifer. "Look, I'm trying to give you some advice," he said. "Older kids find out Billy's dad is a tough guy, everyone will want to take their shot. Billy, he's a sensitive boy, is what I'm saying. No need to put him through that. What if some sixth grader comes to school with a pocketknife? Billy ends up wearing an eye patch for the rest of his life, or missing an ear? See what I'm saying?"

"My son," Jennifer said, "barely remembers his father."

Horace looked up and across the street, Jennifer getting the sense that maybe he wasn't looking to see if anyone was watching him as much as he was making sure someone *absolutely* was watching him. "Problem is other people do." He reached into his jacket pocket and Jennifer recoiled, prepared to have a gun in her face, except Horace came out with a multicolored brochure featuring a girl sitting quietly on a sofa and an older woman looking over her shoulder, approvingly. "Take this," he said.

"I don't want whatever that is," Jennifer said, figuring there was something stuck between the pages—money, some directions out of town, another threat, probably less vague, who the hell knew anymore?

"Suit yourself," he said, and tossed the brochure into the backseat, too. "Used to be a stigma with homeschooling. But plenty of people do it now. That brochure has some info about services that provide study guides, book lists, whatever you need. I'd look into it. Because what if there's a day when I'm not on the job, and one of the kids takes it too far? Imagine having that sitting on your conscience?" Horace whistled through his teeth. "That'd fuck you up but good. Not that you look like you're hanging on to a thick rope, if you don't mind me saying."

"I'll let my husband know you feel that way the next time I see him."

"Oh," Horace said, all fake sincerity, "is he back? I could use half a mil."

"Wouldn't that be a nice surprise for you," Jennifer said. "Walk out to harass me and the Rain Man is sitting here, waiting on you." Jennifer saw something pass through Horace, realized he was just the guy giving the message, that he probably hadn't really considered what that meant, exactly, but now he did. "What would you do then, Officer?"

A horn honked before Horace could answer—just a light tap. Tom Gehrlein double-parked next to Jennifer's car and, when she looked over at him, he hit a button and lowered his passenger window, so she cranked her window down, too. "Everything okay, Jen?" he asked.

Jen. No one called her Jen. "Yes," she said, because what else could she say? Jennifer tried to remember what he did for a job. Copy machine sales? Or maybe it was computers? No. Wind. He worked for a company that was trying to get wind energy turbines installed in Illinois. He literally sold air. Wasn't that a game. "Everything is just fine."

"That's real good," he said, and then pointed at his crying daughter. "You ever have mornings like that with your son?"

"No," Jennifer said. "He doesn't throw tantrums."

"Well, you're lucky," he said. He looked beyond Jennifer, addressed Horace. "If you wouldn't mind, could you let my daughter in? She cries much longer, she'll throw up."

"No problem," Horace said, though he didn't move.

"You going to Open House next week?" Tom asked Jennifer.

"Probably," Jennifer said.

"I'm going to try to have the stomach flu," he said, "see if I can get my ex to handle it. But if I end up well, maybe we can stand together in the library and avoid the reproachful eye of the nuns?"

"Maybe," she said, realizing, *maybe*, that he was flirting with her, or what amounted to flirting before 8:00 a.m. She also considered that he probably didn't know anything about her, which was nice—until she realized that if he did get to know her, he'd probably end up under government surveillance. If he wasn't already an FBI agent. Then the Family might subcontract out a kidnapping on his daughter, pay some pedophile a couple thousand dollars to pick her up. Sal used to tell her how the Family wasn't in that dirty business, but that didn't mean they wouldn't hire out periodically if they really wanted to send a message.

"Great," Tom said, then paused, like maybe he wanted to say something else, and finally settled on, "Well, I'll let you get back to it," then gave both Jennifer and Horace a two-fingered salute and pulled away.

"Looks like you got a boyfriend," Horace said. He'd worked a big ring of keys from his belt and was thumbing through to find the one he needed. "Anyway," he said once he found what he was looking for, "I wouldn't ignore the problem, if I were you. Billy's a bit of a pussy. You're gonna be picking him up in pieces if you don't do something."

He smacked the roof of her car, twice, the sound reverberating like a gunshot, the real echo being Jennifer Cupertine's stunned realization that there wasn't a single safe space left for her.

It also occurred to her, watching him walk off, that she'd probably never see Horace again, that he was the horse's head inside her bed, as it were; nothing original left in the world.

•

THE NEXT DAY, on her lunch break, Jennifer Cupertine walked a few blocks from the museum to Northwestern Memorial Hospital. She took the elevator up to the ninth floor, home to the Ronald J. Cupertine Physical Rehabilitation Center, which occupied a considerable portion of the east wing, more than twenty rooms, most of them private.

All the common spaces were done up in soft, blond wood and recessed lighting, the private rooms had big-screen TVs, DVD players, some even had wider beds, and, if you weren't on a restricted diet, you could order food off an actual menu. Jennifer knew all of this because just like everyone else in the family—the real family—she'd given birth to her son at Northwestern, had been put up in the Cupertine wing after a particularly difficult C-section and complicated recovery, and never got a bill for the services. Ronnie himself didn't show up to the hospital, but his second wife, Sharon, was there every day for a week. Jennifer would wake up and Sharon would be sitting on the chaise sofa across the room, reading *Vanity Fair* or *Architectural Digest*, or at least looking at the pictures, and as soon as Jennifer's eyes were open, she'd get to work, ordering nurses around, fluffing pillows, changing flowers, chatting Jennifer up about whatever the news of the day was, or the pictures she'd seen—for a few days, Jennifer remembered Sharon being inordinately fascinated by rainfall showerheads— just normal, dumb stuff. And for a time afterward, Jennifer and Sharon had been friends.

That time was over.

Jennifer hadn't spoken to Sharon since she'd been enlisted as the go-between for the Family, telling Jennifer that what happened with Sal "was all in the game" and that she just needed to be a good widow and the Family would take care of her.

Like Jennifer was going to let the people who got rid of her husband tell her how to live. Tell her that it was all some kind of *game.* Maybe she'd believed that when she was a kid, thought it was exciting and cool that her boyfriend (and then eventually her husband) was a person others were scared of. But Jennifer Cupertine was almost forty now, plucking a single gray hair from her right eyebrow every two weeks, and some asshole had just threatened her and her child at *school.* Yeah, she'd let Ronnie pay off her house, but only so she could mortgage it for cash, which had been a mistake, since now she was in business with Countrywide, and they were just as bad as the Family, except the Family killed you faster.

She'd tried Sharon at home and on her cell a good ten times, but she hadn't picked up. Neither had the maids or the kids or the answering machine. She even called the number Sal told her never to call unless the feds were kicking down the doors, but even when that had actually happened, that night he disappeared, she didn't call it, because what good would it have done?

That one just rang and rang, too.

So she'd come to the hospital where Ronnie Cupertine was recovering from his sunstroke—the *Sun-Times* even had a quote from him hailing the slate of movies he was sad to be missing at the film festival he'd underwritten, another blurb big-upping the Native Short Film Festival, debuting after the first of the year, where he was "looking forward to being in the front row!"—to let Sharon know this bullshit was not going to work on her. If Sharon wanted to keep her comfortable little life, she'd tell these bastards to step the fuck off. And if Sharon wasn't there? Maybe she'd tell Ronnie directly.

That was the plan, anyway.

Except when she got to the reception area, there was a security guard sitting behind the desk, not one of the usual volunteers she recalled from her time on the wing. Behind the security guard, the floor opened wide into a U of patient rooms with a nurses' station between them, and then one long spoke of a hallway. Nurses milled about, moving in and out of rooms, no one in a terrible hurry. This wasn't the floor where emergencies happened. It was where you recovered from emergencies.

Fat Monte's mostly vegetative widow, Hannah, was also living out her days on the wing. Jennifer had come to see her a few times those first couple months, always late at night, but couldn't bear to return. Hannah didn't have a real head anymore, just a combination of skin and bones that approximated one.

"Help you?" the guard said. He was sitting, but Jennifer could see that he had on a Kevlar vest under his shirt, but no gun, which seemed silly. He had the *Tribune* crossword open in front of him and was puzzling over 4 Across: *Royal elephant.*

"I'm here to see Hannah Moretti," Jennifer said.

"Your name?"

"Jennifer Cupertine," she said.

The guard tapped at his computer. "You have ID?" She gave him her license and he examined it under a light, then pushed his chair back from his desk to a small copier, made a quick photocopy of it then gave it back to her, made out a guest pass and slid it into a lanyard, handed it to her. "You're on the list," he said, like he was a bouncer at a club, "but I'm going to need to look in your purse."

"For what?"

"This is a private floor," he said.

She pointed at the gilded CUPERTINE on the wall. "That's my name."

"Not my rules," he said, so she opened her purse and let him shine a pen light over its contents. "Room 913."

Jennifer started to walk off, thought about something, came back. "What do you do with the copy of my license?" she asked.

"Stick it in a file," the guard said, "then at the end of the day, we shred them."

"Then why bother?"

"Not my rules," he said again, this time with a shrug. "If it was up to me, I'd be on Navy Pier with my kid."

Jennifer knew the feeling. "Babar."

"Pardon?"

"Four Across," Jennifer said. "You can put that in pen."

JENNIFER FOUND HANNAH Moretti's room toward the back of the wing. When she was first moved to the Cupertine Center, Hannah was in a huge room that looked out over the lake, but now her room wasn't quite as nice. From the hallway, Jennifer could make out the end of Hannah's bed, the tent of sheets and blankets where Hannah's feet were, an understuffed side chair, and a single window that looked out to a parking structure.

"You here to visit Ms. Moretti?" a nurse asked from behind Jennifer. She was young, maybe twenty-five, and had eyebrows that she'd drawn in, not very well. She was preparing an IV stand, the bag filled with a chocolate-brown fluid. Behind her was a three-foot-tall whiteboard that listed each patient's pertinent information: name, room number, day nurse name, doctor. Jennifer scanned it, found what she was looking for: *R. Cupertine/930/Matt/Dr. Biskar/ NA.* She drifted down, found Hannah: *H. Moretti/913/Connie/Dr. Gay/8/29.* There were fewer than a dozen other patients listed, but their last names read like the donor wall of every museum and art institute in the city, including the one Jennifer worked in. The only prominent Chicagoland names missing were Wrigley, Comiskey, and those of governors and senators already doing time.

"Yes," Jennifer said.

"That's a surprise," she said, but not in a nice way. Jennifer wondered who came to see Hannah, who she had in this world. She had a mother in St. Paul, she remembered that, but Ronnie had probably paid her off years ago, to keep her away, keep her quiet. The only family Fat Monte still had around wasn't inclined to visit, Jennifer was sure. His mother had been farmed out to an assisted-living facility in Las Vegas and the son Fat Monte had fathered to a stripper out in Springfield was barely seven, if that. Not that she imagined the kid would be dying to come up to see the woman his father had shot in the face.

The nurse pushed the IV stand from around the station and into the hallway. "She's due to be fed and have her stomach tube cleaned, so maybe come back in fifteen? Unless you want to watch."

"No," Jennifer said. "I'll come back." She pointed at the board. "What does the 8/29 stand for?"

The nurse turned around, looked at the board. "That's the expected discharge date," she said.

That was in two days. "She's being moved?"

"No," the nurse said. "They're taking her off the machines. Maybe tell anyone who cares."

ROOM 930 WAS wedged into the far western corner of the building, down a long hallway off the main floor. There were cameras and closed-circuit monitors all up and down the corridor. No one was going to creep up on Ronnie Cupertine in his own hospital wing . . . especially not with the two guys standing outside his door.

Jennifer recognized Bobby Lopiparno when she came around the corner. The boys in the neighborhood called him Lollipop or Sugar back in the day, because he had diabetes. But then, in high school, he got into selling coke, so Sugar stuck. She didn't recognize the other man, but he was tall and thin, and wasn't wearing a tie, unlike Sugar, who had on a full suit, vest and everything, which made him look like he might be the clergy, though Jennifer suspected he was aiming for some Sonny Corleone bullshit. Both men had on the same hospital lanyard Jennifer wore, which gave them a multilevel-marketing-seminar vibe; no one looks particularly tough with a plastic bag around their neck, turns out, but the thin guy also had on a gold bracelet and had a single diamond stud in each ear, like he was the dangerous one in a boy band.

"Hey, little Jennie Frangello," Sugar said, calling her by her maiden name, like all the boys still did when she saw them, as if she'd never grown up, never become a Cupertine. Would that it was so simple. He sprang his arms open, as if he expected her to jump into them, which wasn't going to happen. There was a closed-circuit TV hanging over him, another at the end of the hall where she'd been walking. Sugar was sweaty, wide-eyed, and as twitchy as a rabbit—*high as fuck*, by Jennifer's estimation—though the other guy looked perfectly at ease. Could be that was just because the skin on his face was so clear and hairless that Jennifer could see the big open pores on his cheeks from a few feet away.

"What are you doing here?" Jennifer asked. She hadn't seen Sugar in a good five years, not since the night he and his wife, Bonnie, came to their house—with a good bottle of scotch—and Sugar and Sal spent the next several hours in the backyard, drinking and talking quietly, their heads close, Sal periodically shaking his head, getting up, pacing. When Sugar and Bonnie finally left, Sal came in and told her, "He's Ronnie's guy in Detroit now. You believe that? He can't count to ten unless he uses his toes, but he's Ronnie's guy in Detroit."

"I don't get a hello?" Sugar said now. "Know me since third grade, you can't even say hi? Gotta come up here all tough girl." He grabbed her up in his arms before she could stop him, hugging her, but really patting her down, around her shoulders, down to the small of her back, not rough, but she could feel his fingers on her skin, could smell his sweat when he pressed her against his chest. Could also feel the grip of his gun poking into her ribs. "Easy, sis," he whispered into her hair when she tensed up. "Be real easy."

He set her down a foot away, made eye contact with her for half a second before he launched into a story.

"You see that, Mike? This girl, she's hundred-percent legit, but back in the day, let me tell you, this was the bitch you wanted, and her old man? He once walked up into the Viewpoint, kicked open that old back door, off the dance floor? The wood one? Kicked right fucking through it, cuz, see, he always wore these steel-toed work boots. What did he do, meat packing or something? Something hard, right? Union man, didn't take a dime wasn't on his paycheck. Anyway, kicks in the fucking door, where they're banding cash from the book, and that motherfucker, he's like, this is my local right here, you start doing your gangster shit in here, I got nowhere to drink, and that was it! Straight up. Everyone on the block knew you didn't dick around with old man Frangello, and then he made sweet little Jennie Frangello and, boy, that was that."

Jennifer didn't know what the hell Sugar was talking about, and from the looks of him, he didn't either. Her father had been middle management at Montgomery Ward corporate, working in catalog sales, first in tools, later in home appliances, was at his desk on the fifth floor of the Mail Order House building on the river when Jennifer's mom died of a heart attack, was at the same desk when he died of pancreatic cancer, which was never even diagnosed. That whole Montgomery Ward building was going to be condos by the end of the year. Great view if you didn't mind being haunted by the ghost of Leopold Frangello, who everyone in the neighborhood knew was the guy you went to when you needed a stove and had to put it on layaway, but didn't want anyone to know, because gangsters were always broke.

"That's right," Jennifer said.

Sugar nodded almost imperceptibly, just a slight dip of his chin, then went on. "You know who she ended up with? The Rain Man."

"For real?" Mike said to Jennifer.

"For real," Jennifer said.

"Mad love," Mike said. He had a slight accent, like he was trying to sound street but had actually grown up in Lincoln Park. Jennifer guessed he was maybe twenty-one; she was almost twice his age and she'd never had diamond earrings so nice. He wasn't Italian, she could tell that much, which made Sugar's deference even more odd.

"What does that mean?" she asked.

"Respect," Mike said. "Like that I respect you for hooking up with him."

"I didn't hook up with him," Jennifer said. "We got married and started a family. It's what normal people do every day." She tried to peer into Ronnie's room, to see if Sharon was inside, but the door was only cracked open a few inches. She heard a man's voice talking, so she tapped it open another inch with her foot, tried to get a wider look. "You know, like your parents?" She made out Ronnie in the bed, propped up, his head encased in a metal halo, keeping his neck in place. His black hair, usually combed and parted like a Republican congressman's, stuck out wildly and Jennifer could see that his silver roots were coming through. His eyes were half open, as if maybe he was in a twilight sleep. How long had he been here? Papers said a week. She guessed closer to a month, judging from his hair alone. She didn't imagine falling on a golf course would put you in a halo, either. She leaned forward, tried to make out the rest of the room, saw the coil of a phone cord stretched out across the bed, realized the man's voice she heard was someone talking on the phone. Mike caught the door and closed it once he realized what was going on.

"Boss is in a meeting," he said.

"Looks like your boss is in a coma," Jennifer said.

"That's not my boss," he said, like they were doing that bit from *The Pink Panther* her dad used to love. *Does your dog bite?*

Sugar cleared his throat. "You here to see Ronnie, Jennie? Because no one was expecting you."

"Sharon, actually," she said.

"She's out of town," Sugar said.

"Since when?"

Sugar shifted from foot to foot. "She went to their place in the U.P.," Sugar said, trying to give her that *keep-your-fucking-mouth-closed* look. Ronnie didn't have a place in the U.P., far as Jennifer knew. "Cool out for a few weeks. Been so fucking hot here."

"Kids, too?" Sugar cocked his head, confused. "She take them out of school?" she said, giving him some help.

"Yeah," Sugar said, "yeah. That's what she did."

"And just left Cousin Ronnie here with that thing on his head?"

Sugar tugged at the lanyard around his neck, didn't say anything.

"I had a thing happen to me at Mount Carmel," Jennifer said. "One of your cops threatened me and my son."

"Not our cops," Sugar said.

"I'm sure," Jennifer said. "Look, I don't care what you people do. It's your problem. But by rights, my son could have this whole family in a few years if he wanted it. So this bullshit? It needs to stop. I'm just trying to get by, okay?"

"I'll tell Ronnie," Sugar said.

"How?" Jennifer asked. "Telepathy?"

Nothing.

What the hell was going on? She looked at Sugar's left hand. He still wore a wedding ring, so that was something.

"How's Bonnie, Sugar?"

Nothing.

"She been to see Hannah lately? Weren't they friends?"

"She don't get down this way much anymore," Sugar said.

"That's good," Jennifer said. "Being a wife in this family turns out to be a pretty dangerous job."

The sound of laughing came from Ronnie's room.

"Why don't you come back next week," Sugar said.

More laughing. Whoever was on the phone in there was getting some good news.

"Boy king and shit?" Mike said.

"What?" Jennifer said.

"Your son. He even walk across the street on his own yet? Or you still holding his hand?"

"What about you?" Jennifer said. "Who holds your hand?"

"Hey," Sugar said. "Be easy, sis."

Mike laughed in a queer way. "You think *birthright* matters? This isn't the old ways, lady." He waved her off with the back of his hand.

The door opened then and a man Jennifer didn't recognize stepped out. He had on a white open-collared dress shirt, a cream-colored linen blazer, jeans, those slip-on shoes people with money wear with everything. He was in his early forties, black hair, smelled like that awful peach body spray strippers liked to douse on themselves. He gave Jennifer a cursory once-over, let out a little snort, maybe of approval, maybe of derision, Jennifer couldn't tell. He slid on a pair of tortoiseshell sunglasses, motioned at Sugar and Mike with a nod of his head, and they followed him back down the hall. Sugar gave Jennifer a sideways glance, but Jennifer didn't know what it meant.

All these guys and their fucking sideways glances. Sal used to come home from work, lie in bed, and stew. It wasn't about the job— he did what he did, he didn't say shit to her about it—it was about what amounted to office politics. Everyone trying out moves they'd learned watching the same five movies over and over again.

Jennifer pushed open Ronnie's door.

The room was empty, save for Ronnie and the litany of machines he was hooked up to, though she saw his hospital phone was back on the otherwise empty table next to him. No flowers. No pictures. The two sofas at the far end of the room had no wrinkles in them. There were no magazines or books. The TV was off. No hint of Sharon and the kids in the least. Ronnie Cupertine, who'd run the Family for decades, who always had two or three guys with him wherever he went, was all alone. Jennifer could make a few calls to old friends who'd be very happy with this knowledge. Might even pay her for it.

She walked up next to the bed, examined Ronnie.

He was missing most of his teeth, his jaw wired up with an elaborate series of what looked like cables and pulleys. His nose was little more than two slits. He had pins sticking out of his cheekbones. It was as if his face had been split in two and all that was left from the original version were his eyes, but even they were wrong, encircled with deep bruising and swollen until the skin looked slick, so that they seemed to melt into his forehead, which was stippled and dented, never mind the contraption screwed into his flesh.

This wasn't sunstroke.

This wasn't a stroke at all.

This was a beat down.

And then whatever came next, maybe *that* was a stroke or a heart attack or a seizure or something, whatever had left him in this state, but it started with something hitting his face.

Who would do that? If someone was going to beat the shit out of Ronnie Cupertine, why wouldn't they just kill him? Who was going to let him live? That wasn't how it worked. People who owed money might get beaten up, lose a finger, lose an eye, but if someone came at Ronnie Cupertine, it would be to take over the Family. Even Jennifer knew that much.

And if someone had tried and failed to put Ronnie down, that person would now be dead. There'd been nothing in the paper about any new Chicago gangland business, no gossip, just old stuff dredged up because of that Miami guy in Las Vegas who lost his strip club to the government, dumb crooks getting exposed, which always seemed to be a good reason to dig up a photo of Sal and put it in the paper somewhere.

Jennifer hustled out of Ronnie's room, found the men on the closed-circuit TV screen, loping deliberately down the corridor, just like they'd seen in the movies. The guy with the tortoiseshell sunglasses was on his cell phone now, Mike a step behind him, also on his phone, Sugar a step behind Mike, head up, looking directly into the camera, like he was waiting for her to notice him. Jennifer sprinted down the hall as the men turned the corner toward the main portion of the floor, the two new guys dipping into the men's room together, Sugar left to stand guard, the Ronald J. Cupertine Physical Rehabilitation Center bustling twenty feet behind him.

Two nurses huddled over a clipboard.

An orderly pushed a cart stacked with meals, Jennifer smelling asparagus.

A doctor, barely thirty years old, sucking on a pen, another pen behind his ear, paced in front of a room.

Jennifer stuck her hand inside her purse. The first couple months after Sal disappeared, she kept a gun with her, as if she were the gangster. What would she do now if she had that gun? Get all of these Gold Coast assholes onto the news, everyone forced to explain why they were getting medical care in a hospital wing paid for by a crook and killer . . .

But . . .

Wasn't that it? They were all part of crime families, in one way or another. Jennifer. Sugar. The university hospital that took Ronnie's money. Even the nurses and doctors. How many gunshot wounds had they treated here? How many beat downs? All of them bound to confidentiality and a blind eye for what? All the lines were kinked in this place. The only legit thing here was the pain.

Sugar took his lanyard off, wound the cord around both of his hands, pulled it tight. "You gonna do something," he said, "do something. Don't wait on it."

"I'm at sea here, Bobby," she said. She put her hands up. "I'm not in this shit, okay? Stop making me a part of it. I want out. Tell that to whoever makes those decisions."

"If I knew who that was," Sugar said, "I'd be in Maui, sipping cocktails. Do yourself a favor, sis." Sugar looked over his shoulder at the bathroom. "Change your area code." Jennie heard two toilets flush. Sugar dropped his lanyard onto the floor, kicked it away.

"I thought we were family. Isn't that the story? That we're family?"

The bathroom door opened and out came Peaches, followed by Mike, both of them still on their phones. Peaches saw Jennifer standing there, said, "Hold on," into his phone, then handed it to Sugar. "You have a nice visit?"

"Who did that to my cousin?" Jennifer said.

"Oh, now he's your cousin?" Peaches said. When Jennifer didn't respond, he said, "You got any ideas?"

"We don't speak."

"He don't speak to anyone anymore." This got Mike to laugh, but Sugar stayed quiet. "Your husband been around?"

"If my husband were here," Jennifer said, "we wouldn't be talking in a hospital."

"You think that?"

"You're not from Chicago," Jennifer said, "or you'd think that, too."

"My family has been here a long time," Peaches said. That got Mike to laugh again. "I am new to the area, that's true, yeah." He got close to Jennifer. Close enough that if she had that gun, she could pull it out and pop him in the head, but she'd be dead in about five seconds, since she could see now that Mike had a bulge on his ankle. No one frisks men's ankles in hospitals. Plus, if she was dead, who would raise William? One of these assholes? Them or someone like them. "But I've been paying attention for a while now. I don't see you out working the streets, not that you couldn't make a few dollars, for a couple years yet, my guess, so I figure you've probably got a little money tucked away. Maybe Ronnie gave you a few dollars? Maybe his wife slipped you some cash? That's over now."

"Ronnie has never given me a cent."

"Except for your house, right? It's a nice house. If it was me," he said, "I'd get a security system. Fix that window that looks out back, too. One with all that rot in the pane? The screen just pops right off. How long until you were in her room, nephew?"

"Twenty seconds," Mike said.

"Nobody talks to me like this," Jennifer said.

"Your husband," Peaches said, "has left you in this position. Do you ever think about that? He climbed into a truck and drove off without you. What kind of man does that?"

"The kind that knows I can take care of myself."

"And yet here you are, looking for help." Peaches leaned in closer now. "I know he talked to the newspapers." Quiet now. "I know that was him. I know he killed that FBI agent. And, girl, I know he's been in contact with you. So go back to your pretty pictures," Peaches said, "you're embarrassing yourself."

•

IT WAS AFTER one when Jennifer finally made it back to the museum, her office mate Stacy already at her desk, eating a salad with her fingers.

"You're late," Stacy said. Stacy wasn't Jennifer's boss, but she spoke to her like she was.

"I went to see a friend at the hospital," Jennifer said. She'd taken a few minutes to sit with Hannah, to talk to her, tell her she was sorry for ever pretending this bullshit was normal. According to the nurse, once they took Hannah off the feeding tube, she'd be dead in a week, probably less.

What had Hannah ever done to deserve this but love Fat Monte? And for him to do her like that? He didn't *need* to do it. He could have driven out to the woods and shot himself. Could have done it in the front seat of his car. Could have done it on the fifty-yard line of Soldier Field, on a Sunday, during football season, while the Bears were calling heads during the coin flip. Could have just cooperated with the FBI, done his time, figured out how to survive in prison for the rest of life, let his wife go, let her have her own life. But he chose to shoot his wife in the side of the head and then shoot himself, as if he couldn't imagine a way she could live without him, as if her only worth was being his wife.

Or maybe Fat Monte thought that someone else would come and kill Hannah after he was gone, or would torture her for whatever information she might have about all the dark shit he'd done, and so therefore what he was doing was mercy. And yet he'd fucked that all up, hadn't even bothered to check to see if Hannah still had a pulse before he turned out his own lights. Sal was always complaining that Fat Monte wasn't detail oriented, and there, in that hospital bed, was proof positive.

Sal would have at least finished the job, Jennifer thought. It wasn't a pleasant thought, but there it was.

Jennifer set her purse down on her desk, where it made a heavy *clunk*, enough that Stacy actually looked up.

"Your phone has been ringing like crazy," she said.

That was weird. Jennifer called her voice mail, hoping it wasn't Mount Carmel, calling to tell her that someone had cut off William's ear.

No new messages.

She checked her cell phone. Nothing.

"When did they start coming in?" Jennifer said. Stacy gave her a blank stare. The woman had three college degrees and frequently couldn't muster even rudimentary language. "The calls. When did they start coming in?"

"I don't know," Stacy said. "Last twenty minutes or so."

"But not before that?"

"I wasn't paying attention," Stacy said. "I only noticed when it started to bother me."

A feeling began to niggle at her, like *she'd* missed some detail, too. She stepped over to the window, looked outside. She made it a point to pay attention to her surroundings, keep an eye out for that man with the long gray beard—or at least the big black RV he drove—who had once come with a message from Sal. But on the street today it was just the normal tidal flow of people working their way up and down Michigan Avenue.

The thing was, no one called her. Ever.

It wasn't part of her job. Her work life revolved around the pictures. No one outside of the museum even knew she existed, at least not in the context of her position. She could go days without receiving a call, weeks without voice mail.

Jennifer went back out into the hallway.

Across the way was her old office—a windowless storage closet, basically, that now held two interns, both of whom preferred to sit just outside the door, laptops on their knees, neither of them even looking up when Jennifer walked by—and then there was a smoked glass door that led out into the museum. It was a slow day, kids back in school, college back in session, end of August, vacation time over. Still, a few hundred people would make their way through the museum between now and five o'clock, each of them walking by the door to the admin offices on their way to the first exhibit—*Burnham's Follies: Chicago Iconic Architecture*—Jennifer only able to make out their basic forms through the tint, not who they actually were. The only thing stopping someone from opening that door, walking down the hallway, and shooting her as she sat at her desk was a sign that said AUTHORIZED PERSONNEL ONLY. The door didn't even have a lock.

Jennifer slowly made her way back to her office and tried to get her nerves under control, did her positive self-talk, which never worked, because the thing was, people *were* following her. People *did* want to kill her. Her husband *was a hit man.* Her rational fears were precisely what schizophrenics had to lose their minds to find, an irony that wasn't lost on Jennifer.

She lingered outside her office door for a moment, working it all through, her eyes settling on her nameplate. All this hiding she did, to keep her head down and do her job, was all for nothing. That man who smelled like peaches knew everything . . .

She slid her nameplate off the wall. It was a flimsy, paper-thin piece of plastic lightly embossed with white letters. They made them upstairs in the HR office. Everyone at the museum knew her name. She didn't think anyone here knew her story. They all just thought she was a single mother who never wanted to go to Miller's Pub after work because she had to get home to her kid . . . not because Sal had killed Vinnie Donnaci right in front of it a few years back, the *Tribune* calling it "an old-fashioned public snuff job," which was the only way Jennifer had known it was his work. And no, she wasn't able to work the Al Capone Casino Night fund-raiser. And no, she would not be attending the Gangsters and Flappers Halloween party.

Because, after all, how would those pictures look?

And there it was. That thing she'd missed. What had that punk said to her? *"Go back to your pretty pictures."* How did he know where she worked? She'd never seen the man before in her life. And if Sugar was Ronnie's guy in Detroit, why was he lapdogging that dumb ass Mike? Sugar Lopiparno, who'd done five years for voluntary manslaughter and eventually ended up with his own fran-chise in Detroit because of it, wasn't the guy who walked behind the guy who walked behind the guy. He was the guy.

How did he know about her money?

How did he know about . . . anything?

She stepped back inside her office, rummaged through a drawer until she found a pair of scissors, then cut her nameplate into a dozen strips, dropped them into the garbage can under the desk. She unlocked the bottom drawer of the five-drawer file cabinet in the corner. Her first month at the museum, before they trusted her with the actual photos, half of her job involved making sure she knew where every signed permission for reproduction was kept; every day someone from the second floor would come down, angry, and she'd solve their problem with a piece of paper.

All this time later, it was still her job, no one else willing to carry the burden.

Story of her life.

Middle of the drawer, she found what she was looking for. The file marked INSURANCE. It was just a single manila folder and inside was the card Jeff Hopper had given her when he showed up at her house. He was dead, she knew that, they'd found his head in a Dumpster a few miles from where Jennifer stood right at that moment. But she'd kept his card. He'd made her an offer. Told her she could help Sal if he came in. There had to be some record of that. Could be his partner remembered.

Jennifer didn't know who might answer his phone if she called his number at the FBI office, didn't know if it was anyone who might give a shit about her in the least, but this sudden confluence of events had her spooked. If the FBI actually were keeping close track of her, wouldn't they have already stepped between her and some of these people? They wanted her safe, so that when Sal came looking for her, they could get their man . . . didn't they?

FEDERAL BUREAU OF INVESTIGATION
CHICAGO FIELD OFFICE
SENIOR SPECIAL AGENT JEFF HOPPER
ORGANIZED CRIME TASK FORCE
(312) 412-6700

He'd died doing his job. Wasn't that absurd. She didn't know if Sal had killed him. She supposed he probably hadn't, cutting off heads wasn't the kind of thing her husband did, but surely Hopper had died because of Sal, and Jennifer couldn't shake that sense of guilt. She knew Sal killed people for the Family, but somehow, when she was younger, she was able to content herself that he was killing other criminals, so it wasn't as bad, though of course that was ludicrous reasoning, since even criminals have people who love them, like Jennifer loved Sal. Like Hannah loved Monte. Like Sharon loved Ronnie, wherever she was now.

She didn't know who might be coming at her, didn't know what side of the law she really was on. She'd never committed a crime in her life, other than the crime of omission, and yet here she was.

You could quit the Job. You couldn't quit the Life. That was the difference between cops and robbers. She could change area codes all she wanted, she'd still be looking over her shoulder, waiting, waiting, waiting. The Life attached itself to you like cancer.

She didn't need to leave.

She needed to be protected.

These people weren't trying to scare her. They were trying to draw Sal out.

They wanted Sal to show his face.

That cop. Peaches. Probably whoever had beaten Ronnie. It wasn't about keeping Sal secret, it was about getting him somewhere they could take their shot. With his wife, with his kid.

If what Peaches said was true—about the newspaper article—it made sense. And she supposed it was a truth she'd avoided all along. Jeff Hopper wouldn't have gone to the press. He would have arrested Sal or he would have . . . failed, and continued searching. Maybe died trying, but that didn't seem reasonable. He didn't seem like that kind of man. Killed? Sure. But not died. Died made it seem like an accident.

So what was the in-between?

That Sal had killed Jeff Hopper and then dimed himself, the FBI, and the entire Family out. That he'd snitched on everyone, including himself, implicating himself in murders going back fifteen years. Why would he do that?

To protect himself.

To protect Jennifer and William.

To keep Ronnie under his thumb. All those years Sal had worked for Ronnie and the end result wasn't that he and Jennifer and William got retired out to some hideaway in the Bahamas when he fucked up on those FBI agents. It was that Sal got disappeared and Jennifer and William got left in Chicago, as collateral.

And now all of that had turned to shit.

Jennifer slipped Hopper's card into her front pants pocket and was grabbing up her purse to leave, because she needed to get the fuck out of there, when the phone on her desk began to ring.

One ring.

Two.

Three.

It would go to voice mail after the eighth ring. Jennifer would be in the lobby by then, and she would never be coming back.

5

"You're crooked," Rabbi Cy Kales said. He reached across the table at the Bagel Café and adjusted David's tie. "Do you keep them knotted or do you redo them every time?"

"I keep them knotted," David said.

"Your first mistake. You must learn that different shirt collars require different knots. What you have on now should be accompanied by a full Windsor. Do you know how to make one of those?"

"No," David said.

"Give it to me," Rabbi Kales said. David took off his tie and handed it to him. Most days, Rabbi Kales still dressed like he was coming into Temple Beth Israel—a suit and tie, or at least slacks, a button-down, and a sport coat—but today he wore a yellow polo shirt and a Member's Only jacket he'd probably owned for twenty years. He turned up the collar of his polo and threaded the tie around his neck with surprising dexterity, flipping the tie to the left, to the right, under and around the knot, until a few seconds later he was finished. "Did you see how to do that?"

"Yeah," David said.

"You'll remember?"

"I remember everything," David said.

Rabbi Kales slipped the tie from around his neck without unknotting it, and David put it back on. There was no fucking way he'd remember how to do whatever black magic Rabbi Kales had done.

"Better?" David said, the tie tightening around his neck.

"It will do," Rabbi Kales said. The waitress came and dropped off their order. Rabbi Kales was having yogurt and a bagel and cream cheese with a side of lox. David wasn't bothering to eat, his face hurt too much this morning, so all he got was a cup of coffee and a wan smile. Later, he'd make himself a protein shake, some oatmeal, maybe crush up some Aleve and sprinkle it on top, swallow a handful of multivitamins and Cipro, since he was pretty sure he had some kind of infection. Which is why they were here today, on a Tuesday, instead of what had become their usual Thursday get-together: Midway through his morning bar mitzvah training class with Sean Berkowitz—who preferred to be called OG Sean B, leaving it tagged over half the fucking city—David felt something pop somewhere behind his nose, like a spring had come loose, then immediately felt blood rushing down his pharynx and into his throat, followed by a fresh, new pain that radiated from between his eyes, through the back of his head, and then out his nose. Or that's how he imagined it, anyway. He went into the bathroom and looked around his mouth, half expected he'd see a waterfall of blood, but there wasn't anything. He sent Sean to class, told him they'd meet after school, the fucker needing as much training on the Torah as possible, the kid not exactly a natural with Hebrew, or morality.

He explained all of this to Rabbi Kales once the waitress was out of earshot. The Bagel Café was the only place David was pretty sure Bennie hadn't bugged. And by the transitive property of Bennie, that also meant the feds, since whoever Bennie was listening to, there was a good chance one day the feds would get wise, hack into Bennie's surveillance system, and become privy to all of his operations. David was under the impression that the bugs in his house fed into some kind of Soviet bunker buried under Bennie's house, where he sat with his headphones on, listening to everything. But now, in the Bagel Café, of course that all seemed ludicrous. Where the fuck did Bennie's bugs go? Surely not his house. Which meant he probably had some safe house in town where it was all fed. David couldn't think about that shit. It would drive him mad.

"You got a doctor I can see?" David asked.

"What about your friend with the RV? Isn't he a physician?"

He was talking about a guy David knew only as Gray Beard. And he wasn't David's friend. He was a guy who did favors for Bennie, like cutting the wires in David's jaw after some dental surgery had gone bad when David first got to town. He was also a guy who'd done two favors for David, one involving a dead body—Dr. Kirsch, who'd done the *farpotshket* plastic surgery on David's face in the first place—and one involving getting Jennifer some money in Chicago. In both cases, Gray Beard had come out with a nice cash profit, but David hadn't been asked for a favor in return, which made him reticent to use his services again. Gray Beard already knew too much; if he'd bothered to do any investigating at all, he knew exactly who David was. Not that David thought Gray Beard gave a fuck. Still. It wasn't a well he could keep drinking from.

"I need someone with a medical practice," David said. He shifted his jaw from side to side, reflexively. When Gray Beard fixed his mouth, he went in with bolt cutters to get the wires out. David hadn't seen that much of his own blood, ever. "Not a GP. A surgeon. Someone with an outpatient facility. I'm not going into a hospital."

Rabbi Kales spooned some yogurt into his mouth, made a face. "I'm told I should eat yogurt every day," he said. "That it is good for my digestion. But I don't understand how eating rotten milk is good for anything."

"It's not rotten milk," David said. "It's actually the opposite of rotten."

"The point," Rabbi Kales said, "is that I have lived nearly eighty years without it and I still live today. You would think that if I truly needed it, I would be dead already."

"That's not what's keeping you alive," David said. "And I'm not worried about dying. I'd like to eat solid food without needing a sedative. I'd like to not be worried that I'm going to wake up in the morning with my eyeballs underneath my cheekbones." David had read about this happening to people. Get a fucked-up facelift, end up looking like the motherfucker at the end of *Raiders of the Lost Ark*. He learned forward, lowered his voice. "People are starting to ask questions."

Rabbi Kales pushed away his yogurt, spread some cream cheese on his bagel, took a bite. There was a dollop of cheese stuck to the corner of his mouth. Out in public, it made Rabbi Kales look a bit more fragile, so David let it be. "Dr. Melnikoff still practices, yes?"

"Far as I know," David said.

"He has a gambling problem," Rabbi Kales said, matter-of-factly.

David wasn't surprised. Irving Melnikoff was one of the founding members of Temple Beth Israel, which meant he was in his late sixties or early seventies. If you were still practicing medicine at that age, that meant you had some shit in your closet that wasn't hanging right.

"He might be open to a cash transaction." Rabbi Kales took a sip of water—no ice—and the dollop of cheese fell into the glass. He shook his head, took a napkin from the container at the edge of the table, dug the cheese out, then pushed the glass away. "I could talk to him for you."

"And tell him what?"

"That you were Mossad," Rabbi Kales said, "and therefore treating you would be of the utmost service to Israel. And that he must keep it secret, because of the nature of your previous work."

"That's crazy."

"David," Rabbi Kales said, "look around. Every Jew in this room thinks their Israeli cousin is Mossad. The nice thing is, no one can prove it one way or the other. He will believe me, and when you have no medical records, he will believe you. And if he does not, he will believe your cash."

"I'm not Israeli," David said.

"Feh," Rabbi Kales said. "We all look alike. You have your backstory, he won't press you on it."

David thought about it for a moment. "I feel like I'm going to need continuing care," David said. "Like if I get a sore throat, I don't want to get arrested at Rite-Aid when I pick up my prescription. I need to normalize this."

"This is something you should discuss with my son-in-law."

"Your son-in-law is under surveillance. Even when he's off house arrest, he's going to be looked at, okay? The feds, they don't view him as a onetime criminal who has been reformed by his incarceration, I assure you. You, you're just a sick old man. I can't keep stealing your medications."

Rabbi Kales sliced his lox in half, waved over the waitress. "Bring Rabbi Cohen a small plate," he said to her.

"I'm not hungry," David said when the waitress left.

"You're being looked at, too," Rabbi Kales said. He lifted his chin just slightly. "Jews who don't eat are suspect."

David looked over his shoulder. Harvey B. Curran, the *Review-Journal*'s Mob gossip columnist, was sitting a few booths away, working on the last bits of an omelet, three newspapers spread out around him, a reporter's notebook by his left hand, a pen keeping it open, another notebook in the pocket of his shirt, an old red Day Runner stuffed with scraps of paper and cards. Weird thing was he had on an eye patch. That was new. Last time David saw him, which was the week previous, over at the Chicago-style pizza place over on Fort Apache where the Temple was cosponsoring a charity event for a fireman who'd lost his leg in a house fire, he looked like he always did: tan pants, white pinstriped shirt, same notebook in the pocket, mustache, sandy blond hair that was turning gray, jacket thrown over the back of his chair. Harvey was sitting with his daughter, sharing a pizza, both eyes in working order.

Curran didn't take part in any of the actual charity events—like the silent auction, which included a Diamond Experience from the Millionaire Detail Club—but at the end of the night, he stopped by the table Temple Beth Israel had set up and dropped a twenty in the donation box.

The waitress returned with a plate and Rabbi Kales slid half of his lox onto it. "Have you developed a taste yet?" Rabbi Kales asked.

"No," David said. He scooped up a piece, put it in his mouth, swallowed without chewing. Anything raw or rawlike made him want to vomit. Even three years later, all that time spent in the meat truck had given him fucking PTSD for uncooked meats. Didn't matter if it was cow or chicken or salmon or fucking roadkill on the side of the highway. These days, on the rare times he went grocery shopping, he got premade food as much as possible.

"Did you read the book I gave you?" Rabbi Kales asked.

"Most of it," David said.

"What do you mean most of it?" Rabbi Kales said.

"I knew how it ended," David said. The book was an account of the Jews in Warsaw during World War II, Rabbi Kales of late stacking the Holocaust books on him. David had read fifty books on the topic in the last nine months or so. Fact was, reading the books left him so enraged, he found himself questioning the effect on his mental health. Like he needed anything else.

"Did you get to the part about the 1943 rebellion in the Warsaw ghetto?"

"Yeah," David said. A couple hundred Jews, armed with ten rifles among them all, put on a guerrilla campaign for a month against several thousand German soldiers, managing to kill just under two dozen of them and hastening the wholesale killing of hundreds of Jews, which included the Germans setting fire to the ghetto and then filling the sewers with poisoned gas to drive out whoever might be hiding.

"What did you make of that?"

"From what point of view?"

"As a Jew."

David picked up a piece of lox with his fingers, as he'd seen other people do in the past. Jews liked to eat with their fingers, picking raisins out of a kugel or an apple from a Waldorf salad. He put the lox in his mouth, chewed it this time. It was smoky and salty and tasted too much like . . . fish. He swallowed it down, followed it with a gulp of coffee, which now tasted like it had been spiked with a salmon farm.

"Here's what I don't understand," David said. "They knew they had no chance. Right? They had two automatic weapons. Two. Germans had tanks and planes. So what was the use? Wouldn't it have been better to hide? Tactically? They'd already seen the trains leaving and not coming back."

"True, true," Rabbi Kales said. "And there are some who say the rebellion only hastened the extermination of other Jews. That it made the Germans realize that putting the Jews to work, even for a short while, was foolish. That as long as they lived, they would fight. Never mind the substandard labor they performed. So why do you think they did it, Rabbi? Answer your own question. Why would they stage a rebellion they knew would fail?"

Whenever Rabbi Kales referred to David as "Rabbi" he knew he was attempting to impart something larger, to remind David that no matter how much he wanted to pretend he wasn't a rabbi, he was, at least functionally. David looked around the restaurant. There were plenty of non-Jews in the place today; the medical offices nearby had emptied out for lunch, so there were Asians, Mexicans, African Americans, young people, old people, the place filled up with people who had an hour for a sandwich and weren't particularly invested in the cultural history of the food—they just wanted some corned beef on decent bread.

"To show the rest of the world that the Jews were dangerous," David said. "That even if they knew they were going to get killed, they'd resolved to take as many Germans out as possible, too." It was an edict David found appealing.

"Why? What's the use of killing other people when you're dead, too?"

"So maybe word would get out?" David said.

Rabbi Kales nodded once. "Go on, Rabbi."

"So ten thousand years later," David said, "some other Jew would hear the story and fight back, if there were any Jews left."

Rabbi Kales smiled. "I believe that all to be true. Because, you see, there was no postwar for them," he said. "They were doomed." He reached over and took David's water, spooned out all of the ice, then took a sip, coughed, took another sip. "This was vengeance. The only vengeance worth anything, in my opinion, is holy vengeance. It wasn't personal, it was historical. You should finish the book."

"Not business?" David fucking with him a little bit.

"No," Rabbi Kales said. "There was no business in this." He took another sip of water. Coughed again. "But that is another thing I have been thinking about of late. What is the value of business if it does not provide some other, larger worth? This place, for instance." He took a bite of his bagel, chewed it. "It's a business, but it feeds us, it provides a place to gather, you go into the bakery and buy a dozen black-and-white cookies, it gives you joy." He pointed out the window, toward the Strip. "Even my son-in-law's gentleman's club has some larger worth, if you examine it absent of its prurient qualities. A lonely man can spend a few dollars to feel an approximation of love for four or five minutes. That is not without its worth. Business should always be about something larger than itself."

"But let me ask you something. In this little morality lesson, what about the girls at Bennie's club?"

"They are there by choice," Rabbi Kales said. "They are not slave labor, are they? Do they not pay their rent by providing a sliver of emotional well-being to these men? Can they not pick their own shifts? Work when they choose?"

There was something at work here, Rabbi Kales trying to get to a point, David only now seeing the steps he was setting up, from giving him the book in the first place to this shift in conversation. "They pay for it down the line," David said. "Deluding other people isn't the sort of thing that stops bothering you."

"Then you must always be aware that the larger good should outweigh the potential bad. The Jews in the Warsaw Ghetto understood that."

There it was.

"That's how you do it?" David said. "Just like that?"

"That's part of it," Rabbi Kales said.

"I don't think that's gonna work for me."

"You have a long life to lead, Rabbi."

"Not if my face collapses on Rosh Hashanah." He scooped up some of Rabbi Kales's cream cheese, spread it on a piece of lox, ate it. That was a little better. He could see the appeal, kind of. "What do you think Dr. Melnikoff will charge?"

"That, you'll need to discuss with him," Rabbi Kales said. "Whatever the amount is, I'm sure my son-in-law will approve the expenditure."

"I can't take any money from him," David said. "I walk out of his house with a duffel bag of cash, we're all going to prison. He was crying poor to me the other day, anyway," David said.

"That's the nature of *your* people, isn't it? That crime doesn't pay?" Rabbi Kales smiled then. A joke. That's where they were now. Men who joked. Because they'd gotten away with it. "I will speak to Irving on your behalf," Rabbi Kales said, "as your rabbi and his. How you choose to proceed will be up to you. All will be confidential, however you decide. If need be, you front the cash and I'm certain Benjamin will reimburse you."

"What makes you think I have a bunch of cash sitting around?"

"You're a man who waits for a rainy day, aren't you?"

David didn't have much of a choice either way.

"You'll do it this week?"

"Yes, of course, Rabbi," Rabbi Kales said. "If my mind doesn't go completely before I remember to do so."

"I heard you pissed all over your daughter's sofa."

"Technically," Rabbi Kales said, "my son-in-law's sofa. No self-respecting Jewish woman owns a leather sofa."

"You want to talk to me about it?"

"It was just a bit of show," he said. "Doing as I'm asked."

"Okay," David said. He didn't believe him.

Rabbi Kales finished his bagel, sat back in the booth. "Now I need something from you."

"What's that?"

"I would like to take my granddaughters to see Israel," he said. "While I can still travel."

"Bennie won't have that," David said. There was no fucking way Bennie would let Rabbi Kales out of the country, much less out of Las Vegas, not at this point. He sure as fuck wasn't going to let Rabbi Kales takes his two daughters with him, too.

"My son-in-law can't even walk to the end of his driveway," Rabbi Kales said. "How could he prevent me from getting on an airplane?"

"Just try to leave. See what happens."

"I want you to come with me," Rabbi Kales said. "In fact, you need to. If you intend to do this job, legitimately, you must go. You cannot run the largest Reform synagogue in Nevada without being expected to visit Jerusalem on occasion. There are duties related to that job. This is one of them."

"We're not the largest," David said.

"We will be," Rabbi Kales said. "I have faith in your methods."

"It's a moot point. My paper isn't good enough. Not to get into Israel, anyway. Out of Vegas, maybe."

"We will get you paper that is."

"How?"

"That would be my son-in-law's problem. If you tell him this is something we must do, it will be incumbent on him to figure that out for you. His Chinese friends I'm sure could help. I do not expect that he'd want you to be arrested in front of his children."

"He won't let me walk into a casino," David said. "He's not going to let me near an airport." America was a good ten years behind Israel when it came to things like security. He'd never make it out of customs.

"This stage we've built," Rabbi Kales said, "is useless without actors. Benjamin must be made to understand this. You are a rabbi. Rabbis go to Israel. If you wait until I am unable to travel, or I am gone? Rabbi Cohen, I promise you, the play will be over. Let Benjamin solve this problem."

David thought about this. "My Jewish isn't good enough, either."

"Going to Israel will help with that," Rabbi Kales said. "Plus, now that you are Mossad, it will give your story more credence with Dr. Melnikoff if you needed to visit Israel periodically. And imagine how much easier it would be to teach your bar mitzvah student— what was his name?"

"OG Sean B."

"Charming," Rabbi Kales said.

"It's the Berkowitz family. They're new."

The Berkowitzes had moved from Cleveland into one of those dirt-yellow starter mansions in the Trails early last year, Sean's father, Casey, some big shot in the MMA world. First couple months, everything was cool. They came to temple, donated money, got Sean into the Academy, everyone got free tickets to cage matches, Sean's mother, Kate, spearheaded a cystic fibrosis fund-raiser, Sean made friends with the boys who played soccer. David sometimes ran into them at Northside Nathan's, his pizza spot, splitting a veggie pizza and a platter of antipasto. Or he'd be wandering the aisles of Organized Living, imagining what Jennifer would be buying if she were next to him, and he'd come around the corner and there they'd all be, a cart full of containers, big smiles. A normal life. Everyone seemed happy.

David fucking hated them.

Back then, Casey looked like he'd been born inside the menswear section of a Dillard's, always in a navy-blue suit, black wingtips, and rimless eyeglasses, always wanted to talk to David about how MMA was actually less brutal than boxing, that he worked in the sport only because the business model celebrated the fighter, not the promoter, and was more fair all around. "I can get you front row to anything. You just tell me."

"I don't believe in fighting as a sport," David told him. "It's barbarism."

"I get it, I get it, I get it," Casey said. In David's experience, if you had to say something out loud three times, you probably didn't believe dick. "But let me know if you ever want to go, just for the spectacle." Then he leaned in. "Or if you want to make some money, I sometimes have the edge on a match. You know. Who is injured. Who is 'roiding. No guarantees, but better than what the *Review-Journal* knows."

"Steroids aren't going to stop someone from kicking you in the face."

"No," Casey said. "But they help when you're choking someone out, in my experience."

Not in David's.

"I'll keep that all in mind," David said. And he would have, but before he got the chance to explore that money angle more directly, Casey ran off with a ring girl named Lexus, moved into a house that looked like a Nagel print over in Desert Shores, and then everything went to seed. Casey jumped deep into a new life as a full-time ass-hole. All slicked-back hair, Hugo Boss jackets over white V-necks, distressed jeans with holes in weird places, and facial hair designed to look threatening. Lexus was the kind of woman who wore cowboy hats and boots but had never ridden a horse.

Back in Chicago, the Family had a rule that if you left your wife, you bought her a house in another fucking city, you shared custody of the kids, you paid your share of alimony and child support, plus something extra around the holidays, you kept it nice, didn't freak the fuck out if she got remarried, everyone civil, for the good of world peace, as it were, and that way, no one got murdered watching a Cubs game at Harry Caray's. You left your wife, you didn't rub it in the whole family's face. You built in some distance. Casey Berkowitz didn't get that memo, so he was living three Starbucks away from his old life, and his wife, Kate—they weren't even close to being divorced yet—was living in Charlie's Down Under, a bar and video-poker shithole over on Lake Mead.

David spotted her car there three or four times a week, which was easy, since she drove a red Mercedes with personalized plates—FLYBENZ—and tended to park backed-in wherever she went. David considered Kate's backing-in the adult equivalent of her son's obsessive tagging, which not coincidentally had started about a week after Casey walked out. Kate didn't have a job, so sometimes David would see her at Charlie's at 9 a.m., sometimes he'd see her there at 9 p.m., sometimes he'd be unable to sleep and would go for a drive, keep himself away from the telephone or the TV or any other bad decisions, and he'd see FLYBENZ backed into a space in front of Charlie's at 3 a.m. David was tempted to go in and sit beside her, have a drink, tell her he could help her.

Because the fact was, David thought it was just a matter of time before Kate got into her car after a few too many White Russians, drove over to Desert Shores, and took a tire iron to her husband and his girlfriend while they slept. That's how normal people end up in prison. David understood the compulsion. It was a fucking embarrassment to be cheated on. It was better to be a widow. Widows got casseroles and rugelach.

It was, David thought, a favor he could do.

It was a favor he would *like* to do.

Corporate guy like Casey, he'd have life insurance. Kate Berkowitz and her son, OG Sean B, could get out of Las Vegas, go back to Cleveland, start a new life before Casey got indicted for fixing fights and they lost everything. Give them a chance Jennifer and William never got.

Maybe, it occurred to David now, this was that chance. Could he get his family to Israel eventually?

"And then what?" David said. "We get there and you disappear into the Dead Sea?"

Rabbi Kales laughed. "David," he said. "It's a salt sea. I would need to wear cement shoes to disappear into the Dead Sea."

"You know what I mean. How do I know you'd get back on a plane?"

"How do I know *you'd* get back on a plane?"

"I'm not staying anywhere alone," David said. "I'm already alone."

Rabbi Kales clapped his hands lightly in front of his face, tapping the tip of his nose with his index fingers, then spread his fingers out like a peacock. It was something he did when he was thinking. At first

David thought it was one of his stalling techniques, but the longer he spent with him, the more he saw it was one of his authentic moves.

"There is no postwar for you, Rabbi Cohen," he said, quietly. "If this is the life you're going to have, it is going to get smaller and smaller, until you're underground, waiting to die. That is your fate. You must embrace that if you are to survive. You are to be a real rabbi? A real rabbi goes to Israel. We convince Benjamin first. But it's something you must reconcile."

"Rabbi Kales," David said. He was himself for just a moment. "The only way I get on a plane is if my wife and kid are on it, too. You figure out a way to make that happen, I'll fly to fucking Tehran with you. I don't care. But I'm not risking my life to do *you* a favor that gets *me* deeper into this life. That ain't happening. I understand your point, about being a rabbi, I do. And I respect it. I want you to know that. But if the Chief Rabbi of Israel comes to town, wants to sit here and have blintzes with me, and then asks me a question I'm uncomfortable with? Or indicates that he does not believe I am a real rabbi? I will follow him to the bathroom and I will drown him in the toilet. I will kill his entire security team. I will blow up his plane. Whatever it takes. No questions. Don't ever think otherwise." David paused, let Sal Cupertine go back where he belonged. "Now, if you want to go to Israel with your granddaughters, I will advocate for that. If you think it will help Temple Beth Israel, absolutely, you should go. But your daughter, Rachel, will stay here. And if Bennie tells me to keep you here and you try to leave, I will do my job."

Rabbi Kales spread a bit of cream cheese on another piece of lox, ate it slowly. "You know, David," he said, "there will come a time when there is no one for you to threaten, when people are no longer frightened of you. If you're lucky, you will be my age and, *b'ezrat hashem*, your family will be with you. But you will still be looking over your shoulder. You will always be looking, waiting. You must figure out how you will live *then*, when this romantic notion of yours is fulfilled. You have figured out this idea of how you might die, how you will take out all the people who attempt to do you wrong, but you have not figured out how you might live. Your wife, your son? There will always be a gun pointed at them, David. You will not always know who is pointing it." He sighed. "My advice? When they come for you? Surround yourself with other Jews. They will die to protect you." He raised his chin again, pointed it toward the window. "In the meantime, help your friend."

Harvey B. Curran had finished his breakfast and was now in the café's parking lot, attempting to pick up pages of newsprint, bits of *The New York Times*, *Los Angeles Times*, and *Review-Journal* sprinkled around him like dandruff, his notebooks, pens, his Day Runner, his keys. It was like he'd been turned upside down and dumped onto the ground. He knelt down to pick up what he could, but it was apparent that depth perception wasn't currently his friend.

"Fuck him," David said.

Rabbi Kales raised his eyebrows. "You've not met?"

"No," David said. "Not officially." David's name and Temple Beth Israel had appeared in Curran's column a couple dozen times, however, all connected to Bennie Savone's case. And Sal Cupertine showed up a few times, too, Curran's thing being about drawing these lines of controversy between the families operating in Las Vegas and their parent companies in other cities. He thought it was pretty fucking funny that Sal Cupertine had last been seen inside of a truck filled with ground beef. Which wasn't actually true. There was a shit ton of steaks and filets in there, too.

Rabbi Kales pointed at David. "The reason you are so sharp, Rabbi Cohen, is that you grew up watching men's backs," he said. "Imagine how wise you would be if you'd spent that time watching their faces."

BY THE TIME David got outside, half of the newspapers were in the intersection and Curran's Day Runner looked like a crime scene.

"Let me assist you," he said. He put a hand on Curran's shoulder and the reporter twisted around to see who was there.

"Oh, thanks," Curran said. "I'm half an invalid right now. I tried to unlock my car and ended up spilling my work onto Buffalo and Westcliff." David got down beside him and retrieved one of his notebooks and a stack of papers, set them on top of Curran's car, and gathered up his pens, neither of which had caps. "Watch the ink," Curran said. "You don't want to get it on your suit."

"It sticks to you," David said, "but it washes out. Eventually."

Harvey B. Curran chuckled. "I suppose that's a good thing."

David retrieved the front-page section of *The New York Times* from beneath a Honda Accord. There was a page-one article about "The Summer of the Shark." He handed it to Curran. "What is your take on this?" he asked.

"Shark attacks?" Curran asked.

"Yes," David said. "They seem to be on the rise. There was the boy in Virginia Beach this weekend who was eaten. Those people in Florida earlier this summer." He pointed at the newspaper. "Important enough that *The New York Times* is devoting their front page to the question."

"I think, technically, they're just being bitten, not eaten."

"Does the shark not swallow?"

Curran looked at David quizzically. "I don't really know, actually. It's not my area of expressed interest."

"Ah, I see," David said. He walked over to the sidewalk, picked up three business cards that had flown away:

Steven Dickensheets, Forensic Accountancy.
Sheriff Geoff Sebelius.
Scott Schumacher, Editor, The Public Record.

Good people to know. He handed the cards to Curran. "Do you have an opinion as to why it happens?"

"We're still talking about the sharks?"

"Yes."

"Okay. Well," Curran said, "I guess it's probably like being in the grocery store. Someone grabs the last bunch of bananas, or if you think they're about to, I guess that might piss you off. Probably the same basic idea. People getting in the way of food."

"Interesting," David said. "What should be done?"

His hand went up to his eye patch, adjusted it. The skin directly around the patch was red and angry. "I'm sorry, I guess I'm confused as to why we're talking about shark attacks."

"I can see why that would be the case," David said. "Since we're strangers who don't know each other, don't know what each is interested in, or what we might like to read about in the newspaper. Or anything else about each other, for that matter."

"Ohhh," Curran said. "I see."

"Do you?" David pointed at the eye patch. "That seems to be affecting you."

"I developed some kind of infection," he said. "My daughter came home with pinkeye or something; a week later, I'm like a horror film."

"That happens."

"You have children?"

"No," David said. "But I am surrounded by them at our school. You know. The one you frequently disparage in your column because of who happened to pour the concrete."

"It's not about you, Rabbi, I hope you know that," Curran said.

"I do," David said. "Which is why I have come over here to help. To show you that I am a man who understands what it's like to have something dropped at your feet you cannot quite pick up." He gathered up the rest of the papers and handed them to Curran, like a parting gift.

"I hear what you're saying," Curran said, patiently, a speech he'd probably given a hundred times over the years. "I'm just doing my job. If I covered sports, I'd talk about how mediocre UNLV's basketball team is this year, would probably throw in a shot about them being crap since Tark left just to keep on Tark's good side. But I cover the Mafia." He shrugged. "Confidentially? I'm sure you recognize that Bennie Savone is an unsavory fellow." He waved two fingers at Rabbi Kales, who was watching the show from inside. Rabbi Kales raised a fork of lox back at him through the window. "Or at least your boss does."

"Former boss," David said. "He's retired."

"How do you retire from God?"

"He is not involved in the day-to-day operations of the temple," David said.

"Is he well? I heard he wasn't well."

"He's a man in his seventies," David said, "who doesn't need to read conjecture concerning his own deterioration in the local paper."

"I just report," he said.

"Or speculate," David said.

"The Mafia doesn't send out press releases."

"The temple does," David said. "I saw you at our event not ten days ago."

"I'm the kind of guy who buys his daughter shitty pizza when she wants it, particularly if it's on the one weeknight I get her. Just a coincidence that I was there that night."

"On the pizza, we agree," David said.

Harvey B. Curran stared at David for a few seconds, not speaking. David had seen Curran's photo in the *Review-Journal* three times a week since he arrived in town, his "Street Sense" column always spread across the bottom of the Opinion page, the only column that put people's names in bold type. He'd also seen him at the Bagel Café at least once a week for three years now, periodically saw him inside Smith's buying groceries, had parked down the street from his house a few times, watching it, making sure he wasn't putting shit in his column because someone was paying him to do it. Someone other than the newspaper. But Curran drove a 1994 Toyota Corolla, had a half-furnished home on a cul-de-sac that backed up to Cheyenne, a block off of the Rainbow intersection, and seemed to spend most of his free time writing books about corrupt casino owners, which kept him in and out of court fairly regularly. David would be surprised if Curran had more than five hundred dollars in his bank account.

"I'm sorry if I've offended you in some way," Curran said. He patted his own chest with the tips of his fingers. "I feel like I have."

"You have," David said. "Torah says, 'Buy the truth and sell it not.'"

"I'm not Jewish," Curran said.

"It's also in the Bible," David said.

"I'm not much of a Christian," Curran said. "Mr. Savone's crimes are public record."

"Mine are not."

"I understand what you're saying, Rabbi," Curran said. "I'll see what I can do."

"That's all I can ask." David extended his hand. "My name is David Cohen. I'm the rabbi at Temple Beth Israel. It's a pleasure to meet you after all of this time I've spent in your column."

Curran took his hand, shook it. "I'm Harvey Curran," he said. "I write for the *Review-Journal*."

"Aren't you missing the B?"

"Honestly? It's not really my middle initial."

"What is?"

"A," Harvey said. "When the paper hired me, they wanted me to use a middle initial, make me sound a little older. This was fifteen years ago and I was just out of journalism school, see? Once they realized people would have open license to call me 'hack' they decided B was a better choice. Now here I am, stuck with it."

"Have ye not seen a vain vision? A lying divination?" David said. "It's not the worst I have heard."

"I suppose not," Curran said. He took the papers and notebooks off the roof of his car and tossed them in his backseat. "Thanks for your help. I'd be running in traffic right now to save yesterday's news and tomorrow's column."

"Good luck with your eye," David said. "Next time you're in the neighborhood looking for Jimmy Hoffa's body in the foundation of the Performing Arts Center, stop by my office, I keep wine for just such occasions."

"I'll do that," Curran said.

David started back toward the restaurant, but before he got inside, Curran said, "What about the sharks? What would you do?"

"My view is that the proper authorities should find the sharks and all of their close associates," David said, "round them up, and kill them on the shore, for the public to see."

"SO?" RABBI KALES said, when David was back across from him. "What says his face? Golem or Gabriel?"

Out the window, Curran sat in his running car, jotting something in his notepad, David thinking it was probably a bad idea he was driving himself around with only one working eye, then wondering if he even really had something wrong with his eye, if it all was some con. But then Harvey attempted to back his car out of a moderately tight space and ended up making the process into an eleven-point turn before he got his Corolla faced the right away.

"He's not going away," David said, "is he?"

"No," Rabbi Kales said.

6

Rabbi David Cohen's job at Temple Beth Israel most days simply entailed Lighting the Way, which wasn't exactly his skill set, but he made do. Tried to fake a good example. Which meant he'd come to appreciate that he couldn't fix every problem by getting rid of the part he found distasteful.

Like this whole thing with Harvey B. Curran.

It was after four and David was sitting at his desk, looking at the *Review-Journal* online, scrolling through Curran's old columns, trying to figure out how he might just use him for good.

Well, a kind of good.

Talking to him today, David found himself feeling a sense of grudging respect, for the one guy he'd met in town entirely on the level. Curran did his job and he did not give a fuck who was angry about it. Yeah, he had his pat answer when David pressed him, but it also seemed like he understood his role in the world: bad shit happened, he brought it to light.

In Las Vegas, Curran didn't have to go searching for it, it was all right there, the Mafia such a shitty organization locally, they couldn't even transcend cliché: They owned the strip clubs, they ran the girls, they broke legs for numbers guys, and they still tried to fuck with the unions, which was next to impossible now, so they ended up pressuring the culinary union rank and file and ended up getting cut to shit, literally, by a bunch of cooks and waiters who didn't want some dumb guido in their kitchen unless it was a celebrity chef in from Florence. And it was *all* public record: Just last week, Rick Cazzetti, who owned a strip club called the Black Puma, was arrested for beating the shit out of a guy who owned a notary-and-mailbox joint in his same industrial park because the notary had taken him to small claims court over some beef with Black Puma patrons pissing on his door. Cazzetti got bailed out by a guy named Randy Hermano, who was a sitting city councilman.

It baffled David.

Cazzetti was Genovese from way back, had done fifteen years of fed time in the '70s on a variety of RICO charges, none of which stopped him from owning a strip club in Las Vegas, so as soon as this hit the blotter, his old mug shot and new one were in Curran's column, and now Curran was digging into Hermano, too. Hermano was a local personal injury lawyer who'd been elected to the city council based largely on the fact that in his commercials he walked through the empty desert in slow motion while the voice-over announcer said four words: "Progress. Integrity. Family. Hermano." Curran was now looking at Hermano's voting record in relation to anything even tangentially related to Cazzetti and it wasn't looking good for anybody, Curran now calling Hermano "Soon-to-be-Indicted City Councilman Randy Hermano" and putting his every move in bold type.

Bennie Savone was the one guy doing something different, and Curran was so close to it, he couldn't see it, because it was new. David could use that. He just wasn't sure how.

In the Torah, the Hebrew words for *was*, *is*, and *will be* were the words that made up God's name, not because Jews thought God foresaw the future, but because He *was* the future, which was some Einstein shit. But not even Maimonides thought that meant everyone was destined to some predetermined fate. No, God wasn't sitting around manipulating each living soul like a marionette. Maimonides believed people more often than not suffered from self-inflicted evils and then ascribed them to God's master plan when they couldn't reason with their shitty decisions.

Everything happens for a reason?

Fuck no. You brought shit onto yourself.

So he'd brought Curran to himself today. He'd figure out how to use him.

David clicked off the *Review-Journal*'s page and spent a few minutes watching the security camera feed. He had cameras surrounding the temple, the Barer Academy, the funeral home, and, farther up the street, the Performing Arts Center, so from here at his desk, David could watch thirty different angles of suburbia's slow crawl. Most days, there was nothing to see, but that didn't mean David didn't keep looking, which is when Casey Berkowitz came screeching into the parking lot with his son, OG Sean B, a mere ninety minutes late for the continuation of Sean's bar mitzvah class.

"It's this dumb shit's fault," Casey said when they eventually reached David's office, one hand clasped on the back of Sean's neck, like a Rottweiler without a leash, the other on a can of Red Bull. David had watched them arguing in the front of the temple for five solid minutes but didn't bother to get up from behind his desk. He was going to Light the Way. He also had the first idea of a plan coming into play. "Tell him you're sorry for being late, Sean."

OG Sean B wore the same basic outfit every day: baggy jeans belted at his groin, plaid boxers pulled up over his hips, a plain white T-shirt, and a Milwaukee Brewers baseball cap pulled down low over his eyes and cocked slightly to the right, not that he was from Milwaukee or knew anything about baseball, but because the logo, an M and a B and a baseball, spelled out MOB. He also rocked a Star of David the size of a lampshade around his neck. David had seen Gangster Disciples in Chicago wearing the exact same outfit, right down to the Star of David, since the six-pointed star was how they identified one another, difference being they were black and legit hard knocks, not twelve-year-old Jews caught up in a divorce.

"Yo, dawg, I was faded this morning, so I just went home, got my grub on, and was out," OG Sean B said, David reminded suddenly of

Slim Joe, who he'd lived with for his first few months in Las Vegas, before he had to shoot him in the face. He'd liked Slim Joe, as much as that was possible. Or missed having someone to talk to, anyway.

"Speak real English," Casey said, and gave his son's neck a shove. Sean's head snapped forward, knocking his hat off.

"I'm sorry, Rabbi Cohen," OG Sean B said. "I got to my pops's and forgot I was supposed to meet up with you. So I went to bed." He probably *was* faded this morning, on his mother's Klonopin or his father's Xanax, or maybe Lexus had some Vicodin left over from her latest boob job. When David was twelve, he was already running errands for the Family, old-timers like Pete Divarco giving him nips of Jameson, but David didn't try any drugs until he was a little older, fifteen, sixteen, seventeen. He found he liked the way coke made him feel before he had to fuck somebody up, started to get a fondness for H in his twenties, which made him feel good for about fifteen minutes, and then made him want to pull strangers' eyes from their skulls. He kept that shit from Jennifer, though, and then when William came around, that was it. He didn't fuck with any drugs, just a taste here and there for business, like on the day in Chicago he lost it on those Donnie Brascos. Hardest thing he did now was scotch, even though most days his face felt like someone was driving an ice pick through it.

"It happens," David said, suddenly in a forgiving mood, because Casey's face was pissing him off. His handlebar mustache was perfectly manicured, he was too tan, wore too much shitty cologne, and his pants were held up with a white belt that had the "Joy and Pain" masks for the buckle. He'd put on about fifteen pounds of muscle in the last few months, which made David think he was probably hitting some of his fighters' HGH.

The barbed-wire tattoo on his left biceps was new. *This fucking guy.*

"That hurt?" David asked, pointing at the ink.

Casey looked at his arm, then pulled his sleeve down. "It doesn't mean anything," he said.

"Good thing it's permanent, then," David said. He had a tattoo of an eight ball on his shoulder for about fifteen years until one of Bennie's surgeons dug it out of his flesh, not even bothering with the laser treatment, David waking up with an oozing hole that took six months to heal. He had a gnarled scar there now that looked like he'd been bitten by a wolf. Not that he missed the tattoo. These days he had a deeper appreciation of his own flesh.

"Anyway," Casey said. "He failed to mention to me that he had this appointment. Then his bitch mother called fifteen minutes ago to make sure he went, and so here we are, here we are, here we are." He let go of his son's neck and Sean rubbed at it absently, picked up his hat, but didn't put it on. "I don't suppose there's a discount for missing half a lesson?" He was bullshitting, David recognized, but David wasn't in a place where he was hearing that.

"No," David said. And then David was gone and Sal Cupertine was sitting there for a few seconds, assessing. "There's a penalty."

"A penalty? Like, what, no blintzes on Hanukkah?" Still bullshitting.

"You've wasted my time," David said. "Every five minutes you're late, it's another twenty." He looked at his watch. It was 4:17. "You're in for three hundred right now. You keep standing there with that look on your face, it's gonna be fifty every five minutes."

"The look on my face?" Casey asked. "What about the look on your face?"

"You see something you don't like?" David said. He steadied his gaze on him. "Something that doesn't meet your approval?"

"I didn't mean . . ." Casey started to say, but he didn't know what he didn't mean, so David let him stew on it, because he had him now. "I was just kidding around, Rabbi Cohen. Like we do. The way guys talk."

"I don't like the way you talk," David said. "It's disrespectful to me. It's disrespectful to yourself. Also, you ever bad-mouth his mother in front of me again? You're going to have a problem." He paused, let that sink in. He opened up his desk drawer, came out with a roll of masking tape and a pair of long silver scissors. "And that ink is disrespectful to us all." He pulled out a foot of tape, cut it with the scissors, put it flat on the desk, sticky side up. "My family didn't get tattooed in the camps so you could come here and put barbed wire on your skin, you understand?" That was a new wrinkle, David adding some Holocaust history to his family on the spot. Fuck it. Now that he was gonna be Mossad, why not? Plus, there were survivors who attended Temple Beth Israel and they didn't need to see that shit. "So you're gonna put this tape around your arm and you're gonna leave it there until you're back home. You ever show up here again with that tattoo showing, I won't bother with the tape. I'll just use the scissors."

"I don't come to temple to be threatened," Casey said.

"You don't come to temple," David said, which got OG Sean B to mutter "Damn, G." David looked at his watch again. "You're now at three fifty. You want to go to four?"

"I want to talk to your boss," Casey said, because he was one of those guys who always wanted to talk to the boss, the ploy of business travelers everywhere. "I donate a lot of money to this temple. This is bullshit."

"You don't donate that much," David said. "Your wife does, though."

David came around his desk. He wasn't as big as Casey, in fact David never really was one of those weightlifter types, but it was about presence, and David had the gravity of man who wouldn't mind killing you, because he wouldn't, and so he wasn't surprised when Casey took an instinctual step backward. He picked up the tape, grabbed Casey's arm, wrapped the sticky side onto his skin, tourniquet-tight.

"Go outside," David said. "Stare up into the sky and make your complaint. My boss will get back to you upon his return." David put his arm around OG Sean B's shoulder, the kid sweaty. "When you're done," he continued, "you can leave a check on my desk, or Esther will be here tomorrow morning and she can run your credit card. I'll be in the small shul with your son, getting him ready for manhood." He tapped his watch. "Let's call it three seventy-five."

Maybe Rabbi Kales was right. Maybe he wouldn't always be able to scare people into doing what he wanted. Maybe he didn't want that, anyway. But the point was, today, while he still could, Rabbi David Cohen was going to get his, so he could get out. There was no postwar? Fine. Then he'd just fight the entire time.

When he got back to his desk an hour later, there was a stack of twenties on his desk, a yellow Post-it note stuck to the top bill, Casey's block-letter scrawl filling it up, margin to margin:

SORRY FOR ALL THE MISUNDERSTANDING. PS: NEIL DIAMOND IS PLAYING THE MGM ON NEW YEAR'S EVE. YOU'RE INVITED TO SIT IN OUR BOX.

David wondered what kind of Jew got a barbed wire tattoo and then he figured it was the same kind of Jew who thought David wanted to ring in the New Year with Neil fucking Diamond.

Thing was, New Year's Eve, a lot of people got drunk and got into tragic accidents. David made a note of that.

"Why does this office look smaller with you in it?"

David looked up and saw Rachel Savone—Bennie's wife and Rabbi Kales's daughter—standing in the doorway. She was dressed in a sky-blue Ralph Lauren Polo dress, her arms and legs perfectly tanned. Her sunglasses were up in her hair, which looked lighter, and she had a purse dangling between her elbow and wrist.

"I changed the furniture," David said.

"That's not it," Rachel said. She stepped inside, closed the door behind her, then sat down in the chair across from David. "My husband says you have photos for me?"

"Yes, right." He opened a drawer in his desk and came out with sheets of proofs from the Rosen/Solomon wedding.

"I finally get to see the wedding my husband paid for," she said. She took a tube of pink lipstick from her purse and began silently marking any potentially incriminating photos of guests or property. After she was gone, David would go through and X out any pictures that showed his face. "Do you think they'll lie and say the baby was premature?" she asked after a while, not looking up.

"I doubt it," David said.

"What a *shanda* it would have been if I was pregnant on my wedding day," Rachel said.

"Times have changed," David said.

"No," Rachel said. "*People* have changed. No one wants to offend anyone anymore by saying anything directly to them. My mother would have sent me to live on a kibbutz before she'd have me pregnant under a chuppah." She paused, brought a proof page close to her face, then finally made eye contact with David. "Do you have a magnifying glass?" David did. Rachel hovered it over several photos. "Who let this asshole bring his mistress to the wedding?"

"The weathergirl?"

"Yes, the weathergirl," Rachel practically spit. "Did you say something to Jordan?"

"No."

"No? You see? This is exactly what I'm talking about." She flipped back through the pages, crossing off photos. "And in a red dress. Disgusting." When she was finished, she gathered up all the proof pages and slid them across David's desk. "Looks like it was a great party."

"The bride and groom seemed happy."

"Well, that's nice." Rachel sat there for a moment in silence, as if she was mulling over some offer. She didn't know the absolute truth about David—didn't know his real name, didn't know his backstory, and, crucially, didn't know what she didn't know—but she knew enough that whenever David saw her, he spent most of the time calculating in his mind how, precisely, he might kill her to get out of whatever trap she was about to set for him. Problem was David sensed that she knew *that*, too. "I figured it out," Rachel said eventually. "The thing that's missing in this office is God."

"He's here," David said.

"Oh, I know," she said. "You've read all the same books, believe all the same eschatology. But in this room, Rabbi Cohen, you lack the presence of my father. And so you lack the authority of God." She dropped her lipstick back into her purse, then came out with a photocopy of a newspaper article, set it on top of the photo proofs. "My husband wanted me to bring this to you," she said, "which means I've probably just committed a felony."

It was a story from the *Chicago Sun-Times* about a film festival. David wasn't sure what the fuck it was all about until he scanned to the bottom and read the news about cousin Ronnie—who in the paper was identified as "Philanthropist Ronald J. Cupertine," as if no one knew he was a murderer, but then Ronnie did always tend to buy full-page ads for his car lots in the *Sun-Times*—being hospitalized with some neurological problem. If the newspaper was reporting he was in the hospital, that meant it was serious. Back in the day, Ronnie would never let anyone say he was sick, unless it was looking like there might be some legal trouble about to come down, in which case he'd develop an arrhythmia, get himself checked into his own wing at Northwestern, where he could make phone calls that he knew couldn't be tapped, hospitals one place where the feds couldn't just put ears on somebody, because of all the privacy and confidentiality laws.

This didn't look like that.

He read further, saw that Ronnie was now underwriting a Native Short Film Festival, in partnership with the Chuyalla tribe.

So.

Not Russians.

Shit.

"Tell him I said thanks," David said. "These look like interesting films."

"It's as if you don't think I have a brain," Rachel said. She stood up then, walked over to the window, looked outside. "Can I tell you something in confidence, Rabbi Cohen?"

"Of course."

"No," she said. "Actual confidence. Not the thing where I tell you something and then I get a call from Vincent Zangari telling me he's had my passport canceled, or how I find out that my father's will has been changed and that Temple Beth Israel now owns the family business, which, I might add, my *mother* paid for originally. Because

I'm a little light on friends right now, Rabbi, and could use a learned person's point of view on something."

"I'm happy to be that person," David said.

Rachel nodded, considered that. "I don't know what you told my father to convince him to move into an assisted-living facility," she said. "But it's been appreciated. I think he's getting good care there. Making friends. Eating right for the first time in his life. I think, mentally, he's in a pretty good place, but he's having more and more . . . spells, I guess you'd say. He's not progressed into full-blown dementia as yet, obviously. So, I keep thinking, when his disease does progress, and his mind really starts to go, what do I do?"

"You love him," David said.

"No," Rachel said, "that not what I mean." She tapped the window. "When my father designed this building, do you know why he wanted a window here?"

"No."

"He said it was so he'd always have a view of the setting sun," she said.

David walked over and stood beside Rachel, looked out. All he saw now was the school. "Talmud says nothing will ever satisfy the eye until it's covered by the dust of the grave."

Rachel forced out a sigh. She turned and looked at David. "What I mean," she continued, "is when he starts talking. When he doesn't know who he's talking to. When he says things that are true to people who shouldn't know the truth." She tapped on the window again. "When he starts talking about where the bodies are buried, Rabbi."

David reached past Rachel and drew the blinds down. "You bring him home," David said. "You care for him yourself. And then if he needs to go, you help with that, too."

"How?"

"If it comes to it," David said, "I'll show you."

Rabbi David Cohen, who used to be a hit man named Sal Cupertine, watched those words sink into Rachel Savone. He'd lived in Las Vegas for three years now, and in that time he'd thought of his wife and son every single day. He tried to imagine what Jennifer's life must be like, the loneliness she must feel, the fear that surely accompanied that loneliness. But he never could quite picture it, until today, until right now, when he saw a flicker of his own wife in this woman.

Rachel blinked once. "It's late. I should probably let you go."

"Come anytime you need to talk, Rachel."

"I'll be sure to do that." She smiled wanly, then took her sunglasses from her hair, slid them onto her face, tucked the long strands of her hair back behind her ears. Rachel and Jennifer were the only two people in the world who might understand what it was like to be in each other's skin. Sad thing was, if both were lucky, they'd never lay eyes on each other. "Thank you for listening, Rabbi."

After Rachel left his office, David picked up the photo proofs from his desk. She'd gone through and cut nearly twenty photos, including every single one in which he appeared.

7

"Why aren't we going to school?" William asked.

Jennifer and William walked up Michigan Avenue, where she had the cab drop them off, checked if anyone was following them, then swung west two blocks, to State Street, went inside Carson's department store, in the old Sullivan Building, took the escalator to the second floor, women's cosmetics. It was funny. A hundred years Carson's had been on that corner and she'd never once bought anything there. Her mother used to take her to the store during the holidays, when the entire building was done up in gold and red, the building's brass fixtures all shined to a glow, the display windows on the street filled with scenes of small-town Christmas. They'd try on expensive clothes, do a little fashion show for each other, twirling in front of the three-way mirror, then her mother would take her to the Parker House for tea, which seemed extravagant for just hot water and a bag of herbs.

By the time Jennifer had a little bit of money, could maybe afford to shop at Carson's, back when Sal was starting to do well, that's when they bought a house and had a kid, acted sensibly, put everything back into the family, Sal telling her that one day they'd retire out west and she could shop on Rodeo Drive, like she was in *Pretty Woman*. It was an idea Jennifer appreciated, even if it was the opposite of what she'd grown to want out of life.

Carson's was a little dingy now—still classy, sure, the Sullivan Building was architecturally stunning, no matter how many mirrors and mannequins you shoved inside it—but the floors were stained in places. She spotted water damage in the acoustic tiles above her, which, when paired with the security cameras over every register, gave the impression that she was in a detention facility.

She'd never once brought William here—she couldn't imagine a reason why she ever would have—but now that they were inside, she felt sorry for that. She could have told William about her mother, about how they didn't have very much money but still liked to do little special things that *seemed* expensive, and how that had made Jennifer feel like she had an exciting secret life.

She didn't feel that way anymore.

"Mommy," William said, "shouldn't we be at school?" This was a question William had asked every day for the last week, since Jennifer decided she needed to keep him with her, every moment of every day, until today, the first Thursday of September.

"We're on a field trip," Jennifer said.

"Why aren't we with the rest of the school?"

"It's a special field trip," Jennifer said. "It's one big game of tag."

"I don't like to be 'it.'"

"Then we'll play hide-and-go-seek instead. I know you like that one."

"Will you let me hide this time?"

"Yes," she said. At home, that wasn't possible. There were too many things he might stumble into. "Just this one time."

Jennifer headed over to the M.A.C. counter, where lanky blond women in tight black tops and gay men with asymmetrical haircuts in equally tight black shirts applied makeup to women who'd never be able to replicate the look at home. Jennifer slid around the counter to a display of lip liners, pulled out a sample of Spice, ran the color on her hand. It was off-brown, muted, not terribly exciting.

"That would look great on you." It was one of the blondes. She was doing up a woman in her thirties talking on her cell phone. The blonde was taller than Jennifer, or at least her platform heels made her that way, and her lips were painted a blood red, her eyes done up smoky, which, when combined with the fact that Jennifer could see the nobs of her hip bones from her exposed midriff, made her look like she was heading into either rehab or the ground.

"You think so?"

"Yeah, totally," she said. "Try it on your lips. It looks way better on your face than on your hand."

"I don't know," Jennifer said, "I sort of have an aversion to germs."

The blonde grasped at her collar, like she was looking for pearls. "Ohmygod, I feel the same way. You don't know where they've been." She held up a finger. "I could open a new one and if you like it, you buy that one, and if you hate it, we'll just pretend it came damaged."

"That would be great," Jennifer said.

The blonde reached under the counter, pulled out a box, opened it up, handed the liner to Jennifer, left the box right there. "Try it."

The woman on the phone hung up, threw her phone into her purse. "Heather? We gonna finish or what?"

The blonde—Heather—gave Jennifer a conspiratorial eye-roll, like they were in this together. "Give me one sec." She reached under the counter and came out with a small rubber ball. "Can I give this to your son? It's a superball. One of those that bounces to the ceiling? Is that okay?"

"Of course," Jennifer said.

"Here you go," Heather said, and William took the ball from her hand. It was colored to look like the Earth and William was at that stage where he was fascinated by maps, so his attention was immediately grasped. He didn't even bother to bounce the ball. Instead, he started pointing to places on the globe and naming the countries at random. Papua New Guinea. Yemen. Haiti. Vietnam. Switzerland. *Has strong metaphorical thinking and amazing memorization skills,* his school report had said, *but must control his irritation at the pace of learning.* That was both William's curse and his gift: He was never bored, only frustrated, which Jennifer recognized was her fault. She'd closed the world around him so tightly that when he wasn't in school, he was only with her or with his books. Not even the kids in the neighborhood wanted to play with him now, or maybe their parents wouldn't allow it. Which made sense. Still, that was no way for a boy to grow up. She knew that.

It wasn't that Jennifer was paranoid. It was that she knew she was being followed.

"I'll be right back," Heather said.

"Take your time," Jennifer said. She ran the liner around her lips, found a mirror. It *did* look nice. Not that Jennifer was in the market for a new lip liner. No. She was on a job. She looked up, into the camera above her, then over her shoulder, to make sure she knew where the escalator was, so she'd know exactly where they'd be coming from. Then she dropped the liner into her purse, casually, like she knew what she was doing, because she did, and then took the sample, slid it into the empty box, waited for Heather to come back. It took a few minutes. Jennifer wanted Heather to remember her, be able to pick her out of a photo lineup, all that, just in case. She wasn't trying to be forgettable. Too many people had walked into police stations in Chicago never to be seen again. So she wasn't going out like that. Real people needed to see her. People who didn't know enough to be afraid of the Mafia, the crooked cops, or feds on the take. She knew Jeff Hopper hadn't been any of those things. She assumed whoever took his place was the same.

But still.

Doing this here? There'd be a record. She would be remembered.

"So?" Heather asked.

"I don't think it's quite my color," Jennifer said and slid the box back across the counter. "But thanks for going to the trouble."

"No worries!" Heather said, and Jennifer thought, yes, this is a person with no worries. How old was she? Twenty, maybe. She should be in school. Getting a degree in something useful so that she doesn't end up depending on someone else for her well-being. "And you can keep the ball," Heather said to William.

"I'm not allowed to take gifts from strangers," he said, and began to hand it back to Heather, but Jennifer stopped him.

"It's all right this time," Jennifer said.

Heather gave Jennifer one of those looks young women often gave her when they met William. That "He's such a little man!" face, not knowing that having a little man in your house meant that you also had an alien being in your family room, a silent, brooding, carefully constructed tool of destruction. One minute he was sweet and quiet, the next he was running into walls, pretending to play football, both offense and defense at once. *He needs to live where he can have friends.*

Jennifer and William wandered around the floor for a few more minutes, letting all the cameras pick them up, letting everyone who wanted to see Jennifer see her, and in case they didn't, she paused by a display of scarves, found a nice black one with a prominent security tag—it was Hermès, after all—and wrapped it over her shoulders, grabbed a pink one, wrapped it around William, a big game, grabbed a nice angora twinset, too, stuffed it into her purse, right on top of her gun.

Well, not her gun.

Sal's gun.

Had he killed people with it? Probably. It was a Glock, one of a dozen left in the carpeted-over crawl space inside the hall closet; it's not that she didn't know they were there. When the cops and feds searched the house after Sal killed those four men, she assumed they'd find them, like they found everything else they'd carted from her home and never returned, not that she gave a shit about most of it, except her old photo albums. But they hadn't. Maybe they didn't want to find them.

Jennifer grasped William's hand. "Now, when I say run, I want you to run," she said, "like when you play football at home, okay? And then hide."

"You'll come find me? You won't make me look for you, will you?"

"Never," Jennifer said. "And listen, if we get separated, it will just be for a few minutes, okay?"

"Okay," he said.

"And you have grandma's phone number in your pocket, right?"

"Yes."

"Show it to me."

William reached into his pocket, pulled out a crinkled piece of paper that had Sal's mother's Arizona phone number on it. Jennifer had called 411 and was surprised to find her listed, just outside Phoenix. She called the number yesterday from the pay phone in front of the new Quiznos that had gone into the space where Tino's Pizza had been for twenty years. Voice mail picked up, and there was Arlene's voice, the Chicago so thick in it, she imagined people in Arizona must have found it amusing. It meant she was really there, not hiding, and that was good. If somehow Jennifer misjudged this situation, William wouldn't end up in some Social Services nightmare. He still had family. Real family. Not that he'd ever met the woman.

"I've memorized it, too," William said.

"Of course you have," Jennifer said.

She took a deep breath, double-checked that Jeff Hopper's card was in *her* pocket, and headed for the emergency exit next to women's shoes, the one marked ALARM WILL SOUND IF DOOR IS OPENED.

She spotted the security guards right away—matching cheap blue suits, bad haircuts, nine bucks an hour to bust heads not going too far, she supposed—converging on her from every side of the store. The crime of the century had been perpetrated. Colored wax and fabric were about to be stolen.

What she didn't expect, however, was to see Sugar Lopiparno and a guy with a tattoo on his neck step off the escalator.

Or maybe she did. She didn't bring that gun for nothing.

"Hey, little Jennie Frangello," he said.

"Run," Jennifer said, and they took off. She even managed to push open the alarmed door before two security guards were on top of her, another was grabbing at William, shoving them both to the ground. One asshole put his knee into Jennifer's back, then slammed her face into the tile. Jennifer's nose exploded beneath her and she felt a tooth slice into her tongue, and everything went white, and then her mouth filled with blood, and she knew, right away, that this had turned upside down. That she'd fucked up, that this wasn't good at all.

The fire alarm blared, emergency lights flashed. Jennifer managed to turn her head slightly to the left, her face slipping across the floor, her own blood greasing the way. The other asshole told her to stop resisting, though she wasn't, she wanted to be arrested, that was the whole plan. But she couldn't say that out loud, couldn't open her mouth wide enough to speak. Where was Sugar? Where was her son?

And then William was screaming and pulling at her arm, pulling at her purse strap, trying to get her up, and another asshole was telling him to let her go, let it go, *Stop fucking around, kid*, and then her purse was gone and she knew what was happening before it even happened, as if everything in her life had been leading up to the inevitable moment when William Cupertine, son of Sal Cupertine, grandson of Dark Billy Cupertine, pulled his father's Glock out from his mother's purse and shot one of the security guards in the back of the head.

8

" **W**hoever did this to you was a quack," Dr. Melnikoff said.

He held an X-ray up to the light, like doctors always did, as if you knew what the hell you were looking at. It was Thursday afternoon, a few days after David had lunch with Rabbi Kales, and David was in Melnikoff's office in Summerlin. It was just down the street from David's house, in the Village Center Medical Plaza, which meant it was crawling with Temple Beth Israel people, so David got an appointment first thing in the morning. He didn't realize he'd be there all goddamn day, but Dr. Melnikoff ordered a battery of X-rays and blood and urine tests once David told him of all his complaints, and once Melnikoff started pressing his fingers into David's soft tissue.

"This part here? The expander across your nasal cavity? That's what we'd do for someone while they waited for extensive surgery, to stabilize their face, not to go about their life with." Dr. Melnikoff shook his head. "Here, along your jaw, the rods have not been placed with the idea that you might gain or lose weight, or that you might ever have dental work, or that you're an animal that chews." He shook his head again, muttered, "Butcher, really."

He pulled out another X-ray, held it up. "Here, by your right eye? I'm going to guess you have nerve damage. Possibly irreparable. We'll see. I'm not optimistic." Melnikoff set down the X-ray, pulled a printout from a manila folder, read it, then took off his glasses, folded them into the pocket of his lab coat, sat down on a stool, the kind with wheels. "You have an infection. Probably have had it for a while. I'd guess three to six months, judging from your blood work. You're taking Cipro?"

"Yes," David said.

"Who gave that to you?"

"I had it," David said and left it at that.

"Fine," Dr. Melnikoff said. "It's the wrong antibiotic. Stop taking it unless you're afraid you'll be poisoned by anthrax in the near future. I'm going to put you on a heavy dose of both probiotics and sulfamethoxazole-trimethoprim. It's going to mess up your stomach. Not that you probably feel much like eating anyway."

David did not.

He wheeled over. Took David's chin in his hand, moved David's head back and forth. "You have any pain when I do that?"

"No."

"Good, good," he said. "The chin implant looks pretty standard, so that's a plus." He sat back. "The beard is doing you some favors. A few months from now, you could very well look like a basset hound without it. You have scarring underneath?"

"Some," David said.

"Figured. Well, we'll see if we can do a little cosmetic work, too." He touched David's hairline, across from his left eye, where it didn't grow right. "I don't know what's going on here, but I can take a look if you're worried about it. Once we put you under, may as well fix what needs to be fixed."

"Put me under? For what?"

"You need surgery, Rabbi Cohen," Dr. Melnikoff said. "Your nose and cheekbones are collapsing. The rods in your jaw need to be replaced, but that's not as pressing a matter at the moment." He reached up and put his index finger and thumb on David's cheekbones. He flexed his fingers and David almost threw up from the pain. "If you got into a car accident, or if you tripped and fell, you could have a real problem, Rabbi." He reached back and grabbed an X-ray again. "You see your orbital bones here? Beneath them, you're basically held together by Pixy Stix right now. You get a blunt-force trauma to your face, or you sneeze real hard for all I know, you could be in a dire situation. I'd be inclined to replace what you have here with cadaver bones. It's more natural-looking. Certainly more stable."

"From where?"

"Pardon me?"

"The bones. Where do you get them?"

"Oh," Dr. Melnikoff said. "No one has ever asked me that. I suppose you're concerned about getting materials from non-Jews? Is that the case?"

It wasn't. "Yes."

"I'll look into that. We typically work with a local tissue bank."

"LifeCore?"

"Yes. Why do you know that?"

"Jerry Ford supports the temple's programs. And he happens to be my neighbor."

"Oh, right, right," he said. "Of course. He doesn't actually come to temple that often, does he?"

"No," David said. "He's a casual member." He thought for a moment. "When would this need to be done?"

"We need to get this infection under control first," he said. "Six weeks for that, would be my guess. That gets us to the middle of October. I'd like you to gain a little weight, because we're going to wire you back up for a month after the surgery, since I'm going to need to rebuild your palate. Realistically, I think that puts us into December."

"Hanukkah is the ninth," David said.

"Fine," Dr. Melnikoff said. "We'll schedule you for the eighteenth. That fit into your schedule?"

"I have the Berkowitz bar mitzvah on the twenty-second," David said. "Will I be ready for that?"

"No," Dr. Melnikoff said, "unless you want to do it lying down and bleeding from your eyes." Dr. Melnikoff pressed a spot below David's right eye. "Does that hurt?"

"Yes." In fact, it was all David could do not to grab the doctor by his throat and choke him until he bit off his own fucking tongue.

"We wait too long, it will become an emergency, not an elective. So we'll do it on the twenty-third. Will that work for you?"

"I guess it will."

"You're going to need someone to care for you," he said. "You have a relative or someone that can come stay with you for a few weeks?"

"I'll work it out," David said. He didn't know how.

Dr. Melnikoff exhaled. "Now we come to the uncomfortable part," he said.

"You've been wonderful," David said. "Tell me the price."

"This is just my cost," he said. "I want you to understand that." He rolled a few inches away. "Rabbi Kales explained the situation and I understand completely. *Completely.* This is my honor and you can depend on me for total confidentiality."

"The Hippocratic is a fine oath."

"Right, right," Dr. Melnikoff said. "That, too. The other thing. I'll have nurses working on this, of course, and an anesthesiologist, but they won't have access to any of your extensive records or, for that matter, lack of records."

"Dr. Melnikoff," David said, "man comes naked into this world, naked he must leave it. I appreciate the sensitivity and I trust you."

He did, actually. Because yesterday, David broke into his house. He was old-school Las Vegas, so he didn't live behind a gate. Instead he had a mid-century modern home on Alta Drive, the kind that still had all of its original furnishings but had been augmented with nonperiod items over the years: thick white shag carpeting in the living room, a hot tub in the master bathroom, wood paneling in his home office, a stainless-steel refrigerator in the kitchen, which David saw was filled with corned beef, mustard, sweet onions, challah bread, orange juice, and pickles. In his freezer he kept five bottles of Stoli, a stack of frozen dinners, and about twenty steaks, which immediately made David want to throw up. Melnikoff lived alone, his wife, Connie, dead now for five years—her headstone at the cemetery always had fresh daisies on it, a delivery coming twice a week—and his children, Pam and Julie, lived in Los Angeles, came up for the holidays, so David saw them at temple periodically, though he'd never spoken to them. He was dating Lydia Penzler these days, the two of them showing up to events at the temple once or twice a month, now that her husband had finally croaked from Alzheimer's last winter, but she lived over at TPC. There weren't any photos of her in the house, which David thought was maybe a bad sign for the longevity of the relationship. Not that David came looking for that. No, what David was looking for was something small: a carbon monoxide monitor. He didn't think he'd find one in house like this, but he had to be sure, not leave that shit up to chance. Because if anything went wrong with Dr. Melnikoff, his plan was to either suffocate him with carbon monoxide or simply blow him up. Old man, living alone? That's how shit happened sometimes.

"Please," David said, "don't worry."

Dr. Melnikoff exhaled from what seemed to be the bottom of his feet and his whole demeanor changed. "If everything is as I expect once I get inside, I think we're looking at fifty thousand."

David didn't respond. Dr. Melnikoff was now just a guy named Irving who needed some cash. And David didn't just give up cash to guys named Irving because they asked for it. He'd looked into Irving's gambling problem, made sure he wasn't in deep with some Gambino fucker running games, and it turned out that, in fact, it was worse: He owed the Mirage, the Rio, and the Palace Station $400,000 on markers and was paying $7,000 a month on them, which he'd pay until he defaulted or died, since he was still gambling. A marker was like an interest-free loan or an IOU, depending upon how the casinos were feeling about your ability to pay. They thought Irving would keep giving them cash, it was a loan, but soon as he missed a payment, it was an IOU. And if you defaulted on an IOU over $250 in Nevada, you were looking at a felony, like you'd written a bad check. But at $400,000, he was looking at jail time for major theft. He'd lose his medical practice, his house, everything.

Problem was, casinos knew that, too. Knew that if you were doing time, you weren't earning any money to pay off the debt, so first they'd go after you in a civil manner—attach liens on your property, try to garnish your wages, blacklist you, take you to court, compel you to pay by talking to the press, the *Review-Journal* and the *Sun* happy to do favors for the casinos, which propped them up with ad revenue every month, by writing stories about motherfuckers who'd defrauded them. A little public shaming went a long way toward getting paid. A guy like Irving, though, he'd rather pay a lawyer to negotiate his bill, pay pennies on the dollar if he could on the debt, while paying his lawyer five hundred an hour.

Back in the day, when the Mob ran the casinos, Irving would be dead and his daughters, Pam and Julie, would owe his debt, and then they would be dead, and their kids would owe the debt, and eventually, they'd either be dead or they'd figure out a way to get the debt paid. They could go to the cops, of course, but it was still illegal to default on the IOU, even back then; the debt would still be real, the crime would still be real. So if you went to the cops, they'd arrest you.

When people talked about Las Vegas being better when the Mob was in charge, that's really what they meant: Some motherfucker named Irving took out a marker, he was marked.

So David waited. And waited. "But," Dr. Melnikoff said eventually, "I think we can make it thirty-five thousand."

David waited some more.

"For Israel, though, I guess thirty thousand is appropriate."

"For Israel," David agreed.

"And I'd prefer to have that up front," Dr. Melnikoff said.

"I'll pay ten up front," David said, "and the balance after I'm content that the surgery has been successful. I suspect if this were being handled through insurance, there would be a thirty-day billing period, correct?"

Dr. Melnikoff shifted in his seat. "Yes, of course," he said. "Of course. That's fine."

Fucking shtunk. "Fine," David said. He reached into his pocket, came out with a rubber-banded roll of bills. He got up and set it on top of his X-rays. "That's five. Come by the temple tomorrow and I'll give you the balance."

"Yes," Dr. Melnikoff said, "yes, that sounds perfect."

David took out his wallet and thumbed through the bills. Put another five hundred directly into Dr. Melnikoff's hand. "I'd like you to find a different tissue bank," David said. "For privacy purposes."

"We'll find the best tissue bank. World class." Dr. Melnikoff put the money into his pocket.

"Thank you," David said.

"Rabbi Cohen, can I ask you one question and then, I swear, this is the end of any awkwardness on the topic?"

"If you must."

"I've never worked on anyone like you and so, of course, I have a million questions that I understand you cannot answer. So, this comes from a place of great suffering. My wife, Connie? You never met her?"

"No," David said. "She passed before I arrived here."

"Right, of course. Well, her family? Most of them died in Poland. Lodz. She got out just in time, went through Ellis Island, the whole thing, had a very clear memory of it. But her grandparents, aunts, uncles, cousins, the entire family never got out. Very sad. Very sad. She carried them with her forever."

"I understand," David said.

"So, I just want to know. For her, you understand." Dr. Melnikoff lowered his voice, and for a moment all David saw was Irving Melnikoff, a man who loved his dead wife. "Did you ever get to kill any Nazis?"

9

The south-facing guest rooms on the ninth floor of the Chuyalla Indian Casino and Resort had the best views in the whole place, which wasn't saying much. During the day, if he squinted, Matthew Drew was pretty sure he could make out the glint of the sun off Mill Lake Falls in the distance, though that might have been wishful thinking, since it was five miles away and across I-41. Below, a phalanx of orange earth movers tilled the land for what was going to be a championship golf course and, one day, a hundred condos and time-shares. The Chuyalla had a master plan for the area that also included a movie theater, a resort-style trailer park, which sounded like a misnomer, an outlet mall, maybe even a water park. At the moment, though, all they had were mounds of dirt and huge billboards with fanciful renderings of what the future might look like, all with the same slogan: *The Chuyalla Difference: Tradition. Family. Excellence.*

"Can you imagine living out here?" Matthew asked his sister, Nina. She was packing up her school books and an overnight bag. Since the week after he beat down Ronnie Cupertine, he and Nina had stayed in adjoining rooms in the hotel.

"They'll never build all that crap," she said. "And spoiler? *You* are living here."

"You know what I mean," he said. He pulled the curtains back a few inches and surveyed the land, looking for . . . what? Snipers?

It wasn't that he was worried.

Not really.

He'd erased all the video. The cops hadn't shown up. No foot soldiers from the Family arrived with bats. Management hadn't even come to him with questions about yet another ambulance showing up at the property.

None of which seemed right. At first, Matthew waited for someone to poke their head up, if only so he could bash it in. As the days wore on, he started to worry that the silence was worse. But then newspapers in Chicago reported that Cupertine was sadly going to miss the film festival he underwrote as he was hospitalized with some "minor issue," which Matthew obviously knew was a lie, and then carried a jaunty quote from the man himself, which Matthew also knew was a lie. Because at the very least, Ronnie was going to need full facial reconstruction surgery. He might not see the light of day for six, nine months. Maybe longer. So that got him thinking: Why would the Family put Ronnie's name and physical location into the press unless they wanted people to know where he was, that he was alive, and that if you'd taken your shot, you'd missed.

Letting Matthew know he'd failed.

Letting him know they knew he was looking for information.

Whoever *he* was.

Matthew doubted the two fucks tasked with guarding Cupertine had been forthright with *their* bosses about what they'd seen that night, doubted they could even pick Matthew out of a lineup, but that didn't mean the Family wouldn't start poking around, maybe start looking to see who the Chuyalla employed, cross-referencing that with people who might have a legit beef with Ronnie Cupertine. How long would it take for them to figure out that Matthew Drew once worked at the FBI? That he'd partnered up with Jeff Hopper? That he'd been looking for Sal Cupertine? How long until every motherfucker Matthew had sapped on the game floor was holding a contract on his life?

Which is when Matthew got . . . concerned. He started thinking about his sister, started worrying about some hard knock kicking down her apartment door and putting one in her face, too. That if Jeff Hopper had been concerned enough to force Matthew out of town after Fat Monte killed himself, maybe Matthew should be concerned for his own skin. Or at least his sister's.

Better to be safe.

Nina walked over to where he stood, yanked the drapes open wide. "Get some light in here. You're going to get rickets." She walked off into the bathroom, started to gather her belongings, so he cinched the drapes a few inches. She had class tonight, back in Chicago, and then all day Friday, so she was going to spend the night with her friend Veronica, then be back Saturday. Maybe Sunday. There was a party she wanted to go to.

"Okay," Nina said a few minutes later. She looked around the room. "I think I have everything I'll need. You'll get the rest of my stuff moved?"

"Yeah, no problem," Matthew said. The Native Mob had the entire ninth floor rented out this weekend, including the Presidential Suite, where they had a full buffet and open bar working, and were taking bets on all the football games, the NFL season kicking off on Sunday. So Matthew and Nina needed to find new digs. Plus, Matthew needed to have some plausible deniability: It was one hundred dollars just to get in the door with the Native Mob's sports book, but then you could bet whatever you wanted—the spread, over-unders, prop bets, straight up—provided you had cash or chips. This wasn't a leg-breaking operation, since you had to pay up to make the bet, no credit offered, and the Native Mob paid out immediately. At least that's how it had gone this summer during the NBA finals, which went off without incident. They were quiet, professional, and tipped.

Basically, it was a service to the community.

The Chuyalla said it wasn't Matthew's problem. It all seemed sort of quaint. If you were in Las Vegas, you could bet on the number of times someone scratched their ass in the Super Bowl and it was legit, but 1,700 miles away, it was a federal crime. Matthew didn't mind looking the other way on victimless crimes like betting, but he couldn't very well pretend not to see something that was sleeping next door to him.

"I'm going to be up in the Eye in the Sky all weekend," Matthew said, "so when you get back, just wait for me in the lobby, and then we'll get a new room for you."

"Why don't I stay in Chicago? Veronica would let me crash for a week if you're still worried about the security at the apartment."

The apartment they rented in Chicago was your average six-story box with a buzzer entry. The building was filled with UIC students, which meant you could walk in with an aircraft carrier strapped to your back and no one would say shit. Matthew didn't stay in it very often these days, but he still paid most of Nina's bills. That was one thing this job was good for: He made money. He could put a little away every month, keep Nina feeling comfortable, not have his mother stressed out in the process.

"Not yet."

"Then when, Matthew? Because the drive back and forth to campus is getting old fast."

"Another couple of days," he said. "I want to make sure there's nothing to worry about."

"I'm not worried about anything," Nina said, "other than your propensity to jail me in a casino."

He hadn't told Nina what, precisely, he had done. He couldn't. If she knew Matthew had beaten up the head of the Family, then he'd need to explain everything else. So instead he said some shit had gone down at the casino and some bad guys had threatened his family and the Chuyalla took this seriously and insisted Nina come stay with him while the tribal police investigated.

It was, in a way, the truth. Or at least true enough to get her to move upstate for the last few weeks of summer, with the idea that the hotel was the safest place they could both be, since Matthew had a whole security team working for him here. But now school was back in session and she wasn't going to miss her senior year of college—particularly not since Matthew had already helped her out with the tuition—for something as nebulous as a threat.

"Let me give you something," he said. He went into his room, unlocked the closet safe, came back holding a Glock. "Take this."

She put her hands up. "Really?"

He popped the magazine out, examined it, popped it back in. "This has a full clip. You want an extra one?"

"Jesus, no," Nina said. "Who do you think I'm going to need to shoot thirty times?"

Matthew handed her the gun. "I want you to keep this on you at all times."

"You want me to bring a gun onto a college campus?"

"No one is going to search you," Matthew said, "because you're not going to be breaking any laws. But keep it in reach. So, not at the bottom of your backpack. Keep it in the front pocket. Or in your purse. Okay?"

"If I decide to roll up into a club on Friday night," she said, "do I shove it under my belt? Is that how you do it?"

"This isn't a joke, Nina," Matthew said.

"I'm sorry," she said. "But it's been three weeks, Matthew. If I eat another BLT from room service, I'll kill myself." She hefted the gun in her hand. "Or take out twenty-nine bystanders and *then* kill myself." It wasn't the first time Nina had handled a gun. When they were kids, their father used to take them hunting, and after that shit with the Family a few years ago, Matthew took her to the range, got her comfortable with a gun again. Nina was pretty good with an AR-15, tended to go wide and to the left with a Glock, but she'd gotten better the more she did it, and soon enough was plugging center mass. She dropped the gun into her purse. "Satisfied?"

"Anything weird happens," Matthew said, "don't fuck around. Pull the gun and shoot. Even if you just shoot into the ground, they'll know you're serious."

"*They.* Great." She gathered up her bags and headed to the door. "When's your next shift?"

"I'm on an overnight," he said. He was going to his little apartment in town today, maybe pay a bill, maybe eat a sandwich, catch a nap. Then he'd be back on at 9:00 p.m. Saturday and Sunday he'd be pulling twelve-hour shifts, the casino expecting big business. "You need something, call me on my cell."

"A shower wouldn't hurt you, bud," she said.

Matthew pulled up the casino's security cameras on his laptop and watched Nina wind through the hotel and then out into the parking lot, where she loaded up her car and drove away. He clicked back over to the parking lot cams, waited to see if anyone took off after her. All he saw were two old women with matching oxygen tanks and cigarettes shuffle into a minivan.

He needed to get the fuck out of Wisconsin.

•

"HEY, SKIP," PURVIS said. "You maybe want to check this out?"

Matthew Drew pushed away from his desk in the surveillance room and stood behind Purvis. He was one of Matthew's better guys—he'd been on a Stryker Brigade team in Desert Storm and was the only halfway decent Chuyalla on his team, meaning he actually didn't mind kicking his own people out when they did stupid shit— and so Matthew scheduled him whenever he thought things might get thick on the floor.

"What do you got?"

"I don't know. Could be nothing. Could be we're about to get wet up."

On screen, Matthew saw a line of blacked-out Suburbans pulling into the parking lot. It wasn't an undercover operation, that much Matthew could tell when he zoomed in on the SUVs and made out their government plates. Standard FBI practice was to cover those up on a covert operation, not that it was ever covert to show up in five SUVs, but it meant there was no element of surprise involved.

It was 10 a.m., the first Sunday of the NFL season, which meant the hotel and casino was teeming with people—a couple hundred were in the convention hall to watch the Packers play the Lions on four giant screens, the three bars inside the hotel were decked out in green and gold and rammed full of drunks in cheeseheads, hollering for blood, and the gaming floor was wall-to-wall with high rollers and nickel-slot players alike—so if the FBI were showing up, it was because there was someone here they really wanted to embarrass. If they wanted to pick up Matthew for that Ronnie Cupertine thing, they'd just kick down his apartment door and grab him whenever they wanted.

Matthew thought they'd be respectful about it. He still had friends in the Bureau. Guys he'd gone through the academy with, junior agents who used to eat lunch with him in the Roosevelt Building cafeteria, go out for a drink at Fitzgerald's, talk about how when they ran the Shop; they were going to get Geraldo Rivera back in town to bust open another of Capone's old vaults, then shove Ronnie Cupertine inside.

Just a bunch of jokers.

Playing at this thing.

It wasn't even real to most of them, because of course it was ludicrous. Everyone thought they'd end up working for Jack Crawford in the Behavioral Science Division, because they didn't realize *Silence of the Lambs* wasn't based on a true story. Thought they'd be Joe Pistone, doing that Donnie Brasco deep-cover operation, stomping people to death, hoping they'd get the chance to talk like gangsters, even though they all had degrees from the best colleges in America. Thought they'd be doing hostage negotiations and bank robberies and talking Libyans out of hijacked 747s, which made sense. They'd all wanted to be FBI since they were ten. Matthew had been the same way, thinking he'd be on tactical assaults, and then ended up here, a Sunday in September, working at a casino.

And anyway? It wasn't a federal crime to beat an old man up. Someone wanted to arrest Matthew, they could just send a street cop.

"You want me to contact tribal police, Skip?" Purvis asked.

"Give me a sec," Matthew said.

The Suburbans parked and ten guys in FBI windbreakers stepped out. None of them took out their guns. That was a good sign. Matthew shifted the feed to the cameras on the private roads leading into the facility. There were three black vans idling on the side of the road. Paddy wagons. Another white extended van was pulling down the road, along with a tow truck, but neither was close enough to pick up their plates.

Matthew zoomed back in on the group of agents.

He recognized Lee Poremba walking abreast a taller man he didn't recognize, then the other eight held back a few steps, moving in single file. They all wore polo shirts under their windbreakers, a couple looked to have Kevlar, all of them radioed up, but Poremba and the other guy had on shirts with ties under their windbreakers. Neither wore tactical gear.

Poremba was the senior special agent in charge of the Organized Crime Task Force in Chicago. Matthew had met him during the time he spent in Springfield on Kirk Biglione's aborted trial, and before that, Jeff Hopper had vouched for him, told Matthew he was the only decent guy left in the Bureau, that he'd given Jeff and Matthew a head start to apprehend Sal Cupertine first, once they knew how he'd escaped, because Poremba thought Jeff had earned that right. One morning in Springfield, a year ago now, Poremba sat down next to him at the Ramada coffee shop, the two of them not supposed to be talking, since Matthew was there to give damning evidence of the FBI's incompetence. If he'd gotten the chance, Matthew was prepared to lay out exactly how the FBI had fucked up the whole Cupertine affair, but that chance never did come. But that morning, Poremba just sat there, eating his two fried eggs and sourdough toast in silence, until right before he got up to pay his bill. "Wanted you to know," Poremba said, counting the bills in his wallet, not looking up, "that if I had any say, you'd be on my team, right now."

"Okay," Matthew said.

"You did good work on Cupertine," he said. "You're solid with me, just so you know." He turned and looked at Matthew then. "I think about Hopper every day. I shouldn't have let him go out there. I'll always regret that." And then he was up and gone.

Matthew believed him. On both counts.

"You ever seen this guy?" Matthew asked Purvis now. He zoomed in closer, to the agent beside Poremba. On his windbreaker was the logo for the Milwaukee field office.

"No," Purvis said.

"He's never come in on gaming issues?"

"Not to my knowledge."

Which meant they were probably here for the group upstairs. The Native Mob was running their operation, as planned. There'd been no issues. Last night, Matthew went up to the ninth floor around 10 p.m., before he clocked out and went back to his apartment, just to make sure nothing untoward was happening. Hallways were empty. Clean. Down by the Presidential Suite, there was a guy standing by the double doors wearing a suit, cell phone in his hand, didn't look strapped. When Matthew approached, name tag still on, the guy stepped from the door and met him a few feet away. "Everything cool, sir?" the guy asked.

"I don't know," Matthew said. "Everything cool with you?"

"Badgers lost to Fresno State. So everyone's a little pissed off."

"They cover the spread?" Matthew asked.

"I don't know about that," he said.

Matthew didn't know who was staying in the Presidential Suite. Didn't really care. Because the truth was simple: Matthew's job was to protect the property. Not the people. He didn't give a fuck about the people. Next job he took, maybe he'd be doing some kind of paramilitary security in the Middle East, the kind of job guys who'd washed out of Quantico ended up taking all the time. Be expected to stand between an armed insurgent and some asshole from Exxon, be willing to take a bullet so he wouldn't have to pay more than three bucks a gallon for unleaded.

"Let management know they're here," Matthew told Purvis now. Purvis nodded. "Should I make an anonymous call to the ninth floor, in case any of them are up there?"

Matthew clicked on the ninth-floor feed. The hallways were empty, save for a maid pushing a cart filled with dirty dishes back toward the service elevator.

"No," Matthew said. If the FBI wanted into one of the rooms, they'd need a warrant or a guy already inside, which was possible. Probably likely. But in that case, they'd have marshals with them, a tactical team, a couple guys with door rams. The Native Mob would be armed, but Matthew didn't see them or the FBI engaging in some Waco siege. "They want to go up there, they're going to have to show papers. And if they have paper, they're on our phones already. That's not a problem you want to have, Purvis."

"On our phones? How? Wouldn't we know?"

In his mind, Matthew ran through a million different entirely legal tapping scenarios. Thought about how easy it would be to have CIs working in every part of the hotel and casino. Considered it was highly plausible that the feds had bugged this place during construction, that every feed Matthew had, the feds had, too, that the whole casino and hotel and surrounding property was marked as probable cause for investigation from the moment it broke ground. The Chuyalla had been involved in bingo rooms since the 1980s, and during that time, there'd been half a dozen murders related to people adjacent to the tribe, including an unsolved case where the vice president of the bingo operation ended up buried upside down outside of Iron River.

It was, Matthew realized, probably why he'd been hired in the first place. To think about these things.

He captured a photo of the agent beside Poremba, sent it through the recognition system, but only statewide. Nothing showed up.

"No," Matthew said, "you'd never know."

TEN MINUTES LATER, Matthew's gun and sap locked up in a file cabinet, Senior Special Agent Lee Poremba and his partner were standing in his office; the weekend day manager of the hotel, a fifty-year-old Chuyalla dupe named Del, shifted nervously in front of them. "This man," Del pointed at Poremba, "is from the FBI office in Chicago. He has some questions for you. Our lawyers are on their way and they've advised us to wait for them."

"Okay," Matthew said. He made eye contact with Poremba, who, as ever, seemed entirely impassive. His partner seemed cut from slightly different cloth. He'd taken his windbreaker off already and had it folded over his arm, rings of sweat visible under both of his arms.

"Okay you want to wait, or okay you'll talk to them?" Del asked.

"Am I personally being charged with anything?" Matthew asked. Poremba shook his head once. "You can go, Del," Matthew said.

When Del was gone, Poremba pointed at the man beside him. "This is Special Agent Zane Wilmore," he said. "He runs the Gang Task Force up here. You mind if we sit?"

"Be my guest," Matthew said. He'd never met anyone from the Gang Task Force in Wisconsin, not when he was on the job, and not since he'd taken this new one, though now that he was looking at Special Agent Wilmore up close, he seemed familiar. Poremba and Wilmore sat down across from him and took in the surroundings. Matthew had five TVs mounted on the wall, which at the moment were all tuned to the casino floor and its surrounding bars and restaurants, and he had two computer monitors on his desk, a wall of bookcases filled with binders. His window overlooked the employee parking lot and the row of Dumpsters he'd banged Killer's face against.

"When Matthew was an agent, he worked with Jeff Hopper," Poremba said to Wilmore. He didn't say anything about the months that followed, which made Matthew think this introduction was intentional and not just the sort of territorial pissing everyone did in the Bureau, where you let everyone know how they were connected, so that you might get something accomplished based on who you knew or where you'd been.

"For a couple days," Matthew said. "Before I got fired."

"He was a good agent," Wilmore said.

"You ever tell him that?"

Wilmore looked at him curiously. "I worked with him a million years ago. Rochester. Then again when all three of us were in Kansas City for a little while. You were probably in middle school."

"Rochester. Who bothered to organize in Rochester?" Matthew asked. This was the kind of conversation he used to overhear in the office, senior agents bullshitting on confidential information like they were talking about the Cubs and White Sox. No one had these conversations with Matthew back then. He was just "kid this" and "kid that." Until you had war stories, you weren't shit. Matthew had stories now. He just didn't have anyone to tell them to. He'd never mentioned Sal Cupertine to anyone.

"You familiar with the area?"

"I used to play club lacrosse out there. When the fields weren't frozen."

"Last ten, fifteen years, the Bonanno Family muscled in, but there wasn't anything to take. Rochester was always independent and it's so damn cold, no one wanted to be involved up there, anyway. Crap place to be an agent, crap place to be in the game, honestly."

"Wisconsin is better?"

Wilmore cocked his head, like he hadn't heard him right, then like he was sizing Matthew up. "It's changing," he said after a while.

"Have we met?" Matthew asked.

"Yes and no," Wilmore said. "I came through here last month. You showed up on the tour for a few minutes, told us about how you could keep our conventioneers safe."

"What was your convention?"

"Model trains," Wilmore said, and Matthew suddenly remembered him. It had been a day when the Native Mob was having their council meeting downstairs. Which is probably why the FBI was back today. Everything was starting to come into view.

"That's a good one," Matthew said. All that gear. All the machinery. Nothing but men in overalls. They could have bugged the whole place. And probably did.

"I thought so. You didn't background check us?"

"No," Matthew said.

"That's too bad," Wilmore said. "All that groundwork for nothing."

"You like your job here?" Poremba asked.

"I like the salary."

Poremba got up from his seat, looked at one of the TVs. "You catch a lot of card cheats?"

"No," Matthew said. "I wouldn't even know what I was looking for. We've got people who do that. My main job is throwing people out by their hair."

"That must be nice," Wilmore said.

"I haven't heard any complaints."

Poremba leaned close to the TV screen, his face just an inch or two away, then tapped it with his two middle fingers. "I need glasses," he said. "I can hardly make out anything on this." He slid his hands between the TV and the wall, up along the top of the TV, down each side, under the front, didn't say a word.

"By the time someone is at a table," Matthew said, "if they look suspicious, I already know who their parents are." He pointed at his computer. "We run everyone through the facial-recognition database. If they're local, or in the database tribal cops use, we'll have them."

"And yet," Wilmore said, "you've got every shot caller in the Native Mob upstairs."

"I'm only responsible for the casino," Matthew said. "And even still, Native Mob, they don't shit where they eat. Most of the time, if there's a problem, it's Latin Kings or Gangster Disciples or the odd Vice Lord who we end up putting back on the street. We had a situation with the Sons of Silence not long ago. Biker gang from Colorado? Came out for a Broncos preseason game with the Packers, ended up getting into a knife fight in the buffet with some Mongols down from Ontario."

"I didn't hear about that," Wilmore said, indignation creeping into his voice.

"We kept it in house," Matthew said.

"Mongols and Sons don't usually beef," Wilmore said.

Matthew could tell something was pissing him off and that made Matthew want to piss him off more. But at the same time, Wilmore was also trying to be . . . courteous. It didn't seem like a natural series of emotions for him.

"What about the Family?" Poremba asked. "Any known associates up here?"

"Not in a while," Matthew said.

"Since when?" Poremba asked.

Matthew examined Poremba and Wilmore for a second. Neither of them had cuffs on their belt. Matthew took Poremba at his word that he wasn't personally being investigated for anything. If Poremba was here, though, that meant there was a crime going on that was larger than simple gang activity, which made sense, because the Chuyalla were surely running a skim operation, which operated on a few levels. They had a rigged poker table that Matthew had witnessed personally, there were at least three slot machines that were chipped, and the mere act of renting out space to the Native Mob for meetings was probably illegal, though it wasn't as if they listed Native Mob LLC on their rental agreements. No, instead, it all went through a tattoo parlor called Demon Dogz in St. Francis, so that, technically, the Native Mob's monthly meetings were a gathering of tattoo artists and their subjects. They even had insurance. A credit report. All of it legit. The Chuyalla also sponsored a powwow every July, right on the fairgrounds located just east of the hotel and casino. Ten thousand people would roll through over three days for a lacrosse tournament, singing, dancing, food, games, crafts.

That was the public show, which the public paid fifteen dollars a head to view.

The private show was more elaborate. Tribes throughout the country used the powwow circuit to move prescription drugs, coke, weed, money, and guns in and out of the reservations, all of it being taxied in tour buses filled with kids and seniors and sporting equipment and giant tenting materials. Not that the buses were being searched. They drove right onto the property, through the gates of the fairgrounds, and then the gates were closed at night. Tribal police guarded them to make sure no one tried to break in to steal the lacrosse nets.

The Chuyalla also offered up more than fifty thousand in prize money for the singing, dancing, and lacrosse competitions, and that looked rigged to Matthew, too. At least the singing and dancing. The lacrosse matches looked legit. That was something Matthew knew something about.

"Why don't you tell me what you're doing here," Matthew said, "and then maybe I can answer your question with a little more accuracy."

"I have you on surveillance, carrying a weapon, stalking Ronald Cupertine pretty much every day for six months," Poremba said. "Fifty to hundred feet away, sometimes. I have you at his children's dance recitals. At his job. *Everywhere.* I've got a complaint from his wife, describing you right down to your dimple, saying you showed up at a school book drive, that you followed her and her children inside the Field Museum, and that you used to watch her from a Starbucks about a block from her house. She thought you might be a child molester. I even have the warehouse on Wolcott. I don't know what your idea was with that and, honestly, I don't want to know." He stopped, dug a Kleenex from his pocket, blew his nose, tossed it in the trash. "Then you just stopped. Fell off him completely. So what brought me here, first, was trying to figure out if you were lying in wait when you hobbled Ronnie Cupertine in your high-roller toilet. Convince me that you didn't take a job here because you knew you'd get this chance."

"I didn't *take* a job here," Matthew said. "They called me. Said I got referred to them."

"By who?" Poremba asked.

"I kind of thought it was you."

"It wasn't," Poremba said.

"Must have been someone at the FBI," Matthew said. "I don't know anyone else in Chicago." Even as the words came out of his mouth, Matthew realized how absurd this was all beginning to sound.

"Are you aware who owns this place?" Wilmore asked.

"The Chuyalla sign my checks," Matthew said.

Poremba shook his head slowly. "You ever hear of the Chuyalla before you got this job?"

"I don't know," Matthew said.

"I'll give you a hint," Wilmore said. "You didn't. There's maybe two hundred Chuyalla. They don't have the capital to be opening casinos and water parks, so you gotta work that backward, ask yourself who has that kinda cash, who might they partner with to open up an operation this big, even get an ex–FBI agent to run their security for them." When Matthew didn't respond, Wilmore said, "I'll give you another hint. They're having a party inside your casino right now."

"If they had that kind of money," Matthew said, "why would they bother to run a book upstairs, knowing you'd find out and come looking for them?"

"They don't have that kind of money," Poremba said. "But Ronnie Cupertine does. The Family does."

"Look," Matthew said, "if I'd known I'd get the chance, I would have killed Ronnie Cupertine. And then I would have quit. But here I am. Showing up to do my job on a Sunday. Just like you two."

"Why didn't you kill him?" Wilmore asked.

"Did you know Jeff Hopper well, Special Agent Wilmore? Like, did you know anything about him, at all?"

"He was hard to get to know."

What did Matthew know about Jeff Hopper? That he was alone by choice. That he'd come to Chicago and made no lasting relationships, would date a woman for a month or two, but when it got close to being serious, he ended it. He'd only really learned that much after Hopper died and Matthew was living in his place in Walla Walla and the cards and letters of condolence showed up and Matthew, the only thing like a close living relative, answered them, and suddenly he was thrust into Hopper's private world. He'd known Jeff Hopper in one context only: as a man who was seeking some justice for the death of his friends.

"When his agents got killed by Sal Cupertine," Matthew said, "when you heard about that, what did you think?"

"I thought it was an avoidable tragedy." Wilmore paused. "I went to the academy with Cal Hodel," Wilmore said, one of the four men Sal Cupertine had killed. "So it's a little personal for me. They found Cupertine's spit on him. He'd choked him."

"You planning on tracking down and killing every other member of the Family to exact your vengeance, then?"

"Of course not," Wilmore said.

"But I am?" Neither man responded. "Ronnie Cupertine didn't deserve the honor of being killed by me. I'm not going to give him or his bullshit Family that respect. Yet you come here with three paddy wagons and an entire assault team to talk to *me* about beating down a guy who has deserved it since *you* were in middle school? The guy who called the fucking hit? Jeff Hopper died to bring justice to those men Sal Cupertine killed. Got his head chopped off. And you're here sweating me?"

Poremba pointed at the TV again. "You make him on this?"

"No," Matthew said. "I ran into him in the bathroom. But do you want to know something funny? I put his picture through the database the next day, because I was worried that maybe he'd been coming in and no one had noticed that he was pinging. I came up with zero hits. Guy's been running a crime family for thirty years, has his own television commercials, but doesn't have a file that local law enforcement can access through facial recognition. If he walked into a police station armed with a bazooka, they'd need dental records to figure out who he was. That struck me as odd."

"He show up on your own database?" Wilmore asked.

"No," Matthew said.

"That didn't make you wonder why?" Wilmore said.

"No," Matthew said, but it should have, it should have made him start to piece together what was only now becoming clear to him. That he wasn't here by some happy accident. "But you didn't show up on the system either, Agent Wilmore."

One by one, Poremba unplugged each of the five televisions, then sat back down next to Wilmore, yanked the power cord out from the back of Matthew's computer, then did the same with Matthew's telephone.

"If someone were listening," Matthew said, "it would be me."

"I wouldn't be so sure of that," Poremba said. He pulled out a slim pack of Kleenex from his pocket, took one out, blew his nose, set the rest of the pack on the desk. "The second reason I'm here," he said, "is to do a health and welfare check. Cops pulled a car registered to you out of a pond in Lynwood yesterday."

"What are you talking about?" Matthew said. Lynwood was a village thirty minutes south of Chicago. Matthew had driven through it, but never stopped. "My car is parked right out back." He turned around in his chair, to point out his Mustang in the lot, which is when he saw an agent standing ten feet from his car, a blast shield at his feet. The white van he'd spied earlier was pulling up. "Is that a bomb unit?"

"Your other car," Poremba said. He pulled an envelope out of his jacket pocket, opened it up, unfolded a two-page report. "A '91 Honda Civic."

"That's my sister's car," Matthew said. It had been his car when he was in high school and college. He'd given it to his sister Nina when she moved out to start at UIC. Hadn't even bothered to get it reregistered in her name.

Poremba and Wilmore shared a look. "She live in Lynwood?" Wilmore asked.

"No," Matthew said. He stood up. Went to the window, watched as a man in a full bomb suit stepped out of the white van, along with a German shepherd. "She's in an apartment by UIC. Where I used to live. Last few weeks, she's been staying with me. Up here."

"Why's that?" Wilmore asked, but Matthew was already out the door, Poremba catching up to him at the service elevator, sliding between the doors just before they closed.

"Where you going?" Poremba said.

"I need to go," Matthew said. "I need to find Nina." He wasn't thinking straight. He pushed the button for the first floor. He needed to get out of this building. This fucking place. Did he understand Poremba right? Was he . . . working for *the Family*?

"When was the last time you talked to your sister?" Poremba asked.

"Thursday." Was it Thursday? No. Wait. He was getting confused. He'd worked an overnight this week. Matthew took out his cell phone, scrolled through the numbers. "Friday. I talked to her on Friday." He turned the phone around, showed Poremba the call log. "I called her. 9:47 a.m. I was coming off shift."

"What did you talk about?" Poremba asked.

"Bullshit. You know, whatever. School and work and . . . and . . ." Matthew stopped himself. "What the fuck is going on?"

"I need you to calm down," Poremba said. "I'm sure it's just a misunderstanding."

"Why are you here?" Matthew asked. "The other guy. What the fuck is he doing here?"

"I came to talk to you," Poremba said. "Like I said. If I just showed up by myself, that would look suspicious. So I picked a day to come out where we could have a conversation, Special Agent Wilmore could handle his business, and you wouldn't be endangered." He paused. "I've been waiting for the right time." He paused again, Matthew aware that he was reading him, working through the playbook for a situation like this. "And then another thing happened and my timeline changed. And this happened, with the car, so we moved everything up. Now. You talked to your sister on Friday. Was she going somewhere?"

"She was at the library, studying," Matthew said. "She had class that day."

"What time?"

"I don't know. Ten?" He tried to concentrate. They passed the fourth floor. The third. "Yeah. She has a ten o'clock class on Monday, Wednesday, and Friday. Criminology. Sometimes she calls me after class, if she has a question."

"Okay," Poremba said. "She the type of person who goes out at night?"

"She's in college."

"Okay. Is she the type of person who wouldn't notice her car was missing for a day or two?"

"No. She hid with me in Walla Walla for two weeks while Jeff was working with your office chasing down leads on Sal Cupertine," Matthew said. "She doesn't know everything, but she knows enough that she came with me when shit got bad, okay? She'd be alarmed if something was out of whack."

"Okay," Poremba said. "Okay."

"She's not some sorority girl," Matthew said. "She knows how to handle herself. I taught her. She's got a gun. She's . . . she's not an idiot, Special Agent Poremba."

"I know she's not," Poremba said.

Matthew hit the call button on his phone. There was some mistake here. Maybe Nina met someone at a bar last night, hasn't even been back to Veronica's yet. Or got drunk and slept at a different friend's place. That's what college students do—they meet people at bars. They sleep on friend's couches. They don't answer their phones at 10 a.m.

No service.

Fucking elevator.

He pushed the 1 again, again, again, until finally the doors opened.

"Hold on," Poremba said, but Matthew was already gone, past the laundry, the break room, the staff kitchen, then out the double doors to the loading dock, into the sunlight, the air cool, barely sixty, fall finally here, and then broke into a run, arriving in the staff parking lot at the same time Agent Wilmore came sprinting out from the opposite direction.

The German shepherd was circling Matthew's Mustang, the agent in the bomb suit a foot behind the dog, the leash taut.

"Ease up," Agent Wilmore said. He put a hand on Matthew's chest. "Let's ease up."

Matthew grabbed Agent Wilmore by his wrist and snapped it. One move.

Poremba ran up behind Matthew, out of breath.

"Agent Drew," he shouted, "stop."

But Matthew was almost to his car now, he hit the call button on his phone, put the phone to his ear. Took out his car keys.

The German shepherd and the agent came around to the back of the Mustang.

"Agent Drew," Poremba shouted, "get away from the car. We need to clear it."

This would all be figured out.

The German shepherd reared back on its hind legs, began to claw furiously at Matthew's trunk. The agent in the bomb suit pulled the dog away, turned, and shouted something, but Matthew couldn't make out what he was saying from inside the blast helmet. The agent let go of the dog, started to rip at his suit, unfastening it at the neck, peeling it back, shook his helmet off, screamed, "Get the fuck away!"

But Matthew was there already.

He heard what the agent heard.

The sound of a cell phone ringing in the trunk.

Matthew pulled his phone from his ear.

Five rings.

Six.

He hung up. Hit redial.

There it was again. Unmistakable. The German shepherd howling now.

10

Tuesday mornings, Rabbi David Cohen met OG Sean B at Temple Beth Israel at 7:00 a.m. to go over his bar mitzvah curriculum. Which meant David had to get to his office around six if he wanted to prep, have a cup of coffee, take a decent shit before the kids started showing up for school next door, which brought the parade of parents, each of them with some new problem only David could solve through his deep interpretation of the Talmud. That his interpretation usually boiled down to some variation of three edicts— *Don't be an asshole; Clean your own house;* and *Sometimes, you look the other way,* which was actually a line from a song—didn't seem to bother anyone, since none of them had read the Talmud anyway. So by 5:57 a.m. on the second Tuesday of September, David had already done five miles of road work, hit the heavy bag for thirty minutes, bundled four grand in cash to drop in a safe deposit box, and was now in his Range Rover, driving through the still-dark streets of Summerlin, headed to the temple.

To get his mind right for twelve hours at work, he was listening to yet another bullshit book-on-tape about Kabbalah—his third— since he couldn't bear to read the pretentious shit. But Kabbalah was all the congregation could talk about, half the people thinking it offered them some profound enlightenment, the other half believing it was the end of the Jewish faith. Today he was learning about the mystical uses of self-mortification to purify the evil in one's soul, an idea David was sure wouldn't land particularly well with anyone, since it would require a relationship to shame that simply wasn't present these days and recognition that their problems were not, in fact, part of God's grand plan.

It sure wouldn't work on OG Sean B. His tag was multiplying across the city; everywhere Rabbi David Cohen went, he saw another reminder of this niggling problem. Coming out of the funeral home, David saw it on the transformer box facing Hillpointe. Reading a magazine in the toilet at the Barnes & Noble on Rainbow, it was etched into the grout at David's feet. Even up on the Summerlin Parkway overpass, which David was pulling toward now, the tag was there in front of him, three feet high and upside down, just as it had been for the last ten days or so:

OG SEAN B 187.

What kind of OG let someone dangle them upside down off a fucking freeway overpass?

The kind that really wanted to be noticed, David thought, which wasn't all that different from how plenty of real OGs acted, like Cousin Ronnie in his absurd used-car commercials, though in this case it was probably less of an elaborate con and more a cry for help. OG Sean B wanted someone, anyone to pay attention to him, didn't matter if the attention was negative. He was like a dog that pisses on the rug just to get punished for it.

Also, 187 didn't even mean anything in Nevada. It was the penal code for murder in California. Here it was just another number that had been co-opted to mean you were tough. And it wasn't clear to David if the 187 was meant to indicate Sean was going to murder someone or if he was about to be murdered.

"How do you know someone isn't framing me?" Sean asked last week when David confronted him about the overpass, the kid not smart enough to get the spray paint and Sharpie ink off his hands before playing dumb. He was like his father in that regard.

"You need to have an enemy in order to get framed," David told him. "You have any enemies?"

"Would I know?" Sean asked. Since school resumed in August, David had encountered a steady run of teachers, parents, local businesses, and neighborhood HOA presidents asking for the kid's head. The HOAs were the more pressing issue, since they were threatening to have OG Sean B shot if they caught him alive, which was technically legal in Nevada, the state's Use of Deadly Force laws being pretty lenient, particularly as it related to people committing crimes on private property. David didn't care for most laws, but that one seemed fine. Still. It made him look weak, this bullshit, and eventually, someone was going to call the cops, because eventually everyone called the cops when someone fucked with their property.

It was an accumulation of tsuris without an easy solution. And then, yesterday, it came to a head.

"He's a menace, Rabbi," Roberta Leeb, the seventh-grade math teacher, told him. She'd stopped him on the sidewalk in front of the funeral home, David coming back from putting another Triad body into the ground. A teenage boy, judging strictly from his torso, since he didn't have a face, the whole thing sliced off, a seam around the ears and scalp, meticulous, surgical work, but a fucking waste of time as a torture device, since the only person horrified by it was the one doing the work. "A real criminal, if you want my opinion," Roberta continued. "Having him anywhere on the campus is tantamount to a violation of Hebrew law."

He wanted to go home, take a shower, get the bits of dirt out of his hair and from under his nails; every funeral they did was a soil-throwing affair, even on a windy day. Didn't matter what end of the death spectrum he worked on, end of the day, David was picking someone else from his skin.

"Tell Dr. Lupus." Dr. Lupus was the principal. He was in his seventies, had known Rabbi Kales since they were kids in New York. He came to work about twice a week, spent the rest of the time at his place in Sun City either playing gin or drinking it. David didn't think he'd make it through the year. He was mostly a series of tremors.

"Please," Roberta said, in that *way*. "Let's take some responsibility here, okay?"

"How's his attendance?" David asked.

"Perfect," Roberta said.

"If he were such a major criminal," David told her, "he wouldn't come to class." David hadn't gone to a day of high school after the eleventh grade. "He'd be too busy moving his weight."

"What does that even mean?" Roberta said.

"A man, however fallen, who loves his home," David said, "is not wholly lost."

"He's not a man," Roberta said. "I'm asking you to handle this situation. He's beyond my reach." She leaned forward and brushed dirt from the arm of David's jacket. "Anyone I know today?"

"No," David said. "Out-of-town guest. Someone who always wanted a view of the mountains."

Roberta was in her forties. Rabbi Kales had recruited her from the Levine Torah Academy in Henderson, a private school David was busy putting out of business. If they didn't close up shop by next semester, there was a good chance there would be a significant structure fire on campus. "I could be next if I have to deal with that little fucker one more day, pardon my language." She dug into her purse, came out with a pack of cigarettes and a lighter. "Do you mind?"

"Yes." David didn't like the teachers smoking near the school. Bad optics. She shrugged, shoved the cigarettes and lighter back into her purse, came out with a pack of Nicorette, pushed a square of gum into her mouth, David watching her hand shake the whole time. Hard to work a full-time job with a full-time addiction. "You interested in Kabbalah at all?" David asked.

Roberta actually recoiled. "You're not one of them? All spiritual cleansing and the Light of Hashem?"

He was not. But it occurred to him the thing that pissed people off about OG Sean B was the same thing that pissed them off about Kabbalah: Both showed a lack of respect for the faith. Jews weren't supposed to act *that* way, and by doing so, did damage to everyone, and God wasn't going to be able to unfuck it for the rest of them.

This Kabbalah problem he blamed primarily on Madonna. She was all Jewed up these days, kept talking up the healing powers of the Zohar in interviews (at least according to the Casual Torah Study Group ladies who couldn't shut the fuck up about it), and had started to wear a scarlet thread bracelet to ward off the *ayin hara* in every photo. The Casual Torah Study Group ladies kept bringing in *People* to show David *the horror! the shanda! khas vesholem!* like he needed some evidence apart from their fervor, ironic since he was pretty sure they hadn't given a fuck when she was covered in crosses, writhing on a stage in a wedding dress.

That was the thing with Jews, David had learned: They didn't really trust converts all that much. They abhorred their iconography being co-opted, which made perfect sense, historically speaking. The problem with being hunted for the last two thousand years was that they were always waiting for the wolf to once again show up at the door, dressed just like them.

Two of the most aggrieved Casual Torah ladies, Joanie Helms and Millie Meltzer, even convinced David to join them at the community college over on Charleston to watch a free speaker pimping himself as Yehuda Da Truth Tella prattle on for ninety minutes about numerology and the Ten Spheres of the Sephirot. He was purportedly from the Kabbalah Center in Tel Aviv, though David was pretty sure he'd seen the same guy hawking cell phones at the Meadows Mall. Not that Joanie and Millie seemed to care, both of them taking notes like high school freshman the whole time. The grift was done so expertly that, ten minutes in, they'd both forgotten their Talmudic grievances and were openly sighing and nodding in agreement, just like everyone else in the room.

David caught Yehuda's eye about midway through, no easy task in a room of 250 people, and held it for a few seconds, let Yehuda take him in in full, con man to con man, but Yehuda didn't flinch, his patter so tight that when he looked into the face of an actual contract killer he still trundled forward. David could have pissed on the floor and Yehuda would have said it was a sign from God.

It was all bullshit. A mixture of cheap mysticism and Reiki healing with a little Hebrew tossed in, basically Scientology for Jews, without the thuggery, spacemen, or the booth at the farmer's market. David saw nothing revolutionary in the "truth" Yehuda was telling, Kabbalah had been around since the Middle Ages after all, but he did appreciate the hustle. At the end of his talk, Yehuda passed out registration forms for a three-day seminar taking place at the Mirage in October—with the promise of "Enlightenment, Engagement, and a Healthy and Wealthy Future!" The Yentas flopped their black Amex cards out like they were dealing blackjack.

Soon, David was stocking scarlet bracelets in the Judaica store at the temple. Thirty-five bucks—cash only—got you a piece of red string that David snipped from a ball of yarn he bought at Joann's. He then had Linda Barris and Ed Geyer, the thousand-year-old volunteers who worked the spot on Saturdays after services, make little signs that said the string had been personally blessed by both Rabbi Cohen *and* Rabbi Kales, who'd taken on an exalted position in people's minds since his "illness," as if his proximity to death somehow made him all the more holy, with all proceeds going directly to the Barer Academy's Scholarship Fund. The fund was bullshit, since no Jews in Summerlin wanted to be known as the "needy Jews," and yet the fund was a money tree, the dead being particularly kind to it, always good for a few thousand in their wills.

David was pocketing that bracelet money directly, averaging about a G a week—in fact, the money he'd bundled this morning and had stashed in the passenger seat of his Range Rover, along with his gun, was mostly bracelet cash—everyone in the congregation was wearing the bracelets now, even the men. Jordan Rosen had one on either side of his Rolex. It was shit work making the bracelets—though David sort of liked the monotony, found it psychically calming—and in that way, it was just like the old days, David happy to do an odd job if it meant something in his pocket. But it was also like the old days in that people thought something David did was actually protecting them, when in fact it was all an elaborate con: You were going to die. You were always going to die.

"Personally," David said to Roberta, "I think Kabbalah is a scam. But I read something interesting the other day."

"If it involves crystals or vortexes," she said, "I'm not interested."

"No," David said. For someone who didn't believe in Kabbalah, she sure knew a lot about it. "The Safed, every night before they go to sleep, do a meditation forgiving anyone who has made them angry or damaged their property, either wittingly or unwittingly, as well as anyone who has pondered such an action."

"So they even forgive people who *think* about doing things to them?"

"Right," David said. "And they ask that no one be punished by God for having done or thought about doing bad things to them. Basically, they absolve the whole world, every night. Start fresh the next day."

"I don't agree with that," Roberta said.

"I don't either," David said. "But maybe try it for a week."

Roberta chewed her nicotine gum for a few seconds, contemplating.

"Where are you from originally, Rabbi?" she asked eventually.

"All over," David said. "My father worked for the military." He had the whole backstory he'd been given memorized, little details added over time to flesh out the small things, as many things that were kind of true as possible, so that he wouldn't slip up. The military part Rabbi Kales gave him. Jews in Israel served. Jews in America did not. He'd never need to worry about anyone asking a follow-up question, because they didn't want to sound like weaklings, and the fact was they thought military service in America was beneath them.

"See, I grew up here," she said, which David already knew. He knew where every single teacher at the Barer Academy had come from and where, in a way, they were headed: Bennie's lawyer delivered a dossier on each of them when they were hired, including information David might need down the line, details on their addictions, who they were fucking on the side. Roberta was relatively clean. Smoked a little weed her husband, Don, got from a coworker at UNLV. No children. Labrador named Lucy. Owed $189,000 on her house, which had an ARM loan, which was like getting sharked by the Bank of America. "I remember when where we're standing was still desert. We'd come out here and drink on Friday nights. The cops would let us mill around for a few hours, then they'd show up and we'd all have to pour out our beer and go home. No one ever got arrested unless they really mouthed off. And even then, they wouldn't get charged. Their parents would have to come down to the station and pick them up, which was a whole production."

"You were kids."

"That's right," Roberta said. "But you know what the difference was? The cops didn't think we were jerks. They'd grown up here, too, so they knew getting wasted in the desert was just what kids did. Rites of passage are important, Rabbi."

"I agree."

"Then you'd agree pretending you're a gangster is not a rite of passage," Roberta said. "It's something you do when you're seven. Cops and robbers, all of that? You keep doing that after puberty hits, you're not pretending anymore. You're a budding sociopath."

"Maimonides said . . ." David began to say, but Roberta cut him off.

"Save your quotes for Shabbat," Roberta said. "Not everything is about the twelfth century. If that kid isn't out of my class by end of business this Friday, I'm quitting and you can teach pre-algebra, Rabbi. I'm not having some trench-coat Columbine wannabe in my classroom. His other teachers feel the same way, so brush up on your history and French, too."

The problem David had, other than his empathy for OG Sean B's living situation, was that OG Sean B was going to stand in front of a few hundred of his closest friends and relatives on his thirteenth birthday in December and speak Torah. Temple space was already booked, along with the ballroom at the Performing Arts Center for the after-party. The temple had also contracted the DJ and the catering, the bartender, the flowers, secured a magician, reserved a "hype man" to get the kids dancing, Cold Stone Creamery was doing a pop-up ice cream parlor, and then there was going to be a paintball tournament on the undeveloped grounds west of the cemetery, some sort of desert warfare simulation. Ninety-five thousand dollars out the door. It wasn't all profit, of course, but David was going to get his. Roberta Leeb was not going to stand in the way of his money.

"I'll see what I can do," David said. He heard something move into his voice, didn't try to stop it, having seen how well it worked with Casey Berkowitz. He leaned down toward Roberta, about five feet nothing and a lot of that was frizzy hair. "Meantime, don't threaten me again, Roberta. I don't react well when people threaten me."

"Don't make me," Roberta said. She stepped off the sidewalk then and headed back toward the Academy's parking lot. By the time she reached her car—a red Miata—she was already smoking.

IT WAS, RABBI David Cohen considered now, how it always went in Las Vegas. No one was ever willing to just walk away with credit on the machine. The proof was all around him. A steady stream of SUVs exited off the Summerlin Parkway and headed south toward the half-built gated communities that now advertised NO DOC LOANS! on the billboards. When the Howard Hughes Corporation started to build out Summerlin, the idea was that the neighborhoods would be filled with doctors from the Summerlin Medical Center, lawyers from the Village Center Legal Park, gaming executives from the Resort at Summerlin, maybe a few white-flight types coming in from Los Angeles to buy golf course homes at TPC, but certainly not the strippers, professional Texas Hold 'Em players, and other cash-only professionals they were attempting to lure in now.

The stethoscopes and white collars had come, sure enough, but there weren't enough of them, which is how all master plans got ruined, David had learned, particularly from reading Rabbi Kales's books about the Holocaust: Once you ran out of the people you wanted, you either diluted the pool or started killing the minorities. So now the developers had to pimp to two diametrically opposed lifestyles: the luxury set who spent their disposable income on golf, tennis, teeth whitening, and hair plugs . . . and the aspirational existence of upwardly mobile charlatans.

You had cash these days, the developers didn't give a shit if you got it bouncing your ass on tourists' dicks, going all in on pocket twos, or treating brain cancer. As long as you were prepared to pay a variable rate of interest, as Roberta Leeb was, you could have a brand-new home with an unfinished yard and access to a community pool, no questions asked. It was ruining the neighborhood. The Jews of Temple Beth Israel were already getting restless, moving farther and farther west into newer and more expensive developments opening in the foothills of the Red Rocks, places with exorbitant HOA fees, which kept out the riff-raff who could only afford their homes and not the land around them, ghettoizing their own exclusivity. Places like the Lakes at Summerlin Greens, where David lived, were equally filled by wealthy families, geriatrics who thought Sun City was one step from a feeding tube, girls named Star, and vampiric twenty-five-year-old poker players who wore sunglasses at all hours and flew model airplanes over the common areas.

Most of the SUVs streaming by David this morning were driven by young women—strippers and cocktail waitresses coming back from their shifts—and middle-aged, tanning-bed-orange white guys in red shirts and black ties, Gotti haircuts, cigarettes burning between their fingers. David really saw these young women only in the early morning, but he ran into these corporatized pit bosses every day, at all hours. They still talked and dressed like mobsters, except they didn't have to kick up, were content to pull six-figure salaries from the MGM and Steve Wynn in exchange for paid vacation and a 401k. Used to be a pit boss had some actual sway, maybe would smack the shit out of you for some card-counting bullshit, but the assholes David saw were just costumed performers, guys so tough they answered to Human Resources and handed out punch cards for free steak dinners. No one was smacking the shit out of anyone for Steve Wynn's bottom line. That was up to the lawyers, like the ones Dr. Melnikoff was surely dealing with regularly.

Not that David thought it should be different.

No, in fact, what he felt was simple pity.

It was going to be part of the lesson he taught OG Sean B today. *He who humiliates himself will be lifted up. He who raises himself up will be humiliated.* Casey. OG Sean B. These assholes? All the same, all playacting at the shit David had done. And if they knew what David knew? If they had to sleep with that? There was a difference between mitigating a dispute at the pai gow table and killing four Donnie Brascos in one night, and yet these guys spent their lives fronting like they were the kind of people who did wet work. *Pitiful.* What was a kid like OG Sean B supposed to think? The whole culture of this town was upside down, and the longer he lived here, the more David began to believe that Las Vegas festered and abided evil. In Chicago, yeah, the Family sold drugs and killed people, extorted money and ran rackets, but if you didn't come looking for the Family, you'd never see them. The Rain Man wasn't going to show up at your house and kill you for cheating on your taxes or running a red light.

Maybe Israel was the place he and his family *should* go. The wars there at least had precedent, and everyone had a gun. A fair fight. Wouldn't that be nice.

These men driving by him craved the stink he couldn't wash from himself in a thousand Days of Atonement. And frankly, David wasn't sorry about a lot of the things he'd done, which made him pity these men more. They wanted to be Al Pacino, not Sal Cupertine. That would be in the lesson, too, David thought. The Jew is born civilized, he'd read that, and though he didn't believe it, it's what made mensches out of meshuggeners.

The light changed and David caught the eye of the driver of a black Ford Expedition lagging through the intersection. He was olive-skinned, which wasn't something David saw much of on this side of town—maybe a Mexican or Persian, hard to tell precisely in the coming dawn. His hair was cut close, and he had one of those thin goatees favored by douchebags everywhere, his face illuminated by a glowing TV screen mounted next to the rearview mirror, the blonde beside him watching it with a kind of slack-jawed wonder. The Expedition was going maybe fifteen miles per hour, slow enough not to be terribly dangerous, but it had been raised up on monster truck tires, like it was going to assault Gaza.

David gave the man a nod as they passed each other, and the man nodded back. The night shift and the day shift crossing at the time clock, punching in and punching out, everyone driving tanks. The grind was real and, man, it was armored.

•

WHEN DAVID PULLED into his parking space at the temple, a quarter after six, there was already a car in the lot, which was strange. It was a black Cutlass, white water spots on the hood, windshield a corona of dirt from the wipers, and it was parked at the edge of the lot closest to the street, perpendicular, covering three spaces at once.

This time of the morning, there were usually a few cars up the way at the Barer Academy, janitors and the rent-a-cops getting the place turned on.

At the funeral home and mortuary across the street, the morning guy, Miguel, would be coming in around seven to start the pickups from the hospitals and hospice facilities around town, if he wasn't already doing an emergency from the overnight, someone waking up to find their spouse dead beside them. Ruben and the rest of the staff came in around eight, unless there was an early service on the books. If there was a body coming from one of their partners, Ruben handled that himself, drove the hearse to the pickup—usually the private airfield in Henderson, or the muni out in Boulder City, or if it was coming in a car, they'd meet out in the desert—brought it inside, handled the paperwork, removed the organs if they were getting repurposed, had the staff clean the corpse, or not, get them into their coffins so David could do his show.

Jerry Ford and his LifeCore van usually showed up around nine thirty for any donations from the morning shift, and then walk-ins would start at ten, crying families looking lost and afraid.

This morning, however, there wasn't a soul anywhere. No one jogging. No one walking a dog. The American flag hadn't been raised in front of the school yet. There weren't even any planes in the sky, which was odd, since 6:00 a.m. was when Southwest and United and American started launching people back to their lives, seven days a week.

Just this black Cutlass and David.

It was probably nothing.

David got out of his Range Rover, walked over to the Cutlass, peered inside the driver's side window. There was a small clipboard stuck with Velcro onto the dash, marked MILEAGE LOG. Each line had a place to put the date, the beginning mileage, and the ending mileage, and then a place for initials, David seeing the same two up and down the page: MM.

Today's mileage started at 45,912.

The day before: 45,427.

Almost five hundred miles in one day.

On the passenger seat sat a red accordion folder filled with carefully filed documents. Maybe fifty or seventy-five pieces of paper, also what looked like glossy photos, though he couldn't make out anything specific, and then maybe a third of the documents and photos had yellow or pink sticky tags jutting off them. Next to the folder was a phone charger, a ripped-open package of Tide Sticks, a Nikon camera. There was a foam cup in the cup holder, an inch of coffee in the bottom.

A wire coat hanger dangled from a hook in the backseat.

There was a lint roller on the floor, next to a lockbox.

Shit.

David walked around to the back of the car, looked at the plate.

US GOVERNMENT

FA34119

FOR OFFICIAL USE ONLY

FBI? ATF? Maybe U.S. Marshals. Maybe all three.
He couldn't kill them all.

He had two choices. Run or fight. He had a Glock in the Range
Rover, full clip, fifteen rounds. He had the four Gs in the car, plus all
that cash in safe deposit boxes around town, including one up in
Pahrump, an hour away. If he could get that far. He doubted it. Fifteen
rounds weren't going to be enough to take on a full federal assault
team. He'd take out a few, sure, and then what? He'd be the guy who
killed six feds instead of the four already on his sheet. So they'd give
him six lethal injections instead of four? If he made it that far. They'd
probably just plug him right here. Save the taxpayers some cash.

If the feds were on him, it would be a production, even if he got
away. Spike strips. Planes. Sharpshooters. CNN motherfuckers
tracking him like O.J. This car? It was the tip of the spear. Maybe a
diversion. When they grabbed Tony Camelia, a New York guy in
Niagara Falls, they told him he'd won a free trip from his grocery
store loyalty points, put him up in the Sheraton, even gave him the
free breakfast buffet, then twenty-five agents put AR-15s on him at
the waffle bar. All he'd done was kill a snitch. What would they
bring for Sal Cupertine?

"Maybe you can help me?"

David turned and saw a woman in a black pantsuit, blue shirt
opened two buttons, tall, almost six foot in her boot heels, walking
across the street from the funeral home. Red hair pulled back from
her face in a thick ponytail. Thirty, thirty-five years old. She didn't
have anything in her hands, no purse, no phone, but walked like she
had something on her hip.

"Is this your car?" David said.

"I'm looking for someone," she said. Not unpleasant. Not pleasant. Maybe didn't even hear the question, still thirty feet away.

In the distance, David thought he made out the bleating of a siren. He looked to his right, past the Academy, to where Hillpointe bled into Hills Center Drive, watched the intersection. A black Suburban crawled by, going north. A couple seconds later, another Suburban, going south. But then a Honda, a minivan, a Lexus. Nothing with a siren bar on top.

Where were they?

He turned back. The woman was only a few feet from him now.

His own car sat twenty yards away, which meant his gun was twenty yards away, behind a locked door. His knife was in his pocket, but he couldn't exactly gut a person in the temple parking lot. For one thing, her screams would wake the neighbors. For another, he didn't know how he'd explain the pools of blood to OG Sean B, never mind the kindergarten kids when they began to show up in two hours, if he somehow managed to hide her body in time. And he wasn't keen on killing women. In fact, he'd never done that. He needed to figure this out, fast, without getting shot.

"Are you lost?" David said.

"Rabbi David Cohen?" A question in her voice.

"Is that who you're looking for?"

"Is that who you are?"

"No," David said, but then thought better of it. What if he got out of this situation? The lie would be a problem down the line. He looked to his left. No Suburbans there. But now he heard another siren. He was sure it was a siren. He tried to smile. It nearly worked. "Not until nine. I'm just David Cohen right now."

"Ah, okay," she said, and nodded her head. She was in front of him now, a foot between them, professional distance, but didn't put her hand out to shake, instead she put both her hands in front of her hips, index fingers pointed down, palms open, ready to move. She had freckles on her nose. A coffee stain, looked like, on the lapel of her shirt, those Tide Sticks probably coming in handy. He couldn't see her gun, but the way her belt slung low around her hips, he knew it was there. "I'm Agent Moss. You're in charge here?"

"As much as a man can be," David said. He closed his left hand into a fist, felt the leather strap of teffilin there. It was wrapped all the way up his arm, around his wrist, over his thumb, and then encircled his middle finger three times. It was going to be part of today's lesson for OG Sean B, about the harmony of spirit and action, the rule of intellect over emotion, that the heart ennobles any calling. He slipped the strap from around his finger, felt it spool into his palm. "Is there a problem?"

"There is," she said. "We need to talk about your operation here." She pointed over her left shoulder with her thumb, toward the cemetery. David could see her pulse beating in her neck. Where was the backup? Already inside the temple? Or maybe there was a sniper on him from inside the Academy? Another from inside the funeral home? It made sense. That's why no one was here yet. They'd cleared the buildings. Probably blocked traffic behind him. David looked up into the sky.

Nothing.

Nothing.

And then . . . he heard it. The *whoop-whoop-whoop* of a helicopter. He couldn't see it. But he could hear it. And the sirens. Were they getting closer? It was hard to tell. But there were three or four of them now, he was pretty sure.

"I have a student arriving shortly," David said. "Will it take long?"

"Depends," Agent Moss said, "if your answers satisfy me."

"Then maybe you should come back," David said.

"That's not an option," she said. "Is there some place private we can do this?"

"Right here is fine," David said. He wasn't walking into a building to get shot. He got killed inside the temple, they'd have to knock the whole place down, or else it would end up a stop on a tour, like the Marie Calender's on Sahara where Lefty Rosenthal's car got blown up, or the stoplight on Flamingo where 2Pac got hit.

"Okay," Agent Moss said. "If that's how you want to do it." She took a step to the right, toward the passenger side door, and for a brief moment, David was behind her, which was all he needed.

He pulled the strap of leather teffilin tight between his hands and yanked it around Agent Moss's throat, twisted it in an X, compacting her carotids and knocking her out before she could even start to fight, spun her around toward the temple, where he figured the first gunshots would come from—if they were going to shoot him, they were taking Agent Moss out, too—reached down with his right hand and went for the agent's gun, to give himself a fucking chance, yanked it from the holster.

He came up with a Blackberry.

Shit.

He dropped the Blackberry, felt along her back, her left hip, kicked at her ankles. There had to be a gun somewhere.

Nothing.

He stood there, facing the temple, the agent hot against his chest, her legs twitching, waited. One. Two. Three. Tightened the strap.

Waited.

Nothing.

He spun Agent Moss around toward the Barer Academy. If there was a sniper inside there, David would already be dead. He knew that. He also knew that he had about fifteen seconds before this woman was a fucking vegetable.

He spun toward the funeral home.

Maybe her partner was coming up behind David now. It wasn't like in the movies. They wouldn't shoot you in the back if you had an agent in your arms. They weren't Navy SEALs. They were guys like Jeff Hopper, who didn't even come at him armed. Or those three Donnie Brasco motherfuckers, geared to the teeth in a hotel room, and they couldn't manage to hit him with a single bullet. They weren't killers. They were office workers. Difference between shooting at a target and shooting at a person was that a person would always shoot back.

Nothing. Nobody.

He looked up into the sky for the helicopter, made one out in the distance, flying low, toward the Strip. He listened for the sirens.

They were getting farther away now. Were they even sirens? Or was that only a ringing in his ears?

He dragged Agent Moss back around to the driver's side of the Cutlass, away from the street, dumped her on the ground, let the strap go. Tried to gather his thoughts. Let Agent Moss breathe for a second, before it was too late.

It was 6:19 a.m.

Why wasn't David dead yet? Something was off. He rifled through Agent Moss's pockets, looked for a wallet, some kind of ID, but she had nothing, just her keys. No handcuffs, zip ties. Wasn't wearing Kevlar. He picked her Blackberry up off the ground, clicked open the mail. A page of messages scrolled down, all to a @nv.gov address. Which meant this was probably a government phone. Which meant it was probably chipped with GPS. Which meant she was being tracked. Or could be, anyway.

Thing was, Agent Moss, she wasn't missing. Not yet. She was where she was supposed to be.

David pocketed the phone, then unlocked the Cutlass and pulled out the lockbox, which wasn't locked. He looked inside, found a store-bought sandwich wrapped in plastic, a banana, two oatmeal cookies. He tossed it back into the car.

Agent Moss's right foot twitched, brushed against David's heel. He looked down, watched her eyes, to see if they opened. A pool of fluid began to spread out on the pavement under Agent Moss. She'd pissed herself.

David stepped around the car, popped open the trunk. A Samsonite overnight bag. A black Nine West purse, a worn hardback copy of *The Bridges of Madison County* inside it. Jennifer read that. Kept it on her nightstand for a year. He dug the woman's wallet out of her purse, found her driver's license. Melanie Moss lived at 1418 Snowflake Lane in Carson City. She was thirty-five years old. Had forty-seven dollars in cash, five credit cards, a Costco card. A Blockbuster card. A receipt from the Chevron on Rainbow. Twenty-seven dollars in gas, eleven dollars in snacks. A receipt from dinner at Houlihan's, a shitty restaurant next door to the Courtyard Inn on Rainbow. She had a receipt from there, too. One night, government rate, eighty-nine dollars.

Where the fuck was her FBI ID?

Where the fuck was her backup?

Why the fuck did they send her out here alone?

Agent Moss let out a sound akin to someone trying to swallow wood chips. David walked over and nudged her with his shoe. She didn't react. Red foam on her lips.

He'd tried not to snap her windpipe. It was like asking a shark not to swim. Even Harvey B. Curran would understand that.

It was 6:20. In forty minutes, OG Sean B would be here. In less time than that, teachers would start showing up to prep. The gym teacher would be outside, washing down the basketball court. The one goy on the whole faculty. Mr. Landers. If he saw David, he'd walk over, coffee mug in hand, would want to know about getting some new metal basketball hoops.

And then he'd be dead.

That's how it worked.

Wasn't even a question.

David hadn't killed anyone since that FBI agent. Two years without killing. The best run of his adult life. Yeah, he *wanted* to kill Casey Berkowitz. But he hadn't. He'd shown restraint. A little restraint. An iota. The best of him, he realized. That single iota that stopped him from walking up behind Casey Berkowitz and putting one in the back of his head. It was the difference between him and some Jeffrey Dahmer motherfucker.

And now this.

David pulled the bags from the trunk, tossed them in the back-seat, then knelt down beside Agent Melanie Moss, felt for a pulse at the base of her neck. It was there. Weak. A whistle of air escaped from her mouth. He might not have snapped her windpipe after all. Not completely. Not that it mattered. David lifted her eyelids up with his thumbs, made sure she wasn't playing dead, that she was unconscious.

Sal Cupertine had been in the game pretty much since the moment his father hit the pavement in front of him. Thirty years now. Not a day had gone by when he hadn't thought of someone he'd like to kill, someone he'd killed, or someone he'd seen *someone else* kill. And in all that time? He'd never hurt a woman. Not physically. Never imagined a situation where that seemed like the thing he had to do. Did it happen? Did other people do it? Sure. But Sal Cupertine, he wasn't that guy. Never would be.

The difference between never and once? That could be your whole life.

Rabbi David Cohen wrapped the teffilin around Agent Melanie Moss's throat one more time, pulled the strap tight, put a hand over her eyes, and snapped her neck.

11

Rabbi David Cohen parked the Cutlass behind the funeral home, locked the sliding metal gate behind him, went inside the mortuary, and called Ruben Topaz. It was 6:30 a.m. There wasn't anything on the calendar for the day, which didn't mean anything. Jews liked to get in the ground fast. If someone needed a funeral, it was just a matter of digging a hole and saying kaddish.

"*Estás viendo esa pendejada?*" Ruben said when he answered.

"Pardon me?"

"Oh," Ruben said. And then a pause. "Rabbi Cohen?"

"That's right."

"I thought this was Miguel," he said, his words coming out fast. "You seeing this?"

"There's a client here," David said.

"A family?" Ruben asked. David could hear the TV on in the background, could hear a baby crying, Ruben's wife talking in Spanish, another voice, a boy.

"Not a family," David said.

"Miguel should be there in a minute," Ruben said. "He can do a coroner intake."

"This isn't something Miguel can handle," David said. He never talked to Ruben about the bodies he was burying. They'd talk about the logistics of the ceremony, about whether or not Jerry Ford should be contacted about possible donations, about scheduling. But if there was a nineteen-year-old Chinese guy without a face and a fifty-something white guy with a bullet through his neck

193

in the refrigerators, David didn't ask Ruben if he thought it odd they were named Suzanne Adler and Anne Haber. Did Ruben think David was a rabbi? Yes. Did Ruben think David was at least as morally compromised as he was? Probably, or, at the very least, that Bennie Savone had some dark shit on him. Did he think David was a former Mafia hit man? David doubted it, highly. Rabbi David Cohen was just another in a line of dupes. The last one, Rabbi Gottlieb, ended up in Lake Mead, and Ruben probably thought David would eventually end up there too. "I need you to come in."

"Are you serious? Are you watching this?"

"I'm at the mortuary," David said. "I haven't watched anything."

"We're under attack, man! They're blowing up New York. You need to turn on a TV."

David set the phone down and walked to the lobby of the mortuary, to the small TV mounted on the wall. All day long, a receptionist sat and watched game shows and read magazines and answered the phone. Her name was Bridget or Tania or Maggie. They never lasted long. He dug through her desk and found the remote, clicked the TV on. Watched the news. The president, a bunch of little kids standing behind him, said that terrorists had flown planes into the World Trade Center, that he was getting out of Dodge, and that God was blessing everyone. And then they were showing footage of a plane smashing into a building, over and over again. Confetti falling out of the sky, or maybe that was walls or bodies, the anchor saying all air travel had been canceled, that there were planes still out there, and no one was quite sure which were being flown by pilots, which were being flown by hijackers, maybe they'd start shooting planes out of the sky.

David clicked the TV off, tried to piece together what he'd seen, what the fuck it meant. Took out Agent Moss's Blackberry, turned off the ringer, because someone would be calling, eventually, then went back into the mortuary, picked up the phone.

"Are you still there, Ruben?"

"Yeah, man, Jesus, you see that?

"Ruben," David said, "I need you to listen to me. Are you listening to me?"

"Yeah, man, yeah," Ruben said. "What if they're coming here? We got all these big-ass buildings. They could be here right now."

"Ruben," David said, "the client is in the trunk of a car. I need you to call Miguel and tell him to stay home."

A baby screaming. Ruben's wife—Carla? Carlene? Cara?—speaking Spanish, fast. The TV too loud. More screaming from the baby. The sound of Ruben breathing. Now two boys talking. Kids getting ready for school, everyone watching cartoons or Al Roker and then, boom, planes into buildings. William would be at school already, Jennifer on her way to work.

"This coming from Mr. Savone?" Ruben said.

"No," David said. He thought about his next words carefully, decided it was the only solution. He'd figure out what was on the other side of it once Ruben got there. "This is coming from Rabbi Kales. And he says that if you're not here in the next twenty minutes, you and your entire family are going to be in the trunk, too."

•

BY THE TIME Ruben arrived, five minutes before seven, David had already canceled school, told his assistant, Esther, to notify everyone who worked at the temple to stay home, put up a CLOSED sign on the funeral home, and caught Kate Berkowitz on her cell phone in the car to cancel bar mitzvah class, "in light of the morning's event," and even recommended a part of the Talmud she could read with OG Sean B instead, "to help understand the existential questions he will surely begin to ask"—*Whoever destroys a single life is as guilty as though he had destroyed the entire world*—and was standing outside, beside the Cutlass, waiting.

Ruben usually drove a tricked-out red Ford F-150, being the kind of guy who liked to drive down to Laughlin with his wife and kids, hitch his boat—the *Loco Motion*—and a couple Sea-Doos to the back, spend the weekend on the river, David always hearing him tell Miguel how lucky he was, maybe he'd start hitting those dice again, like back in the day. David always wondered when that day was, exactly, since Ruben Topaz was no more than thirty-two, even though his oldest boy was already ten, then a five-year-old and a newborn, and probably another on the way, because he was Catholic. But David and Ruben kept it professional at all times, nothing personal. Both of them in their roles.

Bennie Savone had known Ruben since he was a teenager, put him through mortuary school in Arizona, set him up at the Kales Mortuary and Home of Peace, trusted him to run the entire shop, both legit and criminal. Families liked him. He was a good boss to the funeral home staff. Got shit done. Even volunteered to help coach the temple baseball team, since the Jews, man, they needed help with that. Was respectful to everyone. Firm handshake. Looked you in the eye when he spoke to you. Didn't rip off the public on caskets, even cut prices for people who really couldn't afford it— most Jews, all they wanted was a simple pine box, as per Jewish law, but those simple pine boxes had upgrades, too: silk lining, gold handles, inlaid platinum design work, make it nice for the graveside bit—or told them they could get a deal at Costco, since the real money was in the service. Plus, a lot of the dead were goyim who had married Jews, and so they didn't want to be buried without them, thus they'd get the full open-casket show, which was more money, but Ruben, he was fair about that, too, didn't gouge senior citizens burying their spouses or shocked out-of-towners tasked with getting their relatives into the ground. He was pretty good with flowers and linens, could arrange a plate of oranges to look like a rose; for five hundred dollars he could make a reception in the Home of Peace for twenty-five people, make it seem like it cost five thousand. Push came to shove, he'd bake cookies, cut up some apples, run down to the Bagel Café for a bagel and challah platter, some lox, comfortable and home-style. Whatever had to happen, Ruben Topaz handled it, always immaculately dressed, always empathetic, always ready with a tissue or a hug.

A mensch, if David was being honest about it.

This morning, though, Ruben rolled up in a black minivan, baby seat still in the backseat, UNLV sticker on the rear window, and got out wearing a pair of Adidas sweatpants, black Chuck Taylors, and a white tank top.

David had never seen Ruben without a suit. Now he understood why: Ruben's left arm was a full-sleeve tattoo of the Stratosphere hotel, the point of the tower disappearing under the strap of the tank top, and his right arm depicted the Virgin Mary tossing dice and coming up with the hard eight. Across his chest, just above the line of the tank and creeping up toward his neck, was the number 13. He was from the Barrio Naked City gang, which made sense. The Wild Horse was technically in BNC territory. Not a bad strategic partnership. Explained why there were never any stories of Gs from BNC shaking down anyone at the club or shooting it out with Rolling 60s in the parking lot—a thing that happened at Cheetahs every other weekend—not that Bennie would put up with that shit. And not that David thought Ruben would be out calling shots or doing drive-bys, seeing as he lived on the outskirts of Summerlin in a nongated development called the Vista at Terra Lago, across the street from St. Anne's Catholic school and church. David had a hard time imagining someone with two-carat diamond studs in his ears, or the diamond-studded cross around his neck like Ruben was also sporting this morning, getting much traction with the homies anymore. He was about as street as Rodeo Drive, even if he still had the ink from his old life.

"You looking at something?" Ruben said.

"You don't have a shirt with sleeves?"

"That's where we at?" Ruben said. "We're talking fashion? I wasn't even working today, right?" It looked to David like maybe Ruben had a gun tucked under his tank top, shoved in his waistband, though now he didn't trust his judgment on these matters. Not like David blamed him. Today was getting more and more fucked up as each minute passed. "My wife barely let me walk out. She's scared as shit, so let's do this, okay? I'm here."

"You have a gun there in your waistband?"

Ruben looked down at his stomach like he wasn't sure. "If I do, that change something?"

"No," David said. "Not unless you pull it out."

"Rabbi Kales here?"

"No," David said. "He sent me."

Ruben considered this. "Then no," Ruben said. "I got nothing on me."

They stood there for a few seconds, both of them sizing each other up, Ruben in his gangster leisure-wear, probably a loaded nine on his body, David in his suit, his Glock now inside his jacket, both coming to some conclusions about the other, though David suspected Ruben's were wrong.

David shrugged, popped open the trunk.

Ruben leaned in, got a better look. "Oh shit," he said, and recoiled. "I know her."

"What?"

"She's an inspector," Ruben said. He shook his head, like he was clearing something out. "Melanie." He pulled a pair of latex gloves from his pocket, snapped them on, tipped her body on one side, then the other. "She's wet. She shot?"

"No," David said.

Ruben put her back down, manipulated her head and neck. "Man, she's still warm." He looked up at David then. "What happened to her?"

"She stopped breathing," David said. "Then her heart stopped. Then she died."

"Her neck is broke." He held her chin between his thumb and index finger, like Dr. Melnikoff had done to David, moved her head back and forth. "Who dumped her off?"

"No one."

"She drove herself?" Ruben looking at him again, talking to him like he was a fucking dupe.

"That's right."

Ruben shook his head again, like he didn't understand what David was saying, went back to the body. "There's some ligature shit on her throat. Fuck, man." He sniffled. "Gotta find someone to torch this car," he said, more to himself than to David. "She's leaving material everywhere."

"What kind of inspector is she?"

"Huh?"

"You said she was an inspector. She a sheriff?"

"No. From the state."

"Gang enforcement?"

"No, man. Funeral homes," Ruben said. "Mortuaries. She comes through every couple months, makes sure everything is up to code. Been on the job, shit, five years?"

Five years. And David had never seen her. How had he missed this? "Like a health inspector?"

"Yeah," Ruben said, "but for the dead."

"What was she doing here?"

"I don't know," Ruben said. "Inspectors show up when they show up. They don't make appointments. That's the whole thing."

"She was looking for me. Do you know why?"

"You saw her before this happened?"

"That's right," David said. Ruben was maybe in a little bit of shock this morning, maybe wasn't computing all the numbers, was leaving remainders all around, trying not to get it all right, because Ruben, he was not a guy who wanted to know everything.

"I don't know," Ruben said again, but he didn't sound convinced of that, but then something else clicked and Ruben cocked his head, took the measure of David again, maybe really saw him, his face, his body, his suit, the way he was standing, how he wasn't scared, and that wasn't normal, for a person not to be scared in a situation where there was a dead body in a trunk, a man with a gun, and then everything that was stretching out on the other side of those things, all the possible endings.

A simple motherfucker would be scared.

"I really couldn't say," Ruben said.

"I need you to *know*," David said. "It's important. So think for a second. Why would she be looking for me?"

"Last time, maybe," Ruben said, still thinking, putting together his strategy. "She said we had to get Rabbi Kales off of some of the paperwork and get you on."

"Did you?"

Ruben took a step back. He didn't look like the killing type, David thinking that when he got those tattoos and bought that gun, he probably thought he could be the killing type, could be the kind of guy who would drive up on you and put a bullet into your house or your car. Today? If he was the killing type, he'd have pulled out that gun already. Because he was realizing he'd fucked something up, was trying to walk it back in his mind, because this dupe had murdered a girl and stuffed her in a trunk and was calmly standing in front of him.

"I thought I did that," Ruben said finally. "I thought I submitted everything."

"You think so because *you* did it," David said, "or because you had someone in the office do it for you?"

"It doesn't matter," Ruben said. "It was my job. If it didn't get done, that's on me. I take responsibility for my actions."

Huh.

"Okay," David said, momentarily content for the first time all day. "I respect that attention to duty."

Ruben looked at the body, spit on the ground. "Man, this is out of pocket. This is not how we do business."

It wasn't. David had fucked up. He recognized that. What the fuck was in his head?

The politics and territorial grudges of Temple Beth Israel. No one stabbing anyone in the back, everyone going straight for the face. Messy, ill-considered, hoodlum shit, that exposed everyone for who they really were. No one looking big picture.

David had let it distract him. Living in this ecosystem, David was angrier at Roberta Leeb than at the fact his plastic surgery was collapsing. Mad at Al Roker for talking shit on TV, not at Bennie for being too lenient with other families in town, this open-city bullshit allowing for one dumb fuck to cast everyone in a bad light. Mad at Casey Berkowitz for being a shitty father and husband, not mad at himself for being worse. At Sal Cupertine, for being dead, or missing, or on the news.

And now Ruben, standing there with his diamond earrings, the absurd topaz pinky ring he wore, tacky as fuck, but probably two Gs out the door. The boat. The Sea-Doos. The truck. Even the minivan was nice. Chrome rims. Professional tint job. Motherfucker wasn't getting rich, but he was comfortable enough to not give a shit about whatever detail this Agent Moss needed him to fix. Bennie had given Ruben such a long leash, it had turned into a noose around David's neck.

At least Ruben was taking responsibility. David appreciated that.

"This is how we do business now, Ruben," David said.

"This girl," Ruben said, "people know her here. I can't have her up on the table or in the refrigerator. Her picture is gonna be in the paper. People are gonna miss her. She's got a kid, man. You hear what I'm saying?"

David did, though he had a feeling nothing was going to be in the paper for a while, in light of what he saw on the TV. "She lives in Carson City?"

"Yeah, I mean, that's home base. She makes a circuit. Comes down here, goes out to Boulder City. Goes all the way up to Winnemucca." Ruben closed the trunk, but not all the way, just so he wouldn't have to look at her. "She comes down for the convention? In May? She's just a real nice person."

"She married?"

"No," Ruben said. But then he stopped himself. "I don't know. I guess maybe she was. I don't know."

David inched the trunk open, looked at Agent Moss's hands. She had a silver ring on her right thumb, which David should have noticed. No FBI agent was going into the field with a thumb ring.

An antique ruby number on her left middle finger. No flashy diamonds, two small understated studs in her ears. Ruben's were nicer.

"How old is the kid?"

"I don't know," Ruben said. "Six? Seven? She already had her when I met her."

"So it's a daughter?"

"Yeah," Ruben said. "Yeah, I think so."

"Okay." David thought for a moment. He couldn't just let this woman disappear, make this kid think her mother ran off and left her. That would be worse than knowing your mother had been murdered. You grow up thinking your mother went ghost on you? There was a generational guilt attached to that. Die tragically, it's a fucking shame, but a kid isn't gonna grow up blaming themselves for that. He'd killed a lot of motherfuckers in his time and yeah, they had kids. But part of how David reckoned with it was by picturing how much better those kids lives were without their scumbag fathers. And most of the time, it wasn't like these assholes just disappeared—their bodies were left right in the open. That was all part of the mythology. The Rain Man would walk right up and shoot you in the back of the head, didn't matter where you were standing. Kid found out about that, they started to ask questions, started to figure out the truth, understood it wasn't some random occurrence.

That wasn't the case here. He fucked up. He owed a debt. Physical and spiritual.

But by the same token, David wasn't gonna drop her body off at her house, dressed for church.

"I need you to get this body into the ground," he said eventually. "We got any holes dug?"

"No," Ruben said. "We didn't have anything on the books."

"Okay," David said again, still thinking. And then another thought: "You tell your wife I called you?"

"No," Ruben said.

Too fast.

"Think hard," David said, "because you've got that gun on you, which makes me think you left the house worried. Maybe told her there was a problem and you were gonna take care of it. Something like that didn't happen?"

"You said Rabbi Kales was putting me and my family in a trunk," Ruben said.

"If you were worried about them," David said, "you should have stayed home."

"My girl," Ruben said, "she's not one of these do-nothing *chavalas*. She needs to handle business, she handles business."

"What about your kids? They handle their business? Your five-year-old handle business? They know how to duck a sniper round? Your baby know what that red laser light is on his chest?" Ruben didn't say anything. "Something goes upside down with me? Those kids, your wife? They're already dead. Nothing you can do about that."

David watched Ruben figure out what it meant, or what it could mean: that there were people outside his house right now, baby and wife killers, waiting on some word from David. In real life that was some pussy shit, David did his own work, but Ruben, he'd grown up watching movies, this was a situation he'd envisioned before, so the scenario seemed more likely, since he'd probably seen it fifty times on Cinemax.

"So here's what happened," David continued. "Start getting it right in your head. I called you, told you the inspector was here. You came in, by the time you got here, she'd heard the news on the radio and she was worried, told you she was going to go home, be with her kid. And then she got in her car and drove away. You understand?"

Ruben stood up straight. Looked around. "Yeah," he said, this making sense to him. Wiped his nose and eyes with his forearm. Shit. Was this fucker crying? "So, I saw her?"

"You did. You can even describe what she was wearing. She waved at you as she drove by. Put you on a lie detector, you'd pass. But it's not going to come to that. Maybe a cop comes out here, maybe not. But if one does, tell the truth. You saw her, she was in her car. That's the truth."

"Man, this isn't some shit I know how to deal with, okay?" Ruben said. "Like mentally. She has a kid. I got kids. You know, I put myself in her place."

"You're going to take her inside," David said, and he was in full rabbi mode now. He was in charge. It was God talking. And God, He knew how to solve your problems. "You're going to clean her, every inch, from scalp to toe, then you're gonna black light her. Then you're gonna get a nice coffin ready. One of those fifteen-thousand-dollar numbers, okay? I'm going to go back to the temple, go through the clothes donations, find a nice outfit for her. You're gonna strip her, put all her effects in a medical waste bag, cinch it up tight." A plan coming into place. He'd done something like this before. A freelance job in St. Louis, a city councilman, except it ended up being an unsolved murder in Milwaukee. "Then we're going to put her down near a good family. There someone out there you like? Someone you admire?"

"Like personally?"

"Like personally."

Ruben wiped at his face again. "I guess I liked Mr. and Mrs. Zarkin."

Clark and Zadie. Zadie went first, Clark followed her a week later. Both in their eighties. No kids, but half the city had turned out for their funerals. Clark owned United Discount Mattress over on Spring Mountain. Everyone conceived in Las Vegas in the last four decades had him to thank.

"Good choice," David said. "You'll go out there with the backhoe and dig her a spot with them. You'll go home, be with your family, and this is over." David looked at his watch. "You move quickly, you can be home by nine thirty. You can move quickly, can't you, Ruben?"

"I don't know," Ruben began to say, but David put a hand up to stop him.

"Ruben," he said. "You *know*. You *know* everything. So if you say you don't know, that tells me I need to worry about you. I need to worry about the way you're feeling. I need to worry about who you're talking to, what you're saying to your wife, what you might say when you get home. And if I'm worried about it, Rabbi Kales is going to be worried about it, and Mr. Savone is going to be worried about it." David opened the trunk wide again. "Take a good look, Ruben, and then decide whether you *know* or you don't *know*."

Ruben stayed quiet for a few seconds. He reached into the trunk, adjusted Agent Moss's pant leg, which had ridden up a few inches, her calf showing. "Man," Ruben said, "I didn't show up for no senseless murder."

"You think those guys we've been burying cut their own faces off?"

"That's different," Ruben said.

"Not to their loved ones," David said. "You think grandma sleeps well with her grandson gone missing? There is no different. There is only alive and dead." He paused. "And whatever comes next, that's for God to know."

Here was this guy, trying to make moral equivalencies. Here was this guy, trying to figure out where he fit into all of this. Here was this guy, with his big truck, his boat, his van, his diamonds, his gun, his ink, his past, his present, his future, all tied up in the game, no way out now, probably never was. Born into a Mexican gang in the shadow of the Stratosphere, now an indentured servant to the Mafia, if Bennie was even really that. He was in a crime family, all right.

"I got a line, Rabbi," Ruben said. "I just try to keep it. Everybody got a line."

"When you're getting shanked in the prison showers for all you've done? All the bad motherfuckers you've crossed just by coming in here every day and doing your job?" David said. "Well, you tell them about that line. They'll get it. I promise. Meantime, my advice is get this shit done."

He let his words sit there, let Ruben hear his old voice in full, then began to walk toward the temple. David wasn't scared of getting shot in the back, because Ruben Topaz wasn't prepared to give up everything for that dead girl.

Which is what it came down to these days. What you were prepared to give it up for. David, he was prepared to give it up, every day, to see his wife and kid again.

It was a little after seven now. He needed to get this Cutlass back to Carson City. It was a seven-hour drive. Eight if you stopped for lunch, David thinking he'd need to check a map, figure out a midpoint, make it authentic on the GPS. People knew where Agent Moss was, she was a person with a schedule, which meant after she disappeared, cops would backtrack on her, get her on camera checking out of the Courtyard Inn, getting gas, maybe even ask to check the cameras at the temple or the funeral home, which was fine, they didn't record anything. They'd play it step by step. GPS on her phone was pinging right now, which meant Agent Melanie Moss was still alive, digitally, so they'd be able to ping her way home, too. Which worked out perfectly.

David was thirty feet away now, about to unlock the gate leading to the front of the funeral home, when Ruben called after him. "Or what?"

David turned back slowly, half expecting Ruben would have his gun out, frankly surprised to find Ruben where he left him, not running up on him, or in a crouch, or back in his van. Just standing there covered in shitty ink, beside a dead girl in a car trunk.

"Or try to quit," David said.

•

WHEN DAVID CAME back to the mortuary half an hour later, Melanie Moss was naked on the table and Ruben was cleaning the right side of her body. Her face and neck were already clean, all her makeup gone, and David could see that she had acne scars high up on her cheeks, as well as a C-section scar running under her belly, a tan line on her right pinkie toe from a ring. Ruben had changed into his scrubs, wore glasses and a surgical mask, was using a sponge that fit comfortably in the palm of his hand to scrub her. Ruben would work down to her feet, then start over on her left side, turn her over, clean her backside, right to left. Doing his job, as per Jewish law.

Well, except for the radio on the floor, news coming out in a steady hum.

"Put the clothes in the coffin, please," Ruben said, not looking up from his work. The coffin was already in the corner. Cherrywood. Platinum fixtures. The kind they sold to the goyim with real cash. The kind who wanted their bodies preserved, just in case all their sins were eventually forgiven and they got to come back. They normally put the Jews and war dead in unsealed pine boxes, which accelerated the dust-to-dust aspect.

"Don't worry," Ruben said, as if he'd read David's mind, "I cut slits into the bottom. Decomp will be the same."

"Good," David said. He set the clothes he'd found flat into the box. He'd picked out a nice St. John sweater set and black slacks that he vaguely remembered seeing on Helen Kellerman. "That's good thinking."

"Your bag is in the corner by the cold storage," Ruben said.

David found the bag, opened it up, looked inside. Shook it. Looked over at the body. Something wasn't right.

"Where's her jewelry?" David asked calmly. Ruben looked up, confused. "Her rings." Nothing. "Her earrings." Nothing. "Her fucking jewelry, Ruben," David said, not so calmly anymore. "Where the fuck is her jewelry?"

Ruben pulled down his mask, snapped off his gloves, dumped them in the garbage, walked back to the small metal desk where they kept forms and a manual typewriter, slid open a drawer, rifled around a bit, like he couldn't find what he was looking for, though David knew better, so he kept his eye on him, and eventually came out with a Ziploc bag containing Agent Moss's two rings, two diamond earrings, a toe ring, and an ankle bracelet. "Mr. Savone lets me keep what I find," Ruben said, though he handed the bag to David like it was contagious.

David couldn't believe this shit. Ruben was pulling six figures and was pinching from the dead on top of everything else. "Have some fucking respect for yourself."

"I got a family, too, man," he said.

"Yeah," David said, "that's my point. You shame them."

David unzipped the bag, shook the jewelry out into his hand. The silver thumb ring was the kind of thing you could win for doing particularly well at Skee-Ball on Navy Pier, same with the toe ring, a turquoise number. The earrings looked real, since they were too small to be cubic zirconium—no one faked having a quarter-carat diamond, after all. The ankle bracelet was three bands of intertwined gold, probably valued at a hundred bucks in a kiosk at the Meadows Mall right now, worth a third of that.

The ruby ring, however, was raised up in a gold base designed to look like a flower, though the gold had turned rough in places, dimpled with age. David ran his pinkie through the inside of the ring, felt how smooth it still was there, as if it had never been off a finger. He slipped it into his pocket, put the rest of the jewelry back in the Ziploc, looked over at Ruben. He had his shoulders hunched forward now, arms loose in front of him, was shaking out his wrists, like he thought maybe they were about to go at it. Fact was, if it came to a fistfight, David would probably have his hands full.

He handed Ruben the bag. "That's yours," he said. "Do with it what you want."

"Okay," Ruben said, "whatever you say." David didn't think he believed that.

"You ever open the Talmud?" David asked.

"No," Ruben said.

"Well, there's a line in it that says it's better to join the company of lions than assume the lead among foxes," David said. "I've always liked it. You know, found ways to apply it to my life in situations where I'm unsure about my actions. This minute, Ruben, you're a lion. Later on, you're gonna need to decide if you're a fox or not. I'm sorry Rabbi Kales had to threaten your family to get you here. I'm sorry you're afraid now. Living with dread is no way to live."

"How would you know?"

"Fear is physical. It's normal," David said. "Dread, that's your morality showing through. That's about you as a man, Ruben. That's something I understand."

"I worked hard to get to this place in my life," Ruben said, "so I don't react well to this kind of activity. I left that behind. I'm about family now. Not that G shit. That's not me. Rabbi Kales didn't need to get down like that with me and then send you, you know, because that could have turned bad for you. You could be on this table right now, but I respect Mr. Savone too much for that. So I do my job, I go home, I see what this bullshit is with the planes, and I try not to think about this shit here. So I'm a fucking lion, homie. Don't even question that." He lifted his chin toward Agent Moss's body. "But just to say? I do not condone what you did to Melanie."

"I'm getting that," David said, thinking, *But not so much that you ask why I did it.* Ruben was smarter than that.

"Okay," Ruben said, then he wiped his hands together like a blackjack dealer coming off shift. Hands clean. "Last we talk about it, then."

David tried to imagine what it must be like to be Ruben Topaz. To spend most of your waking time with the dead but have no control over your own life. Dread was indeed moral, but Ruben had made his deals, too. Still, David had to plant a tree before he left. It was something Rabbi Kales had taught him. *Talmud says to plant an acorn so that someone else may rest in the tree's shade or eat the tree's fruit, not so you may climb it.*

"You get her into the ground, everything looks good," David said, "I'll have a bonus for you. More valuable than that jewelry. Something for the holidays. Spread it around to the staff. That something you could make do with?"

"Probably," Ruben said. David thought Ruben likely had a pretty lucrative side business going with the personal effects of the dead, something he'd not considered before, something he couldn't believe he'd missed. Jews were buried covered in their jewels. He doubted most of it made it into the ground. Mob guys? They had more gold chains than Liberace. Triad fuckers wore every gem you could imagine. These last few months had probably been good to Ruben. "Yeah. Could be that would help. The hourly people, they'll want to get paid for today, even though we had to close." Ruben planting his own tree.

"Good," David said.

Ruben put the Ziploc bag back into the desk, found a new pair of gloves, and returned to work on Agent Moss's body without saying another word, David watching him clean her for a few moments. He needed to get on the road, but there was something bothering him.

"Was she religious?" he asked eventually.

Ruben looked up. "I didn't know her like that."

She wasn't wearing a cross, but David supposed that didn't matter. Not everyone wore their faith.

"Are you?" David asked. Ruben's giant cross was under his scrubs now, same with the Virgin Mary and her hard eight.

"I have my beliefs."

"You mind if I say a prayer?"

"I don't think she was Jewish," Ruben said, "whatever she was."

"It won't affect her passage into the next life," he said. "The prayer is *for* the living."

Ruben shrugged, so David went and stood beside him, stared down at the body. The cleaning solvent Ruben was using had a light lemon scent, like Pine Sol, and David was reminded of how quickly a body went from a person to a thing to a problem. In our wickedness, Talmud said, we are utterly consumed. And yet, the body. Always the body, left behind for those with earthly problems to worry on.

"In your hands, O Lord, we humbly entrust our brothers and sisters. In this life you embraced them with your tender love," David said. "Deliver them now from every evil and bid them eternal rest." He paused. Not like how he paused during Naomi Rosen's wedding ceremony, but because he found himself imagining Agent Moss's daughter, the evil she would believe in, the evil that was real, the evil that was him. "The old order has passed away. Welcome them into paradise, where there will be no sorrow, no weeping or pain, but fullness of peace and joy with your Son and the Holy Spirit, forever and ever."

"Amen," Ruben said.

"Amen," David said.

He gathered up the bag of Agent Moss's clothes, checked that he had her keys in his pocket, her ring, her phone. Pulled out his gun, let Ruben see it, ejected the clip, inspected it to make sure it was full, jammed it back in. Kept it in his hand.

"I'll be back tonight," David said. "The Temple, the school, and the funeral home are closed. I'll reopen the temple in the morning for services; we'll see about the school, depending upon what the news is. Either way, I expect it to be a busy day. Could be a big day for heart attacks and strokes. If it gets bad, could be some suicides, too, so maybe place a call to Jerry Ford first thing tomorrow, get him ready for an influx." Ruben nodded slowly, watching him. "Soon as you're finished, go be with your family. I'll expect you here first thing in the morning. We clear?"

"Yes," he said. The radio on the floor bleated out a warning. There might be a plane headed to the White House. "What do your books say about aliens blowing up New York?"

"It wasn't aliens, Ruben," David said.

"Whatever, man," Ruben said. "You got something I can take home to my wife and kids? Some prophecy?"

"I don't believe in prophecy," David said.

"What do you believe in?"

David had a day in front of him. Could be he'd need to come back and kill Ruben Topaz and his entire family, though he hoped it didn't come to that. "Kingdoms arise and kingdoms pass away," David said. "Israel endures for evermore."

"We're not in Israel," Ruben said.

"It's the idea."

"My kids," Ruben said, "they don't get *the idea*."

"Everything dies," David said. "But maybe everything that dies someday comes back. Tell them that."

Ruben took this in, David wondering if Ruben would ever hear "Atlantic City" or even remember this conversation . . . though David had a sense maybe the things happening today would be hardwired. His kids would just want to know that all the dead people might show up again one day. A little magical thinking. And, if David was any indication, the dead coming back happened with more frequency than people really thought.

David stuffed his gun back into his coat, picked up the bag of clothes, and headed out.

"You even really a rabbi?" Ruben asked before David got to the door.

"You really an undertaker?" David asked. He thought of something, came back a few steps, grabbed a box of disposable gloves.

Ruben looked around the room, at the body of Melanie Moss, back at David. "I suppose I am," he said.

"Then I suppose I'm a rabbi," Rabbi David Cohen said.

12

Eight hours from Las Vegas, David pulled off the road in Dayton, a few miles outside Carson City. He'd made one stop already, thirty minutes in the parking lot of the Mizpah Hotel in Tonopah, just to make sure the bread crumbs were being left in the right places, Agent Moss's Blackberry plugged in the whole time, ringer off, the GPS pinging into outer space, tracking him, watching the phone glow with each new call. He answered the phone a few times, stayed silent, heard a man, a woman, another man, a child, all saying some variation of "Hello? Can you hear me?" and then he would hang up or wait a few seconds for the phone to lose its signal, the northern stretch of desert through Nevada a cell phone graveyard until you went through the little towns that sounded like country songs—Coaldale to Hawthorn up past Walker Lake into Stagecoach. He'd come this way once before, so he knew the path, except he'd ended up in Reno that time, where he dumped Hopper's car, made some phone calls, stole a car from the airport, and drove home. He'd need to make different plans today. He had a feeling people would be looking at every car and truck that came in and out of airports for a while, had a feeling some darkness was coming down, the news on the radio growing more bleak by the minute, the Towers now dust, the Pentagon all fucked up, that other plane ditched in Pennsylvania, government in a fucking bunker somewhere.

Talmud said not to be daunted by the enormity of the world's grief, pay attention, finish your fucking job, which David was trying to do. Still, David understood that this was one of those days that people were going to remember with crystal clarity, the kind of day where you remembered precisely where you were when you first heard the news, where even small, insignificant things would seem larger in memory. He'd need to get his story straight. *The radio. On the way to work. Canceled school immediately. Went home and called my family. Stayed glued to the TV all day. Couldn't believe it.*

Except Rabbi David Cohen didn't have any family. Yet another inauthentic moment he'd need to create in order to seem normal. David couldn't even share real horror with real people. And wasn't that some shit. If he were home, what would he be doing? Telling Jennifer it was going to be fine. Keeping William away from the TV. Thinking about where all of his guns were. That if some motherfuckers showed up in Chicago, he wouldn't wait around. They'd get in the car and head north. What was Jennifer doing on her own? What was she telling their son? Had she bothered to call Sal's mom? Christ. His mom. She'd be out of her mind. She was scared of flying as it was, said it was dangerous. Maybe she was right.

That said, he'd picked a good day to fuck up. Better than the last time, at any rate. What is one murder on a day of so many? He wouldn't be heading out of town in a frozen meat truck, but he also wasn't going to chance anything by rolling into Reno, not with cameras everywhere, so midway through the trip he decided Dayton would be a good place to execute the first part of his plan.

It was an Old West town on Highway 50 that hadn't been sufficiently revitalized into a tourist trap yet. It was still just old and west, hardly looked like a town: two gas stations, Dotty's Casino, the Pizza Factory ("We Toss 'Em! They're Awesome!"), windswept clapboard houses with shitty boats on blocks in the driveway, and an actual Main Street, which had the old red-brick Union Hotel in the middle of it, a saloon and flophouse from 1870, according to the sign. The rest of the street was dotted with similarly decrepit buildings that David imagined one day would become art galleries, gelato stores, places to get saltwater taffy and fudge and various kinds of jerky, one of those joints that sold candles with your name on it, a

Starbucks, a handmade jewelry shop, or something else called a shoppe, David never sure what the dividing line was.

He'd picked Dayton for a reason, and on the other side of Main Street, he found what he was looking for: Across a two-lane frontage road, where yellow flags snapped in the wind atop twenty-foot-tall poles, a giant billboard touted new starter mansions surrounding the EXCLUSIVE! ARNOLD PALMER–DESIGNED SIGNATURE COURSE AT THE DAYTON VALLEY GOLF CLUB! EASY ACCESS TO THE DAYTON EXECUTIVE AIRPARK! IF YOU VACATIONED HERE YOU'D NEVER LEAVE! THIS WAY! He'd been getting real estate mailers about this place every week for the last year, an outfit called YourDesertHomeSource.com mailing him postcards of his very same Summerlin home cut-and-pasted into the countryside in Dayton. Get *away from it all*, the mailers said, *in your own home!*

David wound through the development—it was already mostly built out, a hundred-plus homes encircling a verdant golf course— until he found the remaining model homes, all lined up along La Costa Avenue near the intersection of Palmer and Royal Troon.

David crept slowly around the block of perfect homes filled with no one, the fake street empty even though the houses kept their blinds opens, lights on, TVs running. That was the con, David knew, to imagine that house was yours, those blinds ones you chose, that light your safety, that TV your escape. There were no cars, no people, even the real estate developer's trailer was closed, just a flapping yellow flag out front, a closed sign hung in the window. David didn't see any cameras anywhere, and why would there be?

Everything inside a model home was an imitation, and even still, the developers locked the good-looking stuff down. Back in the day when he and Jennifer thought they might move to Batavia when he got straight—whenever that was, since it was more her dream than his—Jennifer would drag him to open houses of new developments and they'd imagine their lives, Jennifer pointing out how couches were anchored into the carpet, TVs screwed into the bureaus, even pillows were tied discreetly into place. He had the vague notion then, even still, that getting some boys together and robbing model homes might be an easy score, breaking into a house where no one lived the sort of thing that seemed like a no-brainer; but then he saw that the leather sofa was pleather, that the TVs were off-brand, that the refrigerators were hollowed out, just shells, no motors. The boys could come in with pickaxes and take out the copper wiring, but no one wanted to sweat to get paid, they wanted the score, and the score wasn't something you rolled up your sleeves on. It was something that dropped at your feet, you turned it around the next day, or the next hour, and then you bought what you wanted with the cash, which was usually some H, or a girl, or you tossed it on some dice and it was gone, all the same.

When he and Jennifer did buy a house, in Lincolnwood, it was older—built in the '60s—and had some character, nothing granite inside, nothing stainless steel, just 1,600 square feet of dark wood floors and drafty windows, fully grown trees in the front yard where he hung a tire swing, a backyard you could have a BBQ in and not feel like your neighbors could hear your every word, a single-car garage, which was fine, because they only had the one. It wasn't Batavia and he wasn't a Straight Guy, but it was normal enough that he could raise a family, not run into the wives and sons and daughters of the people he had killed.

Not often, anyway.

His Summerlin doppleganger was the last model, the largest they currently offered: two stories, 4,500 square feet, a home theater, a built-in gym, imitation hardwood floors, a three-car garage, RV-compatible parking. It didn't have the six-foot wrought-iron gates or the cherub fountains David had—people in Dayton didn't seem like cherub people, much less people who needed an extra level of protection in case the U.S. Marshals came crashing through the gates—and he was also pretty sure it hadn't been wired up with CCTV and bugs that fed directly into Bennie Savone's home. Nor did the house have a closet that had been retrofitted into a soundproof gun safe, racked to the ceiling with handguns and rifles, nor did it have a

bookshelf stacked with the holy books of the Jewish faith, or a portable foundry in the backyard to melt evidence . . . though the sign out
front did say all the houses were LEED certified and customized to fit
any buyer. That got David wondering who'd done the original construction upgrades on his house in the first place.

David parked alongside the white picket fence to his fake yard,
across the street from a green belt. It was surrounded by hip-high
iron fencing, put up to make sure no one got too close and smudged
the paint, or fucked with the flower bed, or yanked at the artificial
grass. You could only look at your future. Touching wasn't allowed.

He put on his hat, snapped on a pair of disposable gloves, got out
of the car, took Agent Moss's purse from the backseat, wiped it down
with a handy-wipe, dropped the antique ring into it, zipped it up,
and tossed it over the fence.

Someone would find the purse tomorrow, someone decent.

Someone looking to buy a house.

Someone that would eventually get that ring back to Agent
Moss's daughter, if Ruben was even right about that. Or maybe it
would be the next day. Maybe next week.

He'd been listening to the radio for eight hours and he wanted
to pretend that he was feeling fine, that he'd seen some shit in this
life. That people had shot at him and he'd never been hit. That he
should be fucking dead, really. That he always thought he'd end up
buried in a field somewhere, if he was lucky enough to get a burial;
more likely someone would chop him up into little pieces, because if
you catch the Rain Man you're not going easy on him, and that
prepared him for the unexpected things the world might offer. He'd
seen pictures and videos of tornados and earthquakes and war and
suicide bombers and all that real-life CNN shit. Everyone had. But
he'd *witnessed* a body go off a building. He knew what that looked
like. He knew what that sounded like. Most people? They didn't
know. And a part of him thought that witnessing his father that way
had turned him into this . . . thing. The Rain Man. A man who
doesn't forget.

And maybe it did. Played some role, anyway.

But it got him wondering today, specifically, if everyone was watching the TV, seeing all those bodies hitting the ground? Or even the people in New York. Thousands of them, all seeing that shit. Would there be, after this, thousands of people like him? Millions? Would it devalue what it meant to be a human?

Like what he'd done today. To a woman. That wasn't the job.

That was Sal Cupertine, thinking he didn't want to go to jail. That was Sal Cupertine, thinking he'd never see his wife or kid again. He'd done it for personal reasons. Not business at all. He'd killed her and he felt . . . not good. Bad, if he was being honest. It took him back to sitting in his father's car, waiting with his mother, and then, boom, there's a fucking puddle on the sidewalk. Thirty years he'd been dealing with that puddle of shit.

Used to be he'd drive five miles out of the way just to avoid seeing the shadow of the IBM Building. But as time went on, the streets of Chicago filled with places he'd rather forget, so he stopped avoiding anything. Jewish custom taught that you should meet all sorrow standing up. Sal Cupertine didn't know about that shit, but he did it anyway, tried to impart that to his son, tried to show that to Jennifer, that they'd chosen a kind of life and there was no turning back on it now. You did something? Live with it.

"It's a great place to live, if you're wondering."

David turned to see a man in a golf cart with a standard poodle sitting beside him. The dog hopped off the seat and ran over to the greenbelt, immediately squatted and pissed. How long had David been standing there, looking at his ersatz house? A minute? Five? His head wasn't right. He was sure of it now. Or maybe David was just getting soft. Too many days spent listening to people talk about their problems, not enough days solving them. He was getting lax. Letting shit stand that could not stand.

That wouldn't do.

David put his arms across his chest, let his right hand rest on his gun. If this was going to be his day, well, he'd had worse.

"Looks like it," David said.

"The HOA is a bunch of Communists, but you get used to it." The man was in his seventies, at least. Looked like the kind of guy who was in a former life maybe an airline pilot or a Southern governor. Aviators and a zip-up sweater sporting the logo of the golf course. His golf cart looked like a miniature Bentley, leather seats, dark wood dash, fat tires with rims, the whole deal.

"You live here full-time?"

"No," he said. "I'm a snowbird. Down from Manitoba. Winnipeg."

"That so," David said, an idea taking root.

"Except now," he said, "we don't wait for the snow. Perk of being retired. Go back and forth as I see fit."

"You going home soon?"

"End of the week was the plan," he said, "but then I saw the news today and me and Mitzy," he nodded toward the poodle, "are probably going to pack up tomorrow and hit the road. I've got an RV, so we're portable. No sense waiting around for some lunatic to drop a bomb on Reno."

"If it's just the two of you," David said, giving him a chance, "you should leave now."

"Confirmed bachelor," he said. "Never did see a good reason to get tied down." The man lifted up his glasses, put them on top of his head, so David tipped his hat down, cast a shadow over his face. "You single?"

"Married."

"Too bad," the man said. "Surprising amount of tail here. Divorcees. Widows. You fix a sink for one of them, you're basically in the system. Young guy like you, you'd have your pick."

"That's not me."

"That's every man." He whistled and Mitzy came bounding across the street, hopped back into the cart. "Anyway. Day like today just confirms the whole world is a bucket of shit," the man said, like they were in the middle of a different conversation. "I see you work for the government." He pointed at the license plate. "You got a busy week in front of you. You undercover? CIA or something?"

"Bureau of Land Management," David said.

"Oh yeah? What's that like?"

"I enjoy being outside."

The man nodded, considering this. "Yeah, but then you got all of those militia people causing trouble to deal with, right? Grazing rights and whatnot? Sovereign nation this, sovereign nation that. We got some of that in Canada, too. French separatists and the kind."

"Every country has something."

"You won't be seeing anyone flying planes into buildings in Canada, that's for sure." He patted his left hip and that's when David saw he had a little holster and gun there. Maybe a .22. Good for shooting pheasants. Not much else.

"You think that will stop a plane?"

"No," he said.

"You should leave," David said, "while you still can."

"Yeah," he said. "It's getting worse. But what can you do? Not many undesirables here, even with the golf," he said. "Anyway, look me up if you buy. I live over on Snead Place."

"What number?"

"Eight two one," he said. "Got my own block at this point. Bunch of Chinese came in and bought up the other houses. They're just sitting empty. Prospectors, I guess. Like the Gold Rush, but the Chinese already have all the gold, right?"

"Maybe I'll come by later tonight," David said. "Sure would like to get a look inside one of these before I head back."

"Where's back?"

"Las Vegas."

"Can't stand the place," he said. He reached up and scratched at his nose. The skin on his hands was pink and scaly.

David stripped off his gloves, stuffed them in his pocket, came over to the golf cart, let Mitzy smell him, then he scratched the top of her head, along her neck, made sure she was comfortable with him. She began to lick at his wrist. Good. Passive. He rubbed inside her ears, until she made a cooing sound deep in her throat. He put his face in front of hers, held her head in his hands, let the dog sniff his face, lick his nose. The man turned in his seat, watched the whole show.

"That dog," the man said, "would roll over if Charles Manson showed her some attention. Indiscriminate bitch, that one."

David could reach over right now, grab that .22, and shoot this asshole in the face. Could tip over the golf cart, crush this old man under it. But he'd probably kill the dog, too. He didn't want to do that.

"Seven too late to come by?" David asked. "I need to drop my car back off at work before the boss gets on my ass."

"Seven's fine," the man said.

David stood up, snapped his gloves back on. Took back hold of the dog, see if she'd try to wrench out of his grasp with gloves on, but she didn't. He kissed her on the top of her nose, let her go.

"Mind if I ask what's with the gloves?"

"Psoriasis," David said.

"Me, too," he said, brightening. "Part of why I come down here in the first place. Weather agrees with my skin."

"Nice weather," David said.

He patted Mitzy on the back. "You know where to find me. Happy hour starts in five minutes and goes until dawn." He gave David a wave and pulled off, but then the cart stopped and the guy put it in reverse, rolled back up to David.

"I'm a real asshole," he said. "I didn't even ask your name. I'm Roger."

"You can call me Sal," David said.

"All right," he said. Mitzy the poodle turned in her seat and watched David intently as the cart drove off, David thinking Ruben Topaz's kids were about to get a present and that Mitzy would finally get some unconditional love.

•

BY FIVE THAT evening, David was parked across the street from a Walmart Supercenter only a few blocks from Agent Moss's house. It was in what looked to be a relatively gentrified part of Carson City, a new subdivision hacked into an old neighborhood and surrounded by big-box stores. It was, David thought, a vast improvement. Carson City was another in a series of shitty state capitals David had visited in his life. Springfield? Shithole. Jefferson City? Shithole. Lansing? Shithole. A few years back, he flew to Jamaica and killed five guys in one day in Kingston, and Kingston was a shithole, too. Tonight, parked in the shadow of a closed henna tattoo shop called Inkt, the storefront of a psychic reader, and a Sir Speedy Printing, the news radio scaring the living fuck out of him, David found the sight of the Walmart Supercenter oddly soothing. Civilization kept moving, even when it seemed like it was about to close up shoppe.

He unplugged Agent Moss's Blackberry, opened the back panel, slid out the green battery and the SIM card, then dropped the phone on the pavement outside the car, stomped it to pieces, kicked the remnants into the street. He wiped down everything he'd touched inside the car with handy wipes, even though he'd worn gloves the entire time, rolled down all the windows, left the keys in the ignition, put Agent Moss's suitcase on the front passenger seat, got out, yanked his hat down.

David walked up the street a few blocks, which had him in an older neighborhood of mismatched houses on pockmarked streets. There was a stop sign covered in gang graffiti a block from a model-home development called Winter River Creek Estates—"estates" apparently now houses on a quarter-acre parcel of scrub, but with parking for a boat or RV that would never materialize—and David had to pause to decipher the codes, figure out just who might be coming around the corner. Not that he was worried. He had his gun. He had his knife. He had more than half of a fucking brain. Street gangsters would spend ten minutes talking shit to you, asking where you were from, who you were with, before deciding if they were gonna jack you, stomp you, shoot you, whatever. David saw someone who even looked vaguely threatening on his walk? He'd put one between their eyes. It wasn't even a thing. Not today.

No one seemed to notice David, the sun still out, air hot and sticky, at least eighty, and still, no breeze. Fall was coming up, but in this neighborhood, with the heat pushing up from the concrete, it still felt like a summer.

Couple more blocks, he was in an area of mixed-use housing, which just meant shitty apartments on top of vintage clothing stores and coffee shops—a new name for living in a fucking tenement above the Goodwill and the greasy spoon—and then a few minutes later, he was back in the glow of the Supercenter, entering the shopping plaza from the opposite direction to where he'd left the Cutlass. The car wouldn't last an hour by David's estimation, not with the lot lizards he spied wandering around, the twenty-four-hour Supercenter like a regional hub for trucker speed, runaways, and tweaks of all measures, plus there was a shitload of minivans, Ford trucks, and eight different kinds of cars that looked like Honda Accords, which meant bored teenagers stuck with their parents, who might wander off, see the car, call a friend. Everyone was a potential thief these days.

David tugged his hat lower. Put a hand to his mouth. Rubbed at his cheeks. His whole face covered, nothing facial recognition would be able to make out, at least not according to what David had learned reading up on the technology, which had become one of his favorite hobbies, second only to figuring out the decomposition rate of the human body and how it could be hastened. A camera might catch him—he was a six-foot-tall white man with a beard, wearing a hat, a big coat. He adjusted his gait, gave himself a slight limp, like a pulled muscle in his hip.

He was as unmemorable as a hangnail. Perfect.

There was a greeter standing just inside the door of the store. He was old, white, and had eight hundred stickers and buttons on his blue vest, David thinking about the humps retired out in Sun City, Mob guys from all over the country who'd settled in a master-planned senior citizen community in Las Vegas that had a private movie theater, book clubs, bunco tournaments, pancake breakfasts, even put out a sexy beefcake calendar touting the hotness of men who hadn't pissed in a single stream in twenty years. Fucks who'd made their bones on shakedowns and loan sharking now cheating at canasta for kicks.

David craned his head to the right of the greeter, found what he was looking for—the battery disposal bin—next to a display touting discounts on all Hostess items. Walmart getting three and a half bucks to slowly kill small children. Not a job David would take, but everyone had a price.

There were four cameras pointed at the door.

Angle was poor, nothing straight on, because the footage was probably being fed into some massive database in Kansas, run through by market researchers once a week, looking for trends, not criminals. Walmart didn't care if you stole something from their stores. They didn't want some kind of takeover bullshit, but anything short of that? They half expected it. It made the whole enterprise safe.

If people thought they could lift some razors or cold medicine without catching a bullet, it built community trust, so crooks would come back when they had money to buy a blender or microwave or a Mr. Coffee. But to Walmart, it was all just a ploy to stop neighborhood assholes from doing a strong-arm robbery. Make the store an important part of the ecosystem, a place you could do a little petty theft *and* buy your mother a card on her birthday? That made it sanctuary.

In Chicago, the Family had bars and strip clubs spread out across the region, made sure if the boys wanted to go out and fuck shit up, they'd do it in a friendly establishment, no cops, no unvetted girls. Not that the boys knew that, but Cousin Ronnie understood the *omerta* didn't mean shit once most people got loaded or fell in love, most humps not exactly CIA, so they'd end up giving classified intel up for a bit of pussy or a bit of H, so Ronnie, he made sure no one was getting into shit by controlling the flow of people, drugs, and liquor. If you rolled up into Miller's in Andersonville and weren't in the Family, they'd let you in, might even let you stay a bit, but the bouncer would have run your driver's license number, the bartender would have your Visa, and if you stepped out of line, your fucking house would burn down and your credit would be ruined.

He grabbed a cart. He had a kit to put together. He went through his list. Ax. Bleach. Tarp. Rain pants. He'd get dog food. That would be a nice detail and one he could use. In his mind, Roger was already dead and David was already in his RV driving back to Las Vegas, but he still had to handle that shit. He'd bring the body with him. So he'd need some ice. Best to maybe get that in Dayton afterward. Hard to explain to a cab driver why he needed to put fifty pounds of ice in his trunk, in addition to the ax and whatnot. But that was the only reasonable way to do this, that way David could sell Roger's parts to LifeCore, make a profit on the deal, give the money—and the dog—to Ruben. See if Gray Beard could use another RV. Or just torch it.

He dropped Agent Moss's battery and SIM in the recycle bin, wheeled past the pharmacy, past the display of Halloween costumes and candy, not even the middle of September and everything was orange and black. Past the party supplies, past the office supplies, and into the electronics section, where he thought he'd pick up a black light before he headed to the garden section, which is where the bulk of his murder kit was housed, David having bought enough kits in Walmart over the years to have a system down. Except this time there was a wall of TVs all tuned to the news, the sound low, New York City exploding over and over again. People were huddled there, their carts overflowing with bottles of water, shotgun shells, lanterns, all manner of camping supplies, more Spam than David had ever seen in one place, the end of the world apparently meaning you had to eat potted meats.

"What are we waiting for?" a teenager in a backwards red UNLV hat asked the crowd. He was a white kid whose jeans were belted too high, and he was chewing on a straw.

"President is coming on," a man in a fake-fur lined denim jacket said. "Everyone else is in an undisclosed location, I guess."

The teenager nodded. Flipped his hat around. Bent the bill nervously, turned the hat back around. Gnawed on his straw.

A few seconds later, when the president appeared on the screen looking like a guy who wasn't even supposed to come in that day, a young black guy in a blue vest walked up with a remote control, turned up the volume on the biggest TV—a 50-inch LCD—and everyone pushed a little closer.

David hadn't voted, of course. Never had. He wasn't real fond of this guy, wasn't real fond of the last guy . . . or the guy before that . . . or the guy before that, but he wasn't real fond of anyone who worked in the government.

He had operated under the belief that you could walk up and shoot a guy in the back of the head in public because people couldn't make sense of it. And if they could—if they were an off-duty cop or had been in Desert Storm or Vietnam or Korea or some covert ops shit—no one was inclined to get involved with a motherfucker who'd kill a person in broad daylight. It wasn't the order of things. Maybe the whole world was becoming like that.

David, though, was always watching, because Cousin Ronnie had taught him that calamity was an opportunity. Extortion and rackets worked only when people felt like there was no one to enforce the laws. This shit in New York would have Chicago going bananas.

Motherfuckers would start disappearing, because the gangsters in Chicago had institutional memory, and David wasn't just thinking about the Family. He was thinking about the Russians. The Mexican gangs. The Vice Lords. These were legacy businesses. The time to make money, the time to get over on everyday people—which is where real profit lived, not stealing from other gangsters—was when they were scared about something else.

Russians would be doing mortgage scams on old ladies first thing in the morning, would have fake charities for the victims by sundown, would be boosting expensive cars from the driveways of Streeterville redbricks by midnight, the blue glow of TVs in windows the sign that no one was paying attention to what was happening on their own street.

The Latin Kings would be selling protection to the migrant workers worried that they were about to be rounded up, because when war came along, Americans had a rich history of looking to put brown and yellow people into camps or drive them to the border.

The Vice Lords would turn on their credit card fraud game, park themselves in the suburban gas station mini-markets with card duplicators, ready for the rush of people like the ones standing in front of David right now. Buy twelve gallons of unleaded in Peoria, five hours later, in St. Louis, your entire bank account would be drained.

The Family? They'd be open 24/7 now. They'd amp up their marijuana and opiate distribution, since bad news meant people wanted to feel high, not paranoid, so they'd push their coke game to the side for a bit. They'd get their Gangster 2-6 corner boys loaded up with some good shit, or give their old shit a new name, rebrand existing products. They'd up their business in the colleges around Chicago and Milwaukee and Detroit, college kids always seeking an influx of drugs when the social order seemed tenuous, the Family learning that going back to the sixties. They'd get their guys who ran the high-priced girl business some pills—Oxy, Klonopin, Viagra—so visiting businessmen could have a real party, but maybe give them a roofie instead, take the motherfucker's Rolex and black American Express and snap a few photos of him nude, with some girl riding him, start up that blackmail business, make some cash on the regular. Then they'd get some fresh girls into the highway strip clubs in the corridor between Chicago and St. Louis, start selling blow jobs at a cut rate for a few weeks, then make the product scarce, turn up the price, make that demand come alive again. Stock market would drop, the Family would start making lower-than-usual-interest loans. A month from now, the Family would come to collect, start moving that interest up, start taking cars, start taking jewelry, start taking electronics, start taking teeth. Two months, fuckers would be getting second and third mortgages to pay off the Family, but by then it would be too late. The Family would have someone make you a cash offer. For your five-hundred-thousand-dollar home, they'd offer fifty thousand and a clean debt, and you'd take it, quit-claim the house to some motherfucker named Gino, because you'd rather owe the bank whatever was left on your mortgage than owe the Family your fucking life. The Family would then sell that house and keep the profit, or they'd set it on fire, or worse, they'd live in it.

"Immediately following the first attack," the president said, "I implemented our government's emergency response plans. Our military is powerful, and it's prepared."

"That's right," Denim Jacket said. He looked at David, nodded his head like they'd agreed to something. Maybe they had, just by standing there together. "No one fucks with us." David wanted to point at the screen and ask if this wasn't someone fucking with us, what was? Everyone got fucked with. That's what David had learned. What mattered was who had your back afterward. Last two thousand years or so, Jews had learned the hard way that it was easy for people to push their empathy to one side, the whole world a mob when no one was willing to stand up for you. Which, David thought now, was why Israelis were obligated to serve in the military. For days like today. You had to be in the company of lions.

"I have directed the full resources of our intelligence and law enforcement communities to find those responsible and to bring them to justice," the president said, and David immediately felt worse. They couldn't find Sal Cupertine. How the fuck were they going to find who did this? Audacious acts were committed by confident people. That was the whole thing. Naming them meant nothing.

It was how the system worked.

Responsibility meant nothing.

The money was in retribution.

The FBI knew the Family was responsible for killing hundreds, probably thousands, of people since the turn of the last century, just in Chicago. All that happened as a result were a lot of movies, shitty

TV shows, novels, and true crime books about guys named Vinnie the Ice Pick. Only a couple dozen consequential people did any real time. Mostly, it was only foot soldiers rotting in prison. David couldn't see how this would be any different. Murder was an industry, from the street up to the White House. History didn't sleep on this sort of thing. It fed on it.

He remembered his dad telling stories about listening to Pearl Harbor on the radio with *his* dad, knew all the stories about how the Five Families and all their associates helped the government for those few years. New York, Chicago, Miami, even those Dixie white supremacist fucks geared up. Sentences got commuted so guys who spoke Italian could assist on the docks with spying. Capos took to planes in the Pacific theater to bomb Japs. Humps were sent out to do up-close fighting in France. Cupertines and Gambinos and Bonannos crossed the Rhine and shot krauts in the back as they fled.

Everyone came back heroes, the whole nation saved by gangsters.

Except a lot of those motherfuckers came back from the war with a taste for killing, knew how to do it more effectively, passed that shit on through the generations, figured out that if you could desensitize a young guy, you wouldn't have to worry about him getting tossed up, end up going state's because of the night terrors and shit. David was nineteen the first time he did a legit hit, but by that point, it was semantics only, seeing as he'd beaten and tortured dozens of motherfuckers by then, had left plenty of people for dead.

Thinking on it now, surrounded by these terrified people in the fucking Walmart Supercenter, it seemed stupid.

When he cut off Otto Agostini's right hand and left foot, did he think the motherfucker just got a hook and a peg leg and then moved to St. Louis or Memphis or Detroit, went to college, got married, had a couple kids, everything was cool? Or what about when he and Fat Monte were dispatched to stomp out a Bandido who'd come up from Springfield to try to move girls and coke up around UIC? He and Fat Monte were both barely seventeen, amped on speed themselves, giddy to fuck someone up. They'd found the Bandido on his chopper parked out on Taylor Street, pulled him off, went to work on him right there in front of Pompei, left him with his fucking hip bone pushed out through his jeans, one eye in the gutter, all his fucking teeth in his throat, set his bike on fire, dinner crowd watching like it was a mime show on Navy Pier. Fat Monte maybe even cut him with his knife, he wouldn't say afterward, but Monte, he liked knife work, slice a guy in the ribs, he might not even feel it, then twenty minutes later, he'd be walking down the street, fall down dead, his spleen bleeding out into his gut.

And truth was, no one was safe anywhere. Everybody dies, baby. That's a fact.

Which was the problem. Sal Cupertine was alive. Sal Cupertine's wife was alive. If motherfuckers in Chicago started to make moves, if Ronnie was already in the hospital, then that meant someone might come for Jennifer, close that circle up tight. David had Ronnie's guys at bay, but if Ronnie was done, whomever he'd trussed up in the past might want to make a statement, kill the Rain Main's family, show that they were scared of nothing, because, really, who the fuck was gonna be upset if the Rain Man's family was on a slab somewhere, what with the whole fucking world coming to a burning end?

That's what David couldn't shake. He'd missed so many days with Jennifer and William. Knew that when he eventually did get back with them, nothing would be the same. Maybe they wouldn't love him anymore. Maybe he wouldn't know how to love them anymore. How many shitty days had they experienced alone? And then today. If Sal Cupertine came to Rabbi David Cohen, what would David tell him? That Talmud says you know a man's true character by his anger. That a hero is one who converts an enemy into a friend. That one must not wait for a miracle, one must create his own outcome.

"Tonight, I ask for your prayers for all those who grieve," the president said, "for the children whose worlds have been shattered, for all whose sense of safety and security has been threatened. And I pray they will be comforted by a power greater than any of us, spoken through the ages in Psalm 23: Even though I walk through the valley of the shadow of death, I fear no evil for you are with me."

David closed his eyes and recited the prayer along with the president, whispering the words in Hebrew: *Gam ki aylaych b'gay tzalmaves lo ira raki atah imadi, shivt'cha umish-antecha, haymah y'nachamuni. Ta-aroch l'fanai shulchan, neged tzor'roy, dishantah vashemen roshi, kosi r'vayah. Ach tov vachesed yird'funi kol y'may chayoy, v'shavti b'vayt Adonoy l'orecha yamim.* David opened his eyes and the others watched him curiously, a guy with a fucked-up face canting and muttering Hebrew probably an unlikely thing in the Carson City Walmart. They didn't even have a Jewish cemetery in town. David knew that well enough. The Kales Home of Peace advertised in the local paper; Jews were always willing to go the extra mile to be buried with one another. They ended up putting three or four dead Carson City Jews into the ground a year. That was about a hundred thousand. Easy cash.

"Amen," David said, figuring, well, build that bridge before it burned down behind him.

"Amen," Denim Jacket said.

The TV went black and then Tom Brokaw was there. David peered around. Everyone was in tears.

"We're totally fucked," UNLV said. "Did you guys watch that shit? We're fucked. We're totally ass fucked here."

"Language," a woman hissed. David turned, saw a young boy, maybe six or seven, holding his mother's hand, tears streaming down his face. The mother was in her twenties, still dressed in her cocktailing outfit—a low-cut black dress under a Carson City Nugget Casino windbreaker, though she'd ditched her heels for a pair of white New Balance sneakers—and had a cart filled with groceries. They'd stopped to watch the news just like everyone else, but now the kid was crying. "It's all right, Evan," the woman said. "Just listen to the man on the TV, nobody else." She glared at UNLV. "Have some respect, okay? Jesus."

"Whatever." UNLV stalked off.

"Maybe this isn't the place to bring your kid," David said, before he could stop himself. One thing he didn't abide, ever, was people telling him and Jennifer how William should behave in public. And really, David wasn't even talking to this woman, wasn't talking about this kid—he was talking to Jennifer, telling her in his head that she needed to get William out of the room, that he didn't need to be seeing this shit, and somehow, it just fell out of his mouth when he saw the crying kid, who was now wailing.

"It's okay, Evan," the woman said. Now she was glaring at David. The kid was howling like a part of him was pinched in some farm implement. The woman put her hand over the kid's mouth, which only made it worse, no one ever quieting down when someone tried to cover their mouth, that was the shit that made everyone crazy, in David's experience both as a father and as the kind of person who had to muffle screams periodically. "That was very rude of you," the woman said to David. "On this of all days? Unbelievable."

"You're right," David said. He shouldn't speak to her, he shouldn't speak to anyone. "I apologize."

This seemed to take the woman by surprise.

"Thank you," she said.

Tears welled up in her eyes.

Shit.

David was in it, just like he'd been in it all day, like how he'd been in it his entire life. This woman, though, no rings on her fingers, this kid Evan at her side, was fucking him up. Was this what Jennifer looked like in public now with William? She worked in a museum, he knew that, so maybe she didn't wear some uniform that made her look like a cross between a stripper and a hostess at Denny's, but was she spending her nights buying groceries in a fucking Walmart with her crying kid? Would Jennifer let William cry in public? William, he was sensitive, not like Sal had been. Sal remembered him, three years old, already staying up all night in bed worried about the world. Sal found him one time, eyes wide open, sweating, Jennifer thinking he was sick, but no, he just had questions, so Sal sat down on the edge of the bed, held his hand.

"Why are we here?" William asked, and Sal thought, *This is not what I'm paid to do.* Thought: *How the fuck should I know?* Thought: *I'm too close to this question.* But William wouldn't close his eyes, wouldn't stop asking that question, over and over again.

"We're here to love each other," he told William that night. "That's it. Just the three of us. Everyone else? I don't know their purpose, but this family? It's for that."

That seemed to satisfy William, but it fucked up David, because now, when he tried to figure out that very question—Why are we here?—that was the only plausible answer he could come up with, no matter how much of the Torah he read, no matter how much of the Talmud he studied, no matter how much theology and liturgy he processed, all the world's religions, none of them had satisfying answers. And then this shit? People flying planes into buildings? David strangling some innocent woman to death for parking in the wrong place? David planning on killing someone else, just for an RV to get himself back to Las Vegas?

"This day has been so fucked up," the woman said, and then she was ugly crying—snot, shuddering, gripping her kid to her body, like someone was trying to wrestle him away from her. She reached into her cart, ripped open a box of Kleenex, blew her nose.

David looked at the woman, then down at the boy. "You're fine. We'll all be fine."

"Are all the people dead?" the boy said to David.

"Evan," the woman began to say.

"No," David said. "It's a natural question. Because he should know that man is born with his hands clenched but that he dies with his hands wide open. That's in the Talmud. It's a lesson to learn early. Death is just . . . another thing. That is all. Nothing to fear."

"The what?" the woman said.

"Talmud," David said. "Jewish holy book. Like a study guide to the Bible." The kid stopped crying for a second, tried to process what

David was saying. So David added, "You can cry as much as you want." He looked back at the woman. "There is meanness in the world. That is what I'm trying to say. Wise to reckon with it head on."

"That's the Talmud, too?"

"No," David said. "Bruce Springsteen. It's just something I think about."

"Are you a . . . priest?"

"No," David said.

David left because it was becoming clear to him that he wasn't himself, that something had come undone today. He pushed his cart outside to the garden section. There was a teenage girl working the register, gauge earrings, a pierced nose, hair shaved up one side of her head, black eye makeup. She'd come to regret those things, David knew, just like how he'd come to regret a lot of the choices he made before he turned eighteen.

"May I borrow your phone?" David asked the girl.

"I'm sorry?" she said.

"I need to call home," he said. "I don't have a phone." She didn't answer him, like she was computing his words. "I need to call my wife and child. I need to do it right now."

"Okay," she said. She dug into her pocket, came out with a cell phone, handed it to David.

"No," David said and gave it back to her. "The store phone."

"That is against policy," she said, but she handed him the receiver. "Dial nine," she said. "I'll give you some privacy. I'm going to smoke a cigarette."

How long would that give him? Five, maybe seven minutes. He'd timed it out before when he'd had to take out a guy on his smoke break. "Maybe have two."

She undid her apron, put it on the counter, then dug a pack of cigarettes from her pocket, a Zippo, walked over to a gate that led out to the parking lot.

All of David's exit plans had been predicated on the world staying pretty much the same. Cops and robbers and all that bullshit.

But this was new. This was a problem. It would take him a couple days, but he could get most of the cash out of the banks. But then what? He didn't have the proper paper to get out of the country, just like he'd told Rabbi Kales. Oh, he had a fake birth certificate, a fake social security card, a fake Nevada driver's license, all enough to get around in Las Vegas, enough to pass muster if someone came looking for him at home, but that shit would wilt under real scrutiny, and David had a feeling real scrutiny was about to come.

He had about two hundred thousand in cash back in Las Vegas. So maybe he takes Roger's RV, drives it back to Las Vegas, hits his banks in the morning, gets all he can, drives to Chicago, picks up Jennifer and William, the three of them on the road for the next year, maybe two, maybe three, never put down any roots at all, wait out history. That kind of cash could last a while, but if he needed extra, he'd do some jobs. Not hit jobs. He could rob a bank. That would be easy. He could rob drug dealers. That would be easier. Some Boise coke dealer? He could rob him twice a week.

Bennie Savone would come looking for him. Ronnie—or whoever replaced Ronnie—would too. The FBI, they'd now be looking for three people, one of whom was a kid, which meant it would be national news, again. THE RAIN MAN KIDNAPS WIFE, SON. He could see the headline already. If the press unraveled his Las Vegas story, then he'd have every client Bennie had searching for him, too. So he'd have the Triads on him. Crime families in Cleveland and Memphis and Detroit. Some pimp shit from LA. The tribes in Palm Springs got rid of three people this year, two the previous, their casino business starting to take off, which meant they'd be pushing bodies more and more often. Not a lot now. But enough that they'd send someone to make sure David didn't say shit. Then he'd have the Jews looking for him, too. Pissed off Temple Beth Israel congregants he'd fleeced would hire private detectives, retired Mossad motherfuckers chasing him to every corner of the planet, the Jews taking that blood oath seriously.

Then there was whoever would eventually come looking for Agent Moss's killer, plus every other person he'd killed in Chicago.

It wasn't even about law enforcement, really. It was about mother-fuckers with sons. Motherfuckers with brothers. Motherfuckers, far and wide, everyone would want a piece of Sal Cupertine once they knew he was out there, on the run.

Or maybe tomorrow the rest of America would be under attack. Tanks rolling across the prairie and shit. Everything *Red Dawn*.

Fuck it.

David hit 9, then dialed his home number. It was about seven in Chicago. Jennifer would be home. William would be home. He'd tell her he was coming, not to worry, and then he'd get off the line. By the time the FBI went through their wires, the whole family would be in the wind. He only needed a day. He had the sense the FBI was going to be busy for at least a week. Maybe a month. Maybe more. If there was one day to call home, it was today. David suspected that today, Sal Cupertine didn't seem like such a big fucking deal.

The phone picked up and David started talking immediately. "It's me," he said, but before he could continue, he was interrupted.

"We're sorry. You have reached a number that has been disconnected or is no longer in service. If you feel you have reached this number in error, please check the number and try your call again."

He hung up, called again. Same thing. One more time. Same thing.

Jennifer wouldn't change the phone number. She knew he would contact her again. She knew how the game worked. You waited. When no message came, that was still a message.

David peered outside at the smoking girl. She was on her phone now, too. Smoking and talking and pacing. She was maybe halfway through her cigarette.

He looked through the sliding glass doors, back into the Walmart. People milled about. It could be any day of the year. It could be any day of their lives.

He could call Jennifer's cell phone.

He didn't want to, because he knew the FBI could clone those phones with no problem, you'd think you were calling one number, but you were really calling a phone bank in Quantico. There were fewer regulations on cell phones, something to do with the law not catching up to the technology, and really, for someone like Sal Cupertine's wife, they probably weren't terribly concerned about any violation of civil rights.

But it was just a Walmart calling.

They'd let that go right through.

Take one look at the number and decide they didn't want to get patched into a credit card call center and end up in conversation with some asshole in Pakistan speaking Pashto/English. Not today.

Fuck it.

One ring.

Two.

David imagined Jennifer fumbling through her purse, looking for her phone.

Three.

He'd be fast. He'd tell her to turn the bath on and just let it run all night, let it flood the house. First thing in the morning, take William to some reasonably nice hotel—Courtyard Inn in Highland Park, the Residence Inn in Evanston, somewhere like that—check in, use your real name, put down your credit card, make it obvious, call the home insurance company, make a claim and an appointment for the next day, all of it a minor horror, but that's why you have insurance, for when your kid turns on a faucet and floods your house. Have that exact conversation, which would be recorded, because insurance companies record all their calls, because they expect everyone is trying to defraud them. Order a pizza, get it delivered. Let people see you. FBI, if they gave a shit, wouldn't have the resources to get the Courtyard Inn tapped, wouldn't have someone in Highland Park ready to sit on a hotel all day, since that would really be three to six guys, a car in the front, a car in the back, maybe a car watching the parking lot, all when obviously it was just your average homeowner calamity. They'd track her credit cards, maybe even use whatever construction crew was about to come fix everything to get some fiber optics inside the house, but in truth, what the fuck had Jennifer done? Nothing.

Which meant they'd do nothing. There were actual bad guys out there, blowing up buildings and shit.

Four rings and David was telling her that the next day, she'd go to the Chili's in the parking lot, because there was always a Chili's in the parking lot, get a booth, order lunch, normal day. Pay, walk out, and there'd be an RV in the parking lot. Inside would be the future. She'd have to trust him. They were going to make this work.

Five rings.

Six.

Seven.

Eight.

Nine.

Ten.

And then . . . nothing.

No voice mail. Just a disconnection.

He put his finger on the hook, kept the receiver in his hand. Thought: *That's not what happens.* A phone doesn't stop ringing. If there's no voice mail, you get a message that says the user doesn't have voice mail set up. If the service has been disconnected, it says the number is out of service. Cell phones don't just ring into eternity . . . and then stop.

He could call again to be sure.

But.

No. He was Sal Cupertine. He wasn't a guy who fucked up the small things.

Oh, sure, he fucked up a couple big things, but a small thing, that's how people ended up fucking dead. Big things you could construct a plan around. A small thing, that came apart fast.

"Any luck?"

David looked up. It was the smoking girl.

"No," he said. He wiped down the phone using his sleeve, hung it up, the girl watching him with a interested look on her face. "I've got a cold."

"It's cool," she said. She put her apron back on. "I hope everything is okay. With your family. My mom is freaked."

In the distance, David heard a siren. It wasn't for him. There was always an emergency somewhere. He knew that. His wife and son were gone. He knew that, too.

13

Matthew Drew unloaded his Glock into the motherfucker in front of him. Fifteen shots, center mass, filling the same hole over and over again. He popped out the clip, reloaded. Fifteen more into the forehead, the eyes, through the mouth. Set the Glock aside. Went to his case, got out his .300 Winchester Magnum. Pushed his targets back thirty feet. Worked on single-shot accuracy for fifteen minutes. *Head shot. Body shot. Head shot. This motherfucker dies. That motherfucker is paralyzed. This other motherfucker never eats solid food again.* Getting that repetition down, snapping off shots. Loose now. Went for his AR-15. Sprayed those motherfuckers. Took them all out. Everyone was dead. Men, women, and children. Matthew Drew did not give a fuck. You were in the Family? You were fucking dead.

Back to the Glock.

Back to the Win Mag.

Back to the AR-15.

When his hour was up, Matthew took off his safety glasses and earplugs, packed up his guns and his ammo, zipped everything into the slate-gray travel case the FBI gave all new agents when they completed training. The seal was right there on the side: Fidelity. Integrity. Bravery. He wasn't FBI anymore. Which was fine. That shit never did apply.

Matthew looked down the line. The shooting range at Second Amendment Sports Club, all the way out in an industrial park in Des Plaines, was doing big business today. Twenty people setting it off. Nines. ARs. .357s. Men. Women. All ages, other than children.

White. Black. Asian. Latino. Behind him, lingering in the teak-and-leather waiting area nestled behind the triple-paned safety glass, were another dozen, waiting their turns. Flat-screen TVs ran ESPN and FOX News. Middle of a Monday afternoon and it was like a sports bar on Sunday.

He hefted the bag of guns up over his shoulder, made his way out, exiting through the retail space, past the glassed-in racks of guns for sale, past the leather jackets, past the target-practice posters—clowns with hatchets in their hands, zombies, white men, black men, Asian men—past ammo displays, past the T-shirts, past posters of women in bikinis holding AKs. He looked every single person he crossed paths with in the eye, made them look away. Everyone was a suspect. Everyone would always be a suspect.

A few months ago, in that casino bathroom, Matthew thought he was looking infinity in the eye. But now he knew the difference. Infinity wasn't boredom. Infinity wasn't ennui. Infinity was grief. He was always opening that trunk. He was always seeing his sister's severed head. He was always in that moment right after, Senior Special Agent Lee Poremba pulling him away, telling him not to look, to close his eyes. The German shepherd howling, the bomb tech throwing up, Agent Wilmore's radius bone popped through his flesh. All of it, over and over again.

If only he'd listened.

He'd been back in Chicago for a week, after the police finally unsealed Nina's apartment. Nearly two months of fruitless investigation later and Matthew was able to clean her stuff out, get his shit out, too, including the rest of his guns, though they never did find the Glock he'd given Nina. The coroner released what they'd found of Nina's body a few days later, so she could be buried back home in Maryland. Matthew and his mother flew back with her body in the luggage compartment of a Delta flight into Dulles; then, the next day, they laid her down beside Matthew's father. Dad had purchased the family plot years ago, and the day they put Nina in the ground, Matthew couldn't stop staring at his own tombstone, already in place, his name and birthdate right there. The only thing missing was his body and date of expiration, though he felt like the cemetery could save some time and just finish the job now, make it the same as Nina's: September 8, 2001. Though, fact was, that date was probably wrong.

Cops had figured out a basic timeline of her death. She'd made it to class that Friday morning; cameras in the parking lot tracked her walking onto campus at 9:26, back out at 11:17, her classmates corroborated seeing her, her professor reported that she'd waited after class to ask a question about a paper that was due in a few weeks. Nothing out of the ordinary. Her last electronic trace was at 12:39 p.m. when she used her debit card at Lou Mitchell's Diner, where she paid for a Royal Burger Delight, a Diet Coke, and an oatmeal raisin cookie for lunch. Her waitress reported that she ate alone, as she often did, Lou Mitchell's the kind of place where eating alone was normal. Her next class was at 2:30. She never made it. A day later, a woman walking her dog noticed tire tracks going into a retention pond below a frontage road, walked down to the shore, and saw the car submerged in about twenty feet of water. The inside of the car had been blasted with bleach and hydrogen peroxide in heavy doses, probably through a hose, which meant whoever had the car wasn't in a place where they felt comfortable torching it, even though they set fire to his sister. The coroner estimated that Nina had been dead for at least a day before she was put into Matthew's trunk sometime late Saturday night or early Sunday morning, the eighth, while he slept. He'd driven from his shitty studio apartment all the way to the casino and hadn't even noticed anything was amiss. But why would he? The perpetrators didn't even need to break into the car: Nina kept Matthew's spare keys and alarm fob on her keyring. And since Matthew didn't have underground parking, all they had to do was walk up, pop the trunk, and dump a duffel bag filled with pieces of his kid sister inside. It would have taken fifteen seconds. Maybe less. She was only five foot two. Weighed 110 pounds. They hadn't even managed to get her whole body in the trunk. Final inventory said she was missing a leg.

Matthew's mom didn't need to know. No one did. And the feds wouldn't put that out into the world. The story everyone got was that Nina had been carjacked, that her body had been found in her own car. A tragedy. But in Chicago? It was a local news tragedy, if it made the news at all.

Which it hadn't. Nina had the ignominy of being murdered three days before the biggest terrorist attack ever on American soil. Even more, the FBI didn't want to acknowledge the murder lest they tip off the Family or the Gangster 2-6 or the Chuyalla or the Native Mob or the tweak that had been hired for the job, if they were able to pull some quick evidence. Instead, that day, they busted up the illegal sports book, took fifteen Native Mob guys into custody for a variety of minor offenses, but with the maximum number of press photos of them being cuffed and dragged out of the hotel. Matthew's car was loaded onto a wrecker, and the whole investigation happened off-site. A bullet point showed up about Nina's car being pulled out of the pond in the local paper with a request for anyone with information to contact CrimeStoppers, but Nina Drew's murder was never reported. Her obituary ran in Chicago and Maryland, but none of her Chicago friends made it out. No one was getting on a plane these days.

Matthew pushed through the gun shop's double doors and into the afternoon light. It was the last week of October. He was due to fly back to Chevy Chase in a few days. He wasn't sure that was going to happen. Ronnie Cupertine was still in a Chicago hospital. Alive. Matthew could finish that job. Then he'd start moving through the Family systematically. Then the Native Mob. Then the Gangster 2-6. Then maybe he'd fly to Detroit, put one in Kirk Biglione. That fat fuck had to know something . . .

By the time he got to the parking lot, Matthew had killed two hundred men, which was too bad, since Senior Special Agent Lee Poremba was standing beside the rental, reading the newspaper. Matthew hit the key to unlock the car, which got Poremba's attention.

"You're a little far from home," Matthew said.

"So are you," Poremba said.

"Yeah, well," Matthew said, "I didn't want to go anywhere I might run into someone I know. End up shooting them."

"Then you should look in your rearview mirror more often," Poremba said.

"You here to give me some good news?" Matthew asked.

"No," Poremba said. "I'm not even here." He put down the paper, moved aside so Matthew could open the back passenger door. Matthew had rented a red Cadillac Seville STS, like his father used to drive. The feds still had his Mustang. They could keep it. Matthew tossed his bag in the backseat. "There somewhere we can talk?" Poremba asked.

"I'm pretty busy," Matthew said. He closed the door and leaned against it, arms crossed.

"I see that," Poremba said. "You practicing or gearing up?"

"Little bit of both, I guess," Matthew said.

Poremba watched Matthew for a moment. "You have anyone to talk to, Matthew? Priest or therapist or something?"

"No," Matthew said.

"It's confidential," Poremba said. "I've seen someone in the past."

"I go in and tell a priest my problems, he'll end up in a cornfield somewhere. No thanks."

"You on anything?"

"I got some Ambien to help me sleep," Matthew said. "But I haven't been taking it." After a while, he asked, "What are you doing out here? I thought you'd be long gone."

"Tying up some things," Poremba said. "I've been back and forth between Quantico and New York. Hopefully back here before too long, but I don't know. They're moving everyone from Organized Crime to Terrorism, at least for the time being. We need to get these guys trained up on some of the observational measures we've been using, see if it transfers over. Domestically, at any rate."

"Wilmore, too?"

"Already gone. All the section heads are getting called back to base. See where we can best be utilized. Personally, I'm hoping to get on a crew looking at the movement of the hijackers and the money, something I'm good at, but we'll see."

"How's his wrist?"

"He's got another month before they take the pins out," Poremba said.

"Sorry about that," Matthew said. He was. Kind of.

"I'll tell him that." Poremba waved the newspaper in his hand, rolled it up into a cylinder. "It's all political now. End result is Chicago will be gutted for a while."

Matthew wasn't surprised.

"You even read the Patriot Act?" Matthew asked.

"No," Poremba said. "I doubt anyone has."

"I read it," Matthew said.

Poremba raised his eyebrows. "It's three hundred and fifty pages of small print."

"I told you I'm not sleeping," Matthew said.

"What do you make of it?"

"It's a taxpayer-funded protection scheme," Matthew said. "Give up all your liberties, we'll keep you safe."

"Maybe that's what we've needed all along."

"Would my sister still be alive?"

"Maybe," he said. "We get access to more cameras? Get on more phones? It wouldn't hurt. Track money with less difficulty, without a warrant? That wouldn't hurt either. Be less chance some clerk in a courthouse is on the Family dime if they knew their every keystroke was being tracked. That's what we're dealing with now. It's not dons and capos and all that. It's file clerks getting a grand to slip information on cases to some white collar, don't know the white collar is kicking it out to the gangs and the crime families. We're not talking street hustlers. We're talking educated, employed, career civil servants who can't make their rent, or their kid wants a Playstation, so they sell out information on what one shitheel is doing to another shitheel. The blowback never touches them."

"So the solution is to be the Stasi? We're either patsies or we're East Germany?"

"What's the next bad thing that's out there?" Poremba asked. "What can I anticipate? That's what I'm thinking about these days. I think I'll try to prevent whatever *that* is. I'll try to prevent *that* for as many people as possible." He paused for a moment. "But I don't know, Matthew. People who did that to your sister? They don't care about the FBI. They don't worry about prison."

"All the time you spent watching me, all the man hours," Matthew said, "and no one can explain to me how my little sister ended up in the trunk of my car."

"You should have come to me," Poremba said.

"And done what?"

"Admitted to beating Ronnie," he said. "Told me what you knew about the Family. Told me what you suspected about the Chuyalla. About the Native Mob."

"And been arrested for attempted murder? Get a handful of RICO charges? Fraud? Or be marked for death for the rest of my life? You don't have the kind of sway to keep me out of prison."

"Matthew," Poremba said, "your silence killed your sister. The people who did this to her? They bought your silence first with your job at the casino and next with her blood. You think anything different, you're just naïve."

A man and a woman, both in their thirties, came out of the shop then, AR-15s slung over their shoulders, the man dressed like he was an assistant coach for the Bears, the woman in tight pink pants, a matching Bears sweatshirt, and black headband. Matthew recognized them from the range, where they'd been getting a lesson. News said gun sales were way up since the planes hit, but for some reason Matthew imagined that was all country people adding one more piece to their arsenal, as if Al-Qaeda were about to invade Appalachia. Instead it was this couple, getting into their gold Lexus SUV now, laughing about something. Just a day like any other.

"Why not just kill me?" Matthew asked, once the couple drove off. It was the profound guilt of Matthew's life now, superseding his last profound guilt, which had been that he'd let Hopper go to Las Vegas alone.

"You're irrelevant to them. You've already been replaced at the casino. And before that, you were replaced at the FBI. Your sister's death sends a clear message to people you'll never meet not to step forward, not to investigate, not to engage. Fact is you're worth more alive. You can tell the story. That's what they want."

Matthew didn't think that was how real life worked. It wasn't mentioned at Quantico, the idea that if you were working organized crime or gang enforcement that you needed to consider the safety of your family. It wasn't *encouraged* that you live in the same city as your subjects—the Bureau suggesting a twenty-five-mile separation was usually enough—but even still, they'd suppress your address, keep you out of searchable data farms, depending upon your clearance level, and they swore that if you were at a high enough level, your phones, your house, your car, everything was surveilled to keep you safe.

It was, Matthew learned, unfeasible. The FBI didn't have guys to watch criminal subjects around the clock; they sure as hell weren't watching *him* 24/7. Not even local cops working in the toughest, most gang-infested parts of the country had significant concerns. East St. Louis, South Central Los Angeles, Detroit, Memphis, Oakland. In the last fifteen years, there hadn't been a single instance of a family member being successfully targeted. It wasn't about honor. It was about opportunity. Some gangster wanted to target a cop, all they had to do was wait for him or her to show up on their block. But no Deuce 9 gangster was going to drive out to the suburbs of St. Louis and commit a murder on a tree-lined street. That was so far removed from the game, it called into question the toughness of the man doing the hit. That's what Matthew thought. It's what he believed. Because it had been true forever.

"They made me a pawn," Matthew said. "I thought you or some-one else at the Bureau had recommended me for the job at the casino, but that wasn't it. They'd been watching me all along, just like you had. They set me up, hoping I'd kill Ronnie. This entire time. Killed my sister because they knew they could." Matthew sniffed. Maybe last week he would have cried. But there wasn't anything left in him. "Made me a dupe."

"You believed in old mythology," Poremba said simply. He pointed into the sky, which was empty this afternoon, and brilliant blue, one of those late fall days in Chicago when you're deluded into thinking winter will be pleasant. "Those planes last month? They were aimed at you, at me, at children not even born yet. They didn't fly those planes into aircraft carriers. They didn't crash them into nuclear power plants. They ran them into people. It's the same thing. Don't pretend it's anything different." Across the street, a murder of crows stalked slowly around the greenbelt between a self-storage facility and something called Diamond Logistics. "You can't stop the nature of these things. They're morphing faster than we can keep up with them."

"So that's it, then. Everyone is looking for Bin Laden now? All the other cases are back-burner bullshit?"

"Yes," Poremba said.

"My mother," Matthew said, "what do I tell her, Agent Poremba? 'Get used to the New World Order, your daughter doesn't matter.'"

"There's good police here," Poremba said. "There's good police in Milwaukee. They're going to keep working the case. Someone saw something. They'll shake it out."

"I don't believe that," Matthew said. "And I don't believe you do, either."

"No," Poremba said. "I don't."

They both knew who did it. Or at least who was behind it. The Family and the Chuyalla and the Native Mob had been in business together for at least a year, that's what Agent Wilmore and Poremba had sussed out, what Matthew should have realized. The Family was consolidating its power up through Wisconsin, moving their drugs farther and farther north, so that they could start combating the

Windsor Mafia in Canada, who were pushing marijuana and pills south, everyone trying to capture market share. The Native Mob had its tendrils in Minnesota, Wisconsin, and Michigan, but also in Indiana, Iowa, and Nebraska. All the places no Family guys wanted to go, but the Native Mob mitigated that problem. The Family could provide the financial backing, the Native Mob could move product. And the Chuyalla could open casinos. It was like Las Vegas all over again, except instead of Jews and Italians fighting other Jews and Italians, it was Native Americans and Mexican gangs backed by Cartels, often on sovereign land, with the Family providing the product, the weaponry, and the social infrastructure of compromised human cargo: the cops, the lawyers, the aldermen, all that, but also the truck drivers, the garbage men, the bulk food distributors, those file clerks and receptionists and janitors who worked in civic buildings who could all use a few extra bucks.

Matthew had beaten down Ronnie Cupertine, had taken him out of the game, and all he'd done was unleash something more vicious and more eager.

They didn't care about the established allegiances, the courtesies, the rules and decorum. That shit was gone. And Matthew understood he'd played a role in that even before all of this: When he busted up Fat Monte Moretti and then a couple hours later, Fat Monte had killed himself. Matthew understood then that the stakes were different. That whatever the Family was trying to hide was big enough that a guy like Fat Monte was willing to pull his own roots versus having someone do him ugly. The Family had tried to get Sal Cupertine killed. They couldn't, so they'd disappeared him. What was the Family trying to hide, that *now*, with Ronnie incapacitated, they had to act? All this time Matthew had been here. All this time his sister had been here. But now they acted? It didn't make sense. Hopper—or someone—had revealed the workings of the Family to the press two years ago, and Matthew was convinced even more that it wasn't Jeff who'd made that call. Maybe it had been Poremba himself. Maybe he'd never know.

"Why didn't Ronnie show up on my facial-recognition database?" Matthew asked.

"You're asking the wrong guy." But the way he said it, it was like he was relieved Matthew had finally put it together. It wasn't something Poremba was going to tell him, but it wasn't something he was going to avoid. Matthew just had to ask the right questions.

"Who's the right guy?"

Poremba shrugged. Still not the right question.

"Ronnie Cupertine . . . is a CI?"

Poremba scratched at his cheek, Matthew noticing a hint of stubble there. "You know, a bad thing happens, you run all the scenarios back through your mind, imagining ways you could have answered a question that would have stalled a person for ten or fifteen minutes and that would have thrown the whole sequence of life's events off by just a beat." He looked at his nails, flicked invisible bits of skin off them. "Sinaloa has come up from Mexico and taken over the marijuana, the cocaine, not so much the heroin, yet, or the pills, but that's just a matter of time. Probably a couple seasons away from having decent poppy fields down there. So they won't need the Family to make money out here anymore, but as of right now, they still push fifty, sixty percent of their product through them, for the sake of convenience, keeping the peace. But that time's up soon. Enterprising guy might try to protect his business interests in any way he saw feasible."

It wasn't the most surprising thing Matthew had ever heard. He knew the history of these deals: bosses had been snitching since there were bosses, making sweetheart deals with the government so whatever victimless shit they were doing—*victim* being a fungible term—like selling booze during Prohibition, marijuana since the 1950s, white-collar opiates since the '80s, or simply running high-end sports books and other mostly nonviolent endeavors, like what the Native Mob had going, could keep on going without much interference. In exchange, maybe they put a name on an unsolved murder every now and again, maybe a bank heist got foiled, maybe a shipment of guns was held up. Traffic cop shit.

"So Ronnie does a little snitching," Matthew said, "it's good for his business, and we get to grab up the Mexicans? That's the trade? Even though Sal Cupertine killed three agents and a CI? Four agents if you count Jeff?"

"I wake up thinking about Sal Cupertine," Poremba said, "and I go to bed thinking about Jeff and those men. Trust me on this."

"I want to trust you," Matthew said.

"But I've got orders, too." A UPS truck pulled up then and the driver hopped out, ran around to the back, came out with a dolly, stacked it with long boxes marked with corporate logos: Smith & Wesson; Sturm, Ruger and Company; Bushmaster. The driver pushed the dolly toward the building, his truck still idling in front. "That's the next thing," Poremba said. "These terrorists, they'll show up in big cities, driving UPS and Fed Ex trucks filled with explosives. Stolen ambulances jacked with propane tanks and nails. Anything you trust, anything you recognize. That's the next level of the attack." A couple seconds later, the driver came running back out, hopped into the truck, and was gone. "Or maybe they'll drop off packages filled with bombs. That way they don't have to die." He counted to ten, then snapped his fingers. "Boom. The UPS guy is already down the block." Snapped his fingers again. "Five minutes later, whole building comes down. Would you be able to describe the UPS guy if you had to put out a BOLO?" Poremba asked.

"I think he was white," Matthew said. "I don't know. I wasn't paying close attention."

"That's what the Patriot Act will be good for," Poremba said. "Take the attention out of it. Everything will be empirical. We get these bad guys, we come back and use it on the Family. Lock everyone up. Sal Cupertine. Ronnie Cupertine, if he makes it. Whoever killed Hopper. Everyone."

"I should have killed Ronnie Cupertine," Matthew said.

"They wanted you to," Poremba said. "You're lucky you didn't."

"Why? That's what I don't get."

"There's not a Cupertine left in the Family," Poremba said. "If you'd killed Ronnie, whoever set you up would have been able to slide right into power, not be worried about Ronnie bringing Sal back. If you had killed Ronnie, you'd be in jail right now. Or dead. I promise you."

"I should be in jail," Matthew said. "You should have arrested me a year ago. Why didn't you?"

"You and Jeff were the only people to get close to Sal Cupertine."

"So this is about Sal? All this shit is about Sal Cupertine? I got set up just like he did? Except I got it from the FBI and the Mob." Matthew spat onto the ground. "I never had a fucking chance."

What was it Paul Bruno had told them two years ago about Sal? Bruno was a Family snitch Hopper had flipped years before, then found him living outside of Milwaukee, moving model homes when everything went down. *You put him in a situation where he might kill someone, he's gonna do that.* And: *The only reason Ronnie would send Sal out in the day would be to get caught.* And then a couple weeks later, Paul Bruno was gone. Disappeared.

"You think whoever killed Hopper killed my sister?" Matthew asked.

"No," Poremba said.

He looked at Matthew for a few seconds without saying anything, as if he was trying to make a decision, then muttered, "Fuck it," under his breath.

"Hopper was embalmed," Poremba said.

"What? His head was cut off."

"Postmortem," Poremba said. "Whoever killed him also took out his eyes and replaced them with rubber pellets. But they embalmed him. Or at least his head."

"That's not what the newspaper said."

"We don't give everything to the press, Matthew," Poremba said. "I think you know that."

Matthew tried to process this. "Why would someone kill Jeff and then embalm him?"

"I assume," Poremba said, "so that he could be preserved for identification." Poremba let that sit with Matthew for a few seconds. "You hear about that kid, few days before all this with your sister, that they caught shoplifting at Carson's? Shot a security guard in the head?"

"Vaguely," Matthew said. "I think I saw it on the news."

Poremba unrolled the newspaper, handed it to Matthew. "There was an update in the *Tribune* yesterday. Worth a read."

Poremba slid a cell phone from his pocket, punched in a number, turned his back to Matthew, walked a few feet away, to the curb. Okay.

Cook County prosecutors said Saturday they will not criminally charge a seven-year-old Lincolnwood child for the shooting of Mitchell Thompkins, 27, of Chicago. Thompkins was shot by the child during the course of an attempted shoplifting September 6 in Carson's Department Store. The child, prosecutors said, came into possession of the handgun outside his mother's home, though the gun was not registered to the mother. Charges against the child's parent remain a possibility, prosecutors said, though District Attorney Teri Rhyne suggested that it was all "a terrible tragedy, made worse by the banality of the situation. The store overreacted to the shoplifting. The boy thought it was a toy gun. He just did what he'd seen on TV." Thompkins remains in critical condition at Northwestern Memorial Hospital, where doctors . . .

The article continued, and when Matthew flipped the page over, there was a plain white envelope placed between the pages, unsealed. Matthew looked up and Poremba still had his back to him, phone to his ear. Matthew opened the envelope and found a record of calls coming into Jennifer Cupertine's home in

Lincolnwood, as well as a cell phone registered in her name to the same address over the course of the last sixty days. Five calls on September 11 had been circled in pencil, four to the home phone, one to the cell, from a number in Carson City, Nevada. They'd come within two minutes of one another, between 7:40 and 7:42 p.m. There had been no calls going out from either of Cupertine's numbers since September 6.

"What is this?" Matthew asked. Poremba didn't respond. He was talking on his phone now. Ordering a cab, it sounded like.

Matthew looked at the other incoming numbers. Almost all were from Chicagoland area codes. A few were from 800 numbers. Solicitors. Collection agencies. By and large, Jennifer Cupertine's home phone rang about six times a week. It didn't surprise Matthew. She must have known they were on her phone. But it was the same with her cell. She hadn't received five phone calls in a single day anytime in the last two months, other than in that two-minute period. She rarely called anyone on her home phone, maybe a call or two every other day, usually to the same few numbers, all in Chicago. On her cell, she was on it at least once a day, usually more. But nothing since September 6.

He took his cell phone from his pocket.

"Unless you meant what you said about going to jail," Poremba said over his shoulder, hand over the receiver, "don't call the local numbers."

Noted. He dialed the circled incoming phone number. An automated voice picked up.

"*Thank you for calling your local Walmart. We appreciate your business and look forward to serving you.*"

Matthew hung up, looked at the number again, redialed, the same. Went back to the list of calls. Why had a Walmart in Carson City, Nevada, called Jennifer five times on September 11 and never before or since?

He went back to the news story.

What had he missed?

It didn't say where the kid was, just that he wasn't being prosecuted. But it also didn't give the name of the mother. That wasn't unusual. If the kid wasn't being prosecuted, naming the mother would be a violation of privacy.

Matthew concentrated. Slowed himself down. Imagined he was looking down the scope of a rifle. Position on the target. And there it was, what he'd missed: *September 6*. And then: *Lincolnwood*.

He'd been to Jennifer Cupertine's house. He and Hopper. He'd met that kid. William. He was four then. Matthew, when he'd been talking to Jennifer, pretended to have a kid, too. Tried to build an empathetic bridge to her, like he'd been taught. Matthew didn't think he'd ever have kids now. Couldn't imagine it, anyway. Bringing a child into this world? So that one day he or she could watch their father get killed for some Mob shit that happened years earlier? And now, William. Being charged or not didn't matter. He'd shot a guy in the head. That was a moment he'd remember forever.

Matthew stuffed the papers back into the envelope, folded it all back into the newspaper, walked over to where Poremba was standing.

"They somewhere safe?" Matthew asked.

Poremba closed his phone, nodded.

Witness protection made sense. Whatever had happened with the kid, it surely wasn't the whole story. The Family, or whatever constituted the Family now, was making a move. Jennifer must have come in, maybe staged an arrest so she wouldn't get marked as a snitch, get Sal marked as a snitch, too. Smart. And then . . . something went upside down.

"Do you know where?"

Poremba shook his head.

Matthew supposed it was better if neither of them knew. Two fewer innocent people who might end up dead. Nina should have been so lucky.

"What happens if this security guard dies?" Matthew asked.

"We'll add him to the list," Poremba said.

"Other people saw this happen," Matthew said. "Someone is going to say something."

Poremba laughed, but then stopped himself, like a faucet had been turned off. "No, they won't. There's no good guys anymore, Matthew."

A Fed Ex truck came down the street, pulled up in front Diamond Logistics, the driver sprinted out with a box, hit the buzzer on the front door, left the box, ran back to the truck, thirty seconds.

"Boom," Matthew said.

"You're learning," Poremba said. "Know what's coming for you. That's my policy. I guess judging from all those guns, maybe it's your policy, too."

"The opposite," Matthew said. "I was thinking of going on a hunting trip."

"All those guns registered?"

"Most of them," Matthew said.

"Not the time to get caught riding dirty," Poremba said. "You don't have a lot of friends left in the Bureau."

A yellow cab turned onto the street and Poremba waved his hand in the air. "I was under the impression that now was the time to do something you might otherwise regret," Matthew said.

"Your focus is on the wrong people," Poremba said.

There were, Matthew understood, things Special Agent Lee Poremba could not say out loud.

"Ever been to Carson City?" Poremba asked.

"No," Matthew said.

"It's just outside of Reno," Poremba said. "I was there for three weeks, after Hopper's rental car turned up. Carson City is twenty-five, thirty minutes away. Not far. The kind of town you'd only stop in if you needed gas. But I have to tell you, the drive between Reno and Las Vegas? It's beautiful. You've never seen the color red until you've seen it in the desert. It's like seeing the planet rust. Before you decide to take all those guns and ammo and do something stupid, you should make that drive. Give yourself something to remember in your cell."

"What do I do when I get out there?" Matthew asked.

"Honor your friend," Poremba said. "Walk where he walked. See what he saw. Maybe it will give you some kind of closure. You still have that information, I presume? Where he was planning to visit between Las Vegas and Reno?"

"I do."

"I found it cathartic, Agent," Poremba said.

"I'm not an agent anymore," Matthew said.

"Good for you," Poremba said. The cab pulled up to the curb and Poremba opened the door, got in, but didn't close the door.

"I'm not a good guy, either."

"I'd think about that," Poremba said, closing the door, "because if you find Sal Cupertine, you're eligible for the reward."

14

U sed to be the Purple Hotel in Lincolnwood wasn't a great place to stay. The Outfit ran girls and numbers out of it for years, up until Allen Dorfman caught six bullets to the dome walking through the parking lot back in '83, a couple days before he was due to be sentenced on fraud and racketeering charges. He was killed in case he decided to flip and give the feds information on the casino grift he oversaw in Las Vegas. He'd been on the job going all the way back to Jimmy Hoffa, so if he started talking in hopes of getting a lighter sentence, could be that a lot of people would end up in prison at best, dead at the least. Turned out it didn't matter. The feds knew everything anyway, and within five years, the Outfit was out of business, both in Chicago and Las Vegas. So the Outfit could have let Dorfman live, but the Outfit had no inside intel, so they did what they had to do, which to Peaches Pocotillo was the right way to handle business. Why worry about the potential for liability? Better to solve a problem when it presents itself to you.

That was the difference between the Outfit and the Family, Peaches supposed.

It was after midnight on Halloween and Peaches sat in the lobby of the Purple, waiting for his nephew. The hotel was operated by Ramada these days, a suburban tourist attraction for its classic '60s architecture, distinctive purple bricks, and giant indoor pool. The kind of place where dentists had conferences, where Jews held bar mitzvah parties, where atheists had weddings . . . which meant it was too cute by a mile, what with the pictures depicting the history of the joint lining the walls. Mayhem, avarice, and murder were fond civic memories equal to the exploits of the Cubs, Bulls, and Bears: gangsters in fedoras eating steaks, pretty girls on their laps; row after row of black Cadillacs, gleamed to obsidian shine; Dorfman's body covered by a sheet. Then: artful black-and-whites of Ernie Banks, Michael Jordan, and Mike Ditka, each in mid-victory. In the coffee shop, you could get a Capone Burger (bloody rare), a Lombardo Pancake Breakfast (the cakes looked like clowns, if you squinted just right), and a drink called the Ness, which was a greyhound.

Isn't that cute.

But then, everything these days was too cute. Like how instead of killing Sal Cupertine, the Family tried to set him up, have the feds do the job for them. When that didn't work, they got even cuter, boxed him up, sold him to the highest bidder.

Not that Peaches knew who that bidder was. Ronnie told Peaches from the get-go, almost a year ago now, that he wouldn't give up that information, that if Peaches thought Ronnie needed to tie up loose ends, he wasn't gonna make more of them. Which was probably why the Family was still in business and the Outfit was on the Purple's Wall of Fame. Ronnie Cupertine's business was antiquated, yeah, but his desire for self-preservation remained pretty astonishingly acute.

Peaches was willing to bide his time. Consolidate his power. He'd been doing that for years. It was why he had three kids from three different women from three different tribes—Oneida, Ho-Chunk, Menominee—all under nine, starting right after the state entered its gaming compact with the tribes in '92. All girls. A son would have been fine, the money was the same either way, each getting a monthly nut from the gaming and bingo operations. They were all asleep upstairs, along with the babysitter, whom he was fucking, even though she wasn't connected to anything, other than the Pink Coyote strip club in Stone Park. His girls all lived in small, shitty Wisconsin towns, so every Halloween, he picked them up, drove them down to Chicago, found a nice, safe neighborhood, and let them roam free.

This time, Lincolnwood fit the bill. Every home in the leafy subdivision was elaborately decorated, there were passels of kids on every corner, and five or six houses handed out full-sized candy bars, which Peaches knew was really a protection scheme. No one fucked with the houses that gave out the full-sized Butterfingers. Mostly, he just liked watching his girls shake suckers down for candy. Trick or treat wasn't really accurate. Everyone was getting tricked.

By virtue of his girls, Peaches had his hooks into three different gaming operations, in addition to the Chuyalla. He hadn't started working the skim in the other locations, didn't have the Native Mob fully established in everyone's gaming side, but Ronnie Cupertine had taught him well these last several months. Gave him a blueprint. Integrated Peaches into all phases of the Family. Drummed up some of that Gold Coast money to invest in the golf course and all the commercial and residential construction they were doing on the casino grounds outside Milwaukee. Ronnie took his cut right off the top. Peaches took his cut, too, and it was still enough to get some associates out there to start pushing dirt around. Move a pile from one end of the grounds to the other. Next week, move it back. Spend a week digging a giant hole. Spend the next week filling it back up. Blow up some boulders, spread them around. Couple weeks later, blow up the rocks, turn them into pebbles.

Maybe something would get built or maybe it wouldn't.

No one was going to come after the Family for their investments if it all fell through. Wasn't like people were going to lawyer up against Ronnie Cupertine.

That was the beauty of it all. Because these days, Ronnie Cupertine was shitting in a bag.

Might spend the rest of his miserable life in and out of an induced coma.

Wasn't the outcome Peaches expected, but in truth? It was a better arrangement. Having Ronnie alive but not functional made

Peaches the de facto head of all things without the complications of an assassination. Capos like Sugar Lopiparno just wanted to do their jobs, make their money, kick up their percentage, go on vacation, buy new cars, everyone trading in their Lincolns and Caddies for Hummers and Navigators. And if that action moved through Peaches because Ronnie was in the hospital and couldn't take visitors?

Fine.

For now, anyway.

No one wanted to ruin a good thing. These days, cops and the feds didn't give a fuck what you did, unless you showed up somewhere with a bomb strapped to your chest. Production was up across the board, all phases of the business getting a bump—everything from extortion to mortgage fraud—but it was the pill game where Peaches predicted they'd make real cash. They were charging two or three dollars per milligram on Oxycodone out in the rural areas, a single 30 mg pill going for almost a C-note the farther you got from the city, but Peaches cut prices for the first two weeks after the planes hit, had his boys selling pills at fifty cents a milligram for a week, pushed out full bottles, then started gouging. They were minting cash on Xanax and Ambien, too. No one could stop panicking. No one could sleep. Next move was to diversify even more. Hit up the Indian gaming in other parts of the country. Some old Chicago humps were out west partnering with the tribes in Palm Springs, Ronnie already doing some consulting work when the shit went down, so Peaches slid right in, no problem. Mike was going there in a couple weeks, fix a few things that were troubling them in Indio.

Two women, one dressed as a slutty nurse, the other dressed as a slutty cat, stumbled out of the costume party raging in Sea Gars, the Purple's cocktail bar. They stopped in front of Peaches.

"What are you dressed as?" the nurse asked. "A tourist?"

"Keep moving," Peaches said. He didn't give a shit what season it was. He liked wearing linen now. That's how he dressed. And no one fucked with someone who wore sunglasses inside. Most of the time, people thought he was blind.

"He's dressed as an asshole," the cat said. "And smells like one, too."

Peaches watched the women bungle into the restroom. Their laughter echoed out into the lobby. The girl at the front desk could barely restrain her own laughter, tried to cough through it. Same with the old queen at the concierge desk. Everyone thought he was some kind of joke. He was the fucking boss of Chicago now, and in Lincolnwood, that didn't mean shit. If Ronnie Cupertine were sitting here, people would be asking for his autograph.

Cute.

It would be real funny when he went into the bathroom and strangled those women, came out and popped these giggling assholes, which he'd decided he was going to do . . . right when Mike pulled up in his new Ford Expedition.

"You have a good night, sir," the front desk girl said when Peaches passed her.

Peaches stopped, tipped his glasses down, examined her. "You got lucky tonight," he said.

"Thanks," she said, because that's all these people ever said, their scripts never deviating. *Good morning. Good afternoon. Good night. Thanks.*

"You're welcome," Peaches said. Because one day? When he was long gone? His picture would be up on the wall, too. Holding the Rain Man's head in his hand.

SAL CUPERTINE'S HOUSE was only a mile from the Purple Hotel, just off Birchwood, middle of a quiet street, big lawns, long driveways, Japanese cars, basketball hoops, ghosts and goblins and red decorative lights, toilet paper flung around some old-growth trees and box hedges, a touch of light Halloween vandalism, the kind the vandals would help clean up in the morning. The Cupertine house had a white picket fence surrounding the front yard, but even now, after midnight, and with sunglasses on, Peaches could see when they crawled by that the front lawn was overgrown and the mailbox on the street overflowed with paper. Wasn't a single light on. He'd checked and the electricity hadn't been turned off. Nor the gas. Some bills were still getting paid.

"What do you think?" Mike asked. He was dressed like Elvis in the 1968 Comeback Special. Wig and leather jacket and everything.

"Go around the block one more time," Peaches said.

There were still people outside, mostly teenagers in costume, hanging out in their garages, bullshitting. No cops, though, not out here. Peaches wasn't yet in the position to get an escort during his crimes. If he was going to a meeting, yeah, he could get them to show up, watch the street, make sure he wasn't about to get wet up. A night like tonight, he didn't need any extra eyes.

More important, Peaches didn't make any government agents. Every car they drove by had state license plates. No beefy white guys sat alone in sedans. It had been eight weeks since Jennifer Cupertine and her kid disappeared. Sugar told him the scene at Carson's was chaos and he wasn't about to stick around for it. Not that Peaches blamed him, but shit. The plan had been to grab them both, use them as leverage to get the Rain Man to show his face, then take them all out at once. Now that was fucked, so Peaches had to move to plan B.

If there was no one watching the house, that meant the feds knew Jennifer and the kid's location, weren't worried about Sal Cupertine showing up and whisking them away. Not like they were watching Ronnie's house on the Gold Coast these days, waiting for Sharon and the kids to return. No one in the Family had an opinion on where Sharon might have gone, because even suggesting she'd gone to the feds was like putting the whammy on themselves, everyone in the Family superstitious. Peaches wasn't into that mystical shit. If he were Sharon? He'd have gone straight to the feds the day Ronnie got his ass beat, then stroked out in the ambulance. But that didn't happen. Because Sharon Cupertine, she was one of those Family ladies that thought it was the 1960s, that families were hands off.

Those were the old ways, as Peaches liked to tell Mike, and Mike liked to repeat it as if he came up with it himself.

The only person out there keeping Peaches from total control of Chicago was Sal Cupertine. So fine. If Peaches couldn't find him, he'd figure out something else.

"All right," Peaches said, once they were back at the top of the block, the Cupertine place four houses away, Peaches able to see the tire swing in the front yard from this perch. "Go up to the door. A neighbor comes out and asks you what you're doing, you're looking for a party. You're a little high and you're lost."

"Yeah, yeah," Mike said. He rubbed at his nose with his thumb. He *was* a little high. Still, he'd proven to be an able lieutenant, smarter than Peaches initially thought, willing to take on tough jobs. "And then take them out?"

"No," Peaches said. "You're dressed like Elvis. Tell them thank you, thank you very much, and walk away. We'll come back tomorrow. No one comes up on you, handle your business. Efficiently, understand?"

"A'ight," he said. "Made something special."

He reached into a bag in the backseat, came out with a bundle of construction-grade dynamite. Five sticks. He'd affixed six feet of safety fuse line to it, which burned about an inch every four seconds. That gave them almost five minutes to get moving. Plenty of time.

Mike shoved the bundle inside his leather jacket and got out. Peaches watched him saunter down the block, kept track of the other houses, in case someone popped out with a gun. He'd done his homework, so he wasn't all that worried. None of the houses had been sold in the last five years, none of the utilities records on the block had been shifted to another name, and when Peaches took his girls through earlier this evening, all he saw in every house was people watching CNN.

Still, they had to be smart, which is why when Mike turned up the Cupertines' driveway and disappeared into the darkness, Peaches took out a burner phone from his jacket, dialed 911, but didn't hit

CALL just yet. There was a fire station two miles away. They'd be able to get an engine here in just a couple minutes. Burn down the Rain Man's house? Fine. Kill a bunch of civilians? Not so good. Not in this climate.

A minute later, Mike came back down the driveway, his gait brisk. Not running. People notice running. Just moving at a good clip. Thirty seconds, Mike was in the front seat and they were moving. Three minutes, they were cruising down Lincoln Avenue, windows down, about to turn onto Touhy, a block from the Purple, when Peaches heard the boom. He turned around in his seat to see the night sky fill with a column of thick black smoke.

Peaches hit CALL, waited. "Yes," he said, after a moment, "I think I just saw a small plane crash into a house."

15

Rabbi David Cohen hated Chinese food, which made it difficult to be a Jew. Temple Beth Israel congregants always wanted to drag him to Chinatown to eat every combination of shellfish and pork they could imagine, as if being in a Chinese restaurant somehow made Kosher rules null and void. "You don't want to be rude," Rabbi Kales told him one time, when Stanley Alexander took them both to lunch to talk about starting a music program for seniors at the Performing Arts Center, Stanley some big *macher* on Broadway back in the day. "Pretend the suckling pig is veal. Pretend the crab is salmon."

"That's what you do?" David asked. Not that he actually kept kosher, but he'd grown accustomed to doing so in public.

"No," Rabbi Kales told him. "I simply enjoy the meal. It's Chinatown."

Except it wasn't. Chinatown in Las Vegas was only a master-planned shopping plaza on a seedy stretch of Spring Mountain where the furniture stores, self-storage facilities, and sex shops gave way to a giant faux–Tang dynasty arch and a dozen restaurants and shops, all vaguely themed to express some part of the Orient. A mile away, it was back to the same graveyard of big-box stores, Krispy Kreme drive-thrus, and Manic Al's pit stops as the rest of the valley.

So David tried to avoid Chinatown, even though it was one of the few places in town he felt relatively safe from cameras, the whole block owned by a development company out of Hong Kong and policed largely by private security, none of whom gave a shit about anything short of a murder. Asian gangs had claimed the block, ironic since none of them lived in the area, the neighborhood around Spring Mountain and Decatur mostly working class and white, so the gangsters had to commute to work. Not like these guys were Triads. The papers talked about United Bamboo being in town now, a Thai gang up from LA. Then there was talk of Vietnamese gangs, and Filipino gangs, all of them supposedly running their operations out of Chinatown, though by the looks of the guys hanging out this afternoon, it was mostly teenagers in lowered Honda Civics. They might as well claim Café Espresso Roma or the Boulevard Mall or the old schoolhouse downtown, because, as David saw from inside the tea shop next to the Ranch 99 grocery store, the only game working in Chinatown was overcharging tourists for Boba, which was fucking Japanese.

Five and a half bucks for Hokkaido Milk Tea seemed outrageous, but David paid it to the seventy-something Asian woman behind the counter, and then sat down and waited for Gray Beard and Marvin. David always arrived first, even though Gray Beard had picked the meeting place. That was the key to not having someone walk up behind you and put one in your ear, not that he expected Gray Beard to be the one to get the drop on him. Gray Beard was in his sixties, David guessed, had been a doctor at some point, but he'd been doing favors for Bennie Savone for a good long time. David had inherited him after his first series of dental surgeries required some extra care. In the interim, he'd found that he and his partner Marvin, who was maybe half his age, weren't averse to doing some favors for money and materials. They'd cleaned up a murder scene for David, dropped Jeff Hopper's head in Chicago, and left money for Jennifer. David didn't want to overuse their services, but these were special times. So David contacted him a few days after getting back from Carson City, made sure Gray Beard was still game, even after the world started to collapse from the middle out. Asked him to get rid of Roger's RV, had him run another errand, too.

After about five minutes, a blue-and-white Zenith Medical Equipment and Supply truck pulled into the lot. Gray Beard and Marvin stepped out, both dressed in crisp white uniforms. They came into the tea shop, Gray Bead nodded at David, both of them ordered from the old woman behind the counter and then pulled two chairs over to David's table.

"New truck?" David asked.

"Needed something bigger," Gray Beard said. "Been a real busy time for our business." He reached into his pocket, came out with an envelope, slid it across the table. "That's what's left from the sale of the RV. Needed to have a professional work on the cargo hold. Smell wouldn't come out. Plus Marvin's expenses in Chicago."

David flipped the envelope open. There was about two grand inside. He pushed it back across the table. "Keep it," David said.

"You sure?" Gray Beard asked.

"Holiday bonus," David said. It was two weeks before Thanksgiving, but already Las Vegas looked like a winter wonderland, even the tea joint covered in pictures of Santa and his reindeer, Johnny Mathis coming out of a tinny speaker on the counter, going on about who had a date for New Year's Eve.

"People been losing their minds lately." Gray Beard lowered his voice. "Took a bullet out of a guy's head the other night. He showed up at the office, looked like he had a racing stripe down the side of his face, said he'd changed his mind at the last minute, decided he wanted to live." Gray Beard's office was wherever he parked his own RV, but which was usually Lorenzi Park. "Bullet was lodged in the fleshy part between the skull and neck, behind the ear? Took me five hours, but we did it." He and Marvin tapped their cups of tea. "You been busy?"

"Yeah," David said. Which was true. First couple days after the planes hit, the temple was empty, same with the school, but then everyone started to come out of their caves, wanted to be around people they recognized, wanted David to explain how to keep living in the face of such tragedy. And then the other side of the business became electric, too, just like he thought it would. Debts started to pile up, people started to pile up, too. The Triads dumped off another war casualty, a little older this time. Maybe twenty-five. No fucking fingers on either hand. Then they shipped out three white boys. Then an older black guy, in his fifties. A nice cash haul, but that was twenty dead men in a few months, and that wasn't nothing, plus the white boys and the black guy weren't war dead, they were just dead. No torture. Just a bullet in the eye. Might not be tomorrow or the next day, but eventually there would be a snitch who would offer up one of those bodies, which David added to his list of concerns. Then a tribal gang in Palm Springs made a deposit—forty-something Mexican, bullet between the eyes. Palm Springs was an area of recent growth. The weak-ass LA Mafia, half of whom had been busted in 1988, were finally getting out of prison and had begun to partner up on some casinos and bingo joints and nightclubs and drug routes for the tribes out that way, which meant they were tussling with Mexican Mafia types over territory and influence, which explained the body. An actual OG in the game, judging from the tattoos David saw—old prison ink, nothing flashy or intricate like Ruben had—which meant he must be of some importance, since gangsters didn't tend to live that long.

"It's been a time, all right," David said. He looked at Marvin. "What about my errand?" he asked.

Gray Beard shifted in his seat. "You sure you want this now?"

"Yeah." The news was going to affect some decisions he had to make.

Gray Beard said, "This isn't a situation where the messenger needs to worry, I presume?"

"No," David said. He meant that. For now, anyway.

"Tell him," Gray Beard said to Marvin.

"That address doesn't exist anymore," Marvin said.

David sent Marvin to check on his house in Chicago. And the disposition of one Ronald J. Cupertine, a patient of Northwestern Hospital.

"What does that mean?" David asked.

"Burned down," he said.

"When?"

"Neighbor kid said it was Halloween night," Marvin said. "It had been empty for over a month. Firefighters just let it go, seems like. Kid said people who lived there were cooking meth so no one moved real quick to put the fire out. Firefighters just protected the other houses on the block."

"Meth," David said. Jennifer never let any drugs in the house. She sure as fuck wasn't cooking meth.

"Hey," Gray Beard said, "he's just reporting."

"Anyone seen these tweaks since the fire?"

"Kid didn't say. I didn't pump him, you know? I just acted like I was trying to drop off a piece of furniture. Rented a truck with a sofa in it and everything. Didn't want someone to peg me for trying to abduct an eleven-year-old on Rollerblades."

It did make sense, David had to concede. The adults in the neighborhood surely knew who Sal Cupertine was, probably didn't like the idea that the family of a murderer lived on the block. That the firemen didn't bother to put the fire out wasn't a surprise. First cop who showed up on the scene probably made the situation clear. You didn't save the Rain Man's house. "Okay. What else?"

"I went to that museum? They said the woman doesn't work there anymore. Not since September."

Over two months now. Jennifer and William could be anywhere. He had to hope they were in custody. If she were hiding, David was confident she'd leave some kind of message for him, somewhere. Unless burning down the house was the message, which could be the case if it had burned down when she disappeared, not six weeks later. Federal custody was the best-case scenario, even though that meant she felt so threatened, she had to get off the streets. Which meant she knew it wasn't the feds who were doing the threatening.

But if Ronnie was out of commission, who would give a shit if Jennifer were at home, doing her thing? No one in the Family would move on her. They'd known her since she was an infant. And if they had any loyalty to Sal, they sure as fuck wouldn't touch his kid. What was the name of the guy Bennie had given him?

Peaches.

"Okay," David said.

He was thinking now. Trying to figure out what it meant to burn down his house if Jennifer and William were already gone.

David loved that house. Bought it with his own money. Got a loan and everything. Well, Jennifer did. And it's not like he thought he was ever going to live in that house again. But he imagined William would live in it until he went to college, because William was going to college. He'd made that decision months before William was born. He had dreams about that house, so precise that he could see every knot in the wood floor. Could imagine Jennifer and William in every room. All the boys knew how much Sal liked the place, would talk about how the Rain Man was cleaning his own rain gutters now, the height of fucking wit and irony, but when it was time for a BBQ or a kid's birthday party and all they had were shitty walk ups with no yards? Or apartments on the fucking Loop? Who did their fucking wives and girlfriends call, asking for a favor?

And now it was . . . *gone?* Like it never existed at all? Whoever burned his fucking house down? David wasn't going to forgive that shit. He'd go old school. Like, Inquisition old school.

And there it was.

He'd have to go to Chicago for that job. Would have to go on the hunt. If he wanted to find Jennifer and William? Same deal. And if it turned out they were in custody, he'd have to find someone close to the feds, which would not be easy, in light of everything.

Thing he didn't get was that Ronnie knew where Sal was. If Ronnie wanted someone to kill him, all he had to do was find some dumb fuck willing to take the job. Maybe that wasn't going to be someone in the Family—David felt good about that—but still, there'd be some guy trying to make his name. But they would have done it already. Soon as Sal cut Ronnie out of the Las Vegas con, he would have sent a team if he really wanted vengeance. But that wasn't the game.

Ronnie wanted money. Territory. Advantage. He wasn't going to get that by killing Sal. He'd get that by killing Bennie, maybe. But that hadn't happened either, because Ronnie knew that if Bennie Savone died, cops and feds would start looking at the temple and that would mean Sal's ass and, by association, Ronnie's. If whoever this Peaches motherfucker was wanted to have Sal killed, he could send a fucking pipe bomb via Fed Ex, or send three or four guys with automatic weapons. They could do that right now.

Unless Ronnie wasn't talking. Literally wasn't talking.

"Did you find out if Ronnie Cupertine was still in the hospital?" David asked. He didn't mind saying his name out loud, didn't think it was a curse like if he said Jennifer's and William's names, because Ronnie Cupertine was a public figure.

"Yeah," Marvin said. "That place was secure as hell, though, so I couldn't see him. I called his room, said I was a cousin. Nurse said he was in no condition to speak. Said a good cousin would show up and sit for a bit and then hung up on me."

"This was at Northwestern?"

"Yeah. Where you told me."

"You see any law enforcement on the floor?"

"A few. Plainclothes types." That could be cops, that could be feds.

"Security?"

"Private guys."

"They have guns?"

"Not that I saw. Walkie-talkies and Maglites. Guys like that."

"Any guys like me?"

"With the yarmulkes?"

"No," David said. "Guys like me, but don't look like me." When Marvin gave him a confused look, David said, "Someone who didn't fit in."

Marvin thought for a moment. "I guess I saw one guy," he said eventually, "sitting by the elevator with a magazine, but not really reading it, just kind of flipping through the pages."

"What was the magazine?"

"*Sunset* or *Redbook* or some shit? Like what you find in a waiting room."

"What was he wearing?" David asked.

"That's what made him stand out, actually. Everyone on that floor? Man, they were done up nice. Suits and expensive shoes— those new Jordans? This guy had on a blue sweat suit and had a tattoo of a face on his neck. No one else had any visible tattoos. So. There was that."

That didn't make sense. Even the Gangster 2-6 guys Ronnie employed, like that poor fucker Chema, he made them dress well.

So if Ronnie wasn't talking, if this Peaches was in charge now *because* of that, maybe the problem now was that this Peaches didn't know where Sal Cupertine was or when he might show up.

If Sal Cupertine got arrested, this whole enterprise would come down.

If Sal Cupertine showed up looking for vengeance, same problem.

And if Sal Cupertine was simply out there, unaccounted for, who knew when he might want to come back and get a piece of the action. Because if Ronnie Cupertine died, the Family belonged to Sal. That was the line of succession.

Then something clicked into place, an idea, the machinery of this whole thing starting to grind into position. Ronnie has a stroke. Someone named Peaches takes over, might be partnering with some non-Family types. Jennie and William disappear. Someone burns down Sal's house. Ronnie's still in the hospital, but he's got cops, gangsters, and private security watching him, which means he can't defend himself, everyone thinks someone's gonna show up. Good guys think that. Bad guys think that.

Yeah.

There it was.

Peaches *wanted* him to show up. Couldn't very well run your own crime empire with a rogue actor floating out in the ether. If Jennifer and William went to ground, maybe Sal Cupertine would poke his head back up, just in time for a sword to lop it off.

He had to give these fuckers credit. It was a more elegant con than he'd thought them capable of, which was yet another reason why David was sure it *wasn't* Ronnie's doing. He'd been snitching on himself for years, David knew that, but he wasn't about to bring Sal back to town and be faced with a history of murder that no amount of confidential information could erase.

David had to think now. Figure out his next move. "Anything else?"

"Your face is falling apart," Gray Beard said, "if you don't mind me saying."

"That hasn't escaped me," David said. "I'm getting it fixed next month."

"By who?"

"Dr. Melnikoff."

Gray Beard whistled. "I didn't know he was still with us."

"Yeah," David said. "I don't foresee that changing."

"Well, good. He has small hands. You want a doctor with small hands." Gray Beard leaned forward, showed David his hands. It looked like he could palm a basketball. "You need something after the surgery, you know where to find me." He tapped Marvin on the leg and they both got up to leave, but David followed them out to the truck.

"Something wrong?" Gray Beard asked.

"No," David said. "I just want to take a look inside."

Marvin gave Gray Beard a look, but the older man just shrugged, so Marvin unlocked the back, pulled up the door. David put his head in, looked around. It was empty. It's always wise to make sure. He also had one other question for Marvin. "Did you happen to see a tire swing?"

"Where?"

"Front of the house, near the end of the driveway," David said. "Big blue ash tree." It was one of the first things David had done after they bought the house. Jennifer would swing on it while David mowed the lawn. No. Not David. Sal. While Sal mowed the lawn. Then eventually William tried it a few times, but he wasn't big enough yet and Jennifer was scared he'd fall.

"There was no front," Marvin said. "That shit was all gone. Flat. Could see straight through to the neighbor's house. It was the ghost of a house."

Gray Beard let Marvin get back into the truck before he said, "He's too honest. Hope it's not a fatal flaw."

"It's not."

"I did want to ask about Mr. Savone," Gray Beard said, "but didn't know if that was a subject you were comfortable discussing."

"It's not," David said. "But I can tell you he's getting off house arrest in January."

"Then maybe I'll be leaving town in January," he said. "In case there comes some advanced scrutiny on his movements."

"There will be," David said. "It would be real wise for you to not say his name out loud when that time comes." A thought came to him. "Could be I need you for something else before then, though. Before Hanukkah."

"Always happy to help a man of the cloth," Gray Beard said.

David watched them drive off, then went back to the tea shop, bought another Hokkaido for the road. The Talmud taught that soldiers fight but kings become heroes, and for a long time, David believed that, even before he knew what it meant. He'd been a soldier in a war his entire life, protecting men who would let him die.

It was time to become a king.

16

Grace, the Talmud said, was given to those who were merciful.
Rabbi David Cohen didn't exactly believe that was true. Rather,
he believed that you were either endowed with grace or it was a
thing you spent your entire life searching for, a pure thing recogniz-
able when it arrived. He understood that Christians held grace in a
different view, that the resurrection of Christ allowed for God to
give grace to everyone, which meant each person had the capacity
for grace, even if they didn't use it. You didn't need to do anything.
You merely had to believe. And then you *deserved* grace.

Which David thought said a lot about the world these days. No
one was willing to earn shit. Everything was birthright. It was a
thought that had plagued David of late, thinking about how if he
were still in Chicago, and Ronnie was sick, he'd be running the
Family. Who would come at him? No one. Because even though Sal
Cupertine wasn't a capo, wasn't ranked at all, just did the dirty work,
everyone in the Family understood the nature of things. He was a
Cupertine and so he *was* the Family.

Which is why he was out here, in Las Vegas, with a new face,
even if it was tearing apart at the seams. Ronnie never did want
someone coming up behind him. He would run the Family until
such time there was no Family. He'd die and take it all with him.
Reputation as important to him as anything else in the world. He'd
be the last don. He'd be legend.

Sal Cupertine would have given him that grace. Because Sal
Cupertine didn't want that fucking job.

But that didn't mean he wanted someone else to have it.

The Talmud also said that there were four classes of people who must offer thanksgiving: those who have crossed the sea, those who have traversed the wilderness, those who have recovered from illness, and prisoners who have been set free. In no case was being merciful required, but it reasoned that any of those four kinds of people would naturally be endowed with a *sense* of grace, if not the thing itself. So Rabbi David Cohen preferred to think that grace was given to those who fought through some shit and came out alive. That being trapped somewhere—at sea, in the woods, in your body, or in a cage—required you to perform outside your normal character, contrary to your nature.

It wasn't about belief.

It was about action.

•

DAVID WALKED OUT onto the front steps of Temple Beth Israel's Performing Arts Center and watched the children playing across the way at the Tikvah Preschool. Below, the leaders of the largest Jewish congregations in the city pulled into the parking lot, one by one, in their German luxury cars. Rabbi Joseph Sigal of Temple Beth Am in his black Mercedes E-class. Rabbi Sherman Roth of Temple Beth Shalom in his silver BMW 528. Rabbi Jason Goldstein of Congregation Beth El in his white Mercedes E-class, which seemed out of character for an Orthodox Jew, but these were unorthodox times. Even Yehuda Da Truth Tella, now going by the more staid Yehuda Stein, in a tricked-out electric-blue BMW X3, the logo for his new Red Rock Kabbalah Center, which had opened in a space that used to be a Tower Records, splashed over the entire driver's side of the car. Today, the Monday after Thanksgiving, wasn't about grace. It was about protection. The first stage of his exit plan. The safety of the Jewish people of Las Vegas. Because Gray Beard was right. Everybody was losing their minds.

David had called a meeting of leaders of the community, reminding each that the Talmud said you should never expose yourself to danger, since a miracle may not save you. "We must present a united front during these times," David told each man, individually, when he phoned them. "We must be one and the same. We must show that the Torah is our connection, that the tribal segregation of our beliefs is a mundane thing during these dark times." David didn't even ask Rabbi Kales for advice; he knew that appealing to their fundamental mortality was the ticket.

Not that anyone needed any convincing. Security had been a debilitating concern for all the people at Temple Beth Israel since the events on 9/11 . . . and it turned out to be a transitive property valley-wide, all the shuls going batshit once it was revealed that many of the hijackers had visited Las Vegas to plan the attacks and get lap dances all over town. (Girls at Bennie's club, the Wild Horse, had even gone to the press, saying they were pretty sure they'd danced for them and that they were shitty tippers, Bennie telling David last week, "When all this shit blows over? Those girls will know for sure if they danced for those guys, because they'll be together again.")

Everyone at Temple Beth Israel was installing security systems in their houses, sons and daughters were being enrolled in Tae Kwon Do, as if Al-Qaeda were going to show up to do hand-to-hand combat with eleven-year-old Jewish kids at the Fashion Show Mall, and old-timers were coming in to talk to David about building attics in their open-concept homes. Jews had a tendency to horde when shit got bad—it was even in the Talmud: "A person should always have his money at hand"—and the result was that donations were down 65 percent, the giving during the High Holidays almost negligible, everyone bunkered in their houses, waiting to die. And it wasn't just charitable giving: Business at the Wild Horse was down close to 50 percent. The hotels and casinos had picked up a little recently, at least according to what they were saying publicly, though the idea of getting on a plane and flying out to stay in a high-rise in Las Vegas wasn't what anyone wanted to do during that first month. But that didn't stop Las Vegas. The city had rolled out a new marketing campaign—*Freedom to get away from it all!*—because losing your house to Sheldon Adelson was what freedom meant. *Whatever you lost in Vegas, ends up washed into new casino construction in Macau.* That would be a more honest slogan. But as business picked up on the Strip, as more and more people were driving into town from San Diego, Los Angeles, the Bay Area, Phoenix, Salt Lake City, even from southern Oregon, so, too, did the fear. Anyone could *drive* into Las Vegas. What was stopping some lunatic from pulling up to one of the temples with a car bomb?

Nothing, David knew.

Turned out, you could kill someone with your bare hands right in front of a synagogue and no one would notice.

As predicted, the cops had shown up a few days after Agent Moss's disappearance. They simply walked back her last steps. David confirmed that he'd seen her, described what she was wearing, even recounted their conversation as it happened, before he broke her neck, that he'd called in Ruben, who confirmed that when he arrived, she was already gone. Carson City cops didn't even send one of their own—a Las Vegas cop handled it, took a statement, moved on. They spoke with David for seven minutes. They spoke with Ruben for less than that. Fifteen minutes, including the time it took to walk from the temple to the funeral home, and Melanie Moss was someone else's problem. A missing person. A tragedy.

But the world was filled with tragedies big and small these days.

A few days before Thanksgiving, David ran into OG Sean B's mother, Kate, in the Lowe's garden section. Kate cornered him by the pesticides, where he was picking up a few things. She looked a wreck. "Why is God letting this happen?" she asked him.

He wanted to tell her to get the fuck out of town. Take all her money, get Sean, and go. Because she didn't know about bad news. She didn't know what it was like to have squirreled away cash in banks he was scared to walk into now, the government with eyes on where money was flowing. He'd managed to get about one hundred thousand out of safe deposit boxes on September 12, but he had at least fifty K in a bank up in Pahrump, not far from a brothel the hijackers allegedly visited, and another fifty in a run-down Wells Fargo across the street from the Econo Lodge where one hijacker had supposedly stayed, just a block off the Strip. But with the FBI crawling around that entire neighborhood looking for evidence, he didn't want to walk into the wrong place at the wrong time and end up facedown with a gun on his head. He wasn't about to go anywhere near the Strip that first week . . . and then, after that? Well, it had only gotten worse.

He was getting squeezed everywhere.

Last week, sitting in Dr. Melnikoff's waiting room, a show was running on TLC called *Daring Escapes*, and five minutes in, some asshole wearing a zoot suit and a leather duster was shown sneaking into the back of a refrigerated meat truck. David realized he was watching himself, or some fictionalized version of himself where he wore fucking zoot suits. David got up from his seat and turned the volume up, the voice-over saying, "This vicious hired killer had one more job: survive being frozen to death until he could get his hands on the truck driver." David thinking, *I didn't touch that fucking truck driver. It was 43 degrees in that truck and I had ten blankets. And a chair.* The next scene showed him shivering and blue, icicles in his hair, cooking raw meat using a Zippo, shoving it into his mouth like he was starving to death. The next scene, the truck was opening up to a beach in California, "Sal" was jumping out, guns blazing, except "Sal" for some reason had a machine gun and riddled the truck driver with about thirty bullets, before he dove into a waiting Lincoln Town Car and was whisked off.

The show posted Sal's grainy photo, the same one they always used, from the Subway in Chicago, along with information on how to claim the reward for his capture and conviction. David looked around the waiting room. There were two women David was pretty sure were strippers, judging from the pervasive body spray and their ongoing conversation about cup size and tip-outs; a thirteen-year-old boy with a huge nose, who was mostly staring at the two women;

the boy's mother, who was flipping through an US *Magazine* and breathing with such venom that it sounded like she was snarling; an older woman, maybe in her sixties, who kept tugging at her neck. None of them had even noticed the TV. But it didn't matter. It was in the popular culture now. He was no longer the Rain Man. He was Mr. Meat Truck.

Even if Bennie somehow got him a passport, he wouldn't go near an airport. Not now, anyway. He doubted he could get on an Amtrak train or a Greyhound bus. He wasn't thrilled with the idea of giving his fake license to pick up Sudafed at Rite-Aid, didn't like the big sign that said SMILE YOU'RE ON CAMERA next to the CCTV inside Walgreen's, even though he paid cash everywhere, so no one was tracking his cash movements, at least. But it was the proliferating cameras that had him worried. Before, he was pretty sure no one paid any attention to that shit, like at the Walmart in Carson City. Maybe Walmart and Walgreens and Rite-Aid and Target weren't doing black ops for the government, but now? All this Patriot Act shit? He wasn't so sure.

Given all this, his goals had changed. Before, it was about getting his wife and kid and getting the fuck out. Now? It was about staying alive long enough to find them; it was about securing a financial future in Las Vegas, where he was now trapped, so that when the door opened, there'd be no hesitation. That meant keeping Bennie in a place where he didn't control all the money. That meant keeping Rabbi Kales in a place where he wouldn't snitch to Bennie—or his daughter, Rachel—if he began to feel like David was overstepping. That meant no more unforced errors. Safety, above all else.

The Torah said, those who are wise shall shine like the brightness of the sky above and those who turn others to righteousness will be like the stars forever and ever. He was going to do that. Keep the righteous in his sphere, and keep them indebted, so that when it was time to bounce, they wouldn't turn on him.

So, in light of all that, a container of pesticide in his hand, David told Kate, "God does not wish us to know why there is so much bad in the world, why the good must always be tempered with evil, because if we knew, we might consent." It was something the Lubavitcher Rebbe had said, but Kate Berkowitz didn't seem to grasp it.

He took her by the hand. Because he was taking everyone by the hand these days, all of Temple Beth Israel a ball of emotional ruin. "What you need to do is simple, Kate. After Sean's bar mitzvah, you need to leave Las Vegas. You need to leave your cheating husband and his girlfriend behind. You need to not pack any of Sean's clothes when you leave, just put him in the car, and when you get somewhere else, buy him clothes that make him look like a mensch. Because, Kate, if I may say so? He's not tough. He will never be tough. And this is a world where you cannot fake toughness anymore. Let him be articulate and smart, but do not let him be tough. Does this make sense to you?"

"Yes," she said. "Yes. It does."

"And you need to stop drinking," David said. "Sean needs a stable parent. That needs to be you."

Kate tried to take her hand back, but David held on. "I am trying to help you. I am trying to help your son."

She looked away. David let go of her hand. "I'm so lost," she said. "I'm feeling so lost." She was crying now, so David took his handkerchief out from his suit pocket, handed it to her. She blew her nose, folded the handkerchief, put it in her purse.

"Can I," David said, "put a friend in touch with you? Just someone for you to speak with?"

"I'll take whatever help you can find," she said.

He would give her that grace.

•

NOW, AS THE rabbis and Yehuda began to climb the steps, he was more confident than ever about what needed to be done to keep everyone safe. This house would not be burned to the ground.

David greeted each man as they came up the steps with a hand-shake and a grim smile, as much as that was possible, the right side of his face not quite right this morning. He'd been on antibiotics for eight weeks now and the only tangible results, best as David could tell, was that his eyeballs didn't hurt when his lips moved. There was a constant metallic taste in his mouth, like he'd swallowed a gun, but never any blood. Dr. Melnikoff told him it could be a variety of things, most likely that the titanium rods in his mouth needed to be replaced, too, which would be another five grand.

"Sweet place," Yehuda said when he walked in, pulling up the rear. He took off his sunglasses and pointed up at the face of the Performing Arts Center, a solid glass wall stretching three stories high. Inside, the performance hall sat five hundred, plus practice facilities, meeting rooms, banquet space, concessions. It had been the centerpiece of Rabbi Kales's fund-raising for a decade. David imagined it had also been a great way for Bennie to wash cash.

"Have you not been here?" David said. He knew that he hadn't. Rabbis Sigal, Rosen, and Goldstein had visited a few times over the years, each of them at the invitation of Rabbi Kales, who'd known them all for years. Sigal had actually been Rabbi Kales's boss at Temple Shalom, before both struck out on their own. When they saw each other now, they would talk like the old fucks in the game who had somehow survived all the wars and couldn't remember why they'd tried to kill each other so many times. The difference being, Rabbi Kales honestly wished Sigal would die, his every move at Temple Beth Israel aimed at crushing Sigal's congregation.

"I appreciate the invitation," Yehuda said. "I know you and the other rabbis view me as an annoyance at best and a heretic at worst. Right now, this idea of a united front is a welcome development. We're all Jews."

"Except," David said, "all the people who study Kabbalah who aren't Jews."

"Way I see it," Yehuda said, "those are the very people we need to reach. Maybe it starts with a red string, maybe it ends with a bat mitzvah."

"True enough," David said. A white van pulled into the lot. "That's the caterer," David said. "I'll be right in. Will you tell the others?"

"Of course," Yehuda said. "I appreciate you asking for everyone's dietary restrictions."

"Talmud says the belly carries the feet," David said.

David walked down the steps and the van's side door slid open. Gray Beard sat inside, his long beard neatly trimmed but still half-way down his neck.

Gray Beard handed David two covered platters of food.

"That's the order," he said. He wore a pair of plastic gloves. "Soups and hot stuff is on the bottom."

David lifted the lid off the top platter. There were several sandwiches and salads and desserts, each marked with a decorative flag for whom it was meant. "You put it together?" David asked.

"Nah, that was me," Marvin said from the front seat. He also had on gloves.

"I need to wear gloves to serve this?"

"Nah," Marvin said. "It's cool. Precautionary, you know?"

"What about if I have someone take it from the platter and put it on some nice china?"

Gray Beard and Marvin exchanged a look. "Being careful never hurt anybody," Gray Beard said.

IT TOOK THIRTY minutes for the five men, including David, to finish their lunch. They sat around a long rectangular table in the Performing Arts Center's banquet hall, eating their chicken-and-matzo-ball soup—except Rabbi Sigal, who had borscht—their selection of sandwiches, their salads—potato, macaroni, kale for Yehuda—and wide array of cookies: pecan, shortbread, rugelach, black and whites, lemon poppy seed, coconut macaroons. David sat at the head of the table, Rabbi Sigal to his left, Rabbi Goldstein beside Rabbi Sigal. Rabbi Roth sat to David's right, with Yehuda next to him, though with a space between them. The rabbis made idle chitchat during lunch, which meant each man went through a list of who was sick, who was dying, who was divorcing, who was cheating on whom, and, finally, who had gone bankrupt in the last sixty days, while Yehuda kept stepping out to take calls on his cell phone, David thinking maybe in addition to the Zohar, he might also be peddling pills. He'd respect him more if so.

"Sorry," Yehuda said when he popped back in. "We have contractors coming today to set up a hookah lounge and it's just been one problem with the city after another. It was probably better when the Mafia controlled everything. You just handed over an envelope filled with cash? Is that how it was done?"

Naomi Rosen-Solomon came in with a stack of manila folders—she worked part-time at the temple now, planned to stay on right up until her baby was due—and a refilled pitcher of water before anyone dared to answer. It wasn't as if the other rabbis didn't know of Bennie Savone's involvement with Temple Beth Israel . . . it was just that they all had their own version in some form or fashion. It was Las Vegas. Crooked money, in the end, was still money.

"Can I get a Diet Coke?" Yehuda asked Naomi.

"I'm not a waitress," Naomi said, "but I'll see if we have any in the machine. Do you have a dollar?"

Yehuda flipped through his wallet. "All I've got are fifties."

"You can owe me," she said. When Naomi came back a few minutes later with another pitcher of coffee and a can for Yehuda, Yehuda noticed the red string on Naomi's wrist.

"Where'd you get that?" he asked her, all teeth and wide eyes.

"Oh, we sell them in our Judaica shop now," Naomi said, and David saw Yehuda's smile waver. *That's right, motherfucker.* Naomi turned her attention to David. "Do you need anything else, Rabbi Cohen?"

"No," David said. "Why don't you lock up the front and go home. I'll see these fine men out when we finish and get the doors open for the after-school program when the next round of volunteers arrive."

"Of course, Rabbi," she said.

"A little young to be having a child, isn't she?" Rabbi Sigal said when Naomi was gone.

"She's graduated college," David said. "A hundred and fifty years ago, she would have already lost two children during birth and traversed the country in a wagon train."

"I guess it is a matter of perspective." Rabbi Sigal had eaten all of his borscht and his lips were a light pink color. "I remember when she was born. Her father and his father used to come to my shul."

"Times change," David said.

"Indeed," Sigal said. He tapped his lips, a thing Rabbi Kales did, every rabbi a parrot, all the way to Maimonides.

David pushed his chair a few inches from the table, regarded the four men around him with what he hoped was solemnity, but with his face in its current condition, he really had no idea. "So," he said, "gentlemen, first I want to thank you for coming here. I know you each are very busy, that this time in our collective lives is fraught, and that after Thanksgiving, the last thing you want to do is spend an hour in a closed room with a bunch of Jews." David waited for one of them men to laugh, but none did. He didn't yet have the skill Rabbi Kales had of forcing people to laugh even when you hadn't said anything particularly amusing. "But, as you can see, and as I'm sure the machinery of *lashon hara* has provided, I'm in the midst of a small medical problem, which is part of why I've called this meeting today. Time, I'm afraid, is short."

"I didn't want to say anything," Rabbi Roth said, and the other men nodded along like they'd each been holding a terrible secret, which, as it happened, they probably had been. "You must be in terrible pain. Is it . . . a stroke?"

David liked Rabbi Roth. He was only a few years older than David and though his temple was less reformed, there were a lot of mid-level casino executives in their ranks, which equaled a lot of money but not a lot of activism. Rabbi Sigal had the casino owners in his stable, which meant he had endowments and investments in the tens of millions, owned property all over the county—housing tracts, office buildings in Green Valley, even the land under a new shopping center called the Commons in Henderson, anchored by a Pottery Barn, a Restoration Hardware, and a Williams Sonoma. Roth's temple probably had a couple million in the bank, plus investments, including their own small, overpriced school, and some action in the Malibu Grand Prix franchise a few blocks off the Strip, the temple making bank on the video games and concessions, the expansion of their synagogue funded by tourists. David liked the idea of ripping off those who came to Las Vegas to win, not just his congregants, who were merely trying to survive.

"The pain is manageable, at the moment," David said. "It was not a stroke, thankfully."

"Is it . . . is it . . . cancer?" Roth asked.

"No," David said. "Nothing like that." He'd worked on this bit for a while. Was prepared for any question that might come his way. "I was in car accident as a child, in Italy, where my father was serving, and had to have much of my face reconstructed. I don't like to talk of it, for a very simple reason: We lost my mother that day. She was driving and, as was the wont for many in that era, she'd been drinking. A touch of vodka, a glass of wine, a Halcyon to sleep, it was, sadly, predictable."

"Oy," Rabbi Roth said. "I'm sorry, David."

"Medicine thirty-five years ago," David said, "was not exactly cutting edge." The men murmured. Everyone had lost someone in the past to some grave disease or accident or ailment that, today, would be solved with a pill or surgery. "The last few months, my plastic surgery has degraded to the point where I am in this condition. Part of me wanted to avoid it, so as not to think of the displeasure and sadness of my mother's death. Part of me wanted to avoid it because I have an aversion to pain, as I'm sure many of you do." Now the men smiled. Now they gave a fuck. David had to kill his fake fucking mother in order to get the empathy vote. "I am pleased to say Dr. Melnikoff will be working on me in the coming weeks and assures me I will be good as new by the New Year."

"An excellent surgeon," Rabbi Sigal said. He didn't elaborate, because Rabbi Sigal didn't elaborate on anything, generally. His was the word of God, even on matters he had no expertise in whatsoever.

"Oh, mazel, mazel," Rabbi Goldstein said. "You will be fine, Rabbi."

Goldstein was from the Orthodox shul off of Desert Inn, which David always found amusing. Pimping Jewish orthodoxy on a street named for a casino owned by Moe Dalitz, a gangster so notorious he never got arrested, the Ronnie Cupertine of his time. Moe ran Las Vegas for years, did it so effectively he ended up getting philanthropy awards from Israeli generals and the Anti-Defamation League, everyone's favorite Jew in Las Vegas, the big boys of the faith happy to look the other way since he was such a great supporter, an irony that did not escape David's notice. But that was back before the Internet. You could be a scumbag without much publicity. David rarely saw Rabbi Goldstein on this side of town. Which was fine. Goldstein thought what David and Rabbi Kales had done with their progressive Reform synagogue was practically a *shanda* . . . well, until Yehuda came along. Also, Goldstein's Orthodox Judaism made David nervous. He was more Jewish than David, had a deeper understanding of the texts, did not think liberally about the Talmud, and the result was that around him David felt like a fraud.

"That said," David started again, "I feel like we must address this issue of safety before something terrible occurs. I don't want to be in a hospital bed worried about things beyond my control." David stood up and paced back and forth, as if he were gathering his thoughts, though he already knew exactly what he was going to say. "I want to say that, first, I am not afraid," David began. "Are any of you afraid?" If they were, they would never admit it. They were not men who were concerned about death. Their belief was so divine— death was merely another phase of the spiritual existence. They would pass on, and when the Moshiach arrived, they would rise again and stand beside him in Israel, the light of the Torah illuminating the world in peace and freedom. All that prophecy bullshit. That was the basis of their faith: Death was but a station, the train always coming. "But we all recognize that our people, our friends, our neighbors, even unaffiliated Jews, are concerned, yes?"

The men all nodded, except for Yehuda, who sipped at his Diet Coke and watched David intently.

"They want to know what to do next, are bombers coming for them, do Christians fault them," David said.

"It is not new," Rabbi Goldstein interjected. He picked up a napkin and wiped at his beard. "Violence is the only way to get noticed these days. It is no different than every day in Israel."

"Did you serve?" Yehuda asked.

"I did," Rabbi Goldstein asked. "Did you?"

"In a way," Yehuda said. "But I am a pacifist. It was a bad fit."

"I, too, am a pacifist," Goldstein said.

"Did you kill anyone?" Yehuda asked.

"I did," Goldstein said. "In Lebanon."

"That must haunt you."

"No," Goldstein said. He picked up a pecan cookie, blew the sugar off it, ate it in two bites. "Not in the least."

Noted, David thought.

"None of us want to hurt anyone," David said, attempting to keep them on track. This was the problem when Jews got around a table. They simmered. "But most people, all they know of the pogroms, for instance, is *Fiddler on the Roof*." Rabbi Roth *tsked*. "Decades of violence and oppression whittled into song. And what does the world remember if our own Jews can barely articulate it? This ignorance eventually gave permission to do it again, on a larger scale. Which, in its own way, gave birth to these maniacs with the planes."

David let that sit there for a moment.

Rabbi Sigal cleared his throat. It made a phlegmy sound. David walked over to where he was sitting and poured him some water, put a hand on his shoulder, squeezed, felt the man's sweat through his jacket. He'd put the AC in the room to a chilly 69 degrees, since each of the men, save for Yehuda, was wearing a full suit. Yehuda had on tan slacks and an open-collared gingham shirt.

"To make a mark," David continued, "violence must be on a grand scale. So this feeling everyone has? It is genetic and specific.

They fear what they saw on the TV, they fear a repetition of the history which we have so ingrained in our people, and they fear something more existential, which is blame. The mob will not blame itself for inviting this horror upon our country. But they will scapegoat someone if they have to, find some segment of society to say, *If not for these people, we would be safer.* When that time comes, eventually, it will be us." David paused. "We are attacked from three sides and yet none of us have protected our faces."

"Rabbi," Yehuda said, and rose from his seat, "if I can interject, I think this is where I am in tune with how young people and more, shall we say, enlightened people view the world. I just don't see the level of anti-Semitism that you do. People come to the Kabbalah Center, they're not looking to become more marginalized after the experience. They're looking for greater acceptance and I think that's what we're doing. So yeah, people are scared, but I think if we try to get people to look more into the healing powers that exist outside of quote-unquote Western medicine, it demystifies part of the fear, which is of the unknown. I feel like that's a role I could take on, locally, if I had a bit more support from the four of you."

"Sit," Rabbi Sigal said, and Yehuda did. Sigal had a touch of Eastern Europe in his vocal inflection, the benefit of having grown up around immigrants, which gave his words a vague sense of Cold War menace. Rabbi Sigal fixed a glare across the table at Yehuda. "Your role here," he said, "is to listen. When we wish to hear from you, we'll ask. You are among rabbis, not your caftan acolytes. Act like it." He blew his nose into his napkin. His eyes were watering now, too. "Finish up," he said to David. "I'm feeling under the weather and would like to leave."

"Of course," David said. He walked to the head of the table and passed out the manila folders. "We need armed protection," David said. "I am not talking about security guards that flunked out of high school. I mean actual police protection, stationed in front of our synagogues—and the Kabbalah Center—during all business hours, seven days a week, for the foreseeable future. You will see in your folders an extensive budget proposal for us to share these costs. I think it is in our duty, as Jews, to protect one another. I know there are more synagogues in town, and we will pull them into our orbit once we have shown how successful this endeavor can be. As well, in good faith, Temple Beth Israel is prepared to manage this program for all of us." David paused, allowed the men to open their files and read in silence for a few moments, save for Rabbi Sigal, who merely looked at the spreadsheet and then pushed his file into the middle of the table, like he was going all in. It had taken David a few weeks to put together all the necessary numbers, a plan that would create a wall between him and the rest of the world.

Rabbi Goldstein held up the spreadsheet. "This figure," he said, pointing to a number in bold red at the bottom of the page. "This is exorbitant. Eighty-five to one hundred dollars per hour for a single armed man?"

"When you hire a man to keep you from death," David said, "you don't take the lowest bid." David lowered his voice an octave. "The Sincerity Tone," as Rabbi Kales called it. He needed to use it here, since in reality the price was closer to fifty bucks per hour. "I know that these last few months have been difficult. Temple Beth Israel finds itself in good financial standing and we are willing to pay all costs through January 1, to show our commitment to this."

"Do these men come with tanks?" Rabbi Roth asked. He had his glasses on now and was running his finger down the sheet. "This seems like a high price to pay for perception."

"It's not perception," David said. "It's sanctuary. These are all off-duty Las Vegas police and U.S. Marshals protecting us. In uniform and fully armed. If we want them to carry automatic weapons in their vehicles, it is a slightly higher charge, as noted on page two. If you want your congregants to open their wallets to you, you must make temple feel like the most sanctified place in the city. An armed man or two out front will bring our people back into our shuls. And, I should note, our funerals."

The rabbis exchanged looks. There'd been a wave of terrorist attacks at funerals throughout the Middle East, suicide bombers dressed as mourners. None of the rabbis wanted to admit that their attendance was flagging, that their donations were down, that they were worried about sustaining certain programs into the New Year; that they themselves feared standing over an open grave, surrounded by strangers, waiting for one of them to explode. Everyone was watching the terror ticker on CNN.

"So if something should transpire," Rabbi Sigal said now, "these guards can arrest someone?"

"Yes," David said.

"Could they, conceivably, shoot someone?"

"Yes," David said. "That's the law in Nevada."

Being a Jew was inherently dangerous to your health. So you watched your back, you listened for anti-Semitic talk, you identified other Jews in a room, you stayed vigilant. Every synagogue in town, at some point, had fielded a threat. Every synagogue in town had woken up to find a swastika painted on the property. It happened.

"You're going to pay the whole bill for over a month and if we don't like the service, we walk free and clear?" Roth asked eventually.

"We are prepared to, yes," David said.

"That's almost two hundred thousand dollars, David. That's a lot of money." Roth took off his glasses, rubbed at his eyes. "Why would you do this?"

"It's a mitzvah. A small one. And once you decide to stay on," David said, "and we begin sharing costs, according to your ability to pay, I would hope that you'd carry that mitzvah forward to a smaller synagogue that perhaps cannot afford the price either. Maybe you and Rabbi Goldstein agree to pay a bit more so that Temple Ohabai Sholom in Pahrump may be protected a few days a week." There were only thirty Jews in all of Pahrump, so they rented a tiny, windowless basement in a church for services. David had tried to get them to drive into Las Vegas, but they were steadfast in not being driven from their neighborhood simply because they didn't own any land. "I know that Rabbi Sigal and I are in better financial shape than most, so I wouldn't expect you to pay what we can. For instance, Rabbi Goldstein. I know you do not generate revenue like we do."

"To put it mildly," Rabbi Goldstein said. "We don't have an aquatic center. Or even a kid's pool. Much less a cemetery. You're a profit center. We are a religious center. If you don't mind me saying."

"Of course not," David said. He really didn't. If Goldstein had even an inch of ambition beyond speaking Torah, David would be out of a steady cash stream, particularly since David charged Rabbi Goldstein's congregants a fee of twenty-four hundred dollars just for a burial plot, another fifteen hundred to dig and then fill the grave, plus a five-hundred-dollar fee to become a member of Temple Beth Israel's Circle of Donors, which all Temple Beth Israel members who were buried in the cemetery agreed to ahead of time. And then the cost of the casket—a simple pine box was one thousand, which the Orthodox almost always preferred, though a few opted for the next level up, which included some understated satin adornments, and which began at three thousand—and then various fees, costs, and assessments . . . all of which were discounted prices offered to Rabbi Goldstein's people, because Jews took care of one another. When you died you were looking at ten thousand out the door, at least, with the funeral home's cost being around one thousand. A 900 percent markup. Goldstein's Jews also came by for things like swim lessons and art classes, because if the choice was to learn how to swim or scrapbook from a Jew or a non-Jew, Jews always picked one of their own, another ghetto of their choosing. "You will not be charged beyond your ability to pay," David said.

"If that's understood," Goldstein said, "we agree."

That was one.

"Well, I either pay equally or I pay nothing," Rabbi Roth said, just as David thought he would. "The protection of one is the pro-tection of all. I believe my congregation will support this. But it might take me two weeks to get them to support it with a check."

That was two.

David looked to Rabbi Sigal. "Rabbi Kales supports this?" Sigal asked.

"Yes," David said. Kales's choice of support was irrelevant, but at some point, one of these rabbis was going to call him, because whenever David made a move, they called Rabbi Kales, even though he was retired, even though he was losing his mind, even though, even though, even though . . .

Rabbi Sigal retrieved his file, examined it for a few moments, closed it again. "This world," he said quietly, "will turn on us if they get the chance." He cleared his throat again, got a little louder. "You are a good man to begin this process, Rabbi Cohen. I cannot let you do it alone." He rose, but kept his fingertips on the tabletop. "'Let the trumpet be blown, let the standard be flown, now set we our watch.'" He slapped the table. "We will pay half these first days," he said to David. "There is no discussion on that." He pushed the file back to the middle of the table. "The rest of you, pay as you can, pay as you must. This is a time where frugality is tantamount to silence." He grabbed up his belongings—a pair of glasses, his keys, a black-and-white cookie wrapped in a napkin—and Rabbi Roth and Rabbi Goldstein instinctually did likewise. When Rabbi Sigal declared a meeting was over, it was over. That's how it had been in Las Vegas for about forty years. A decision had been made.

Yehuda wisely stayed seated while David walked the men out, Rabbi Sigal a little unsteady on the stairs. He'd be in bed in twenty minutes. Maybe fewer. He lived at TPC in a home overlooking the thirteenth fairway. It was worth about two million out the door. David had gone to a cocktail party there last year. Best as he could tell, Rabbi Sigal did not have a safe room filled with guns, but he did have a medicine cabinet filled with heart-disease, high-blood-pressure, high-cholesterol, and high-anxiety medication.

"Your call to action is pretty tight," Yehuda said once David returned.

"You think so?" David said. He picked up a handful of napkins, cleared Rabbi Sigal's dishes, dumping the remnants of his food into the garbage, did the same with Rabbi Roth's and Rabbi Goldstein's. He'd poisoned only Rabbi Sigal's food, as he was the only one whose inhibitions and emotions David wasn't sure he could control. He needed the man to be a touch addled.

"Do you really think Osama Bin Laden is going to fly to Las Vegas to kill Jews on a Tuesday morning?" Yehuda picked up his folder. "Because I'm doing the math? And we're talking a G a day, right? If I'm spending that much money, at the end, I want to have killed Bin Laden."

David sat down next to him. Took a black-and-white cookie from the platter, bit into the white side. Chewed it as though it didn't make every part of his face feel like a red-hot anvil. "I thought you were a pacifist," he said. "Now you're an assassin?"

"I get you, Rabbi," Yehuda said. "You and me, we're about the same age, right?"

"I'm almost forty," David said. "So, no. We are not about the same age." Yehuda might have been thirty. He might have been younger.

"Why not just take a portion of this money and get every member of Temple Beth Israel a gun and a shooting class? Make your own IDF." He held up the spreadsheet. "This bottom line, that's not gonna work, unless there's some other bounce on the backside. Give everyone guns, there's a bounce on that. You teach these people how to shoot? You bring in a reputable gun manufacturer to sell them the right guns, what's suitable for their situation? That's good for the community, too, not just for your temple. There'd finally be a whole team of good guys with guns."

David tried to imagine where Yehuda learned to talk. It was interesting, though, how he suddenly devolved into a kind of quasi-gangster parlance while talking to David, as if he thought that was their vernacular, as if David was the kind of rabbi you could talk guns with and it would be just fine, perfectly fine. Which made David think Yehuda was smarter than he let on.

"If the Kabbalah Center cannot afford one thousand dollars a day," David said, "I can help you with a loan."

"The Kabbalah Center is *for profit*. I'm not looking to give money away. Here's what I can tell you. If I do a seminar at the Mirage one weekend, say, and you and I talk about responsible gun ownership, bring in some Jewish person from the ATF, for instance, have him talk about why owning a gun isn't a license to commit crimes but to stop them, we'd be difference makers." He took a sip from his Diet Coke, let out a little belch. "We're progressive, we live on the right side of town. We partner up? We help a lot of people. I could even start doing seminars here. It's a great space."

"I'll consider that," David bit into the black side of the cookie. Chewed it slowly. "I don't know if you remember, but I caught your show one time."

"You came to the center?"

"No. The community college. When you were calling yourself Da Truth Tella."

"Oh, that was just marketing for the college kids and the soccer moms who grew up on rap music."

"I came with Mrs. Meltzer and Mrs. Helms. They were very impressed, I'll say that."

"Yeah, yeah," Yehuda snapped his fingers. "I remember. You look different now."

"My face changes," David said.

"You've got a distinctive voice, though," Yehuda said. "Real persuasive elocution."

"What does my voice make you want to do?"

A smile worked at the corner of Yehuda's mouth. "Honestly? It makes me want to pay attention. You'd be a good teacher."

"You graduate from college?"

"I did a couple years at UCLA when I got out of the IDF. It wasn't for me."

"What is for you?"

"Faith?" Yehuda said. "Helping people. Also, real estate."

"I see," David said. He wondered where Yehuda would be in ten years. Prison? Maybe. Or on TV. He wouldn't last long in Las Vegas, that much David knew.

"Joanie—Mrs. Helms—is doing a yoga piece for us," Yehuda said, when the silence got uncomfortable. "You should try it when you get out of surgery. Helps with healing. Mind, body, and soul."

"I look like I need that?"

"Don't know until you get in that mind space," Yehuda said.

"Would that be a good way for me to become healthy and wealthy?" Yehuda looked confused. "That's what you were selling when I came to your show. I liked it, especially the part where you managed to get people to pay *you* in order to make *them* wealthy. *Enlightenment, Engagement, and a Healthy and Wealthy Future.* That's how it went, right?"

"It's just a slogan," Yehuda said.

"To you. To them, it's a path. But that's quite a thing, selling people something they already have. Ice to Eskimos, my father used to say." Actually, his father used to say, *Like selling pussy to hookers.* "But getting Jews to build a pyramid for you? That's a whole different level, Yehuda."

"Look," Yehuda said, carefully, David seeing that maybe this fuck was starting to realize who he was dealing with, at least on some atavistic level, since Yehuda had the street smarts of a mime. "I appreciate your offer here, but it doesn't engage with the center's philosophy. So. We wash our hands of it."

"I will seek that which is lost," David said. "And will bring again that which is driven away, and will bind up that which is broken, and will strengthen that which is sick."

"What's that?" Yehuda asked.

"It's supposed to be your philosophy," David said. "Ezekiel 34:16." David looked over both shoulders, fucking with him now. "Between us, Yehuda, confidentially, as your rabbi, are you even Jewish?"

"Of course I am."

"So," David said, "when I contact my friends in the IDF, they'll have a record of you?"

"Of course," Yehuda said.

"Yehuda Stein," David said. "I guess there'd be ten thousand of you. Who was your sergeant?"

"What is this?" Yehuda said. "Are you Mossad or something?"

"What if I am?"

"You should be out hunting Nazis and you're here, hunting toddlers for your swimming classes?" He started to get up, but David put his foot behind one of the chair's back wheels, pinning Yehuda to his spot.

"You're not excused from the table," David said. "And you don't get to wash your hands of anything. Didn't work for Pilate, not gonna work for you."

"It's not in our profit model to give up seven grand a week for some doughnut eater, whether you like it or not," Yehuda said. "So unless you're prepared to get a letter from my lawyer for falsely imprisoning me here, you'll let me leave now."

This made David laugh. It was, in fact, the funniest thing he'd heard since the fucking meat truck dumped him in Las Vegas three years ago. Motherfuckers and their lawyers.

"Let me explain business to you, Yehuda," David said. "Your *profit* comes out of Temple Beth Israel's bottom line. And the bottom line of Temple Beth Am, Temple Beth Shalom, and Congregation Beth El, as well. It would be a shame if those people found out that the Kabbalah Center is patently unsafe for Jews. That, in fact, it's showed up on a list of places the 9/11 bombers scoped out. Then one day, maybe a swastika gets tagged on your window. Then there's a fire in a Dumpster. A stolen car gets driven into the building. Maybe someone breaks into the center and burns a cross inside your hookah lounge. All of those things could happen, conceivably, in this climate."

Yehuda tried to exact the right words from his mouth. "Is this a shakedown?" He laughed, like it was crazy. Because it was crazy. David had done his homework on young Mr. Da Truth Tella, just for a moment like this, when he could take what he wanted from him.

"I mean. You're basically threatening me? Right? You're telling me you'll put me out of business if I don't pony up for *police protection?*"

David pulled Yehuda's chair closer to him. "I know what you are," he said, his voice just above a whisper. Yehuda swallowed hard, didn't say anything, because up close to Rabbi David Cohen? All you really saw was Sal Cupertine, rippling beneath the skin. "I know your con. I know your escape. I see everything you've ever been and ever will be." David shoved Yehuda's chair away, stood up, began to clear the rest of the table clean. "So pay or don't pay," he said, brightly now; this was just another day at Temple Beth Israel. "That is up to you." He smiled, clasped his hands together, held them under his chin, a thoughtful pose he'd stolen from an interview with Steve Jobs he'd caught in Dr. Melnikoff's waiting room a few weeks ago. "But understand this: I will open a Kabbalah Center right here, on Temple Beth Israel's property, and I will charge double for your miracles, your conspiracy theory numerology, and your red fucking yarn. And because I have the moral authority to teach the bullshit you spout, you will end up sitting alone in that overmortgaged warehouse you call a place of faith. That BMW outside? It will be a constant reminder of your vanity. Your home in the Lakes? All your rented leather furniture? Gone. Your Olympic Gardens girlfriend? Gone. Even your Judaism will be gone, because you'll start to wonder how a Jew could do this to another Jew. It will be a crisis so profound that you may eventually start looking for a gun of your own to end the persistent, nagging feeling in your mind that it all could have been avoided if you'd just said yes to me. But it will be too late."

Yehuda watched David for a long time, not speaking. David wiped off the table with a napkin, put Saran Wrap over the cookies, took the manila folders the other rabbis had left behind—none of them bothered to take the documentation, because it didn't matter, they weren't going to be shamed by not paying, which is what made them different than Yehuda, who wasn't encumbered by such emotions—and dumped them into the garbage, too.

"Who are you?" Yehuda said, finally.

•

WHEN DAVID GOT back to his office, after Yehuda agreed to the protection plan, he found Harvey B. Curran waiting patiently, sitting in the same chair Jeff Hopper had sat in a few years earlier. Esther was at the reception desk with a giddy smile on her face.

"I apologize if I kept you," David said.

Curran still had a patch over his eye, and judging from the indention the strap made on his skin, he wore it constantly.

"No worries," Curran said. He got up and gathered his materials: a reporter's notebook, a small tape recorder, that damn Day Runner that David had reassembled in the Bagel Café parking lot. "I've been telling Esther here war stories."

"I read him every day, Rabbi," Esther said. Of course she did. Esther controlled both the writing of the checks and the flow of gossip in the temple, which meant reading Harvey B. Curran's column was required if she wanted to whisper her concerns about Rabbi Kales's daughter being married to that *goniff* Bennie Savone, a man so corrupt he'd been paying Esther's salary for a decade. The ultimate double cross, David thought, neither of them knowing anything about the other, but being almost entirely dependent on each other's discretion. Wasn't that something.

"I should come here more often," Harvey said once they were in the short hallway leading toward David's office. "Good for the ego."

"Talmud says to be exceedingly humble," David said. "Even if you have to fake it."

"Well," Harvey said, "with this thing on my face, I'll take what I can."

"I'm sorry you're still suffering," David said. He unlocked his office door and let Curran in.

"Me, too," Curran said. He sat down at one of the four chairs around the coffee table and David shut the door behind them and sat across from him. "You've redecorated," he said.

"You've been here before?"

"No," Curran said. "But I've seen surveillance photos."

"Not recently, I hope," David said.

"No," Curran said. "This was before your time. FBI had pictures of Bennie Savone taking a meeting here before the temple opened. He and Vic Acosta? You know, the guy who gifted the government Panthers?"

"I know that situation, yes," David said.

"Fifty years Miami has been trying to make a move out here," Curran said, "and they still haven't gotten it right. Anyway, all the girls at Panthers were needle junkies back then. Place was HIV-on-a-Stick. Mr. Savone apparently called Mr. Acosta for a meeting, held it right here, and advised him to clean up his game before it brought down the whole industry."

"That's good advice," David said. "If it happened like that."

"It did," Curran said. "Acosta was wired. He was an active snitch. Just something interesting."

"Any recent surveillance photos I should know about?"

"No, I haven't seen much recently," Curran said. He waved at something in the air, a bug, or some dust, or a thought. "Screw it," he said, and when he saw that David was observing him with open interest, he said, "I might lose my eye."

"Really? That still happens?"

"That was my thought," he said. "But I can't shake this infection." He waved at whatever was in the air again. "Anyway. That's not why you asked me here. You don't need to hear about my personal problems."

"It's fine," David said. "Maybe you've noticed that I've had some medical work done in the past and that I'm in need of more work?"

Curran put up a hand. "I have no idea what the correct answer is here, so I'm not even going to attempt to parry with you, Rabbi. I've learned in the last couple months that I am both easily offended and horribly self-conscious, both things I thought I'd left behind in junior high."

"Who is your doctor?" David asked.

"Whoever Kaiser sends me to," Curran said. "I've seen three or four different people. They keep shuffling in and out. Today was a new guy. Tomorrow will be someone else. It's the factory system over there. Barely even medicine."

"No, no," David said. "You need a specialist."

"I can't afford that," Curran said. "The paper's insurance is for crap."

David went to his desk, scribbled a number down on a piece of paper, and gave it to Curran. "This is Dr. Melnikoff. He is the best surgeon in town. He will take care of you. Or will know someone who can."

"He's not on my plan," Curran said. "I looked."

"He takes on a few cases every year on a pro-bono basis." Or he'd start.

"I can't do that," Curran said, as David knew he would, but he didn't hand the note back. *Interesting.* "I'd lose my job *and* end up on the front page. But the paper is so short staffed, they'd probably have me write the story before I left."

David closed his eyes. Put a finger to his lips. Humbled himself before God. "See him anyway," David said, when he opened his eyes a few seconds later. "Maybe he would do work on a discounted basis. If you paid for it, irrespective of the cost, that would not be unethical, would it? Even one dollar is payment."

Curran ran two fingers across the edges of the patch, David thinking he probably didn't even notice he was doing it. "I don't know," he said, but it was in there now. An idea of what might be possible.

"He's a good man," David said, "and you're a good man. I could talk to him on your behalf. He's going to work on me shortly"

"When?"

"After Hanukkah."

"You trust him?"

"Of course," David said.

"I've just . . ." Curran paused. "I've heard things about him."

"Harvey," David said, using his name for the first time, "nobody lives in Las Vegas because they hate to gamble. Talmud says all Israelites are mutually accountable for each other, and while I know you are not Jewish, I am, and you would be referred by me, which Talmud says makes you an honored guest in Dr. Melnikoff's care."

"Is that true?"

"Being kind to a stranger is greater to Jews than seeing the face of the Divine," David said.

Harvey B. Curran pondered that.

David clasped his hands together. "So, the business at hand."

"Right," Curran said, but David could tell he was still thinking about the offer. David had, of course, known what he'd find when Harvey B. Curran showed up today. He'd kept a close watch on the man since their meeting at the Bagel Café—he'd been the one who got Bennie's girls on record about the terrorist lap dances. He got the sense that Harvey B. Curran . . . liked him. David tried to remember the last time he'd had someone who appreciated him for something beyond his ability to kill. Paul Bruno had been one of the few kids he recalled liking absent any of this gangster shit, and how had that worked out? David ended up burying him in the temple's cemetery under the name Lionel Berkowitz. Every day David walked out there, didn't matter if he was burying some client's body or someone he knew from Temple Beth Israel, he left a stone on Paul's gravestone. So many now it looked like a fucking quarry. "I've been enjoying your recent reporting. You're doing important work."

"Oh, I dunno," Curran said. "It's tough to break something new when the crime has already been committed and the perpetrators are dead. Cosa Nostra, at least they repopulate. These guys aren't coming back. Though I don't suppose you could help me get video from inside the Wild Horse?"

"I doubt it."

"That's too bad. Getting a shot of Mohammed Atta busting his nut in the Wild Horse's VIP would probably get me the Pulitzer. I wouldn't be surprised if Mr. Savone ended up with the Presidential Medal of Freedom."

David didn't think that's how it would turn out. Least not for Bennie. Hadn't worked for Lucky Luciano, back when he was fighting the Axis powers. It was good propaganda, but by the 1950s, all the crime bosses who had worked for the government were busy getting hauled into court, every Sonny and Tino was Cosa Nostra, every street boss was Joe Bonanno. Even random motherfuckers who just hit diners and liquor stores for the till were capos, the FBI cleaning up America like America had cleaned up Europe, and, likewise, were a good six years behind the curve of the scythe. No one from the families was getting off easy just because they stood up to the Nazis while all the Ivy League fucks were investing in steel companies and feeling cozy with their blue-blood anti-Semitism. That game was rigged to favor the perceived good guys. After all, no one asked for the Mob's help with the Koreans or the Vietnamese. No one came sniffing around Cousin Ronnie to help with Desert Storm. If it came to it, David didn't imagine the Bloods and Crips and Latin Kings and Aryan Nation and Hell's Angels and Mongols and all the Italian families and the Russians and the Native gangs would line up along the border to stop whoever the fuck was attacking us now, unless they thought it might fuck with their paper, everyone out for *that cash*. You could tag up your street, pretend to be about *that block*, but what David understood now was that those tags were no different than the cross on the church or the Star of David on the synagogue or the glow of a Walmart Supercenter: They were all just signs of who was safe where. The whole world was a fucking ghetto, the whole nation filled with gangsters.

"So what's the story?" Curran hit RECORD on the tape recorder, set it between them on the table. "You mind?"

"Yes," David said. He picked up the recorder, popped out the tape, handed it back to Curran.

"This a national security issue?" Curran said.

"In light of your previous reporting," David said, "I think you recording anything in this room would be a bad precedent."

"All right," Curran said. "Notes it is."

David told him how the horrors of 9/11 had brought about an unparalleled level of cooperation among the local leaders of the Jewish faith, how they recognized both the danger of the world and the need to honor the heroic first responders who protect the city, and that they would now be hiring a team of off-duty police officers to patrol their properties, to keep their people safe during these difficult times but also to help these first responders earn extra money, particularly since their pension funds had surely taken a hit when the stock market tumbled. "Temple Beth Israel is also making a sizeable donation to the Firefighters of Southern Nevada Burn Foundation," David told him, "and the Friends of the Las Vegas Metropolitan Police Department Foundation."

"What does sizable mean?" Curran asked.

"Ten thousand to each," David said.

Curran tapped his pen against his notebook. "Not much of a story there," Curran said.

"I'm not asking for a story," David said. "Just a sentence or two in a column. We want to show our appreciation for law enforcement and we want to let the public know it is safe to come and worship again. This is a time when some good publicity for God is probably worth noting. All this death in His name. All this suffering. I want to do some good."

"Mr. Savone know you're doing this?"

"I imagine he'll find out."

"You're not worried you'll end up in Lake Mead?" he asked. "Isn't that where they found your predecessor? Rabbi Gottlieb?"

"Did you know him?" David asked.

"No," Curran said. "I never met the man."

"Neither did I," David said. "His parents came through not long ago. They were nice people."

"You really think he fell overboard out there?"

"People die in tragic ways every day," David said.

"Gangsters do," Curran said. "Rabbis? You guys live forever. I saw Rabbi Sigal walking out when I pulled up. What's he? Close to eighty?"

"Yes," David said.

"I bet he knows where some of the bodies are buried." David didn't respond. Curran tapped his pen again. "You should up your donation," he said. "You want to make an impression, add some color to the stack."

"Fine," David said. "We are now donating fifty thousand. In Rabbi Gottlieb's name."

"That's very generous of you," Curran said.

"A gift to the city," David said.

"Who all is in on it?"

"Temple Beth Israel, Temple Beth Am, Temple Beth Shalom, Congregation Beth El," David said, "and the new Kabbalah Center."

"Okay." Curran snapped his notebook closed, but didn't get up right away. He looked at all the books on the shelves, not in the wondrous way Jordan Rosen had a few months earlier—and it occurred to David, the motherfucker hadn't returned his book—but rather in a seemingly more appreciative vein. "The People of the Book," he said. "You know the Muslims came up with that?"

"It's an apt term."

"You reached out to any of the mosques in town?"

"No," David said.

"You should," Curran said. "Get them in on it."

"That's a good idea."

"No charge," Curran said. "I mean, you think you're worried? Every day, there's assholes with guns parked out in front of the mosque over on Morgan. Just goes to show you how crazy this world has become. People see what they want to see and you can't tell them any different. Makes my job harder, I'll tell you that much." He stood up from this chair to leave, stared down at the note with Dr. Melnikoff's number on it for a few seconds, then picked it up, shoved it inside his Day Runner. "I'll see what I can do to get a little mention in the paper. No guarantees."

"Of course," David said.

David watched on the security feed as Harvey B. Curran exited the facility. He stepped into the shul for a moment, looked up at the vaulted ceiling, shook a volunteer's hand—Max Mendelsohn, who'd served in Korea and liked to tell everyone about it—paused for a second in the Judaica shop, flipped through a couple books, and then finally made his way back out to the parking lot, where, David noted, he was parked about five feet from where Agent Moss had died. No, David thought. Not died. Been killed.

No.

Murdered.

He'd leave a stone for her, too.

17

For the first five days he was in Nevada, Matthew Drew avoided the Walmart Supercenter in Carson City. He tried not to even think about it. Instead, he flew out to Las Vegas, landing there during the third week of December, after a month back in Maryland. He promised his mother he'd be back for Christmas, though the truth was, he couldn't imagine what they'd do on that day.

His only goal was to find Sal Cupertine. And if Matthew died in that fight, fine. But some motherfuckers would be going out with him.

So he walked in Hopper's steps, just like Poremba suggested. Tried to get a room at the Royal Plaza Inn, where Jeff Hopper had stayed, two dingy blocks off the Strip, but it was roped off by the FBI already, since the bombers supposedly stayed there, so he ended up at the Courtyard Inn in Summerlin. It was all that he could find, the city overrun by something called the Power-Gen Conference, 25,000 energy and gas executives, politicians, start-up companies, and finance geeks who thought they could predict the future of energy and power had crowded into every decent hotel room near the Strip and off, the whole town thrilled for the influx of business.

The day Matthew checked in, the *Review-Journal* had a fawning front-page interview with a Republican congressman from Texas and some New Jack energy CEO about how Enron was a blip, how the international heavyweights filling the convention center were about to bring forth a revolution, that the power industry was "on a roll," how a combination of foreign and domestic oil production, wind energy, clean burning coal, and solar could create a "new power matrix" that would bring the world into "an illuminated future where you could always leave a light on."

There was also a tiny counterpoint article, on page three, that talked about the rampant corruption in the wind business overseas, how organized crime was getting its hooks into the building of massive wind farms in Italy, Japan, and Norway, and how the oil business in America, where slickwater fracturing was bringing on a new development rush, was once again riddled with scams, frauds, and crooked land deals, the same pack of hungry coyotes that always followed the industry, the government turning its head so that we all might pay a cent less for a gallon of unleaded.

It disgusted Matthew. All that print for this bullshit. And yet, twelve pages into the newspaper, was an article about a dead kid in a crack house in Boulder City. A human less important than a lightbulb.

He got to work that night.

He walked through Jeff Hopper's days in Las Vegas, tried to imagine what it might be like to know that your last days on earth would include billboards for Siegfried & Roy's white tiger show, Rick Springfield in *EFX*, and Actually Legal Girls, whatever the fuck that meant, or maybe those were harbingers and Matthew was missing the point, that society had already crumbled, that death might be a relief from men in makeup taming a bleached cat.

He visited high-end casinos and resorts like the Bellagio and Mirage, places that used to get their top-grade steaks from Kochel Farms before the company went out of business, no one wanting to get their meat from a farm that was hiding mob killers among their T-bones.

He hit up the boutique hotels and family restaurants and burger joints, where Kochel Farms did a steady NY Strip and tri-tip and filet and premium-ground business. Swung by the delis and sandwich shops and meat markets, Las Vegas one of the few cities that still had butchers. Matthew figured they had to be fronts, though he couldn't discern what you had to front in Las Vegas, where everything was legal. High-end pills and teenage prostitutes, most likely, or identity theft and fraud rings. You came in to buy a sandwich or get some chops, walked out with a mortgage in some other state. It was the kind of low-level racketeering that happened everywhere in the current climate, since neither the feds nor the cops really cared. If you weren't flying commercial airplanes into major American structures filled with civilians, you could run whatever game you wanted.

It was a gold rush for fuckups. You had to rip people off on the Enron level to really gain notice, and even then, who really gave a shit?

A couple times, Matthew tried to sit down in a place, get a feel for the patrons and the proprietors, except Matthew wasn't the undercover type. People noticed him. First there was his size. He got that. He was the kind of guy strangers didn't mind calling a "big motherfucker." But he also recognized that he'd begun to project a demeanor of casual violence.

He'd understood that in a practical way before, when he and Jeff had been looking for Sal Cupertine, and of course when he was at Chuyalla, putting people on the ground once or twice a night. But now, trying to be inconspicuous in these mom-and-pop places in Henderson, Green Valley, and Summerlin, strings of Christmas lights everywhere, he understood the greater truth: On his best days—how long ago those were now—Matthew Drew looked like someone you didn't want to fuck with. But these days? He looked like someone who wanted to fuck with you.

Plus, he was armed for tactical assault. Brass knuckles in his pocket. A nine kept under his coat, already fixed with a silencer, another on his ankle. A shotgun in the trunk of his rental car. He'd flown across the country to fight a war without any apparent enemy, other than someone dialing a phone inside a Carson City Walmart. Was that Sal Cupertine? Matthew couldn't make the evidence line up. If Sal Cupertine was able to call his wife, why was it just this one time? If he was able to call her, why wasn't he able to get her and his kid? It was irrelevant now, Matthew supposed. If the feds didn't want Sal Cupertine to find his wife and son, Sal Cupertine never would. Unless they decided Jennifer and William weren't worth the time and money, which was possible.

On his last day in Las Vegas, before making the drive north, he cruised by the private schools, the churches, and the synagogues that took Kochel Farms' low-end products for their cafeterias: premade hamburger patties, hot dogs, cube steaks, all that. He didn't bother walking into those places, because he realized what Jeff surely had, too: that he wasn't going to find Sal Cupertine hiding in the bushes by the jungle gym at Prevatt Lutheran Prep, wouldn't discover him leading afternoon Bible study at Our Lady of Las Vegas, was unlikely to see him mopping floors at Levine Torah Academy. It was the same empty feeling Matthew had been carrying around for years, and he felt it more acutely following the loss of his partner and now his sister. No one had seen anything. No one was even looking.

After hitting his last spot, the Tikvah Preschool and Barer Academy at Temple Beth Israel in Summerlin, an expansive and well-guarded facility, what with the four paramilitary-looking men spread out in strategic locations along Hillpointe Road, a winding tree-lined street surrounded by million-dollar homes, bifurcated by a sprawling cemetery, Matthew circled back to Bruce Trent Park. He'd passed it on his way into Summerlin, saw the sign for that afternoon's farmer's market, and made a mental note to come back, get some food for the road trip to Carson City, make sure he knew where he was going.

But now, after he parked his rental car and got out, he saw a boy pushing a girl on the swing set and a familiar melancholy landed on top of him. What the fuck was he doing, twenty-five hundred miles from his grieving mother in Maryland, chasing the ghost of his dead partner and the specter of Sal Cupertine through the haze of sadness over his sister? Why wasn't he in the woods somewhere, by himself, getting in tune with nature? Why wasn't he in some kind of institution? Why was he out here, chasing footsteps in sand?

Because that's what Las Vegas really was: sand. Matthew couldn't get beyond the impermanence of the place. The Red Rocks were the only thing that seemed real. Not the sprawl of development he saw on either side of the Strip, thousands of homes being built for people who didn't mind living in a place conceived to con people. Not the absurdity of the casinos built to look like Paris and New York and King Arthur's castle and the pyramids of Giza. Not the tourists quoting gangster movies while they threw dice, as if it were all make-believe. The Mafia built Las Vegas on the bodies of the dead, then Hollywood made that seem glamorous, and then the public made it seem like culture. And a couple thousand miles away, Nina Drew lay buried in pieces.

Matthew bought ten bucks' worth of beef jerky and a bag of saltwater taffy for the drive to Carson City and then headed back to the parking lot. When he got to his rental car—he'd only been gone fifteen minutes—his windshield was stuffed with flyers. Don't miss the two-for-one pizza special at Northside Nathans! Don't miss the move-in bargains at the Adagio Luxury Condominiums! Don't miss the Kabbalah classes that could help you "Energize and Invigorate Your Earning Potential!" A missing thirty-five-year-old woman named Melanie. A missing five-year-old dog that answers to Huey. A missing twelve-year-old cat named Tiger, needs its medication, will die without it. Come to Power-Gen and learn how to harness the future of energy!

Everybody was missing something, all the time. Only energy persisted. He tossed it all into his backseat. He needed to get the fuck out of Las Vegas.

•

AT NINE THE next morning, Matthew checked out of the Carson City Nugget Hotel and Casino, where he hadn't really slept the night before, his nerves shot after being caught in a rainstorm between Las Vegas and Carson City, the rural highways a sludge of red dirt, road-kill, and clouds so low, he could barely get much over fifty miles per hour for fear he'd slam into some wandering cow. Ingesting the entire bag of taffy hadn't helped. An eight-hour drive turned into eleven, Matthew getting into Carson City at two in the morning, a light snow falling around him. He expected to wake up surrounded by drifts, but the morning was clear and chilly, maybe 45 degrees, and dry, whatever snow had fallen in the night melted away.

As Matthew drove the five miles to the Walmart Supercenter, he tried to picture Sal Cupertine living in a place like this. Had he spent the night in the Back on Track Inn, with its free HBO and continental breakfast? Or was he renting an apartment now? Did he walk into Carson City Mattress and buy himself a queen-size Sealy Serta pillow top? Did he stop in at the Bike Smith to get his ten-speed tuned up? Did he wander over to the psychic shop next door to the Bike Smith and ask when the law was going to catch up to him?

Nevada, Matthew was quickly learning, was filled with psychics and tarot card readers and quack religions—in Las Vegas, he saw storefronts for Kabbalah, Scientology, even a Zoroastrian bookshop, and bumped into an Ayn Rand Metaphysical Clarity workshop taking place inside the Frontier when he walked through that busted old dump—which he supposed made some crooked sense. There was a psychic only a few miles from the Chuyalla Casino, too, open all day, every day, so you could find out if your luck was about to show up. That more psychics didn't end up getting murdered was, in Matthew's view, the only sign that they might know the future.

Nevertheless, when Matthew got out of his car in the Walmart Supercenter parking lot, he was surprised to find yet another psychic shop located across the street, maybe a hundred yards away, and already open for business, the blinking neon moon, stars, and open palms drawing his attention, even from that distance. He watched it for a full thirty seconds, thinking maybe it was a sign.

"Can I give you this?"

Matthew turned and saw a man and a young girl, maybe seven, come around the front of the Jeep he'd parked beside. The girl held a stack of orange flyers and the man, who was maybe forty, had extended one toward Matthew. The man was wearing a dark green jacket, collar up, a scarf, and his skin was so pale, he looked sick. He needed to be somewhere warmer.

"I'm good," Matthew said. He zipped up his jacket, aware that he didn't want the kid to see the butt of his nine sticking out, and started to walk off, when the man called after him.

"Will you just take a look at it?"

Matthew stopped. Every car in the lot had an orange flyer on it, he saw now. Some had two or three or four or six—both sides of the front windshield, side windows, back window, wherever a flyer would stick, even in the crack of the doors—and the pavement was littered with them, too. How hadn't he noticed them when he pulled in? There were cameras mounted on light poles throughout the lot, everything being tracked and recorded. Matthew wondered if somewhere, someone was looking at him, capturing his face, running it through a database, checking off a box marked SAFE. How wrong they were.

"Sure," Matthew said.

"Annie," the man said, "why don't you give that nice man a flyer."

Annie had on a blue puffy jacket, hood up, even though it wasn't raining, and Matthew could make out strands of red hair peeking out, along with freckles on her nose and cheeks. She had green eyes, which up against her freckles and hair gave her a kind of haunted look. She'd grow up to be pretty, he could see that already, and despite the fact that Matthew hulked over her, didn't seem to be the least bit put off by him when she approached. That would change, he knew, and that was for the best. Guys like Matthew Drew? They were the people you avoided.

"This is my mother," Annie said, and she handed Matthew the piece of paper.

On the paper was a woman, mid-thirties, pretty. He looked at the details:

MISSING

MELANIE MOSS

Age: 35 Height: 5'9" Weight: 138 lbs

Hair: Red, long Eyes: Brown Race: White

Identifying Characteristics: C-section scar, acne scarring
on cheeks, known to wear toe rings.

Hometown: Carson City, NV

Last Seen: September 11, 2001, Kales Mortuary and Home
of Peace, Las Vegas, Nevada

Circumstances: Melanie Moss was last seen departing the
Kales Mortuary and Home of Peace, 8719 Hillpointe
Road, Las Vegas, Nevada, on September 11, 2001, at
approximately 7:00 a.m. in a 1996 Cutlass (black), government license #FA34119. She was last seen wearing
black pants, a blue shirt, and black jacket. Her whereabouts remain unknown, though she is believed to have
traveled from Las Vegas back to the greater Carson City/
Reno region on or about September 11 as well. If you
have any information concerning Melanie's whereabouts,
or if you should encounter her, please contact the Carson
City Police 775-887-2500.

"I've seen her," Matthew said, before he could stop himself.

"What?" the man said. He rushed toward him. "When?"

"I mean, I got a flyer for her, yesterday. In Las Vegas." Matthew
went back to his car, unlocked it, fished through the papers in the
backseat, found the missing posters of the cat, the dog, and then
Melanie. He handed it to the man. It was a different picture—she was
younger in it, Matthew guessed—and the flyer was yellow, not orange.

"Oh," the man said. "Yeah." He creased the flyer in half and
then in half again, then put it into his pocket. "Her mother is passing them out down there."

"I understand," Matthew said. "I'm sorry for your loss." He began
to walk off again.

"We're not calling it that," the man said, which stopped Matthew. Three months gone? Real people didn't disappear themselves for three months at a time unless they'd committed a crime. And if Melanie Moss had committed a crime, her family wouldn't be handing out missing flyers for her in two parts of the state, and certainly not on a cold December morning, in a Walmart parking lot. That was the thing about people who disappeared because they wanted to. The families were smart enough not to look for them.

"She's out there somewhere," the man said, as if he'd read Matthew's thoughts. "We just have to find her."

"I understand," Matthew said.

"It's okay," the man said. He put his arm around Annie, started to move away. "We appreciate you taking the time."

Matthew watched the man and the little girl as they blanketed another three cars. He looked back at the flyer Annie had given him, read through the details again, felt he owed that to the man, to that little girl.

Disappeared on September 11.

In a way, this flyer was no different from the ones he saw on the news, lining the streets of New York following the attacks. When a loved one was lost, or missing, most people didn't know what else to do. Matthew knew that all too well. Her last known location was . . . a mortuary? In Las Vegas? What was she doing at a mortuary? And then he saw the address: 8719 Hillpointe Road. The Kales Mortuary and Home of Peace. He'd been over there yesterday, on Hillpointe, hadn't he? He didn't remember seeing a mortuary, but then . . .

No, not a mortuary, but he remembered the cemetery, how it spread away from the street into a low, rolling green, so that it looked like just another golf course. If there was a cemetery, it wouldn't be unusual that there would be a mortuary next door. If it was a private concern, it would be more than normal. It would be smart.

Matthew popped his trunk, rooted around in his suitcase for his files, took them out. What was the place Jeff had visited? The Tikvah Preschool and Barer Academy at Temple Beth Israel.

There it was: 8900 Hillpointe Road. That would be right across the street. Jeff had gone there, or at least checked it off his list. Or, well, no. The Barer Academy hadn't been fully built out yet, not according to the records Matthew had in front of him. At the time, there was just the Tikvah Preschool. How much meat could a preschool possibly need that they'd buy it from a distributor all the way out in Illinois?

He flipped the pages, tried to find something he knew he was missing, some little detail that was urging him forward. And there it was: The Tikvah Preschool, managed by Temple Beth Israel, was founded in 1996 by Rabbi Cy Kales. The Barer Academy, founded in 1999, also by Rabbi Cy Kales.

Kales. Same as the mortuary. So the rabbi from Temple Beth Israel also owned the mortuary? That was a business model that seemed surprisingly sustainable.

He looked back at the flyer. Melanie Moss had been driving a black Cutlass with government-issued plates. What kind of government agent was she? And what was she doing at a mortuary at 7 a.m.? If you were serving a warrant or picking up a suspect, sure, get someone while they were still in bed. But at a place of business? If she was missing, that meant she was alone.

So.

Not a cop.

Not a marshal.

If she were either of those, her disappearance would be a thing. Even after 9/11. Cops and marshals didn't just disappear. People got worried when those licensed to carry firearms were suddenly unaccounted for.

Same with the car. If she were a cop, the car would be outfitted with GPS. Must be a civil servant, then. If she was last seen at the mortuary, who saw her? This didn't make sense. Who would have seen her there that early in the morning? Maybe someone at the school across the way.

Or the temple.

Matthew tried to piece together three disparate threads in his mind. Jeff Hopper had come out to Las Vegas to look for Sal Cupertine. He'd gone to visit the preschool at Temple Beth Israel and then, that night, he contacted the *Chicago Tribune* from out of the blue with his story. His car had been found in Reno weeks later, which was only about twenty minutes from where Matthew stood. Jeff himself was never seen or heard from again . . . until his severed head showed up in a Dumpster in Chicago.

His *embalmed* severed head.

Melanie Moss, who lived in Carson City, was last seen at the Kales Mortuary in Las Vegas on September 11. But authorities had reason to believe she turned up back in Carson City at some later point that same day. And then she disappeared, never to be seen again. Same as Jeff Hopper.

And on September 11, someone placed five calls to Jennifer Cupertine from this Walmart, at 7:40 p.m., Chicago time. Which would be about 5:40, Nevada time. More than ten hours after Melanie Moss was last seen at the mortuary. Enough time to drive from Las Vegas to Carson City, even in a storm. What time had the paper in Chicago been called? How long after Jeff Hopper had been spotted in Las Vegas? He didn't know. Maybe Poremba did. But it was the same day. He knew that.

It was too similar.

Matthew slammed his trunk closed. He scanned the parking lot, found the man and his kid three rows away, putting flyers on a Ford Fiesta.

"Excuse me?" Matthew shouted. He jogged toward them. "Mr. Moss? Annie?"

The little girl turned at her name, then tapped the man, pointed at Matthew.

"Yes?" Mr. Moss said.

"What was she doing at a mortuary?" Matthew asked.

"Pardon me?" Mr. Moss said. He took a step back.

Matthew took out his wallet, found the last remaining remnant of his old life, his business card from the FBI, and extended it to the man. "I'm Agent Matthew Drew, from the FBI."

Mr. Moss looked at the card like he couldn't quite believe what he was seeing. "Finally," he said. "She's a state employee, not federal, so they keep kicking it back to the local police, who are useless. They can't stop graffiti."

"I understand," Matthew said. "Maybe I can help?"

"Thank you," the man said. "Thank you. Yes. Please. Whatever you can do."

Matthew took a pen from his pocket, flipped over the flyer. He had to concentrate. Make sure he got his tenses right. Not offend this poor man and his kid. He had one shot at this. "Melanie. She is your . . . wife?"

"Ex-wife."

"And your name?"

"Trevor Moss." He gave Matthew his phone number and e-mail address, too. Told him he was on leave from his job at the Nugget, where Matthew had spent the night, that he dealt craps. "The cops have all of this."

"I know," Matthew said. "This is for me. So I can run it up the chain. Get you and your daughter out of this parking lot. It's cold as hell here."

"I'll come here every day," Trevor said. "This was the last place she was. Maybe she got hit on the head or something, is lost, only remembers this place. If that's the case, I'll be here."

"She was here? In this place?"

"Cops said they had her cell phone tracked right here," he said. "She only lived six blocks over, so I thought maybe they had it wrong, but no, they said the GPS tracker on her phone ended right in this parking lot."

"On September 11?"

"Yeah," Trevor said. "Worst fucking day of my life."

"What time did the GPS cut off?"

"Around five," he said.

"Did they look for her on the Walmart cameras?"

"Nothing," he said. "They don't think she ever walked into the store. They didn't see her on the parking lot cams." He looked down at his daughter. He reached into his pocket, took out a ring of keys. "Honey, why don't you go sit in the car for a minute. And then we'll go get some pancakes. Okay?"

"Okay," she said. She took the keys from him, and Matthew saw that she had an antique ring on her thumb. A ruby inset in diamonds. Too nice and valuable for a kid to be wearing.

"That's a pretty ring," Matthew said.

"It's my mommy's," she said, and then skipped off, chirped the alarm on a black minivan, and climbed inside, Matthew and Trevor watching her the whole way.

"Was your ex-wife a coroner?"

"No," Trevor said. "Funeral home investigator."

Matthew didn't even know that was a job. He flipped the flyer back over, tried to be as casual as possible. "So, the Kales Mortuary? That was what? A client visit?" Even as he said the words out loud, pieces began to fall into place in his mind, the connective tissue that pulled Sal Cupertine, Jeff Hopper, and this woman together.

"Yeah," Trevor said. "She was making her Vegas run. Then the planes hit, she turned around and came home. Except she never showed up." He pointed at the minivan. "Annie doesn't know this, but that ring? A couple weeks ago, a real estate agent found Melanie's purse in the bushes at a country club in Dayton. The ring was inside it, along with Melanie's wallet, nothing missing."

There was something going on with this funeral home, with this temple, with all of these players. Two fucked-up things could be a coincidence. But this was four, five, maybe six things that shared a piece of DNA . . . and all of it was on that street in Summerlin. That much coincidence required planning.

"Let me see what I can do to help you," Matthew said. He circled Trevor's number on the flyer, held it up. "This the best number to call?"

"Yeah." He'd give it to Poremba next week if all of this turned out to be nothing. But he couldn't imagine that would be the case.

"Okay," Matthew said. He shook the man's hand. "Someone will follow up with you, I promise."

"Can I ask you a question?" Trevor said. "Something like this? Do people ever get found alive?"

Never, Matthew thought. *Only bodies get found.* "All the time," he said. "Every day."

18

Rabbi David Cohen couldn't pinpoint the exact moment when Sal Cupertine became a man. Was it when he watched his father pinwheel to his death off the IBM Building? Was it when he did his first sanctioned hit, Rolf Huber, outside the Lamplighter, side of the head, brains all over the pavement, picking skin out of his hair for what felt like three days? Was it when he crawled into that fucking meat truck and ran away from his wife, his kid, his entire life?

What he was sure of, as he stood atop the steps of the Performing Arts Center waiting to greet the bar mitzvah guests to the afterparty, was that it wasn't when anyone ever told him he was a man. Because wasn't that what he'd heard his entire life?

Little man, watch this door for a couple minutes.

You want a sip of this, my man?

You're the man, Sal. For real.

Oh, you're a bad man, now?

Here comes the Rain Man.

And yet, there he stood not twenty minutes ago, in front of the bimah, the Torah ark a few feet away, ensconced behind ornate (and fortified, so if the place burned down, the ark would be safe) doors, and pronounced OG Sean B's ascent into manhood a success, his position among the people of Israel affirmed once Sean's father, Casey, had released him with the ceremonial blessing: *Blessed be He who has released me from being punishable for this boy.*

As if it were so simple. You turn thirteen, memorize a bit of the Torah, and all of a sudden, your family isn't responsible for your fuckups?

And who released the children from being responsible for their parents' mistakes? When did that happen?

Maybe *that's* when Sal Cupertine would become a man, David thought. When he owned his mistakes and didn't pass them on to his kid. His own father hadn't managed to do that. His father before him hadn't either. Hell, Sal was paying for mistakes that had been made by those with his name since the 1870s, the Cupertines running grifts in Chicago since the Great Fire. Maybe disappearing into this new life had been the way to stop that particular strain. Maybe William, wherever he was, would be released from his name; he would certainly never shoot anyone in the back of the head.

That didn't mean David didn't want to find him.

He had to.

And then he'd prove Rabbi Kales wrong, that there was a postwar for him. That postwar would include William living in peace, even if Sal Cupertine had to die to get there. Maybe that was the only way out for William. For Sal Cupertine to finally die, not just disappear. What was left for Sal Cupertine, really? The Family? If David wanted to have a life—a real life—he'd need to give that up. Be content with what he was building here, protect this new empire. If that meant going to Israel, then he would go to Israel. Be in a position where what the cameras saw wouldn't matter. Bennie needed to make that happen. This would mean a real birth certificate. A real driver's license. A real social security number. If that meant someone else named David Cohen needed to die, then someone else named David Cohen would die. Bennie could farm that out to the Triads. Let them find a Jew with a clean name. Maybe they'd only need to buy the man's life. Everyone had a price. But it needed to be done. David would tell Bennie this in January. Give him a deadline. He would have Harvey B. Curran get a story in the newspaper about a birthright trip for all local Jews. He would make it a goodwill mission. He would get the mayor involved. The governor. He would even let his picture appear in the paper. He would be Rabbi David Cohen forever.

Maybe that would be the end, then, of Sal Cupertine. William would be free of him. If someone died by the hand of Rabbi David Cohen, so be it. But Sal Cupertine's ledger would be clear.

David watched as the diaspora moved from the temple to the Performing Arts Center, two hundred and fifty guests ready for the fun part of the afternoon. They'd begun to gather en masse below, in the center's parking lot, about where Gray Beard and Marvin had parked. There were two men at the bottom of the stairs guarding a red velvet rope, per Casey Berkowitz's instructions, their paramilitary uniforms replaced today with black suits, sunglasses, and earpieces. Part of it was just for looks—OG Sean B would be envied for having a couple hard motherfuckers in suits working the line—and part of it was that this was just how these guys dressed for events: The security firm David contracted specialized in black-tie functions and private security for celebrities and dignitaries. David had hired five extra security guards for the day—or, well, the Berkowitzes had hired them—owing to the local luminaries set to attend the party. MMA fighters. Rappers. Rumor was Carrot Top or Danny Gans might show up, but David doubted that.

The head security consultant, an off-duty Las Vegas Metro Narcotics Division detective named Alex Behen, came out of the Performing Arts Center, finger to his ear, listening to something. After a moment, he came and stood beside David, watched the gathering crowd for a few seconds. He was armed with at least two guns that David could make. He also drove a black-on-black BMW that cost more than David's burned-down house in Chicago.

"Problems?" David asked.

"No, no, everything is fine," he said. "Suspicious-looking car down by the temple during the festivities, drove away, one of the patrols picked it up on the back side of the cemetery, which seemed weird, so we called the plates in, made sure it wasn't some white supremacist asshole. It was a rental, which we we've been told to keep an eye on. That and U-Hauls. He came back down by the home, so we knocked on his window. Just a lost tourist from the Midwest, nothing to worry about."

"Thank you," David said.

"Can I tell you, Rabbi?" Detective Behen said. "On my thirteenth birthday? I think there were six of us. Probably cost my pops a hundred and fifty bucks, all in."

"Talmud says that we should not be so ostentatious as to arouse envy," David said. "I do not think Mr. Berkowitz adheres to that axiom."

"I don't judge," the detective said, which David understood immediately to be bullshit. Everybody judged. It was the essence of being human.

Beyond the crowd, David saw one of Jerry Ford's LifeCore vans pull out of the Kales Mortuary and Home of Peace parking lot, passing the Home's hearse on the way back in. This was the mortuary's busy time of the year, the dead tending to pile up after Hanukkah, the old-timers sticking around for one last show before checking out. The temple lost Winnie Kaplan, Howard Edelman, and Alice Apple within forty-eight hours. All in their eighties, all people David knew. None of their deaths was a tragedy, per se, but when combined with everything else, it was all a little depressing, particularly since Alice Apple had died while getting liposuction and David was due to go under the knife tomorrow. There wasn't much for LifeCore to take from them, but the temple had made a nice profit this week on another shipment from the Triads, a sudden increase in business from the Midwest, which David thought was probably a reaction to Ronnie's being off the books for two months now, and more business from the tribes down south, this time shipping another Mexican Mafia OG. This one had an old bullet scar on his right side, beneath his rib cage, in addition the new one through the back of his mouth. Some fucking life. Survive getting shot just so you could live long enough to get shot.

If there were any funerals for the next few weeks while David was out of commission, Rabbi Kales would come out of retirement for them, or they'd get Rabbi Roth to assist, provided the bodies were legal. Most of the congregants would probably prefer Rabbi Sigal in such a case, but he'd been very ill of late. It frankly did not look like he was going to make it. A tragedy.

"Mr. Berkowitz and his lady friend are in the hall," Detective Behen said, "and I've got a guy who'll stay between them and Mrs. Berkowitz at all times. There will be no awkwardness, I promise."

"Thank you."

"I don't want to be out of line here, Rabbi, but I wanted to tell you how much that donation the temple made means to all of us," he said. "I didn't know about it until I saw it in the newspaper the other day, so, just to say, me and the boys here? We appreciate the support. This is a crazy time to be law enforcement. Equal parts honor and fear. You know, before all this with the planes and everything, craziest thing I ever saw was that bank heist in LA when they shot it out on the street. But now? I'm not worried about assault rifles and body armor. I'm worried about sarin gas and anthrax. We're not trained for that."

"Who is?"

"Well, we're gonna be. Feds think Las Vegas is going to be the location of a holy war or something, so every other day, there's another bulletin. Look out for this guy, look out for that guy, look out for a truck filled with manure, look out for a bus loaded with nails and propane tanks, I mean . . . it's a whole new world out there."

"It is," David said.

Behen strode down the steps and unhooked the velvet rope and the celebrants came rushing toward David like ants. Many of the kids had already untucked their shirts or ditched their itchy sport coats and dresses entirely in favor of jeans and sneakers— they had a busy day ahead of them, with the paintball war setup, the rap concert, the MMA demo, the DJ, the pop-up ice cream parlor. It was only noon. The party was set to go until 9:00 p.m. David would be home long before that. He was due to be at Dr. Melnikoff's surgery center at 8:00 a.m. He would be kept overnight and then released back to his house, where he'd hired a series of visiting nurses to take care of him. It wasn't the best situation—that would be waking up to Jennifer beside him, spooning soup into his mouth, but that wasn't happening—but he couldn't be alone for the first three or four days. It meant cleaning up the house a little—he couldn't very well have some visiting nurse stumble into a room full of automatic weapons—but that was a minor inconvenience.

A limo pulled up to the front of the Performing Arts Center and Rachel Savone got out with Kate Berkowitz. Bennie's wife was the one person at Temple Beth Israel who David thought might be able to provide Kate Berkowitz with a welcome ear, and maybe a little help, without spitting out the woman's plight to every other person in the city. So after he'd encountered Kate at Lowe's, he gave Rachel a call, asked her if she could do him a small favor. But now here they were together, in front of everyone.

For the next ten minutes, David shook the hands of his congregants as they came by, then took the praise for the lovely ceremony from Kate's family in from Ohio—grandma, wearing so much gilded shit on her body she looked like King Tut; Kate's brother Logan and his wife, Barbara; Kate's brother Teddy and his wife, Gwen; a sister who didn't give her name, too busy with the screaming two-year-old in her arms—took a dozen more kisses on his cheeks from the yentas, then smiled approvingly at the children, who slowed their running when they got near him, or who hushed their voices, or who dipped their heads in deference.

Maybe he was a good rabbi.

It wasn't something David thought about most days, because the fact was most days he concerned himself with how the fuck he was going to get gone with everyone at Temple Beth Israel's money. Though, in reality, it was money they were going to spend anyway, either at Temple Beth Israel or someplace just like it. He wasn't putting motherfuckers on the street. The Steins and the Rosenbergs and the Coopers weren't going to be on food stamps. David would eventually leave, whether in good standing or in shackles, and Temple Beth Israel might crumble in his wake, but wasn't that what every rabbinical teaching was all about? That the temple never lasted. What lasted was Israel. What lasted was faith. No walls could house it, no single man could possess it. That Rabbi David Cohen wasn't Jewish had ceased to be problem was simply an issue of scale: He was more Jewish than the rest of them.

When most of the guests were inside, Rachel and Kate finally came up the steps, arm-in-arm.

"Hello, Rabbi," Rachel said when she reached David. She let go of Kate and put a hand to David's face and kissed his left cheek gently. Rachel had been in the front row of the service, as she always was. "You did a very nice job with Sean."

"Thank you," David said.

"My father has taught you well. He always was good at getting the least Jewish among us to rise up in the name of the faith when their time behind the bimah came."

"Indeed," David said. This one. She'd try to break him every time she could. David understood that. "Sean spoke Torah truthfully today." He turned his attention to Kate. She had on sunglasses, a slate-gray dress underneath a gray Burberry trenchcoat, and matte red lipstick, a sort of a Jackie O look. "You should be very proud of your son," David said. "I was very moved by his sentiments." Sean had spoken on the topic of freedom and restoration of the spirit as embodied by Judah Maccabee, pretty much the last Jew you wanted to fuck with, the guy who made Hanukkah possible, who told his men to "fight manfully," a quote David suspected OG Sean B would eventually tattoo on his chest in Hebrew, because irony was lost on him. "He's a very bright boy."

"I've been thinking," Kate said, as if they were in the middle of an entirely different conversation, "that I should redo my bat mitz-vah. It didn't mean anything to me when I was thirteen, but I think having the Torah study now would be good for me. Do you think that could be something we could do, Rabbi Cohen?"

David glanced at Rachel. She raised her eyebrows slightly. "Are you planning on staying in the area, Kate?"

"For a little while," Kate said. "I'm not going to let anyone dictate where I live."

David looked again at Rachel. She was done helping him. "We'll consider all of these options after the new year," David said. He lifted his chin up, met the gaze of Detective Behen, who was watching from a few yards away. "Will you escort Mrs. Berkowitz in? Mrs. Savone and I would like to talk for a moment."

"Sure, boss," he said. "It would be my pleasure." He came up, put an arm through Kate's, and took her inside, David and Rachel watching until they disappeared into the assembled crowd.

"She's a mess," Rachel said.

"I see that," David said. "I appreciate your help."

"She just needed a friend," Rachel said. "And Xanax."

"She seeing anyone? Like to talk?"

"Isn't that what you're for?"

"I don't think she views me that way," David said.

"I got her an appointment with a therapist I know," Rachel said. "We'll see if she goes. The Xanax has been helping, anyway. Keeping her out of the bars, which is good. Last thing she needs is a DUI or to be impregnated by a bouncer."

"Don't let either of those things happen," David said.

Rachel stared at David for a long moment. It was something David had grown somewhat accustomed to, Rachel Savone the kind of person who appraised you before speaking. In David's case, he always assumed she was trying to decide whether or not to reach into her purse, pull out the snub-nosed number she kept there, and attempt to put a bullet in his face.

"I don't work for you," she said, "and I'm not one of your sycophants, so I'd remind you to talk to me with a bit more respect. I'm still Bennie's wife, Rabbi."

"Are you?" David said.

"Home detention makes the heart grow fonder," she said. "And anyway, I'm helping Kate despite you, not because of you." She shook her head. "Why does every man I come into contact with think they need to tell me how to be?"

"I know you've made bad choices in the past," David said. "That makes me think you don't always know the path forward."

She stared at him. "Next you're going to tell me it's not personal."

"No," David said, "that was very personal."

She dug into her purse, came out with a pack of Marlboros— shook one out, lit it up.

"You smoke now?" David asked. Her husband, Bennie, had survived thyroid cancer.

"Not at home," Rachel said. She blew out a stream of smoke, turned her back to David, looked down Hillpointe, facing the Barer Academy, the temple, the aquatic center, the rolling greens of the cemetery, the funeral home, the undeveloped property, huge parcels of the desert devoted to Jews, living and dead.

"All this," she said, but didn't complete her thought. Which was fine. David wasn't sure he wanted to hear the rest of it. "You nervous for your surgery tomorrow?" she asked after a time.

"No," David said. "Just happy for the pain to be ending."

"You think the pain will end?" Rachel said. "That's what you think?"

"I understand that you don't like me, nor trust me," David said. "But I am not a man like your husband and I am not a man like your father."

"What are you, then?"

"Rachel," he said, "I am merely trying, each day, to be a better person than I was the day before."

"How is that working for you, Rabbi?"

"Most days? I fail. The Talmud says, either companionship or death, and what I take that to mean is you are either part of something larger or you are part of nothing. I attempt each day to be part of something larger. Do you?"

"If you had children," she said, "you'd know what a foolish question that is."

"Then you should stop smoking."

Rachel took a long drag from her cigarette. "Did my father mention that the assisted-living facility has been sold?"

"No."

"The new group raised prices twenty-five percent," she said. "They own facilities in Wisconsin that look very nice, but no one likes to pay more for what they already get."

"I'll talk to them about it."

"It's fine," she said. "He can afford it. But it got me thinking about that area over there." She pointed to the vacant field, where a group was setting up a vast paintball demo for OG Sean B and his friends. "What would it take for us to open our own care facility?"

"I don't know."

"Something to consider, Rabbi," she said. "The Talmud does say that one who does not visit the sick is like one who sheds blood. No one would have an excuse."

"I'll look into it." He would. "Rabbi Kales wants to go to Israel with your girls."

"It's all he talks about."

"He wants me to go as well," David said.

"So go."

"I need you to tell your husband that it would be prudent."

Detective Behen came back outside then, held open the door, called out to Rachel. "You need an escort, ma'am?"

"That would be fine, thank you," Rachel said. She looked back at David, smiled. "Please don't kill me for talking to the police," she said quietly. "It would be a terrible end to a beautiful day." She touched his face again, this time just with her fingertips, and David flinched. "You're so naïve, Rabbi Cohen," she said. She took one more puff of her cigarette, then stomped it out. "It almost makes me like you."

Rabbi David Cohen's cell phone buzzed in his pocket. It was Ruben.

David watched Rachel walk into the Performing Arts Center her father built, using the money her husband washed, on the arm of a cop that was now on the payroll of the Mafia, and the only person who knew all of those things, and more, was him. Rabbi David Cohen owned them all.

"What is it?" David said into the phone.

"Sorry to bother you," Ruben said, "but we've got a problem."

David went down the steps, walked off toward the street, away from the security.

"What kind of problem?"

"I picked up clients that I'm uncomfortable with."

"That's not something I care about," David said. "And it's not something you should concern yourself with, either."

"Yeah, yeah, I figured that would be your answer," he said. "So what I'm gonna do? I'm gonna leave this lady and this kid right here and you can take care of it. I'm gonna get a job at Arby's, I don't give a fuck."

A lady and a kid.

"How old?"

"I dunno, man. They didn't come with no ID."

David had put down a couple hundred bodies during his time in Las Vegas, legit and criminal. The only nonlegit woman he'd buried was Melanie Moss. No nonlegit kids ever came through. That wasn't the job.

"Boy or girl?" David said.

"You have to put the pieces together to know for sure, but looks like a boy to me."

Nobody would touch Jennifer and William. *Nobody.* He kept telling himself that.

David checked his watch. "Don't fucking move."

•

DAVID FOUND RUBEN in the morgue. There were body bags on two of the three tables. On the third, Ruben's assistant, Miguel, worked on a body David didn't recognize and hadn't been told he'd be burying. A fifty-something man with a profound head trauma . . .

which is to say his head wasn't on his neck, so Miguel was reattaching it.

"Who's that?"

Miguel pulled down his mask. "A referral from Congregation Beth El," Miguel said. One of Rabbi Goldstein's, which meant he'd be doing the service. "Car accident."

"When's the funeral?"

"Tomorrow," he said. "I know no one's going to see it, but, I feel like, it's not a wrong thing to put a person right, yes, Rabbi?" Normally, Jewish funerals, you went in the ground as you were. No embalming, no restoration, since they were all closed casket. They embalmed only the goyim, they usually restored only the goyim, too. Because when the Moshiach came, it didn't matter if you were whole or dust, you would be restored then.

"Yeah," David said. "That's fine, Miguel."

Ruben dug into his pocket, came out with a twenty, set it on the counter. "Miguel, why don't you run to Starbucks, get us a couple lattes."

"Okay," Miguel said. He stripped off his gloves, dumped his bloodstained apron in the clothes bin, washed up. Miguel had worked in the funeral home for five years now, on all kinds of bodies. He used to take the bus to work, but now he drove an Acura with a stereo system that you could hear bumping from five blocks away.

"How much does he know?" David asked when Miguel left.

"He don't ask questions," Ruben said. "But he's not stupid."

David looked at the two bags, tried to stay calm.

If it was Jennifer and William, David would be on the table next to them.

He unzipped the adult and was hit with a wave of stench. The rotten and pungent smell of decomposition, but also sickeningly sweet, like old meat and cut, damp grass. David snatched the yarmulke off his head, pressed it to his nose and mouth, stifled a gag. He'd been around a lot of dead bodies, but not a lot of bodies that had been dug up, put in a bag, and shipped cross country.

It was a woman. Naked. Face side down, long blond hair matted with dirt and blood and the exit wound of a gun blast.

"This is not some shit I'm part of," Ruben said behind David, but David didn't respond. He reached down and pulled the hair from the woman's face, revealed her profile. What was left of her profile. Looked like she'd been shot four, maybe five times. Up close. A Glock, most likely. One bullet would have done the job. You only shot someone that many times for the effect. For this side of the equation. Scare the people who find the body. David pushed away the dirt and debris. Stared into what was left of her right eye. Wiped her face off with his yarmulke.

"Get out," David said to Ruben.

"What?"

"Get the fuck out!" David said.

Ruben took an instinctual step back, didn't say anything, then went down the hallway toward the waiting room, where they left the coffins to be taken to the cemetery.

David unzipped the other bag, let the stench wash over him. Steeled himself. Looked down. There were limbs strewn about, all caked in dirt, falling apart, skin torn away revealing the bright white of bones where they'd been cut from the body. Tried to figure out what the fuck he was seeing. Counted. Three legs. A trunk. Two arms. A head.

A boy's head.

One shot, between the eyes. A burn mark. Fucker put the Glock right on him. No exit wound. Bullet was probably still in there.

A boy whose birth he was present for, right there in Northwestern Hospital.

But it wasn't Jennifer and William.

It was Ronnie's wife, Sharon Cupertine, and one of their four children, their son, James.

Sal had known Sharon her entire life. Grew up two blocks from her. She was Ronnie's second wife; her father was Eddie Castigliano, who they used to call Toto, because he had a little fucking dog. She was the sweetest goddamned person Sal ever knew, other than Jennifer. Raised her four kids to be polite. Before Sal and Jennifer had William, they used to babysit all those kids. James was the second-youngest. He was born with a cleft palate and had fifteen surgeries before he was four years old. A little slow, if Sal was being honest, and that was probably good. Ronnie wouldn't put him in the game.

Fuck.

It didn't matter.

The game was over.

Sal loved that kid. Loved all those kids. The oldest two were girls. Suzanne and Lana. They were teenagers now. Then there was James. And Dana, the youngest, also a girl.

That other leg. Maybe it was one of theirs. The pinkie toe still had a dash of red polish on it.

He had to get his shit together. What did this mean? Who would kill Sharon and the kids and let Ronnie live? Because if Ronnie was dead, it would be news. If Sharon and the kids were dead, that would be news, too. Sending them here meant whoever killed them didn't want that fact getting out. Even if they were missing, that would set off alarms. Bennie would hear something, people would start making moves, Sharon had family, too. Her dad had died in prison. Shanked through the eye at Stateville. Probably on Ronnie's orders.

But there was nothing.

Which meant either no one knew they were dead or no one cared that they were missing, which meant everyone thought they'd gone to the feds.

Next bag that showed up could be Jennifer and William.

Or it could be the rest of Ronnie's kids.

It wouldn't be Ronnie himself. You disappear Ronnie Cupertine, it would be like disappearing Jimmy Hoffa. Geraldo Rivera would show up. Al fucking Roker.

David zipped up both bags, went to the waiting area, but Ruben wasn't there. He looked through the window and saw that he was standing outside, on the phone. When he saw David in the window, he hung up, came inside.

"Who the fuck were you talking to?" David asked.

"Nobody," Ruben said.

"'Nobody' is not the right answer."

"My wife, okay? Chill."

Chill.

"You making plans to get out of town?"

"Nothing like that," Ruben said.

"Your wife and kids like having Mitzy around, Ruben? She a good dog? Where they think she came from? The pound?"

"Man," Ruben said, "don't bring my family into this shit."

"Don't make me," David said. Ruben swallowed. "Now. Where'd those bodies come from?"

"Drove up from Palm Springs in a hearse, like the last couple OGs. Some tribe business."

Someone from Chicago was moving bodies through the tribes. But it also meant whoever was moving bodies didn't want Sharon and James to be found, ever, in Chicago. That they were willing to ship them out meant it was a problem. That they dug them up meant they were worried someone would eventually come looking. But they wouldn't have sent them here if they knew David was going to see them. "That's not where they're from."

"How do you know?" Ruben asked.

"Because I know them."

Ruben seemed confused. "Jews?"

"No." David thinking: *I'm going to have to kill him. I'm going to have to kill him and his whole family.* "How long have they been dead?"

"A couple weeks, my guess. Longer, they wouldn't smell like that," Ruben said.

"Miguel see them?"

"No, I'm not fucking stupid." He started to pace. "Look," Ruben said. "I'm not about this shit, okay? I'm ready to walk." Ruben pointed over his shoulder, toward the cemetery. "You know that bullshit with

Melanie? That's not out of my head, Rabbi. I'm going out to her grave, two, three times a week and saying prayers and shit. I add this into it? No. Not for me. Prison you get out of one day. This shit has me boxed in forever. This is some serial killer shit. And I am not with it. Period."

David thought for a moment. He had to get back to the bar mitzvah or someone would come looking for him.

He had two choices.

Give Sharon and James the burial they deserved or give them vengeance.

Or maybe there were three choices.

"I need you to embalm them," David said.

"No," Ruben said. "I did that shit once for you and didn't ask no fucking questions. But this is a bridge too far, homes. If Mr. Savone knew what I did, I'd be a dead man. You hear me? I'd be fucking dead. Then do it on this woman and whatever is left of that fucking kid? No. I'd be fucking dead."

"Ruben," David said, as calmly as possible, "you are already dead."

"What?"

"You are born to die," David said, calm, everything calm. "You don't get to choose when. You only get to choose how you want to live. Do you want justice for these people?"

"You *know* them?"

David wished he hadn't said that, but he had, and now here they were. "Yes."

"Well?"

"They are my family."

"Your family?"

"That's right," David said. He walked down the hall, Ruben behind him, brought him back into the morgue. He unzipped Sharon's bag, the smell enveloping the room immediately. "That's my cousin Sharon. If you flip her over, you'll find a tattoo of a dolphin on her hip. Got it in college. One of those stupid things people do." He unzipped the other bag. "That's her son, James. He's eleven.

Never had a bad day in his life. I don't know if all that shit in the bag is him, because he's got three sisters, too, and if he's dead, and their mother is dead, and there's an extra leg in there? Well, that means they're all dead. That means, sometime soon? You're going to drive out to the desert and there's gonna be three more bags, except this time, it's gonna be little girls."

"They said Monday or Tuesday they'd have more," Ruben said.

Everything went without a hitch, he'd be at home, recovering, but in no condition to assist with this problem.

"Okay. This is what you're going to do. I want you to embalm them. Don't remove any bullets you find. And when the next bodies come, if they look like what I said, embalm them, too. Then put them in your hearse and drive to Los Angeles or San Francisco or Portland. Yeah. Portland." He wanted him to drive to Chicago, but that was too obvious. Leave the bodies somewhere public, where they'd be found, pictures would be in the paper, get on the news, a hotline would be set up. If he needed to, David would call in a tip himself. You don't kill women and children and get away with it. David was learning that every day. These motherfuckers would, too. "Middle of the night, dump the bodies at the first church you find. Doesn't matter the denomination. Then come home. Can I trust you to do this?"

Ruben said, "Mr. Savone will have me killed, Rabbi."

"If he wanted you dead," David said, "you would already be dead. Mr. Savone is not a man who waits around. So my advice to you is to make yourself indispensable. You do this favor for me, I'll be the guy who warns you."

Ruben nodded his head once, but didn't say anything. He was an inch away from breaking. Maybe less.

"You did the right thing, Ruben," David said. "Do you understand that? You did right."

"It don't feel right."

David checked his watch. He needed to get back. He zipped up the bags. "I go into the hospital tomorrow. You ever get another bag with a woman and a boy? You come and get me. I don't care if I'm in surgery, understood?"

"Yes, Rabbi," Ruben said.

•

DAVID WALKED OUT the front of the funeral home just as Miguel was returning. He had two Starbucks cups and a half-eaten doughnut in his hand.

"I'm glad I got to see you. I wanted to tell you good luck with your surgery, Rabbi," Miguel said. "You need anything, my wife and me, we just got a place over by the Smiths on Lake Mead? So I could get you groceries or whatever, Rabbi."

"When did you get married?"

"Oh," he said, "it was just a small thing at St. Anne's, a couple months ago."

"Why didn't you tell me?" Not that he and Miguel talked much. But it was the sort of thing David liked to know about. He made a mental note to have Esther get them something off their registry.

"Oh, I guess I thought you knew." He lifted up his left hand, showed the simple gold band he had. "We been together almost two years, so, seemed right." He shifted from foot to foot. "Can I tell you something personal, Rabbi?"

"Of course."

"In a way, you're responsible for this." He leaned in toward David, lowered his voice. "Do you remember that night I thought the funeral home was getting robbed?" David did. Miguel had walked in on him while he was on the phone, negotiating the transfer of a body. Miguel almost hadn't made it out alive that night. "You asked me what I had to live for, you know?"

"No," David said, "I asked you what you were willing to die for."

"Yeah," Miguel said, "I guess that's kind of the same thing, but different. I took it to heart, though. Like, what did I *have*. And I didn't have *anything*. Now I do. You know, so, I'm more invested in my actions, is what I'm trying to tell you."

"What are you asking me for here, Miguel?"

"More responsibility," he said. He stood up straight. "I'd like to go to funeral director's school, like Ruben did. So I can grow in the company."

"You want to be like Ruben?"

"Yes," Miguel said.

"I'll talk with Rabbi Kales when I return," David said. "See what we can do."

"That's all I can ask," he said.

David made his way up back up the block. It was a Saturday, so in addition to all of the cars across the street for the bar mitzvah, inside the lush green cemetery David made out at least ten cars parked at different junctures. He knew who would be out there. Cliff Grossman came every Saturday with a radio, sat at his wife's grave, plucked weeds, had lunch. Lenore Pincus would be at her daughter Jackie's grave, reading. Visiting families from out of town, dressed for a day on the Strip and with flowers bought from Manic Al's, checking maps to find Nana's final resting spot.

Jews believed the dead existed beyond life as spiritual beings; however, the only remnant of their time here was their deeds. There were no ghosts, no holy visitations. Jews didn't preserve their dead bodies, because they didn't matter. The simple pine box, the quick burial, it was all so that the corporeal vessel could disappear quickly. But still, the Jews came to witness their dead, both the ones they loved and the ones they'd never known. Even places of massacre had turned holy.

Torah said, Remember thy last end and cease from enmity.

Sal Cupertine couldn't do that.

Talmud said, If not for this day . . .

If not for this day he could be any David. But David Cohen was of the Book. It was in him. It was him.

A gust of wind blew in from the west and David instinctually reached for his yarmulke, but it was gone. He'd left it in the morgue.

David crossed the street, nodded at two of the security guards, passed the temple, passed the Barer Academy, reached the

Performing Arts Center, climbed the steps, and found Casey Berkowitz standing there, smoking, along with a man who looked to be one of the MMA guys. He was short, maybe five-eight, but stout, and covered in tattoos, including what looked like the 23rd Psalm on his forearm, his shirt sleeves rolled up to show it off. His skin was pink and thick with veins. He looked like the kind of cheap meat Paul Bruno's father used to feed to the neighborhood dogs.

"Rabbi," Casey said. "I was looking for you."

"Please put your cigarette out," David said.

"I paid for this space," Casey said. "I can't smoke a cigarette out here? A hundred thousand dollars and you get to tell me what I can and can't do? I saw your friend Rachel Savone smoking like a chimney out here and you said nothing."

Detective Behen lingered about twenty feet away. He was on his phone, but when David looked his way, he gave him a nod.

"Are you drunk?" David asked.

"Everyone's drunk," Casey said. "I paid for an open bar." He blew smoke out toward David. Then he said to the bag of meat beside him, "This is the guy I told you about."

"You're the man who threatened my boy here?" Bag of Meat said. "With the scissors? That's you?"

"I'm the rabbi," David said. They were both drunk, though this motherfucker looked like he was maybe coked up, too. He'd be using someone's else piss if he wanted to fight anytime soon.

"I don't care if you're Jesus Christ," Bag of Meat said. "You don't threaten my boy here, or you and me are going to have problems."

"What does that mean, exactly?" David asked.

"It means you pay Mr. Berkowitz the respect he's earned."

"Yeah," David said. "I'll do that when it happens." He took a step back, created a little distance, made sure Detective Behen saw him. He did. Started to head over. David squared toward Casey and Bag of Meat, showed his full face to both men—what was left of it—and said, his voice slightly above a whisper, "I ever catch one of you motherfuckers alone on the street, you're fucking dead."

Which is when Bag of Meat, who at the time was the thirteenth-ranked middleweight MMA fighter in the world, but who in three days would indeed be fucking dead—found hanged in his garage, because nobody threatened people who worked for Bennie Savone, *nobody*—sucker punched Rabbi David Cohen flush under his right eye, collapsing the remaining structure of his face before David even knew he'd been punched.

EPILOGUE

The Branding Iron Café was the only place in these parts, especially in the snow, where you could get a decent drink and a steak. So at five o'clock on New Year's Eve, Caroline Evans and her father, Levi, piled into his Subaru Outback and made the drive from Loon Lake to Clayton, parked between a motorcycle and Chevy truck, and went inside. There were two men at the bar, ten feet between them, and on the television Washington State played Purdue in a bowl game. Somewhere far away, judging by the weather. Texas or Florida or maybe even California. Certainly somewhere a lot warmer than eastern Washington.

"You all right for a second by yourself?" Levi asked.

"I'm fine," Caroline said.

Levi left Caroline at the table to do the thing he always did: He went into the men's room and checked all the stalls, made sure no one was in them, then cased the rest of the place, acting like nothing was wrong, he was just the kind of guy who liked to get the lay of the land. He looked like active military, what with the haircut, the square jaw, and the way he stared you in the eye with a strange, unblinking intensity even if you were just telling him what the specials were.

After a minute alone—which was golden—the bartender noticed Caroline and came around with two menus, set them down in front of her. "Get you something to drink?" he asked.

"Scotch," she said.

"What about for your dad?" This wasn't their first time in the Branding Iron. Caroline figured that by the time spring rolled around, if they were still living out here, she wouldn't even need to place an order. She'd walk in and they'd just hand her a drink.

"Water," she said.

"It's New Year's Eve," the bartender said. His name was Hank. Said so right on his shirt.

"He's working."

"Tough job," Hank said, and gave her a wink. "Steak?"

"Medium rare," she said. "And a grilled cheese with fries, to go."

"Piece of cake, too?"

"Yes," Caroline said. "The chocolate."

Hank came back a moment later with a generous pour of Johnnie Walker over two ice cubes. Caroline gave it a sniff, to see if her nose worked, if she could recognize all the notes. Not tonight. Maybe not ever. She took a sip, felt the liquor burn that spot on her gum line that was still sensitive, then swallowed it down, waited for that familiar rush of warmth. Caroline didn't drink much, never at home. Used to be she'd have a sip of wine at bedtime, so she could sleep, but she needed to be alert. She always needed to be alert. Even out here.

But it was New Year's Eve, and on New Year's Eve, she had a scotch. That was tradition.

One of the men got off his seat at the bar, smiled kindly at Caroline, then headed to the jukebox, put on something twangy, passed Levi as he ambled back to the bar. It must be halftime.

"He say something to you?" Levi asked.

"No," Caroline said.

On the TV, a marching band morphed into a cougar. How nice that would be. Snap your fingers and transform yourself into something different all together.

"I wanted to revisit with you the idea of getting the boy some help," Levi said.

"It's New Year's Eve," Caroline said. "Can't you give it a rest? For one night?

Levi took a sip of water. "There are no nights off," he said.

"Is that why we're here?"

"No," Levi said, but Caroline doubted that. Get her someplace comfortable, but out of the house, away from her son, act like normal people for a bit. See if it made a difference. "There's a program down in California. At Stanford. Started by some researchers trying to help kids from Rwanda process what they have been through. They've been pretty successful, I'm told."

She swirled the ice around her glass. "He's not some lab rat," Caroline said.

"I know that," Levi said. "And now that I've spent some time with him, I want you to know what a fine job you've done with him. But, ma'am, we're not qualified to deal with this." *This. Her son was a "this."* At least he called her ma'am. "It would be a month to start. We'd bring you down on weekends."

"Not acceptable," Caroline said. She swallowed down the rest of her scotch. "I'm going to get a refill." She got up before Levi could respond, set her glass on the bar, motioned Hank over. The woman on the jukebox was singing about how if she had her way, she'd be in your town, and Caroline wondered if that wasn't how it always was: You always wanted to be somewhere different. That love was invariably about how much missing you could tolerate. In the last three years, Caroline hadn't spent a single day without her son. That wasn't going to change. No man, no government, no university research project was going to stand in her way. She knew he needed help. She knew that. Hell, she needed help. The things she'd seen. But that didn't mean they needed to be apart while it happened. Above all else, they wanted information from her. She'd give it a bit at a time, so as to maintain her leverage. As long as she had that advantage, any decisions about her son had to go through her.

She looked over her shoulder. Levi had his back to her, watching the door. Always watching the door.

Hank came over and poured her another couple fingers, dropped two more ice cubes in the glass. "Think the Cougs are going to pull it off?" The Cougs. That must be Washington State. They were down 20–17.

"For sure," Caroline said.

The halftime show on the TV gave way to a news break. The woman on the screen was in her forties, attractive in an unremarkable way, the kind of woman her husband used to call "weathergirl pretty." Tonight, she appeared grave. A graphic popped up on the screen, blood red. Subtle. GANGLAND KILLING?

"Can you turn the volume up, Hank?"

He pressed a button on the remote and Weathergirl Pretty's husky voice flowed out over a clip of cops standing in front of a church, body bags in the distance, surrounded by banks of snow.

"More information is coming to us about the grisly discovery in Portland last week of five bodies left in the parking lot of First Baptist Church, near Troutdale. Police have identified the body of an adult female as Sharon Cupertine but aren't releasing the names of the four minors believed to be found with her, pending identification. This already unsettling scenario is made more troubling by Cupertine's connection, it appears, to a notorious crime family . . . halfway across the country. Dale Hwang reports from our affiliate in Portland."

Caroline felt Levi's presence before she even saw him. He was beside her in a second.

"Come back to the table," he said quietly.

"No," Caroline said.

"I was going tell you," Levi said. "I was going to tell you tonight." And then he ordered a scotch, too.

IT WAS CLOSE to eight when they finally got back to the cabin on Loon Lake. Levi and his wife, Maryann—who had watched her son for the last few hours, and who wasn't really Levi's wife—retired upstairs. Though retired wasn't right either. One of them was always awake. The cabin across the way contained another husband-and-wife team—Uncle Gus and Auntie Donna—who spelled Levi and Maryann periodically.

"I brought you a piece of cake," Caroline said to the boy. He sat at the kitchen table working on a jigsaw puzzle of the moon. He looked up at her casually, as if she were a stranger. And God, maybe she was. She'd cried all her makeup off.

"You said I was getting grilled cheese," he said.

She'd eaten the grilled cheese herself, in addition to the steak, once she realized they wouldn't be going home for a while. Called and had Maryann make him some noodles and olive oil. The pot was still on the stovetop. She'd wash it in the morning.

Her head throbbed and her eyes ached. In the other room, *Dick Clark's New Year's Rockin' Eve* was on the TV. It was almost tomorrow in New York. It was almost an entirely new year, somewhere else. Always somewhere else. Her mind felt like a broken electrical line, snapping on the ground, sparks flying.

They're all dead, Levi told her. *We think we know who the shooter might be. A former FBI agent who attempted to kill Ronnie Cupertine.* They found his gun. They had his name. They didn't know where he was. He could be coming for her next. She had to expect that her husband was dead, or would be soon.

"You're the only child on the planet upset to be getting cake," she said. She took it out of the foam container and put it on a plate, grabbed two forks, then sat down beside her son, but he didn't seem interested. He'd constructed half of the moon in her absence, the Sea of Tranquility nearly complete. She watched him search for a piece, his tongue pressed between his front teeth. When he found the one he was looking for—they all looked the same to Caroline— he pressed it into place.

She took his hand, stopped him from putting his next piece down.

"What?" he said.

His skin was so smooth. She brought his hand to her mouth, kissed it. Reached over and touched the boy on his cheek, brushed his bangs away from his face. Caroline had known her husband for his entire life. She remembered him at seven. Remembered him at ten, at fifteen, at thirty-five . . . and then nothing else. He was frozen in her mind at thirty-five, walking out the house in a dark suit, promising her he'd be back that night with some cough medicine. She and her son both had a fever and a cough, a terrible spring flu, and so her memory feels like it was filmed underwater, everything slow and hazy until the police showed up, and then, for the rest of her life, everything had existed at hyperspeed.

In her memory, he told her that he loved her, but now she wasn't so sure. He didn't do that when he was leaving to do a job, because by the time he was out the door, he was that other person. The Rain Man. Like she was this other person now. *Caroline Evans.* She didn't even get to pick her name. That's how it worked, she supposed. If you were good enough or bad enough, one day you woke with a new name and it was yours.

But William. He was still William. He would always be William.

She should send him away.

She should let them fix him.

She should stop whatever was inside him now, so that someone else wouldn't do it for her.

The therapist from the FBI told her that William displayed a "slight deficiency in empathetic responses" and yet was "acutely aware of his own emotional well-being," which was just a fancy way of saying he felt, all too often, like "some kind of freak." The shooting, she was told, hadn't been emotionally taxing on him because, as the therapist said, "he felt he was doing the right thing."

What if he was?

She let go of his hand and he went back to his puzzle, found another piece, placed it right where it belonged.

"William," she said, "look at me." William Cupertine looked up from his puzzle. "I want you to tell me what you remember about your father. Tell me everything you remember."

He squinted, as if he were staring into the sun, and Jennifer Cupertine tried to not see her husband in his face, tried to find some element in him that was from her genetic code, something to give her some hope.

"I don't remember anything," he said.

She knew he was lying.

•

THE PRIVATE ROOMS on the top floor of the Summerlin Hospital looked east toward the Las Vegas Strip, so at night, if he was semi-lucid, Rabbi David Cohen could just make out the glow of the city in the distance.

Sometimes he thought that city was Chicago and he was flying in from Detroit or New York, coming in for a landing at O'Hare.

Sometimes he thought he was flying the plane into the IBM Building.

Sometimes he thought he was the Prophet Ezekiel and that he had been sitting on the banks of the river Chebar for seven days and seven nights, looking upon the face of God; that the lights of the Strip were the winking eyes of the Lord, telling him: *I don't want wicked people to die. I want them to turn from their evil ways and live.*

Most of the time, he still knew he was the Rain Man, a hit man for the Family, who needed to keep his fucking mouth closed. Like he had any choice. It was wired up like a bridge.

Tonight, New Year's Eve, all he knew was that he was in excruciating pain. He fumbled for the buzzer on the side of the bed, and in a few minutes a nurse came in, but by that point he was grunting out in pain, tears running down his face, not that he could feel them. The only sensation he had in his face was a radiating white agony. He imagined this was what it would feel like to survive a shotgun blast. At this point, it would be a relief.

"Easy there," the nurse said. "Easy, Rabbi. Come on. We been through this now." She adjusted the bag that dripped into his arm and in a few seconds he was rolling. Dilaudid. He loved that shit back in the day. Clean, smooth, none of the rough edges heroin had, which always left him feeling paranoid at the end of a night, looking to fuck somebody up. The nurse propped a pillow under his head, which relieved some of the pressure, and raised him enough to see out the window, the horizon aglow. It was only a bit after 8 p.m. By midnight, there would be thousands of revelers in the street. Fireworks. Bands. Neil Diamond taking the stage.

And then Rabbi David Cohen remembered what he was forgetting, that motherfucker Casey Berkowitz, that other motherfucker with the 23rd Psalm on his arm. That sucker punch. Sharon Cupertine and the kids. David had been in the hospital for almost ten days now. How many surgeries? Four? Five? He'd lost count and it didn't matter. He'd probably lose count again in a few minutes, because he was hitting that pain button now, rolling, nodding, forgetting about it.

"I'm going to let Dr. Melnikoff know you're awake," the nurse said. "He's doing his rounds, so I'm sure he'll be up to see you soon."

She walked out, and for the next fifteen minutes, maybe it was twenty, could have been forty-five, David watched the lights from the Strip shimmer and fade, shimmer and fade. There was a rap on the door and in came Dr. Melnikoff, white coat, blue shirt opened at the collar, black slacks, like he was going out after this, and maybe he was. The man had debts to pay, after all. "This is a welcome sight," Dr. Melnikoff said. He picked up David's chart from the end of the bed and read it. "Your blood pressure is good now, Rabbi, that's a relief." He closed the chart and then stepped to the side of David's bed, learned down over him. "I'm going to touch your face, Rabbi. I'm going to try not to hurt you. Do you understand?"

David tried to nod his head.

"Good." Dr. Melnikoff spread open David's lips and shined a penlight into his mouth. "Good," he said again. "You are healing nicely, Rabbi. The bleeding and the swelling have both come down considerably in the last two days, which is why we lessened your anesthesia and why you're likely feeling more pain. Are you in much pain, Rabbi?"

David nodded again.

"In an optimum situation," Dr. Melnikoff said, "I think we would have dealt with your infection for another two weeks, but an optimum situation was not what we were presented with. So, we've adapted." He ran his thumbs beneath David's eyes. "Do you feel pressure here?" David did not. He shook his head. "That's very good." Dr. Melnikoff shined the penlight into David's eyes. "We may dial back the Dilaudid just a slight bit," he said, "but we'll wait until after New Year's Eve." He slipped the penlight into his pocket and then pulled over a chair. "Rabbi Cohen, I want you to know that when you see yourself, you may be surprised at first, because the face you recognized as your own is no longer. It was not possible for us to rebuild what was, as you know, shoddy construction. The infection that you had made everything below your eyes like quicksand, and the gentleman who struck you did the rest. It was essential that we fix everything at once, and that means the changes you are going to see will be profound. Your jaw, your chin, your orbital region, and your nasal cavity all required substantial work. Where I could, I reused your own tissue. Where I could not, we used cadavers and synthetic materials." He leaned back in his seat, crossed his legs, tented his fingers. "We are not done, I'm afraid. This will be a process that takes time. Do you understand?"

David did. He'd spent six months getting his new face. He'd been through this before.

"All that to say, Rabbi," Dr. Melnikoff said, "I am exceptionally pleased with how you have turned out. Do you want to see?"

"Yes," David tried to say, but nothing much came out. The Dilaudid had him flying now.

"Good," Dr. Melnikoff said. He looked at his watch. "I have one more patient to see and then we'll get you in front of a mirror. Until then, maybe hit the button a few more times and enjoy the view." He pressed a button on the side of the bed and David rose up at a forty-five-degree angle. Suddenly he could see everything, not just the horizon.

Dr. Melnikoff walked out, or maybe he flew, because one moment he was beside David, the next he was gone. The nurse was standing there again. "You have a visitor. Are you up for it?"

David nodded once, or maybe he nodded five times, because he was back on that plane, flying into Chicago, and in just a few minutes he knew he'd be seeing Jennifer and William. He could see her face so clearly now, right in front of him, could count the tiny freckles across her nose, could feel her lips on his, could smell her hair. It was New Year's Eve, so they'd open up a good bottle of scotch, the Johnnie Walker Black or maybe that nice Macallan, and they'd sit in front of the fire, a blanket over them, William asleep in his playpen, because he's just a baby, and then David knows he's in a memory, but he doesn't care, and David would have to wake Jennifer up at midnight to kiss her, and in the morning he'd do it again, to make sure that her first memory of the new year was being loved, by him.

And then he was in minyan, Temple Beth Israel filled with the dead. Row after row of the men he'd killed and the woman he'd murdered. *I will seek that which is lost and will bring again that which is driven away*, he said, *and will bind that which is broken, and will strengthen that which is sick. I will destroy the fat and the strong. I will feed them with judgment.*

"Now, he can't talk," the nurse was saying. David turned his head to the left and saw that she was back in the room, this time with a man he'd never seen before. He was big, well over six foot, and broad across the shoulders like a power forward. He smiled and nodded solemnly at the nurse, and David saw that the man had a deep dimple in his cheek. "He's in a lot of pain right now, so he's flying pretty high tonight. He might not make a lot of sense."

The man chuckled. "He never did."

A golem. He was a golem.

The nurse came over to David's bedside. "Rabbi, your cousin is here to see you. Came all the way from Chicago."

An assassin. He was an assassin.

David tried to get up, but that wasn't happening. He was attached to so many IVs and catheters; he was essentially imprisoned by his own body.

The man waited for the nurse to leave and then closed the door behind her. Came and stood at the foot of David's bed. "Do you know me?" he asked.

David shook his head.

"You killed my partner," he said. "Jeff Hopper."

Not an assassin. An FBI agent. Except he was dressed like he was coming from the gym. If he was here to arrest him, David would already be cuffed to the bed.

"I've been looking for you for a long time," he said. "I imagined when I found you, I'd kill you. But I guess someone beat me to it." He came around to the side of the bed, examined the five different hanging bags that pumped meds into David. "I suppose I could OD you, but that seems like a pleasant way out. Not what the Rain Man deserves." He sat down in the chair Dr. Melnikoff had vacated. "But I suppose what we deserve has very little to do with what we get. You and me, we have a lot to discuss."

The door to David's room opened and Dr. Melnikoff stood there, looking panicked. "Who are you?"

"I'm Rabbi Cohen's cousin," he said. "Matthew."

"This door is not to be closed." He pointed at the whiteboard on the wall, where it said DOOR MUST REMAIN OPEN AT ALL TIMES/FALLING RISK. He came and picked up the chart again, flipped through it. "And I'm sorry, I don't have you on the approved visitor list. I'm going to need you to contact Rachel Savone if you'd like to come back."

"I'll do that," Matthew said. "The nurse who let me in tonight? It's not her fault. I was just so worried." He put up a giant hand. "Flew in from Chicago as soon as I heard the news. Cousin Dave is so private," he said, and there was that smile, that dimple. "I didn't even know he was having surgery."

"You'll need to get the proper pass," the doctor said, but he didn't sound concerned. "Well, as long as you're here, you can be here for the big moment. Rabbi Cohen hasn't seen his new face yet."

"His new face?"

"Newish," Dr. Melnikoff said. He disappeared into the bathroom, came out with a hand mirror, came to the opposite side of the bed from where Matthew now sat. "Rabbi, this may seem disorienting at first, but understand that you are still very swollen. In a week, you will look different still. But this will begin to give you a sense of where you are in the process."

He held the mirror a few inches from David's face. At first, David thought he was hallucinating again, that he was lost in a memory. He blinked twice. Looked over at Matthew, the FBI agent, whose mouth had turned into a crooked smile. Looked over the top of the mirror, at the lights of Las Vegas, and beyond, east toward Chicago. Toward his past. Toward his wife and his son and the man he'd left behind in that meat truck three years ago.

And then, finally, back to his reflection, at the face now returned to him.

Sal Cupertine.

ACKNOWLEDGMENTS

From the first line of this book to the very last, I have benefited from the persistence, kindness, cajoling, midnight texts, meals, tough love, downright threats, and utter devotion of my wonderful editor Dan Smetanka. We started talking about how this book might evolve from almost the moment we finished working on *Gangsterland* . . . and for the next three years Dan never stopped demanding that I take big risks. I am indebted to your hard work and sleepless nights on my behalf. I may have to plant a tree in Israel in your name if I ever put you through this gauntlet again. I am likewise indebted to my amazing, kind, and supportive agent Jennie Dunham, who has been by my side for nearly twenty years. A better consigliere does not exist and I am so happy to have grown up right beside you. And, as well, I have been so lucky to have the indefatigable Judi Farkas getting my work into the hands of people who make pictures move. I am so thankful for your guidance, your generosity, and your foresight. There's at least one good person in Hollywood.

Thank you to the whole team at Counterpoint: from publisher Andy Hunter; to associate publisher and publicity guru Megan Fishmann (who already helped make my dreams come true once, which is a pretty good record); to associate publisher and marketing goddess Jennifer Kovitz; to Wah-Ming Chang, who makes my words look better than they deserve to look; to everyone else between the two coasts who go to work each day in the service of literature. Special thanks to foreign rights agent Judy Klein, who is charged with selling me around the world and who, inexplicably, has been able to do just that. Thank you in all languages!

No book gets written without the tremendous support of some great people. These are mine: my brother, Lee Goldberg, and my sisters Karen Dinino and Linda Woods; partner-in-crime Brad Meltzer; Club 3012 and all of my great friends in the Low Residency MFA in Creative Writing & Writing for the Performing Arts at the University of California, Riverside, without whom I would be lost, and who make having a day job one of the great honors of my life; Agam Patel, who has my back, my front, and both of my sides, daily; Gina Frangello, who was always willing to give me mundane information about Chicago at a moment's notice; Rabbi Malcolm Cohen, Stefanie Helms, and all of Temple Sinai of Las Vegas, I thank you for having a really, really good sense of humor; Vitaly Sigal provided excellent legal advice without a hint of suspicion; Jim Kochel, as per usual, provided me insight on certain, shall we day, *shady* aspects of the casino industry; Julia Pistell and Rider Strong, my Literary Disco cohosts, are my regular and beloved checks and balances, and I so appreciate you giving me time to finish this book when I needed it most; Mechtild Dunofsky keeps my mind in working order—for that, I and everyone I encounter are grateful. Attending the Writers' Police Academy, run by Detective Lee Lofland, was an indispensable experience, and I would like to thank, in particular: Officer Matt Ninham, who taught me about the operations of Native American gangs, patiently answered all of my increasingly obsessive questions, and who, in the process, changed the course of this novel. I took great liberties with the information Officer Ninham gave me concerning the gangs, so any and all factual errors are mine alone, I assure you. Former Special Agent Randy Clifton taught me just how dead I would be in every single situation I'd ever imagined, so that was nice, and Officer Ian Nishimoto taught me how to shoot handguns and AR-15s (you don't want me coming up behind you . . . or, well, coming up wide and to the left of you), and both men taught me a great deal about how and when people with guns end up shooting each other. I am deeply appreciative of all the law enforcement officers and instructors of the Writers' Police Academy for their practical help and assistance.

As one may suspect, I am not a rabbi. My characters' interpretations of Judaism are not to be taken as the official word of the faith and, as ever, my characters' understanding and application of Talmudic law isn't always what it appears to be. Nor should the views of Judaism in this book be construed to be my beliefs . . . all of which is a long way of saying: This is a work of fiction. However, I did find several books especially helpful in the writing of this story—in addition to the Bible, the Torah, and the Talmud, all of which are quoted or paraphrased throughout—and which illuminated many of the thoughts and actions of the characters, as well as the wisdom they espouse: *Modernity and the Holocaust* by Zygmunt Bauman (Cornell University Press, 2001); *The Holocaust in History* by Michael R. Marrus (Brandeis, 1987); *A Book of Jewish Thoughts*, selected and arranged by Rabbi Joseph Herman Hertz (Bloch Publishing, 1926); *Holy Mountain: Two Paths to One God* by Rabbi Raphael H. Levine (Binfords & Mort, 1953); *Policing Las Vegas: A History of Law Enforcement in Southern Nevada* by Dennis N. Griffin (Huntington Press, 2005).

Finally, my wife Wendy, the great love of my life. She lives for days, weeks, months, and years on end with a rabbi, a hitman, and her husband, all of them moping around the house at once, and loves us all, unconditionally. Your people are my people.

Author photograph by Linda Woods

ABOUT THE AUTHOR

TOD GOLDBERG is the author of more than a dozen books, including *Gangsterland*, a finalist for the Hammett Prize; *The House of Secrets*, which he coauthored with Brad Meltzer; and the crime-tinged novels *Living Dead Girl*, a finalist for the *Los Angeles Times Book Prize*, and *Fake Liar Cheat*, plus five novels in the popular *Burn Notice* series. He is also the author of the story collection *Simplify*, a 2006 finalist for the SCIBA Award for Fiction and winner of the Other Voices Short Story Collection Prize, and *Other Resort Cities*. His essays, journalism, and criticism have appeared in many publications, including the *Los Angeles Times*, *The Wall Street Journal*, *Los Angeles Review of Books*, *Las Vegas Weekly*, and *Best American Essays*, and have won five Nevada Press Association Awards. He lives in Indio, California, where he directs the Low Residency MFA in Creative Writing & Writing for the Performing Arts at the University of California, Riverside.